THE PRIZE PRINCE

DETECTIVE KATE BOWEN MYSTERY THRILLER
SERIES

T. R. CROKE

BLUE DOOR PUBLISHING IRELAND

Blue Door Publishing Ireland

Fisherstown, Ballybrittas,

Laois, Ireland.

www.trcroke.com

Publisher's Note: This is a work of fiction. Names, characters, places, and incidents are a product of the author's imagination. Locales and public names are sometimes used for atmospheric purposes. Any resemblance to actual people, living or dead, or to businesses, companies, events, institutions, or locales is completely coincidental.

Book Layout © 2018 Lizzie Harwood using Vellum

Cover Design by Design for Writers

THE PRIZE PRINCE/ T. R. CROKE. -- 1st ed.

In memory of my father
… and for Eva, always

"Not being able to know something
is no proof that it doesn't exist."
Arab proverb

PROLOGUE

Although the two-hour window for aiding the local population was closing fast, the UN patrol continued its cautious advance. As it neared Nefra village, Corporal Dempsey roared from the rear hatch of the Sisu Armoured Personnel Carrier.

"Katyushas launched, close proximity."

"Firing point?" Lieutenant Fitzgibbon, the patrol leader demanded.

"Wadi south of the village. Permission to return to base?"

As Dempsey saw it the patrol had two choices, find dead ground to shelter from the inevitable barrage of suppressing fire that would pour from the Israeli hilltop firebases or return to camp. Open ground was a free-fire zone and anything in it got cut down.

"Remain on mission," the lieutenant ordered over the noise. "Monitor radio traffic and report."

Dempsey relayed the order to the driver and listened anxiously to the engine's high-pitched whine as the APC struggled to accelerate. The UN convoy of white armoured personnel carriers sported bright red crosses front and rear, clearly heralding their mission as humanitarian. An AML 90 armoured fighting vehicle topped and tailed the convoy. Before setting out into the hilly terrain from their base camp, Dempsey had double-checked that each vehicle had a blue UN flag hoisted high.

They pressed on, striving to complete the final part of their mission, the recovery of a battalion APC with a cracked axle from the previous day's reconnaissance. A mechanic would have to make it tow-worthy before they could move it. When a staccato of desperate transmissions filled Dempsey's earpiece, he flashed an urgent radio message to his patrol leader.

"Camp 56 has taken a hit."

Soldiers in the carrier exchanged nervous glances when the air pressure around the convoy compressed again as artillery continued to shriek overhead. The elderly woman on the floor of the APC jolted the ten-man troop when she cried out in pain.

"For Christ's sake, hasn't the IDF seen the flares?" Lt. Fitzgibbon exclaimed. "Inform Ops and tell them to desist." Red flares were an agreed signal between UN forces and the Israeli army that hostile fire was impacting on UN positions.

"They've done that," Dempsey replied. "To no effect."

It wasn't the first time that deploying red flares made zero difference to the amount of incoming ordnance onto UN positions.

"Inform Operations we're diverting to assist at Camp 56," Lt. Fitzgibbon ordered.

Corporal Mick Dempsey's day had been chaotic. Midmorning bombardments had sent everyone scurrying at base camp, a post right on the demarcation line between Israel and Lebanon. About the size of a football field, it was a patchwork of underground bunkers and single-storey portacabins which served as billets, toilets, shower blocks, and a cookhouse. A blast wall surrounded the post, along with barbed wire fencing and a fortified, sandbagged entrance guarded by two machine-gun posts. It buzzed with activity again at lunchtime as soldiers emerged from bunkers dotted around the compound when the all-clear siren sounded.

Minutes after sitting down to eat, Dempsey doubled back when an announcement over the camp's public address ordered the BMR to report. Leaving their lunch uneaten, he headed with his cavalry squad towards the Operations room. He was among a four-strong group rushing from the mess hall when a football caught him square in the face.

"Someone's goin' to get it now," the squaddies behind him leered as Dempsey bent down and retrieved the ball. He fixed his blue beret and growled, "Who kicked that?"

"Sorry," tittered Hussein, a teen from the Tibnin orphanage.

"Feck off and play somewhere else, will ye," Dempsey shouted at him.

"You say football practice is today." Hussein responded.

"You play now, Mick?" his pal, Abou chimed in.

"Later boys, training is down for seven o'clock tonight. Don't be late!"

Dempsey had chosen soccer to keep the teenagers from Tibnin orphanage out of the clutches of Hezbollah as long as possible. Cash donations and hard work from Irish soldiers had contributed much to keeping it open. Hussein and Abousamra were his star strikers. The regular training also kept Dempsey's thirty-something sturdy frame in good shape. Apart from his ginger hair and pale skin, he merged seamlessly with the rest of his new squadron.

His corporal rank was a consequence of a recent demotion. Texas hold'em caused it. When Dempsey scooped the big pot at the end of a long night of barrack gambling, the other players smelled a rat. It took five military policemen to quell the ensuing brawl, and triggered the loss of Dempsey's sergeant stripes. The overseas tour of duty came with the reprimand.

Lieutenant Fitzgibbon looked up from an AO map as the squad entered the Ops centre. Dempsey liked his new commander. Fitzgibbon told him that the slate was wiped clean when he transferred to his platoon, any transgressions a thing of the past. The senior officers at Camp Shamrock, the transport, logistics, and admin headquarters were a different story. Not as forgetful, nor forgiving; Dempsey steered clear of the place.

"Corporal Dempsey, good!" an urgent tone to Fitzgibbon's voice. "The Israelis have given a two-hour window to pick up wounded."

"Sir, the BMR is ready to roll," Dempsey reported.

The Battalion Mobile Reserve provided a lifeline to surrounding towns and villages. It relentlessly reconnoitred the Irish Army battalion's Area of Operation and recovered bodies of Hezbollah fighters, inevitably cut down in futile attacks against the nearby Israeli hilltop bases.

IRISHBATT held ground, carried out patrols, and manned observation posts in their 100 square kilometres of hostile territory extending from the city of Tibnin to the Blue Line along the border with Israel. Within three weeks of Dempsey's arrival, the Hezbollah attacks became almost a nightly occurrence. In early April, Israeli patience snapped and the IDF invaded south Lebanon in an operation it called "Grapes of Wrath." They sought to destroy Hezbollah camps and arms depots, cut supply lines, and kill its fighters.

As the patrol departed base camp earlier that day, the convoy picked up pace and a headwind battered the blue UN flags. The Israelis kept up sporadic shelling towards nearby hills from a warship as the BMR entered the first village. Locals directed them to a site where a fifty-pound Israeli bomb had demolished a family home. Dempsey's squad helped engineers sift through the rubble. They used petrol-powered con saws to cut through thick concrete slabs until they located and recovered a trapped elderly resident.

"Can we make Nefra and get back to base in an hour?" Lt. Fitzgibbon had queried, as they placed the patient into the APC for transport to Tibnin Hospital.

Dempsey momentarily removed his blue helmet to shake concrete dust out of his red hair. He heaved the con saw back into the APC's equipment store, and slung his Steyr assault rifle over his shoulder.

"If we push on hard, Sir, we should do it."

"Mount up," the lieutenant ordered.

By the time the convoy returned to base that evening, they had spent several hours aiding UN colleagues. The troops filed into the debriefing hut, past the stone gabions at the entrance that protected against shrapnel injury and artillery blast. Most said little, they just wanted to get out of bloodstained combats, and shower.

"Camp 56 took a direct hit," the lieutenant began, his voice shaky. "Most of our time was spent helping collect and stack body parts. Too early to say exactly how many are dead, at least a hundred."

Dempsey added "They were all civilians as far as we know. They perished believing the UN could protect them."

When the debrief concluded, he pushed out along a corridor with his men. He shouted he would buy them all a beer in the NCO's mess later.

"Must have cleared his tab," a soldier commented.

"Ya fuckin' bollix!" Dempsey shouted. He pushed through the troops, grabbed the offender, and slammed him against a wall, his forearm driving hard into the startled soldier's throat making him gag.

"Cut it out," Lt. Fitzgibbon snapped, pulling them apart, "enough violence for one day."

"I'll let it go tonight," Dempsey grumbled, "but only tonight."

Two eager young faces stared up at him when he got outside.

"Jaysus, lads I clear forgot. Hang on, I'll go throw on me gear."

Hunger gnawed at him as he changed out of uniform. However, when he thought about eating, the carnage of earlier in the day re-surfaced and made him nauseous. Most of his troops were calling loved ones as he stepped outside. Dempsey had no credit left on the phone card he used to ring home. He reckoned the television news report that IRISHBATT hadn't suffered any casualties would reassure his fiancé that he was alive, at least.

In contrast to the Israeli firebase shrouded in darkness just over the hill, the UN base was lit up night and day. He walked with Hussein and Abousamra to a corner of the compound where the rest of the group waited impatiently. Before he kicked off the training session, Dempsey pointed out where the bunkers were located. As a five-lap warm-up progressed, laughter percolated through the group, everyone pushed and jostled for position near the front. Dempsey busied himself setting up a line of parking cones to practice dribbling. He ended the session with a five-a-side game. As usual, the Hussein-Abou strike force outscored their opposition.

"Great effort lads," he told the teenagers as they circled around him. The session had helped him forget the afternoon's horrors for a while and he felt grateful.

"Next Saturday you'll be playing an army team," he told them as he threw the football to each boy and they headed the return. "They've told me they're going to kick the shite out you. Are ye going to let that happen?"

"No, no," Hussein, Abousamra and four others replied.

"Who's the best?"

"We are," the few shouted in reply, until a translation elicited a forest of clenched fists punching the air.

"Ye're mighty lads. Our final training session is here on Friday night. See ye all then."

Dempsey showered and changed into fresh combats with a military green tee shirt. Before heading to make good on his earlier offer, he picked up a handful of sandwiches the cook had delivered to the NCO's billet. He devoured the egg and onion combination and then stuck his head into a colleague's room. The Company Sergeant sprawled on his bunk was reading reports, the bright light from a reading lamp bouncing off his shiny bald pate. Before Dempsey had a chance to speak, the CS reached for his wallet, sighed and asked, "How much do you need?"

PART I

1

As dusk approached on a warm September evening, the reinstated Sergeant Mick Dempsey, 'borrowed' a UN jeep from the Camp Shamrock motor pool and set out for Beirut. It was his final overseas tour before age tipped him into retirement. Where had the time gone? It felt like someone pressed fast-forward and his time in the army had zipped by in the blink of an eye. Four tours in south Lebanon had been the highlights. This time around, their area of operation was tense, but Dempsey was relishing his final overseas mission.

The hundred-kilometre journey along the coast from Tibnin to the capital city took him over two hours. Six weeks earlier, a chance encounter had reunited him with kids he had known at a Tibnin orphanage, what seemed like a lifetime ago. When he received their invitation to meet them in Beirut, he willingly agreed. He planned to blow off steam in the casinos over the weekend with $500, borrowed from a fellow NCO.

His friends arrived to pick him up an hour after he checked into the Phenix, a twenty-five dollar a night dump,

approved by the Camp Shamrock CO for soldiers on
R & R.

"Are we going to hit the tables, lads?" he grinned, as he
settled into the taxi.

"Sorry, Mick, not tonight," Abousamra answered from
the front seat, before issuing directions to the driver in
Arabic. Dempsey copped his shoulder tic—still there
whenever he was nervous. In their early thirties now,
Abousamra had mushroomed to almost six foot and
sported a thick black beard. Although smaller, Dempsey
recalled Hussein, seated beside him, as the more skilful of
the two footballers. Even as a teenager, he seemed to have
a permanent five o'clock shadow covering his thin face.
Both spoke good English, partly a consequence of evening
classes he had insisted they attend at Camp Shamrock.

As they left the city centre, Hussein opened a shoulder
bag and took out a canvas hood with a pull cord.

"Put this on," he told Dempsey.

"Still wise-cracking," the soldier replied, uncertainly.

In the front seat Abou's shoulder twitched. "Put it on,"
he repeated. "It protects us and you."

"Jaysus, some welcome to your city, this is," Dempsey
observed, as he pulled the hood over his head.

Hussein cinched the cord as they drove deeper into the
Haret Hreik district. The silent driver dropped them in the
underground car park of a rundown building, and
departed. Dank air in the place was shot through with a
blocked drain stink. Hussein undid the cord and removed
the hood. Dempsey rubbed his eyes and blinked as he
struggled to adjust to the gloom. When he spotted two
uniformed militia men emerge from the shadows, sub-
machine guns at the ready, he silently cursed his misplaced
trust in the foreigners. Both wore balaclavas and signalled a
thumbs-up to the new arrivals. They set out climbing the

concrete stairs and Hussein swept a finger across his lips signalling Dempsey to zip it.

As they progressed upwards, they passed armed, hooded militia guarded each landing. They ascended until they reached the third floor, where a sentry signalled them towards an apartment. Hussein clicked a switch as they entered and instantly, a fluorescent tube threw off flashes of blinding light. The light stuttered and flickered stark flashes that strobed the bizarre scene into which the soldier had been dropped. He took in what he could in the brief explosions of light. A small, battered table with four chairs sat in the centre of the room. Pink paint peeled off the walls and filthy curtains hung redundant over a window shuttered on the inside with plywood sheets. The flashing light started to sting and Dempsey held up a hand to shield his eyes.

"Kill it," the suited, middle-aged man at the table ordered.

A guard appeared with a battery-powered lantern and placed it on the table before extinguishing the flickering main light. As the elegantly attired associate stood to greet Hussein, Dempsey noted the body language. There was no mistaking who was boss.

"*Aslaamo alaikam,*" Hussein said, as they embraced.

"*Walaikam salaam,*" the guy replied mechanically. His eyes hadn't left Dempsey from the moment he entered.

"*Aslaamo alaikam,* Sheikh Nader," Abousamra said, leaning in for the familiar Arab greeting. "This is the man we talk to you about."

The sheikh signalled Dempsey to sit. Abousamra took the seat beside the host and Hussein sat next to their uneasy guest.

"Tell me, are you alone in the world?" Nader opened.

Puzzled, Dempsey replied, "What's it to you?"

"Just answer," Abousamra told him.

"I have three kids, their mother and meself are not together anymore. I support them, as best I can," Dempsey said, his strong Dublin accent alien to this environment.

"You think to go on this way, when you return to your home?" Nader asked.

The dim light cast the sheikh in shadow. Middle-aged, his immaculate grooming oozed money and power.

Dempsey stared across the table at his interrogator. "How d'ya mean?"

"How do you intend to go on when the Army dismisses you?" he continued, stroking his dark goatee.

"I might struggle but I'll think of somethin' to get by."

"What about your family?"

"What does my family matter to you?"

"Pity the man whose family suffers neglect."

Dempsey shifted his gaze to the two young men he considered friends.

"Lads, why is this man havin' a go at me?"

"He's not," Hussein told him. "We're trying to find a way to help you."

Nader looked to Hussein, who nodded, and then to Abousamra, who gave a similar acknowledgment to their leader.

"Your friends tell me you seek salvation," he began.

Dempsey recalled Abousamra quoting the Koran to him about gambling when they ate together in Tibnin. He wished now that he hadn't bumped into them on that checkpoint. What was it?

"Sorry, you've lost me," he told his interlocutor.

Nader paused and looked again to his two young disciples.

Avoid it so that you might get salvation, that's it, Dempsey remembered.

Weeks earlier, he had chatted to his teenage protégés about his impending retirement and his unceasing struggle to make ends meet. He thought nothing of the conversation, just old friends catching up. He recalled that neither Hussein nor Abousamra told him much about their new lives in Beirut.

"Mr. Dempsey, we have a proposal for you," Nader began.

As Dempsey listened, he maintained a neutral expression despite his head buzzing with the possibilities of all he heard. The more he considered what was being asked of him and the rewards it offered, the more he was convinced that he could make it happen. They discussed how Dempsey would set about the task. Introductions would be first, he would lead them to the right people. Modalities was next. Dempsey told them planning was one of his strong points, and the timeframe was perfect. He was due to leave Lebanon at the end of the year and Nader told him, his old friends would meet him before he departed to sort out a method of contact.

"One issue remains," Nader said.

"What?"

"I need to know that you will not betray us."

He aimed a barely perceptible nod towards his bodyguard.

"The lads know me…"

The guard crossed the room swiftly and grabbed Hussein from behind. Dempsey jumped away from the scuffle; wanting no part of an internecine feud. With Hussein's arms trapped behind him, after a struggle, the guard managed to handcuff his wrists.

"What the fuck?" Dempsey spluttered.

"A traitor," Nader said. "He must be eliminated. You must do it."

"Abou, what the fuck?" Dempsey repeated.

Abousamra was behind him, next to the sheikh's body-guard. "My leader is my guide," he replied, coldly.

"Only the trustworthy shall leave this room," Nader shouted, menace stitched into his tone.

Hussein sat silent and motionless on the chair, his slight frame slumped forward.

Nader placed a pistol on the table. Dempsey looked at it and then Abousamra, who held his stare.

Reluctantly, Dempsey picked the weapon up and cocked the hammer. The click thundered in the silence that suddenly shrouded the room.

"You or him," Nader said.

Dempsey's mind was ablaze as he pointed the pistol towards Hussein. "Ah Jaysus, lad I'm really sorry."

A gunshot rang out, ear-splitting in the room's confines. Dempsey looked numbly towards Hussein's slumped head. He hadn't pulled the trigger. To his right, the bodyguard slumped to the floor, blood pulsing from a cavity where his right ear had been. Abousamra holstered a pistol and bent to retrieve keys. He nodded towards the sheikh as he unlocked the handcuffs from his friend's wrists.

"A Daesh recruiter," Nader told Dempsey. "I will not tolerate this."

As he stood up from the chair rubbing his wrists, Hussein stared at Dempsey; the look, a dagger through the heart of his childhood mentor.

"Not a game; remember this Mr. Dempsey," Nader warned as he swept out with Hussein and Abousamra in tow as replacement bodyguards.

Two guards entered and pushed Dempsey from the room. They shoved him into a taxi that took him back to his hotel where he lay on the single bed for hours recycling the earlier events. After a sleepless night he prowled the early morning city centre, uncertain of his next move. He ate lamb kebabs cooked on hot coals by market traders and drank coffee in street cafés. He scoured his surroundings, vigilantly checking if he was being followed. By late afternoon, the lure of Beirut's casinos had pulled him in and on Sunday morning, he returned to his unit with a remarkably clear head. The tables had been good to him. He took it as an omen. To his colleague's surprise, he repaid the five hundred dollar loan immediately. He gave an extra fifty to the motor pool grunt who had sorted his transport, together with the promised slab of Bud.

Mick Dempsey didn't care much for Gene Fulton when they first met in 1988. His wrinkled, hard set face had an unforgiving look but it was his lizard-like tongue constantly darting around his lips that creeped Dempsey out. Their paths converged when Dempsey's options ran out as a debt collection agency narrowed in on him. The criminal behind *Accelerated Cooperation,* boasted a "no nonsense" approach to ensuring debts were honoured. Dempsey didn't need a picture painted. He brought his dilemma to Fulton, who couldn't recall him, although they had attended the same school. He explained to Fulton that what he needed was a few weeks protection until he headed overseas on another six month tour. In return, he offered him two Smith & Wesson revolvers he had restored from deactivated to full working order. Fulton sniffed an opportunity.

"The problem will still be there when you get back," he reminded Dempsey.

He used both hands to sweep back unruly, shoulder-length grey hair as he spoke. The girly habit reminded Dempsey of the teasing Fulton endured as a kid until he stabbed his schoolyard bully and got expelled.

"What you need is to get things sorted," Fulton added.

Dempsey's debts had run out of control. Tired of rarely seeing a penny of his income, his wife finally threw him out when she discovered he had pilfered her Christmas savings. The maintenance order she took out in the family court put a lien on his army income. A credit card company had gotten in ahead of her, taking a chunk of his salary to recoup a maxed out line of credit. The family law court redistributed as best it could and the guaranteed weekly amount, however meagre, copper-fastened her decision never to take him back.

By the time he reached out to Fulton, Dempsey owed over £100,000 to eight private gambling clubs around Dublin. Fulton told him not to worry about his debts and drew a line in the sand nobody dared to cross. When he outlined to Dempsey what he needed in return, the soldier tried to convince him the venture was ultra-high risk and likely to fail. Fulton wouldn't listen.

Seven months down the line, Dempsey needed an emergency operation to treat a peptic ulcer. His bosses put it down to stress; it was just two weeks after his repatriation from Lebanon. They weren't wrong. What Dempsey told nobody was that most of his six-month tour had revolved around figuring out ways to smuggle a ton of highly-prized cannabis resin, *Lebanese blond*, and thirty kilos of heroin. Eventually, he secreted the drugs in five armoured personnel carriers being shipped home for scrapping. As the battalion armourer, Dempsey supervised their repatriation by sea and arranged a stopover, which allowed Fulton's gang to retrieve their cargo. It sky-rocketed Gene Fulton's standing in the criminal underworld and he did a deal with Dempsey's creditors that gave them the option of settling for twenty percent of his debt or nothing. They took the money.

Dempsey soon realised that Gene Fulton didn't go away. In the years that followed, he was forced to acquire and maintain the gang's weapons. Not wanting to lose his ace, Fulton kept it as a one-to-one relationship; none of the gang ever met the mystery gunsmith.

Dempsey used a payphone in a bar, well away from Camp Shamrock to make contact. When he dialled the usual number, a pre-recorded service message told him it was no longer in use. Panicked, he dialled another that Fulton had given him for emergencies. Fulton's son, Slasher, answered and explained that the aul fella had been put away after being caught doing something stupid. Rather than rent out his weapons, he had tagged along on a post office stick-up and gotten himself arrested. Slasher was running the show in the old man's absence. Dempsey weighed up his options. There was nowhere else to go and the kid, even if a bit wired, sounded alright. Dempsey sketched out the bare bones of Nader's proposal to him.

"I need to know more," Slasher told him. "I'll send Don to talk to ya'."

"Okay."

"Somewhere handy for everyone."

"Fair enough," Dempsey said. "No chance you'd travel yourself?"

"We don't need cops gettin' curious, now do we."

"You know best."

"How about that holiday place near ya?"

"Sound."

"Next weekend. Yeah?"

"Dead on."

"I'll text details. Bring your two buddies along."

2

CYPRUS - PRESENT DAY

Something stirred deep in Kate Bowen's memory when she copped the group.

"What's up?" her former Detective Inspector, Dan "Digger" Rooney asked. He had caught the fleeting frown, as they sat under a parasol sipping iced coffee.

"Let's take a selfie," Kate replied, picking up her iPhone.

Digger pushed his chair around the white plastic table in the tiny seating area outside the café and waited as she fumbled with on-screen commands.

"You're all out of focus," he chided.

"Don't rush me," she replied, "Smile!"

He pulled a face as Kate extended the phone in front of them.

"Told you," Digger said, as they checked the screen. "You got the diners in the café across the road, better than us."

His blue shorts exposed greyhound skinny legs that belied their owner's unflagging nature; the nickname had stuck, for his bloodhound style of investigation. His plaid

short-sleeved shirt revealed wiry arms bronzed from a fortnight in the sun.

"Anything strike you as familiar about the coffee
drinkers?" Kate asked.

"Is that...?" Digger began. "Let's try one with
my phone."

Kate shook her hair loose from the ponytail that held it
back. "How's this?"

Under the Mediterranean sun her hair had grown to
almost shoulder length. It fell in brunette tresses on either
side of her face. She wore no make-up, but was tanned
from months of unbroken sunshine and her green eyes
sparkled as she smiled. "One for posterity," Digger said as
he clicked a close-up. He re-focused and took another shot
of the diners across the street. They sipped their coffee and
checked out the result.

"What do you think?" Kate asked.

"That's definitely Don Bailey," Digger replied. "I don't
know any of the others."

Kate knew Bailey was a vicious Dublin thug working
for Slasher Fulton and recognised him on sight. Other than
that, she knew little about him. There were three others in
his group. The one sitting beside him had an Irish tan—
face and arms peppered with freckles. He was close to his
fifties, a ginger, although age had tinted his red hair a fairer
shade. The two fit young men sitting opposite the Irish pair
looked Middle Eastern.

"I need better photos," Digger said, picking up his
camera bag.

Photography was his hobby and an hour earlier, he had
been busy, snapping RAF fighter jets taking off from their
Akrotiri base. Kate's invitation to show him the base location spared Digger another languid morning on the beach
as his family's autumn sunshine holiday drew to a close.

Kate was stationed on the island since May, an abrupt, unwelcome transfer. She was the Superintendent, in charge of a twelve-strong Irish Police contingent, an integral part of the United Nations' longest peacekeeping mission. The twelve months in the *sticks was* an undeclared payback for contentious decisions she made in her last case.

"Why bother?" Kate asked. "Just report the sighting when you get home."

"I'd like to check it out," he replied.

"Like anyone gives a crap."

"Come on, admit it; you love this," Digger goaded. "Let's follow them for a bit."

"Be my guest."

"I'll need a hand. You've got a mobile."

"I have two, but I can't use my work one."

"Why not?"

"Conflict of interest."

"Who's goin' to find out?"

"The UN might and I'm not giving anyone else an excuse to kick my ass."

"They're movin', let's go," Digger said.

"I'll use my private phone but I'm not racking up charges on a whim."

Kate strolled across the road and mingled with shoppers in the brand new My Mall Shopping Centre in Limassol's Zakaki district. The place played like a monument to globalisation; lots of shops exactly the same as she had left behind in Ireland, there was even a Marks & Spencer. When she discovered the mall during her first month on the island, she had relished the retail therapy, and the respite from oppressive summer heat its air conditioning offered.

"They're heading for the mall car park," she told Digger on the phone as she followed the small group.

"Get me a make, colour, and number of their car," he replied. "I'll do the rest."

"But you've no car."

"Just phoned in a hire request to the rental company on the ground floor. I'm pickin' it up in five."

"You're bloody nuts," Kate told him. "Jane will freak if she finds out you're spending your family budget like this."

"Jane doesn't need to know. Don Bailey's a bad one and if he's organisin' somethin', I need to find out as much as possible."

"I'll stay with them as long as I can," Kate replied. "But Digger, this is not like the old days, I'm compromised over here."

"Okay, okay. Gotta go."

Bailey walked ahead of the group as they reached the car park. There was little about him that indicated a criminal background. He was average height; about five nine, Kate reckoned. He walked with a confident swagger and wore a sky blue summer polo shirt, which flapped loosely over khaki shorts. Both appeared new. His arms and legs were well toned, Kate observed, clearly someone who regularly worked out. His face had a chiselled look but was only lightly tanned, indicating that his trip to the sun had been brief. His neatly trimmed brown hair was lank on top, the only hint of an undernourished upbringing.

He sprang into a black Mercedes SUV and reversed out. From the car park floor above Digger clicked off shots of the group as Bailey picked up his passengers. Kate followed in her silver BMW 3 series convertible, hardly ideal for surveillance. She had bought it when she arrived on the island. It came duty-free, the only ray of sunshine she could see from her current assignment. She relayed the direction of travel to Digger. They were headed for the ring road out of Limassol. She waited until they had negotiated a series of roundabouts before being confident enough to give Digger the final heads-up.

"Okay, we're on the A1, heading west, moving fast, direction Larnaca," Kate said. "I'll keep the phone open."

"No, hang up," he told her. "I took a chance that they might head for Larnaca and I'm up the road, ahead of you. I'm in a green Kia; the smallest and cheapest yoke I could get. When you pass me, keep goin' until the first Larnaca turn off and tell me if they take it."

"Roger."

Kate felt a tingle of excitement; once again she was breaking rules, once again entangling herself in someone else's nefarious goings-on. Five months earlier she was convinced this chapter of her career had been slammed shut for good when Redmond "Mac" McEnroe announced her bolt-from-the-blue transfer. Mac had been her boss, the Chief at the Surveillance and Intelligence Unit. His vast experience tempered what some called her recklessness. To Kate, it was getting the job done. She ran SIU's field operations and rated her team the best in the business. Digger, Angie, Zoom and others —people she had counted on to go the extra mile without quibble.

As they left the elongated Limassol suburbs behind, Kate overtook the Mercedes and focussed on staying far enough ahead not to create suspicion, but close enough to react, should anything unexpected happen. She drove with the top down and wore a white baseball cap to keep wisps of her retied hair off her face. The Jackie Ohh Ray Bans were an everyday necessity. To her right, she had an uninterrupted view of the Mediterranean where midday sun bounced sparkles off its warm blue surface. In contrast, the other side of the motorway was a parched brown landscape of hills and valleys, periodically pockmarked black from seasonal bush fires. Ten minutes into the journey, Digger called back.

"Something's off with Bailey's mates. They're fuckin' wired to anyone tailin' them, I'm goin' to have to overtake."

"No worries," Kate replied. "I'll stick with them. Stay on the motorway west, take the second exit, and then come back towards Larnaca Salt Lake."

"Why?"

"I saw travel bags in the car. I think they're headed to the airport."

"Great! Feelin' good to be back?"

"Let's not go there," she replied.

"Okay. There's a chance they made me on the motorway. I can't afford to let them spot the car again."

"Ditch it and take a bus to the airport. If they're catching flights, we'll try and see which ones."

Half an hour after Digger's warning, Kate watched from a lay-by as the SUV took the airport off-ramp. She relayed the news, pulled the BMW's soft top forward, and entered the traffic lane for the airport, five cars back. *She's still got it!* Digger thought.

Kate dumped her car in the car park and observed her targets check in, while sipping a Coke at an arrivals bar. When Digger's bus arrived, she smiled watching him in action as he blended in with other tourists. He stepped off a shuttle bus at the small terminal's set down area and helped a pair of elderly passengers manhandle large suitcases out of the hold. He then grabbed a small bag, a recent purchase, and walked to join her.

"Bailey's checked in on the London flight," she told him.

"What about the other bucks?"

"Looks like they're heading to Beirut."

"Even the ginger?"

"Yes."

"Curiouser and curiouser!"

"Copy the photos to this," Kate said, handing Digger a small USB from her key ring.

"Why?"

"I might be able to do some enquiries here on the Arab pair."

"With who?"

"The Americans."

"You know them here?"

"They've a huge embassy in Nicosia. The Marines who guard it invite us around now and again for a drink. There's sure to be CIA there. I'll talk to Whatney and get a contact."

Dan Whatney was the CIA Liaison in Paris who had worked with Kate on her last case that played out in France. When word leaked out of her exile, he had called to commiserate and offer support.

"Kate, don't go doin' anythin' to get yourself in bother."

"It's like this, Digger, over here the days are long. If I've a project going on under the radar, it's a welcome distraction. Nobody needs to know."

Kate performed her mundane UN duties with little enthusiasm. The nights were still rarely restful for her; stifling heat was one reason; flashbacks to her previous case were the other. Its terrifying conclusion had shaken her and she had to learn to anticipate and manage triggers that might induce post-traumatic stress disorder. Linking up with Digger's family on holiday had been a pleasant change of pace, now it had turned into something different. Kate drained her Coke as she studied the photos on Digger's camera.

"You need to see them on a proper screen to get a feel for the heads," he said.

"I'll view them later," Kate replied. "Bailey looks fit."

"He's a kick-boxer. A vicious fucker!"

"Don't know what to make of the Middle-Eastern pair and the ginger's a total mystery. We better go sort out your car and head back to Napa. You promised Jane you'd get back early."

In the afternoon Digger and Kate stretched out on towels underneath a parasol at Nissi beach in Aya Napa. The Rooney family was using the autumn mid-term break to take their delayed annual holiday. A transfer to a new unit meant Digger was last in line for time off during the summer months. Being able to swim in a warm sea at the end of October was a rare treat and Jane was splashing with the children while Digger sulked. Over a late lunch, she had ribbed him about his upcoming fortieth birthday.

"I'm told this warm weather will last at least another week," Kate observed.

"The kids seem to like it," Digger muttered.

"I'm glad, because this island is the last place in the world I want to be."

"What's done is done."

"Thanks for the sympathy."

"We had a bit of craic this mornin', hadn't we?"

"Reminder of better times, I suppose."

"Put your head down and do your time."

"I'm not even at the midway point yet."

"For God sake, Kate, stop feelin' sorry for yourself."

"Sorry! Jeez, keep going like this and you'll bowl me over with empathy."

"Stop apologising. You didn't cause this, you were exiled," Digger replied.

His phone rang.

"I'm going for a swim," she told him, as she jumped to her feet. "Get over yourself and join us."

The reflected sun off the white sand dazzled, as she headed towards the azure Mediterranean. The water was calm, perfect for swimming. When Digger's children saw Kate they raced towards her, splashing and chasing. She picked up Sean and Maggie in turn and threw them over her shoulder into the water despite their protesting squeals. Far as she could tell, they liked the rough and tumble games 'Auntie' Kate played with them.

The beach was busy but not overcrowded. The last weekend in October attracted mostly families rather than the raucous crowds of summer. Kate had steered clear of Aya Napa during July and August.

"Dan's waving," Digger's wife shouted, as Kate chased the children.

Jane was the only person Kate knew who called him by his given name.

"I think he wants you," she said.

"Okay kids, back in a minute," Kate laughed.

She brushed wet hair off her smiling face as she headed up the beach. Was it messing around with the kids pleased her, or reconnecting with Digger for the first time in months, she wondered? Deep down, she knew it was neither; it was the thrill of the earlier chase. Dipping back into surveillance was an adrenaline rush that lingered.

Droplets of water trickled from her black bikini and glistened on her tanned torso. She had used her free hours on the island to get fit again. It didn't come as easy as before, but a weekly Ju-Jitsu dojo with a British Army

Gurkha company in Nicosia had Kate in the best shape of her life as she approached her thirty-fourth birthday.

Digger sat with elbows on knees, phone still in his hand, deadly silent. She grabbed a beach towel and started to dab her hair dry. She glanced at his furrowed brow and dead ahead gaze. Leaving her hair an unruly mess, she wrapped the towel around her waist.

"What's with the thousand-yard stare?" she asked.

"Zoom's dead," he muttered in reply.

3

As Kate stepped onto the Dublin airport tarmac five days later rain pelted down from a leaden sky that promised more of the same. Driven by a biting easterly, it lashed into the faces of passengers as they scuttled down the ramp and ran into the terminal. Kate had reluctantly rented out her Dublin apartment and during this short stay she planned on spending nights at home in Dundalk. Her mother offered to come pick her up but Kate insisted the bus was just as quick and more convenient. As she waited outside Terminal 1, she removed her tan oversized trench coat and shook it, then powered up her mobile and called Digger.

"You made it," he said.

"Wouldn't miss it," Kate replied. "Anything further on how O'Driscoll managed to screw up the operation?"

"What you read online is pretty accurate. I'll explain the details face-to-face."

"Okay," Kate replied.

"O'Driscoll's fightin' a rear guard action. Your replacement, Strong, has been suspended."

"Jesus, he's already found his scapegoat. What an asshole!"

With Kate's departure, SIU had suffered. Angie didn't stick around. She had witnessed Kate's courage on their last case together and knew her treatment was unjust. She shipped back to her old drugs unit the day Kate left. When O'Driscoll took over the reins, Digger also jumped ship. He sought a transfer to Special Branch and the new SIU boss arranged the switch. Neither he nor Angie could stomach working for the vain glorious Chief.

O'Driscoll convinced Zoom to stay. He was captain at the Garda rugby club, an honour O'Driscoll had shared in the past. The new boss guaranteed him he would go places if he stuck around. Unfortunately for Zoom ambition killed him.

At Mount Argus on Dublin's south side, Kate stood side by side with former SIU colleagues at the back of a packed church. They watched as the Commissioner escorted Justice Minister Patrick O'Hagan down the centre aisle. Press cameras clicked as the pair walked to a reserved seat nearest the altar. Zoom's fiancée, Julie, dressed in black, sat across the aisle beside his distraught parents. The political media circus sickened Kate.

Zoom Duggan had been one of her best operators; a tough, brave cop who never flinched from a challenge. Now the stupidity of supposedly smart people had contributed to his untimely death by putting an idiot in charge of a unit where life or death decisions were a regular occurrence.

Mac, Kate's old boss, sat among the senior officers. Promoted to Assistant Commissioner three months after

Kate departed, his promotion offered O'Driscoll the opportunity to take the reins at SIU. They had not been in contact since. Well into his fifties, Mac's six foot plus frame retained a natural robustness and he looked well in uniform.

When the funeral service concluded, Zoom's remains were cremated. Kate left with Digger and Angie and linked up with SIU colleagues at a pub near their base. It was off the beaten track and the owner had set aside a room for them. During the evening he served ham sandwiches and cocktail sausages, not exactly fine dining but no-one complained. Neither O'Driscoll, nor the goon he put in charge of field operations ventured near the gathering. Still numb from his violent death, Zoom's friends drank copiously to his memory. Late in the evening, Mac slipped in through a side door and joined Digger at the bar. He had changed into civvies and as he signalled the barman, he was aware that the hubbub of conversation was dying around him.

"Fucking eejits will get us all killed," someone shouted from the group huddled together in the centre of the room.

Digger recognised the voice and, kicking stools out of his way, shot from the bar into the middle of the group. He grabbed the loudmouth and propelled him outside where he delivered hard slaps on either side of the offender's face and snarled, "If you've somethin' to say, do it face-to-face, don't fuckin' hide."

"I'm just saying what everyone's thinking," came the reply.

Digger felt a tap on the shoulder.

"No harm done," Mac told him. "Let's go back in; I'm buying."

"No offence, sir," the offender offered, eyes cast downward.

Mac held the side door open. "Come on," he said.

As they got inside, Angie stood up.

"This is for Zoom," she said.

She began singing 'I Know You by Heart', the Eva Cassidy classic.

Tiny, tenacious, and brave, Angie was one of Kate's closest allies at SIU. Her short cropped, raven hair gave her an elfin appearance and the power and beauty of her voice stunned everyone. Nobody had known she was a singer. She hit the high notes effortlessly and by the end tears streamed down her face. Kate walked over and hugged her. Wild clapping erupted, sobs petered around the room as months of unbearable tension found release.

As Kate led Angie to the ladies' room, she nodded to Mac, stood by the bar. He raised his glass in their direction.

"Powerful, Angie," he said.

"Thanks, boss," she replied.

"We should chat," Mac said to Kate.

"Okay," she replied.

Strangely, when she woke next morning Kate didn't have a hangover. Everyone was still adrenaline-fuelled which most likely fended it off. The previous evening had been emotional and strung out until the early hours of the morning. With Mac it had just been chitchat. There were more songs and everyone recounted memories of Zoom's hairy exploits on surveillance operations. She stayed at Digger's house overnight. Jane held the children off from waking Auntie Kate for as long as possible. Eventually, they bounded in on top of her and roused her. She played with Sean and Maggie a while, jumping up and down on the bed, before hitting the shower.

She was due to travel back to Cyprus the following day and Mac had asked her to meet for coffee before returning. No matter what arose, Kate was determined to spend the last night at home with her mother in Dundalk. Her only option was to meet him before catching the bus north. After breakfast Digger dropped her off in Dublin city centre. As she took her travel bag from the boot of his car, she said "I'll give you a buzz if I get anything on those Arab heads."

"Don't make hassle for yourself," Digger replied, "I'll work on it here. Angie said she might be able to convince her boss to do some surveillance on Bailey's mob."

"Does Bailey have his own gang?"

"In all but name; *Slasher* Fulton is the gang leader; but he's doin' so much coke at the minute, people wonder if he's *compos mentis* at all."

"So Bailey runs the show. If they're into drugs, how come Special Branch are interested?"

"Bailey's the ringmaster and drug gangs need guns. We're interested since we picked up rumours that IRA Dissidents are renting out their hardware."

They hugged a goodbye. "Thanks for everything," Kate said, "I'll be in touch."

Mac came to the Stephen's Green shopping centre to meet Kate. The city centre office he now worked out of was a few hundred metres walk away in Harcourt Street. They bought coffees in a top floor café and found a seat near the window that overlooked the park. Kate glanced, nostalgically towards Fusilier's Arch. It formed the main entrance into Saint Stephen's Green, the city centre park she had walked through hundreds of times.

"How are you managing out there?" Mac asked.

"I'm bored stupid," she replied.

He cracked a smile.

"Candid as ever."

"It's a fact."

"Last night was good for everyone, I think," Mac ventured.

"For anyone that matters," she replied.

"Agreed."

"How's your promotion working out?"

He studied her closely. Was she being sarcastic; having a pop at him for not doing enough when she needed help?

"It's a change."

"Good or bad?"

"Different."

"High profile, anyway. You've been on the telly."

The number one cop in the capital always attracted attention. Mac had featured in a number of television reports advising people how to stay safe during public events.

"Did it come across how much I enjoyed the experience?"

"What about Zoom?" she murmured, after a beat.

"Such a tragedy; he was one of the best."

"It should never have happened," Kate came back angrily.

Mac looked around. A number of customers glanced nervously in their direction on hearing a raised voice.

"Kate, everyone's raw at the moment," he whispered.

"You know we successfully concluded similar jobs with the unit, without drama," Kate said, her head inclined closer to Mac.

SIU had been tailing a tooled-up criminal gang when Zoom was killed. They had followed them to a Dublin suburban bank branch. A security van doing deliveries for cash machines had been the target.

"I know, but each op is different."

"Making excuses for O'Driscoll. Shit, I knew it, he's going to get this covered up too. He panicked, for God's sake!" Kate hissed.

The plan had been to take out the gang before they got to the security van. However, a delivery truck blocked a camera that had been giving O'Driscoll a live feed of the action. He ordered his on-scene commander to find out what was happening. Zoom, the unit's best driver, volunteered to investigate and report back. The raiders had hijacked the armoured van by that stage and the driver panicked when he copped the pump action shotgun in the unmarked car. He T-boned it and killed Zoom instantly.

"Kate, my advice is to guard your opinion," Mac snapped. "GSOC is all over this and the media's watching."

Kate picked up her skinny latté and sipped, pondering how much the Garda's independent internal affairs investigation body would relish the publicity the case would bring. She looked away from Mac, out over the autumnal brown and gold palette on the sycamore trees that surrounded Stephen's Green. A sullen silence prevailed between them.

"When do you go back?" Mac eventually asked.

"Early tomorrow," Kate replied.

"You won't feel the time passing once Christmas comes and goes."

"You're not the one over there."

She drained her cup and stood up. "Talk to Digger, one of the drugs gangs in the city is keeping strange company," she said as she gathered her keys off the table and slid her overnight bag out from underneath.

"Stay in touch," was Mac's parting advice, as they went their separate ways outside the shopping centre.

A few streets away off the quays, another tête-à-tête played out.

"Hop in," Don Bailey shouted to the prostitute from the passenger seat of the black car, as it pulled alongside. John 'Twenty' Carew, her pimp and supplier, was hunched in the back seat. Nothing he sold on the street went for under twenty euros. Audrey had been avoiding him for weeks. Now, she noticed his right eye was swelling from a recent blow.

"Don't look at him," Bailey said. "I'm the one talking to you. Get in."

She had never seen this guy before but had little choice. As she climbed into the car Bailey noted the wear and tear to the bright red colour on her nails that matched her lipstick. She wore a tight black PVC skirt, short enough to leave little to the imagination and her red top accentuated what she considered her finest assets. These days her appearance was the reason she didn't make it past the front door of most decent hotels. The managers knew her face and her game.

Cocaine had been her downfall. Convinced she only needed it now and again; she ignored the warning sign that an increasing amount of her earnings went towards feeding her habit. It was a vicious circle. The more coke she used, the more she needed. Her looks faded in tandem. She had to drop her prices. When her access was barred to more hotels she became desperate and began bringing the punters back to her apartment. As the clients increased to fill the gap, neighbours complained and she was kicked out. She wasn't choosy and quickly found another place.

"Twenty here, tells me you owe him a lot of money," Bailey began, as the car drove off.

"I owe him some," she shot back.

"Five hundred is what he tells me."

"It's not da much."

"Are you calling him a liar?"

"No, I'm just sayin, I don't tink it's da high."

"Twenty, are you yanking my chain?" Don Bailey asked. He didn't bother turning to see the pimp's reaction as the car rolled along the docks.

"Upon me soul, I'm tellin ya the truth," he replied.

"Audrey, what do you think?" Bailey asked.

"I'm not disputin I owe him a few bob. It's jus da I didn't tink it was da much."

"Buck, stop the car," Bailey told his driver.

He was out of the car before Audrey could react. Opening the door fast, he pulled her out by the hair and slammed her face into the roof of the car before she could protest. Her lip split and blood flowed down her front. She burst into tears.

"Don't start on me, for Jaysus sake," she cried out. "I'll get your fuckin money."

"Slasher's debts are my debts. If I don't collect, it makes me look like a cunt. Are you saying I'm a cunt, Audrey," Bailey said, maintaining his grip on her hair.

"No, no, I swear ta God I'll get it for ya," she sobbed. "Gimme a chance."

"Time's up, Audrey," Bailey told her, "now or never."

"I don't have da kind of money on me," she said.

Bailey pushed her face against the boot of the car and used his free hand to check her bra for hidden cash. He found nothing, so he yanked her panties down and checked it; again, zilch.

"We'll go to your place then," he said. "Brassers always have a stash."

"Aw righ," Audrey sobbed as Bailey threw her back into the car.

"Don't you get any fucking blood on my car," he warned.

Audrey's flat was a kip in a rundown, redbrick terraced house at Ringsend, close to the docks. Bailey was unsurprised by what greeted him. The place was filthy with left-over takeaway cartons and dirty clothes strewn on the floor. He had grown up with similar; his mother was an alcoholic who turned tricks to feed her addiction right up to the night she choked on her own vomit. He despised anyone replicating the lifestyle.

"Money, now!" he shouted.

"I don't have it all," she said.

"How much do you have?"

"€150."

"€150! You brought me this far, for a 150," Bailey shouted at her. He moved towards her.

"Don't hit me again," she pleaded. "In the name of Jaysus, don't hit me, *plea-as*."

"Stop telling fucking lies. Give me the 600 you owe."

"It's 500."

"You're getting funny now? The price just went up. Now get me my fucking money."

"I don't have da much on me," she pleaded, "but I know how I can get it."

Bailey punched her in the face and she crumbled to the floor.

"I'm done with this," he said. "Give me what you've got and I'll be back next week for the rest."

"I can give ya somethin, if you clear me debt," she sobbed, her hands reaching up towards him.

Bailey raised his fist again.

"No, no I don't mean da," she screamed. "I know ya don't want nothin like da."

"You're right on that score. What are you fucking on about?"

"I'll show ya."

From her bedside locker, Audrey pulled out a photograph of one of her sleeping clients. It was printed on an A4 paper sheet. She had sent it her to e-mail address from her smart phone more than a year earlier. At that stage, her good looks earned her three times what she now charged. She showed it to Bailey.

"Him, he's a copper," she said.

He realised what her long game had been; saving her trump card for a day of reckoning. He was surprised that she had held out this long before trying to cash it in. He thought about it a while and decided it was worth a punt.

"When that face of yours clears up, I want a photo," Bailey warned her.

"Awh righ," she whimpered.

"Mention a word of this to anyone and I'll be back. Next time, I won't be so forgiving."

"I'll keep me mouth shu."

"I'm taking the cash and *you*, you stupid bitch, fuck off and find another supplier," he told her, as he slammed the door on the squalor.

4

As she read the news from home, Kate struggled to keep warm at her modest apartment. Christmas was around the corner and miserable rainy days, followed by chilly nights had become the norm in Cyprus. When deployed months earlier into warm May weather, a UN accommodation officer had shown her a room on the Nicosia UNPA base where they wanted her to billet for the next twelve months. It was a dump and she told them to shove it. Eventually, they agreed to stump up fifty percent rent on a small studio apartment just outside the base perimeter.

She sat wrapped in a duvet feeling vexed, as she scrolled the various Irish news sites. A nervous Taoiseach prattled soundbites to counter the drip feed of negative publicity surrounding Zoom's killing. The head of government was unimpressed with the blustering performances by his Justice Minister during television appearances and had taken over control of the media message. GSOC's enquiry was not making the progress Kate expected and it seemed they didn't get what was at stake. She knew it was a slam dunk. Responsibility for the foul-up that killed her friend lay squarely on the shoulders of the operation's planners, O'Driscoll and the suspended Strong.

"GSOC is exercising due diligence," its head of service repeated, as he batted off media allegations of tardiness.

Newspaper editors didn't buy it and their opinion pieces highlighted errors of judgement by senior management. Crime reporters filled the information void. They made plenty of copy from the discontent they picked up among the Garda's frontline crime fighters. Kate finished reading the last one and plugged in her iPad to recharge. She wrapped the quilt tighter and tried to get comfortable on her single bed.

Regular thunderstorms greeted the New Year, and with them came torrential downpours that worsened working conditions for Kate's peacekeepers. During patrols in the UN-controlled Buffer Zone, she observed how winter rains rejuvenated the parched countryside. The hills and valleys transformed, exchanging dull beige for vibrant green. It meant shepherds didn't have far to trek in search of grazing for their goat herds and farmers with permits could plant cereal crops in their lands that lay within the UN Buffer Zone.

It extended north to south across the centre of the island for 180 kilometres. In Nicosia, it was just a few metres wide at certain pinch points, elsewhere it ran to several kilometres in width and separated the belligerent Greek-Cypriot and Turkish sides.

On a Monday in early January, Kate attended the morning briefing and noted warnings of 'soft going on the Buffer Zone tracks. Nonetheless, the British Army officer gave permission to carry out limited patrolling. Kate decided to observe the driving conditions first hand before giving her crews the go-ahead for extended patrols. When her phone rang, she was stuck in the mud waiting for Army assistance. At first, she figured the call related to their predicament, then she realised that it was her private mobile.

"This is Kate!" she answered.

"Batt Young here, one of Whatney's gang," the American accent greeted her.

"Oh hi," Kate replied. "Can you hold on a moment, please?"

"Sure."

Her patrol crew had gotten busy unloading wooden planks to help the tyres gain grip.

"If you get it moving, don't venture off the track," she ordered. The Buffer Zone was laced with land mines. Most had been mapped by Army engineers but she didn't want her crew finding any they'd missed.

"Sorry about that," she returned.

"Could we meet for a chat?" Young asked.

"Would tomorrow suit?"

"Sooner would be better."

"I can't come dressed as I am."

"I understand," he said.

"How about lunchtime?"

"Lunch sounds doable. The Holiday Inn is good for me."

"How will I know you?" Kate asked.

"I'll wear a red baseball cap."

"Let's hope no-one else has the same idea."

"My one's got a big white 'B' in the centre."

"A Boston Red Sox fan."

"Very impressive," Young laughed, "I'll see you there."

While Kate chatted a fresh-faced lieutenant arrived

with a squad from Roca Camp Support Company and between them they managed to pull the UNPOL jeep clear. The lieutenant warned that the weather outlook had deteriorated and Kate ordered all track patrols cancelled until conditions improved. Instead, she sent her crew to San Martin Camp, the Sector One military HQ, near Skouriotissa to assist the new Argentinean contingent with orientation. They had arrived a week earlier and the Commander had requested her assistance in familiarising his men with their area of operation.

Kate arrived back to her apartment at 12:30 p.m. and changed from UN combats into jeans and a sweater. She borrowed a battered bicycle from a neighbour and set out for the Holiday Inn where she chained it to a lamp post and strolled inside.

A few elderly tourists were dotted around the foyer as she entered. She felt her contact would choose a less public place so she headed towards the L-shaped bar where lunch was on offer. Three men sat at the long section of the L nursing beers. Kate continued around the corner and copped a red baseball cap on a shaded corner table.

"The Red Sox fan?" she asked the guy seated in the booth.

"Bartholomew Young the Third," he said, extending a hand. "Everyone calls me Batt."

"Kate Bowen."

"Would you like to eat something?" he asked.

"Let's chat first."

Young was not particularly tall. Stocky was how Kate saw him, his body seemed to have taken on the bulk that came with middle age. His unruly black hair reached the collar of a green polo shirt and was layered with abundant grey streaks. It framed a cheerful, fleshy, lived-in face. He wore faded blue jeans that matched the colour of his eyes and a grey sweatshirt. He looked like the kind of guy who would be uncomfortable wearing anything else.

"What part of the States are you from?" Kate enquired.

"I'm a Missouri boy."

He pronounced his home State as if it ended with an *a*, rather than *i*. Kate smiled, loving the accent.

"How come you support Boston Red Sox?"

"Grandparents lived there, I spent Easter holidays with them as a kid; baseball season kicked off around then. What a shame they didn't live to see us beat the jinx in 2004."

"Pity!" Kate agreed. "I read about the Red Sox winning the World Series for the first time in almost a hundred years."

"I was in St. Louis the evening they swept the Cardinals in game four," Young replied. "What a night!"

"I can only imagine."

"So Whatney told me about your status. Tricky, eh!"

"Tell me about it!" Kate laughed. "Look, I'm doing this enquiry for a trusted colleague back home."

She explained the unusual meeting Don Bailey and likely another Irish man had with two unidentified Arabs at the end of October. She wanted to figure out what was going on.

"Yeah, Whatney filled me in and sent me the photos. They're interesting."

"Do you know them?"

"Straight off, no, but we know someone in Beirut who might be able to help us identify them."

"That's fantastic."

"We'll need some help."

"How do you mean?"

"I'm going to have to go there and I need cover."

"I don't understand."

"Someone with me to make me look legit. You up for it?" he smiled.

"What's involved?" she asked.

"I rustle us up some American passports and we travel to Beirut on a weekend cruise from Limassol. Once there, you can go sightseeing; I'll do the leg work."

"How many people know about this?" Kate enquired. UNPOL mission personnel were considered the fulltime responsibility of the United Nations. A strict code of conduct went with that duty of care and transgressions were severely punished.

"Just me, you, and my own station chief," Batt replied. "If the job goes ahead, the Beirut station chief will be put in the picture."

"What about after the trip?"

"Depends. If it's just something local, European I mean, we can hold it in Nicosia. If we feel it could be part of a bigger picture we've gotta send it to Langley."

"What about my part? Does that get mentioned?"

"We can keep you out of it, if you like: your call."

"When do you need to know?"

"By tonight would be great. We leave Friday evening, if it goes ahead."

"I'd have to switch my on-call duties with a colleague. I'll call you later."

"Let's get lunch," Young suggested. "We can chat about baseball, obviously you're a fan."

Me and my big mouth, Kate thought.

Kate was obliged to make her UNPOL bosses aware of any plans to leave the island. However, weekend cruises to Beirut and other Middle East destinations were popular with UN personnel, so no-one batted an eyelid when she told them that she was taking up a last-minute offer. By six o'clock she had completed the switches that left her free to travel late on Friday night. She called Young with the news.

"Okay *Ms. Marlowe*, you can pick your new daddy up at six o'clock sharp in the car park opposite where we ate lunch."

"Well, this is going to feel weird," Kate joked.

5

Kate and Young left Nicosia early on Friday afternoon to ensure they made embarkation without drama. He was good company and chatted constantly as they travelled the motorway through the verdant hills and plains.

"Only a few weeks ago this countryside was like the surface of the moon," he remarked.

The soil, baked by months of unbroken sunshine, had been renewed by the abundant downpours turning the countryside green as dormant buds exploded into life. For Kate and her UNPOL colleagues it presented new challenges, from keeping wild asparagus pickers out of minefields when they ignored UN warning signs and trespassed into the Buffer Zone, to supervising a hunting season. Kate hated that the lack of any real action had dulled her instincts. A week earlier, when she sighted an armed group encroaching into the UN controlled zone, she immediately summoned Army assistance rather than checking them out with her unarmed patrol. It turned out to be the same group of hunters they had checked the previous day.

"It's a mud bath out there these days," Kate told him. "You could lose your boots in it."

"Shit, I forgot. You patrol this territory."

For the rest of the trip Kate steered the conversation clear of baseball. She had scraped the bottom of that particular barrel.

Limassol was bustling, with three cruise ships in port, one offloading, and the other two embarking passengers. Kate drove to a railed-off section of dock close to where the smallest of the three vessels was docked. The parking area set aside for *Empress* passengers was miniscule and Kate followed the fussy attendant's directions to one of the few remaining parking spots. As they neared the gangway of the *Empress* they linked arms and presented tickets to a Russian crew member. For the early part of the trip, they mingled with weekend tourists, getting their bearings on the ship. They dined together and Young gambled for a while in the casino. Kate played the faithful daughter at his shoulder, encouraging his efforts to beat the house. After midnight they headed to a two-berth cabin and caught a few hours sleep.

As Beirut came into view, Kate sensed a change in Young's demeanour. She knew the feeling when a mission was imminent. He went quiet, as if gearing all his thoughts towards the mission ahead. The city looked beautiful; some of the four-storeyed sandstone apartment buildings resembling those she had seen on trips to Paris. The bijou cruise liner eventually docked and they joined the queue for the tour bus in the crowded port. Soldiers from the Lebanese national army guarded the enclosure where the bus passengers embarked. When they left their military guards behind, Kate was immediately conscious of large groups of young men milling around. They pressed their faces against the windows of the bus as it nosed through the throng. Their hostile expressions shocked her. As they cleared the port and headed into the city, the upbeat guide began his commentary. At some sites, obviously ones where bombs had exploded in the not-too-distant past, the guide cheerily explained that the area was undergoing a period of *reconstruction.*

"You should have seen the place back in the eighties," Young whispered to Kate.

"I've only seen TV documentaries," Kate replied. "It looked dire."

"I had a front row seat."

"You were here?" Kate whispered.

He nodded. The bus wasn't full and most passengers had gravitated towards the back. Kate took a seat near the front that would facilitate a rapid exit. The nearest passengers were three rows back.

"Until it got too hot," he added.

"Jesus that must have been some experience."

"You know how it is, when you're young you think you rule the world; can handle anything."

"When did you leave?"

"We pulled out on October 30, 1983, seven days after a suicide bomber blew up a US base here, killing 241 Marines. They got fifty-eight French paratroopers that same day in a separate attack."

"Did you return to the States?"

"No, pulled back to the Damascus station and remained active."

"Scary days?"

"We lost good people."

They wound their way slowly through the city. Kate was surprised by the familiarity of city centre shops, Virgin and McDonalds were instantly recognisable. The guide explained that they would drive out of the city to Mapas for a visit to Jeita Grotto, which was he proclaimed was "a wonder of nature in Lebanon."

"I'll split when we get back to town," Young said. "See you back at the boat."

"I'd like to tag along," Kate said.

"Think that's wise?"

"I like to find out as much as possible about the targets first-hand. I promise to keep out of your way."

"Fine with me; Whatney sings your praises."

"He can be flowery by times."

"God, you do know the guy. Why use one word when twenty will get the job done, eh?" Young laughed. "You're going to have to buy something to cover your head. Where we're going, you will stand out without it."

Kate picked up a plain grey head scarf from a hawker near the grotto entrance. On Young's advice she had worn plain colours for the trip, beige linen trousers, and a top to match. They sat onto a gondola for the ride into Jeita Grotto. Inside, the temperature dropped dramatically as they took in the beauty nature had created in the ancient cave. The chill gave Kate an involuntary shudder and she was glad to feel the warmth the sunshine brought when they glided back to the outside world. The bus brought them back to Nejmeh Square in the centre of Beirut and dropped them off for two hours shopping. Young got a cell phone number from the guide who warned him not to be late for the return trip to the port.

When well out of earshot of the rest of the tour party, Young called his contact.

"We have to wait an hour," he said when he hung up.

They browsed the souks. Kate enjoyed the buzz of haggling with the vendors, although unconvinced of the hygiene, avoided buying anything edible. Young's contact picked them up in a taxi near the Crowne Plaza Hotel on

Hamra Street, the main shopping district in west Beirut. He spoke English and clearly he and Young were acquainted.

"Rendezvous will be at Haret Hreik district," he told him.

"That's the southern suburbs," Young explained to Kate.

"Must the woman come?" he asked.

He had only exchanged a nod when Kate entered the cab. Young sat up front with the driver.

"She stays," Young told him, "she can handle herself."

"First we change car," the driver advised.

"Aren't the southern suburbs dodgy?" Kate said to Young.

"Hezbollah control the area. We ain't gonna hang around for long."

As the driver spoke to Young, he glanced at Kate in the rear-view mirror.

"So these men you want to know," he said, "we watch for one whole week. They take lunch in a different restaurant each day."

"Do we know where they're gonna be today?"

"Our observation point can see two restaurants."

"Okay, let's hope they use one of them. When we're done, we're gonna have to split outta there pretty fast."

"We understand. It is arranged."

The driver pulled off the ring road of clogged, honking traffic. He drove fast through streets, thick with pedestrians. The revving of a motor cycle engine spooked Kate. She knew sudden loud noises were a PTS trigger and struggled to maintain an unruffled exterior. She glanced quickly over her shoulder; they had picked up company. Two bikes were hanging twenty metres behind but definitely following them.

Out of the blue, she felt coming on the trip was a very bad idea. Everything around her was unfamiliar; the people, the buildings, sounds and smells; everything. She felt her mind pulling her towards the panic that still sometimes invaded her sleep; the feeling that the odds were stacking up to overwhelm her. Her heart beat grew rapid and irregular. Beads of sweat formed on her forehead and dripped onto her left cheek. She wiped them away with her new scarf and took quiet deep breaths to calm herself.

"Okay?" Young asked, leaning in her direction.

"Fine," she replied. "The car's stuffy."

The taxi sped on before careering into the underground car park of a half-completed apartment block. The bikes followed and descended two levels before coming to a halt.

"Wear this," the taxi driver said, taking a length of black cloth out of the boot and handing it Kate.

"What is it?"

"It's called a chador," Young explained, "not quite a burka, but it covers your head and shoulders. It'll mean you fit in better. Hold it in place at the front."

"Now you go on bikes," the taxi driver told them. "I will take you to port when it is done."

Young shook the driver's hand as Kate pulled the unfamiliar garment around her shoulders and drew a section over her head.

"And I'm supposed to hold this in place, while riding a bike?" she said to Young.

"Tuck it in somewhere," he replied. "You'll be fine."

They rode out fast with Kate holding on for dear life to the lunatic controlling the motor cycle. They seemed to stop for nothing and rarely slowed down until they reached another tower block, a replica of the first. Less work had gone into completing this one and those living in it did so in extreme discomfort. They descended to another underground car park.

"No talk," a driver whispered to Young.

He nodded.

Inside, they climbed concrete stairways that were airless and let in no daylight. Makeshift brickwork had closed off any design features intended to give the residents a view of the outside world. They ascended seven flights rapidly until she could see light flooding in from underneath an eight-storey doorway. They had reached the top floor.

"Wait here," one of their drivers said.

The other walked up, gingerly pushed the door open, and looked out.

"I will call you," he whispered to Young before disappearing out of sight.

Young sat down on the concrete floor.

"May as well take a load off," he said under his breath. He checked his watch and added "they break for lunch in ten minutes."

Kate threw off the chador and sat beside him. He opened the small shoulder bag he carried since leaving the bus and fished out a camera with a telephoto lens. He checked that everything worked before setting it down beside him.

Minutes later, light filled the stairway as the landing door opened.

"Come, now," the driver said, waving urgently.

Young was up in an instant, heading for the doorway. Kate wrapped the chador around her head and shoulders, and followed.

"You stay," the driver told her, gruffly.

Young looked to her.

"I've come this far," she whispered. "I should take a look."

"We do it fast," Young told the driver as he pushed past him pulling Kate behind. On the roof, they squinted as their eyes adjusted to the bright sunshine and scuttled hunched over to a small concrete unit close to the edge, where they hunkered down. The services block was roofless and stripped of equipment.

"Other side," the driver pointed. "Today they take falafel sandwiches."

Young crawled to the edge of the building and clicked off some pictures before re-joining Kate.

"What do you think?" he whispered. "Our guys?"

Kate studied the photos in the glaring sunlight.

"I can't be sure," she said quietly. "Any chance I can take a look myself?"

Young gave her the camera.

"Don't ask, just do it."

The driver was caught off guard; unaccustomed to a woman acting independently. Before he could react, Kate had crawled away and lain flat near the building's edge looking through the camera lens. She focussed on the queue at the sandwich bar in the front of the restaurant.

Furious, the driver hissed at Young, "We must go now."

Kate held up a finger indicating she needed more time.

"Now!" the driver repeated.

Without warning, three shots rang out in quick succession, ricocheting off the wall of the defunct services block. Kate reacted instantly, scrambling back to where Young was slumped. She saw him holding his arm with blood seeping through his fingers.

"Holy crap! Are you alright?" she asked.

"Flesh wound," he gasped. "Concentrate on what the drivers want; do exactly as they say."

"Walk fast, no run," the driver ordered.

They got back inside.

"What was that?" Kate asked.

"No talk," the driver repeated.

As they descended rapidly, Young opened his shoulder bag and took out a bandage and a roll of surgical tape.

"Give it to me," Kate said.

She tore off the bandage wrapping and threw it on the ground.

"Pick up," the driver ordered.

As she retrieved the wrapping, she noticed *US Department of Defense* stamped on it. She stuffed it into her pocket and pinned Young against a landing wall.

"Come now," the driver screamed.

"Thirty seconds," she shushed him, and tuned out his protests while she pressed a bandage onto Young's wound, securing it with reams of tape. She used a souvenir tee shirt from his shoulder bag to wipe off excess blood as they raced downwards.

"Good job," Young said.

"We leave now," the lead driver said as he kicked the bike into life.

They roared out of the building onto the streets. Kate noticed that the drivers watched everything that moved as they wove their way through the suffocating traffic. They drove alongside each other whenever they could, shouting to each other in a language she didn't understand, before blasting off again. Every Mercedes or BMW that approached seemed to unnerve them. In Beirut most people knew that these vehicles, especially the ones with tinted windows were favoured kidnap cars. Kate marvelled at their driving skills; they never seemed to stop. By times she glimpsed the ocean and then they seemed to veer away from it. Eventually the port came into view and they drew up a hundred metres away from where soldiers stood guarding a pedestrian entrance. She saw Young hand over a wad of local currency to the lead driver before they walked sheepishly towards their tour guide.

"What happen?" he said to Young, pointing to his bloodstained shirt.

"A bus mirror clipped my arm in the street," he replied. "Those nice boys gave me and my daughter a ride back from the emergency room."

"I very, very worried for you. Why you did not contact me?" the guide asked.

"I didn't want to delay everybody and those boys offered to help us out."

"Very dangerous! Maybe they rob you."

"They were fine," Young assured him. "Just two good Samaritans."

"Your daughter, she is alright?" the guide asked. Kate's top had a streak of blood down the front.

"Just a bit shook up," Young told him. "She don't talk much."

Kate smiled shyly and the guide stepped aside, before leading them past the military guards to the ship. As they slipped slowly out of the port Young turned to Kate and asked "Well, was they the guys?"

"They certainly *was*," she replied.

"You did good, kid," he said, holding his arm. "Now, I need a drink."

Kate bought Young a change of shirt in the ship's gift shop and changed her own top. After Young downed his first drink, they talked about the gunshots.

"A warning, no more," he told her. "If they wanted to kill us, we wouldn't be sitting here."

"Who's likely to have fired them?" Kate asked.

"Probably a local Hezbollah sniper with orders to be on the lookout for what we were up to; shots like that happen all the time."

"Will it spook our two friends?"

"In Beirut? I doubt it."

"So," Kate said, "don't keep me in suspense. Who are they?"

When they docked at Limassol next morning, Kate was conscious that Young needed proper medical attention as soon as possible. As he sank into the passenger seat of her BMW, his breathing had become rapid and shallow.

"Dial this number, would you?" he asked.

Kate put the call through the car's hands-free system.

"I'm at Limassol and I got a wound that needs tending," Young told the operator. "What are my options?"

"Standby please, sir," the calm female voice replied and put the call on hold.

She came back almost instantly.

"Can you make it to the Apollonion Private Hospital? It's in Strovolos, near Nicosia?"

Young looked at Kate; she nodded, and mouthed 'thirty minutes' to him.

"I'll be there in half an hour," he said. "Silver BMW."

"We'll have someone there to meet you, sir."

"Thank you," Young breathed as she disconnected the call.

Kate drove the sixty-three kilometre journey steadily so as not to attract attention. Young was drifting in and out of consciousness by the time she pulled up in front of the accident and emergency department. The car had barely stopped when the emergency room doors parted and an orderly pushed a wheelchair in their direction. A guy in a grey suit approached and opened the passenger door.

"Thank you, Ma'am," the suit said. "We'll take it from here."

"Take care, Batt," she said as his colleague helped him out of the car into the chair. Young waved a tired arm in her direction.

She knew a hospital visit to see him would not be welcomed by his bosses. She waved again and accelerated away from the set down area.

6

Before she hit on a plan, Kate spent days mulling over how to get the intelligence to Digger. Mailing it from her personal e-mail account would expose it to unnecessary risk of interception. Well aware that telecommunications from Europe channelled into Ireland via the UK, she also knew that some of the traffic was intercepted. She feared that using either suspect's name in a phone call to home might similarly trigger an imbedded UK intercept programme. The claims of any interception were always rebutted by the British until Edward Snowdon, the CIA whistleblower came along and blew the denials out of the water.

So, when she called Digger, they conversed in the Irish language.

"*Tá an t-ádh leat go bhfuil tú in ann do chuid Gaeilge shite a chleachtadh liomsa,*" Digger goaded.

He was fluent; it was the spoken language in the Gaeltacht area where he grew up. Kate was out of practice but having acted in school plays through Irish, she relished the opportunity to dust off her vocabulary and conveyed the intel in a flurry of muddled words. She spelt out the terrorist's names in the midst of general conversation. She had no idea whether her novel approach would work, but she hoped it would frustrate potential eavesdropping programmes sufficiently to signal no interest.

The two suspects were Aazim Hussein and Musharraf Abousamra. Their links to Bailey were unknown, but the very fact of meeting him aroused suspicion of some form of conspiracy. One of Kate's college lecturers described it as the dark side of freedom of association. Whatever logic lay behind the special punishment for a criminal conspiracy, she knew it was a difficult charge to prove in a court of law. It made more sense to figure out what was going on and stop it dead. For an instant, she felt the adrenaline rush of a hunt kicking off. Remembering her part in it would be over before it began left her deflated.

Batt Young passed on everything the CIA knew to her. Details were sketchy but they believed both suspects were Palestinian refugees, whose parents arrived in Lebanon in the eighties, and spent some time at the Mieh Mieh Palestinian refugee camp, four kilometres east of Sidon in the south of the country. During the eighties and nineties the camp suffered repeated attacks from Christian militia forces supported by Israel. Young said they couldn't pin down how they ended up in the orphanage in Tibnin. All he could surmise was that Hussein and Abousamra had been friends since childhood.

Young told Kate that both were believed to be high-ranking members of Hezbollah, a powerful military and political organisation of Shia Muslims. In the Eighties Hezbollah, the "Party of God", emerged from the carnage of the second Israeli occupation of southern Lebanon. Israel had invaded its neighbour on the pretext of securing its northern border from terrorist attack. By the end of the failed campaign all they had achieved was to give birth to another more lethal terrorist organisation.

"What the fuck is Bailey doin' talkin' to them?" Digger continued, in his native language.

"Search me," Kate replied. "Drugs maybe?"

"Too early to say. It's worryin', though."

"That's one powerful organisation," Kate said. "I'm told it cultivates weed on a grand scale in one location."

Kate referred to the Bekaa Valley, controlled mostly by Hezbollah fighters. Acres of cannabis was grown there, sometimes camouflaged behind tall corn stalks, sometimes grown in the centre of fields with tomato and pepper plants surrounding the edges. Despite Hezbollah's denials of involvement, most governments were sceptical that such a trade could flourish without its tacit approval.

"Are Irish crims organised enough to be involved at this level," Kate wondered aloud.

"They might be importin' a load for Britain, you never know," Digger said.

"Okay," Kate replied, "that's my good deed done. I'm out of the picture now."

She didn't dare mention how the suspect's identities were confirmed, or her part in the process. In the back of her mind, she felt maybe it was money in the bank. If Digger could figure out what Bailey was planning and stop it, some kudos might trickle down in her direction. It could help when she sought out another detective posting. That was for another day and most likely only Digger would believe her story.

On her next visit to the Marines' house at Nicosia in early February, Kate chatted to a Company Sergeant-Major. She told him that she was past the midway point in her tour and enquired how rotations worked for them.

"We get people shipping in and out all the time at the embassy," the Sergeant-Major told her.

"With us, it's just twice a year," Kate explained.

"We got a guy heading home tomorrow, in fact."

"Oh," she replied "he must be happy about that."

"Not one little bit. The poor guy wants to complete his tour but it's been cut short."

Kate pushed a little harder and when the Sergeant-Major elaborated on a dubious injury his embassy colleague picked up overseas, she figured out that the unlucky deportee was Batt Young. The guy's boss had grown tired of the daily phone calls from the injured party's wife and eventually told him he had no use for a one-armed man. Young was headed Stateside for physio-therapy to repair shattered tendons.

It suddenly struck Kate that she had not gotten an opportunity to thank him properly. The circumstances in which they parted at the hospital were strained due to his injury and the necessity of keeping their Beruit sojourn under wraps meant that she would probably never speak to Bartholomew Young the Third again. While the thought made her sad, she hoped that their hard won intelligence would one day yield results.

Slasher Fulton snorted two lines of cocaine before leaving his Malaga hotel room. He was buzzing, both excited and agitated, when he took the lead talking to the Arabs in a meeting Bailey had arranged. His left knee jerked continuously while he reassured the Sheikh that he had the men and equipment to do what they wanted in

Ireland. The meeting was at a small apartment at Benalmadena on Spain's southern coast. The apartment was
part of a high rise block, jam packed with one or two-
bedroomed cheap holiday rents, most vacant. Located
away from the seafront, buildings of a similar ilk crowded
the view. Slasher felt at home, he had been to Spain
numerous times; for Bailey it was only his second time
abroad.

Hussein and Abousamra accompanied Sheikh Nader,
although they never called him by name. The more Slasher
talked, the less impressed Nader appeared. He abruptly
broke off and spoke to his two associates. Hussein
approached Bailey.

"The boss needs a demonstration of goodwill, you will
come with us."

"Whoa, whoa," Slasher intervened. "You talk to me,
I'm the boss."

"Sit," Hussein ordered him. "We will return soon."

Abousamra placed his hand on Slasher's shoulder to
emphasise the command.

"I will stay with you," he said.

When they exited at the rear of the apartment block
into bright spring sunshine, Bailey popped his shades in
place. A black S-class Mercedes, with tinted windows
awaited and Bailey was directed into the rear seat beside
the Sheikh. Hussein sat up front with the driver and issued
instructions.

"Your boss," Nader began. "He is a big problem."

"I keep him out of trouble," Bailey replied.

"He insults me by meeting me with drugs in his body. I
cannot abide this behaviour."

"As I say, I look after him," Bailey repeated.

"We are not prepared to take risk."

"As I told the boys in Cyprus, the boss will probably be

in jail by the time the job comes around. He won't be a problem."

"Infidel!" Nader shouted. "Stupid man! You don't realise my people are dying every day."

Bailey was worried, but outwardly remained calm.

"I explained to your lads that we can do what you need in Ireland. We don't need to know anything else about what's going on. So long as we're paid, I guarantee everything will be one hundred percent."

"You guarantee this?"

"Totally," Bailey said.

"How can you be sure with a man such as your boss?"

"I know him, I can manage him."

After a thirty minute drive, the car pulled into a gated villa high in the hills overlooking the town. In the gardens the only sound was the periodic hiss of water sprinklers maintaining the lush green lawns.

"Many people risk their lives for this holy task," Nader said, as they waited for the automatic gates to open fully. "We have traitors who threaten us all the time."

They drove into a garage around the back and Hussein led them through a canopied walkway to the basement via the main house. The sight that greeted them jolted Bailey. A small wretched looking figure sat handcuffed to a chair, arms trussed behind his back, his head swollen from beatings, eyes barely open slits. A stench of urine filled the air and a pool of congealing blood spread around the chair.

"One of the traitors, I speak of," Nader began.

"Not my problem, man," Bailey replied, his hands sweaty.

"Kill him," Nader ordered.

"No fuckin' way," Bailey shouted.

The prisoner raised his head slowly, as if he understood the conversation.

"Do it or take his place," Nader threatened.

As Hussein pressed a weapon against the back of his head, Bailey's biggest fear gripped him. He had never killed anyone. He could pummel a body all day long, man or woman made no difference, but deep inside something steered him away from taking a life.

Nader gripped the grey pistol Hussein handed over. He breeched a round, cocked the hammer, and handed it to Bailey. The metal felt cold. Hussein guided him to a position behind the hapless prisoner. Bailey hesitated, fighting to control his breathing. Then he moved fast; gripping the pistol tightly, he pressed the muzzle against the back of the prisoner's head and squeezed the trigger. A jet of blood spewed from the prisoner's skull and sprayed Bailey's tee shirt. He recoiled and kept his hands clasped tightly around the weapon as he turned abruptly towards Nader.

"Drop it," Hussein warned, pressing the barrel of his weapon hard into the base of Bailey's skull.

Bailey hesitated, weapon still pointed at Nader's forehead, holding his stare.

"It is done, my friend. Be at peace," the Sheikh reassured.

Bailey dropped the hammer and lowered the pistol onto the dead prisoner's lap. They brought him to an upstairs room at the rear of the house and gave him a change of shirt. White noise filled Bailey's head. He didn't think it was the gunshot as he could hear water trickling from a fountain in a courtyard outside the window. He felt numb and tried to focus on what Nader was saying. He listened mutely as the actions expected regarding his boss were outlined in graphic detail. He was angry and resentful at being ambushed in such a bloody manner. While his mind raced considering how to strike back at the Arabs, the sound of the trickling water was strangely soothing.

When Nader finished his curt, precise instructions, he asked "Do you understand?"

Bailey nodded his reply. In the back of his mind was the thought that Dublin was home and few dared threaten him there. The Sheikh was not quite done and Bailey watched in horror as Nader slipped a black and white image from a large envelope. It was a photograph of the beauty salon Bailey's sister, Rachel, owned at Temple Bar in Dublin city centre.

"You know this place?" Nader asked, handing over the image.

Bailey glanced at it and nodded. He held his tormentor's stare for what seemed like an age, aware now that he was a pawn in a much larger game.

"We know it also," were Nader's final words.

7

In the weeks following her Beirut adventure, Kate began to contemplate her uncertain future. Her repatriation date was two short months away. Arrangements for going home had already begun. Earlier in the week, she surrendered her BMW to a forty-foot shipping container at Limassol, hoping the vessel would make port in Dublin by the time she got home. She even looked forward to the fortnight's re-orientation leave she would receive, although in reality, she would be bored within days. She needed to start making enquiries soon regarding where she would work, on her return. Going back to uniform duties didn't bother her, but the thought of having to leave Dublin was troubling. She liked living in the capital and loved her south side apartment. Before going to bed she scribbled a list of people to call. Having to beg for a favourable posting galled her.

She was drifting towards sleep when her private mobile buzzed into life. She sat up with a start and grabbed the phone.

"Yes!" she snapped.

"That's not a very pleasant way to answer your phone," Mac said.

"It's one o'clock in the morning here!" she replied.

"Oh sorry, totally forgot about the time thingy."

The fact that Cyprus was two hours ahead was rarely remembered by friends from home deciding to call for a chat.

"Doesn't matter, I'm awake now."

After a beat Mac said, "Well, aren't you going to ask?"

"Ask what?"

"Why I'm calling."

"I presume you'll tell me at some stage."

"The Commissioner resigned two hours ago. The media haven't got wind of it yet, but they will soon enough."

"I'd be lying if I said I was sorry to hear that."

"Fox is in the chair *pro tem*. I reckon he'll be anointed and get the gig full-time."

Dominic Fox had been the boss at Security Branch while Kate worked in SIU directing field operations. Kate liked him and knew he had fought her corner before she was shafted.

"That'll be a welcome change," she said.

"It'll cause a bit of a sensation when the media get hold of it. He's leap-frogged two Deputy Commissioners to get there."

"Have you spoken to him?"

"I've just come out of a meeting with him."

"Burning the midnight oil!"

Mac chuckled. "He's not hanging around. He asked me to come back and take over at Security Branch."

"What did you decide?"

"I said, yes."

"Congratulations," Kate replied.

"We both want you back in your old job."

Kate said nothing.

"Kate," Mac asked, "What do you think?"

He allowed her time to reflect.

"Isn't there an elephant in the room here," Kate said.

"O'Driscoll?"

"Of course, O'Driscoll. You expect me to work as *his* number two?"

"Kate, Commissioner Fox can't move before the full GSOC report is published."

"So what you're saying is, that the Commissioner can only move against O'Driscoll, if GSOC publish adverse findings against him."

"Kate, I can't pre-judge any of the Commissioner's decisions."

"But, it's likely he'll move O'Driscoll out?"

"I can't guarantee that."

"So, until such time as he *might* be moved on, I'd have to answer to him."

"Kate, I can't guarantee you anything, but think about it; a few months from now what slots are going to be up for grabs?"

"Come on," Kate exclaimed. "Hobson's choice!"

"Reality, I'm afraid. But there's another reason to say yes."

"What's that?"

"Another party requested that you return, immediately."

"Who are you talking about?"

"People you worked with in the past. I'm not going to spell it out over the phone."

"I find that hard to believe. We don't pee in our neighbour's garden — not when it comes to appointments."

"Believe it. There are reasons we can go into face-to-face."

"What about the UN? I can't just jump ship and come home."

"We'll get that sorted."

"Just like that," Kate clicked her fingers. "You want me to drop everything, come back, and forget how I was treated."

"It's a clean slate, Kate. The GSOC report can't be buried and it's unlikely to make good reading for either the ex-Commissioner or O'Driscoll."

"When would you want me to start?" Kate asked.

"Monday week."

"That's only giving me ten days to make up my mind, get packed, and give a new guy a guided tour."

"I'm taking that as a *yes*."

In Kate's head something was telling her to sleep on it and reply in the morning. The manipulation of the old regime and her mistreatment still stung. The thought of working in proximity with O'Driscoll made her physically nauseous, but this was Mac and a whole new ball game. She was used to resolving tricky situations and making quick decisions came with the territory at SIU.

"I'll want Digger and Angie back," she told Mac.

"You'll have full control over personnel."

"Then, it's a *yes*."

"Ring me the minute you're home."

"Okay boss," Kate replied.

When she hung up she stared out her apartment window over towards the Pentadactylos Mountain. Usually cloaked in darkness at this hour, tonight a bright moon lit the foothills. Years earlier, enterprising Turkish students had secretly and diligently painted hundreds of rocks over a number of weeks. Local legend had it that one night they unveiled their masterpiece to the world. The Greek-Cypriot population of Nicosia awoke to an enormous Turkish national flag staring down into their city. Covering a sizeable area of the mountain slope, it had been maintained in the intervening years as an enduring irritant.

Just like me, Kate smiled, as she looked up at the moon.

Lights twinkled in a few houses of the tiny villages and all appeared peaceful. Getting back to sleep wasn't going to be easy. Kate pulled on a sweatshirt and tracksuit bottom, borrowed her neighbour's bike and cycled to Iasonos Street, close to the city centre. She parked the bike outside Babylon, her favourite bar in town.

"Miss Kate," Andreas said when he saw her, "very late tonight. I'm closing up."

The place was deserted.

"What's with the Miss?" Kate said, kissing him on the lips. "Just one and go?"

"What can I get you?" Andreas asked.

"It's got to be bubbles," she replied, stroking his stubbled chin.

"Celebrating?"

She waited until he filled the champagne glass.

"Join me."

"You're so kind," he replied, a mischievous glint in his eye.

Kate raised her glass and Andreas dutifully clinked.

"To old friends and better times!" she smiled. "Andreas, I'm going home."

As they sipped and chatted he said, "Stay tonight."

"Mmm, maybe a little while," Kate replied. "I need a clear head in the morning when I give my UN boss the bad news."

Her final week in Cyprus was a blur. Derry Griffin, her replacement arrived on the island on Friday morning. She had called him, months earlier, to apologise when parachuted, unwillingly, into his slot. She spent the day on briefings followed by Sector orientation patrols.

On a frantic Saturday she did last-minute shopping in Nicosia. In the evening she knocked on her kindly neighbour's door and presented her with a gleaming new bicycle. It was a thank-you for the many times she had borrowed her old boneshaker. The previous evening, Despina had a loud, animated discussion with Kate's landlord which culminated in her deposit being returned although she was leaving early. Having helped lug the last of her suitcases out to the waiting UN truck, Despina hugged her tightly.

"I will miss you," she said.

Larnaca airport was chaotic when Kate arrived on Sunday morning. She had spent the night at a local hotel and already knew that fifteen charter flights were delayed. There was nowhere to stand, let alone sit. As a parting gift, Andreas had booked Kate into the executive lounge and she kissed him goodbye before gliding through the masses. She people-watched as she waited for her delayed Frankfurt flight to be called, silently hoping she wouldn't miss the Dublin connection. Her interest piqued when a Middle-Eastern businessman in his thirties, with two bodyguards in tow, sashayed through the lounge to a private room.

"An Arab prince," a waitress whispered to Kate.

"Is he single?" she replied, with a smile.

She arrived into a dark, drizzly Dublin, late on Sunday evening. The caretaker of her apartment block had secured her a small flat. Her own place wouldn't free up until the end of May when the two junior doctors staying in it were due to return to Dubai. Kate unpacked one case and dumped the rest into a small utility room. She ordered Chicken Pad Thai from her nearby takeaway and savoured the familiar flavours. Clearly pleased to see their regular customer return, they threw in two extra wedges of lime.

Next morning, she left at six thirty in a unit car Pete McNally had dropped to her apartment. Traffic was sluggish as she headed for the SIU base, hidden in the Liffey valley, so Kate cut through the Phoenix Park. A constant drizzle from an overcast sky shrouded the city in a grey veil that obscured the usual vista as she drove down Chesterfield Road, the park's main artery. Plumes of industrial steam from the Guinness brewery billowed through the gloom. She turned right at the Phoenix monument and took the narrow road through the Fifteen Acres where herds of deer grazed languorously on either side. *God, it's great to be back*, she thought.

At quarter past seven she pulled up at the familiar *Government Stores* sign, the only 'official' designation on the SIU building. She buzzed to gain entry to the underground car park.

"Yes!" the voice said brusquely.

"It's Kate, buzz me in, please," she replied.

"Kate who?" the distorted voice came back.

"Digger, stop messing about and buzz me in."

Angie had agreed to return without hesitation but Digger was reticent. Kate had spoken to him on Sunday night having waited a week for him to finally give her a nod of agreement. He regarded O'Driscoll as a contemptuous, dangerous fool. He hated the fact that in the job he loved, naked political interference facilitated O'Driscoll's upward trajectory. By Monday morning his transfer paperwork was non-existent but Kate ordered him to return, anyway.

Pete McNally had told her that O'Driscoll wasn't turning into work before ten o'clock most mornings since Zoom's death. Mac had called an eight-thirty management meeting which gave her an hour to prepare. The Surveillance and Intelligence Unit's mandate was to tackle organised crime groups whatever the motivation, political or purely criminal. Kate intended reviewing current operations and planned on tackling conversations with O'Driscoll as adroitly as she could.

There was a portrait of Zoom in the entrance hall. It was alongside the bravery award Kate had accepted almost a year earlier. She paused and studied both. She touched the photo and once again mourned the waste of a good life and a great officer. She smelt coffee brewing and walked towards the canteen where whoops and cheers erupted. She was shocked and not a little embarrassed.

"Thanks a bunch," she said, "but let's cut the crap and get to work."

Laughter rumbled around the room.

"Welcome back, boss," Angie said "you better cut this; Digger was up all night baking it."

"Jeez, red icing. Reminds me of that big flag I stared at for the past year." Kate said. "This looks more like Jane's talents."

"Well, *duh!*" Angie replied.

"Okay," Kate said, taking a knife. "Let's slice and dice."

"This looks cosy," a voice from the corridor interrupted.

Everyone turned in its direction and the space around Kate parted, Red Sea and Moses-like, as O'Driscoll walked towards her. En route, he dumped a black briefcase on a canteen table. He was fatter than she recalled. The needle nose, now with a purple tip seemed Pinocchio-like in his round face. His dyed brown hair had a parting down the centre with depleting strands plastered either side by excessive amounts of gel. His early morning bloodshot brown eyes hinted at someone not bearing up well under pressure.

O'Driscoll's father decided when his youngest son hit his teenage years, he needed strong discipline to curb his wayward tendencies. Too busy with a flourishing building business to monitor his errant son's behaviour himself, he shipped him off to a private boarding school. A brief spell in the Army followed before, eventually, he housed his wild child in the Garda Síochána and used political connections to push him up the ladder.

Like a popped balloon, the convivial atmosphere dissipated instantly.

"Welcome to my unit, Superintendent," he said, looking at the cake as he shook Kate's hand.

"A Phoenix from the flames, what's that all about?"

"It's just a fucking cake," Digger growled.

"You're back," O'Driscoll replied, his tone sarcastic. "And wee Angie, good to see you."

He paused and looked around the group, as if checking for any other unannounced arrivals.

"I've calls to make," he said. "Angie pet, bring me a slice of that cake with coffee, will you?" He picked up his briefcase, walked up the corridor to his office, and closed the door.

Kate looked towards Angie. She had already dumped a large pool of spit in the centre of a small plate.

"Slice of cake with that?" Kate asked.

The room erupted with barely suppressed giggles.

"Briefing in ten minutes," D-I Ron Sexton announced.

Kate took her coffee into the Superintendent's office, followed by her two Detective Inspectors. It was unchanged, apart from O'Driscoll's recently dumped goon having the walls plastered with framed training course certificates.

"Ask Pete to box that crap and deliver it to Strong," she told Digger, as she took the seat behind her old desk.

"Done," he replied.

Kate placed her mobile phone and a brand new journal on the empty desk. Ron Sexton sat opposite, next to Digger. They were similar height, but Sexton was blocky which gave him a squat appearance, as opposed to Digger's lean and hungry look. A true blue Dubliner, he was born and raised in Oliver Bond Street flats, a four-storey social housing apartment complex near the city centre. Growing up there gave Sexton a unique knowledge of the Dublin criminal scene.

Fashion-wise, the two D-I's were polar opposites; Digger being casual to the point of shabby, whereas Sexton insisted on wearing a shirt and tie to work each day. In his spare time, he played trumpet in a local brass band and this morning's light-blue cravat sported three yellow saxophones down the centre. He focussed on organised criminal groups, having arrived six months before Kate's departure. She hadn't gotten to know him very well, but his work with the unit had been solid.

"So what's doing?" she asked, as she wrote her name and rank on the journal cover.

"How's this goin' to work?" Digger interrupted, hitching a thumb in the direction of O'Driscoll's office.

"I only got back last night," Kate replied. "I'm meeting Mac this morning; be patient."

"Ah!" he exclaimed, slapping the side of his head. "This is one big mistake."

Sexton sat impassive, mutely expecting more verbal ping-pong.

"For the moment, work with Ron on active cases," Kate said.

Digger nodded, his face a mask of truculent acceptance.

"Ron, what have you going on?"

Sexton leafed through his journal and began in a slow, measured way.

"There's an operation on Dissident IRA factions, I know little about because Jack was in charge of it until he was moved out."

"Get one of the D-Sergeants to brief me on it," Kate ordered Digger, who nodded.

"As you know I focus on the organised crime side," Sexton continued.

"How come O'Driscoll and Strong were on the operation when Zoom got killed? That was a crime gang."

"I'd been running the case right up to the day of the raid," Sexton told her. "When they got a sniff of imminent arrests, Chief Superintendent O'Driscoll switched his man onto the case."

"Jesus Christ!" Kate exclaimed. "How stupid is that."

"No comment," Sexton replied.

"What are the Dissidents up to?" she asked.

"From what I know, they're mainly making pipe bombs and selling them to criminals who want to eliminate their rivals," Digger said.

"What about the crime side," she asked Sexton.

"We have a few small jobs on. We're watching a warehouse — possible cannabis grow-house, second job is on a gang that we believe has a contract out on a rival. It's keeping us busy."

"Do we know what Don Bailey's doing at the minute?" she asked.

"He's part of Slasher Fulton's gang. Why would we focus on him?" Sexton asked.

Digger remained mute.

"We'll chat about it later," she replied, checking the office clock.

The first hour of Kate's second coming to SIU hinted at stormy waters ahead. And since arriving home, she had forgotten to call her mother.

8

Mac wrapped up the first meeting of his new management team in fifteen minutes. Intelligence analysis, international liaison, a witness protection programme, and VIP protection all now came under his wing. He outlined priorities to the section heads and returned to his office with O'Driscoll and Kate. The trio settled into leather chairs situated around a circular coffee table.

"Tell me what you know about Cloud computing," Mac asked.

"It's a way of storing computer files, so that you can access them anywhere," Kate ventured. "Why?"

"Dublin has one of the densest clusters of Cloud data centres in Europe," O'Driscoll blurted before Mac could reply.

"Do you know why?" Mac asked.

"Low operating costs, the climate here offers free-air cooling for the servers that are at the heart of their systems, plus the lowest corporation tax rate in Europe," O'Driscoll smugly concluded.

"I'm aware that Google, Microsoft, and Amazon have set-ups in Dublin," Kate added.

"There's something like thirty large-scale operations around Dublin," Mac said. "I know that much from my time downtown."

"But, what's…" Kate began.

O'Driscoll interrupted again.

"Irish companies are getting in on the act. Dad got me in at ground floor level with three IT start-ups this year. When one goes public in a few months, I'll flip my shares and double my money," he grinned, easing back into his leather chair and crossing his legs. He believed demonstrating insider knowledge exhibited strength. The invitation to the Assistant Commissioner's office inspired optimism that his career might be secure.

Mac and Kate glared at him—what did his comment have to do with anything? Tempering his irritation, Mac continued, "Should anything happen in Ireland to disrupt worldwide Cloud services it could impact massively on the country."

"That's why the big companies take on ex-Police as security managers," O'Driscoll interjected once more.

Mac paused and stared at him. Kate hoped he got the message to shut up.

"What's any of this got to do with us?" she asked.

"We know that ISIS exploit social media better than most terrorist groups," Mac continued. "They've also hacked Western business systems."

O'Driscoll was about to interrupt again but Mac cut him off.

"They want to open a new front in cyberspace, a 21st century economic war against Western interests. Their goal is to weaken the allied countries."

The phone on Mac's desk rang and he walked over to answer.

"Five minutes," he told his staff officer.

As he turned around, Mac said, "Raphael, my driver will drop you back to base now. Kate can fill you in on the details later."

O'Driscoll much preferred Raph, but during their rare conversations, Mac always used the long form of his name. O'Driscoll opened his mouth to protest, but thought better of it. Meekly, he replaced his coffee cup on the table, retrieved his briefcase, and retreated. Mac waited until the door closed and not missing a beat, continued.

"Worldwide, it's estimated that the cloud computing business is worth €207 billion. Ireland carves out more than its share and the government doesn't want that revenue to disappear."

"So, where do we come into the picture?" Kate replied.

"The FBI tracking ISIS in the States have detected what they're calling a cyber cell," he said. "Intelligence points to a Dublin connection. Robin Jeffers is handling the European end of the case and he requested that you run the surveillance operation on a suspect who's just moved here."

Kate nodded and waited.

"The top brass in the Justice Department are spooked. The Taoiseach wants total cooperation with the Yanks to get to the bottom of it."

"Why isn't he letting his new Justice Minister deal with it?" she asked.

Mac shrugged. "Just a minute," he said. He walked over to his desk and dialled his staff officer. "Send Mr. O'Neill in now, please."

When the tall, dark-haired stranger walked in seconds later, Kate's initial thoughts were that he was easy on the eyes. He wore an immaculately pressed dark grey suit and crisp white shirt with a purple-rose tie worn in a Windsor knot. After exchanging a firm handshake with Mac he repeated the greeting with her.

"Kate, this is Cody O'Neill from Chicago," Mac said. "We met last night."

He invited everyone to sit and O'Neill took the chair vacated by O'Driscoll. Kate noted his hands as he placed them on the armrests; they were almost elegant. As he settled, she caught a scent of his aftershave, subtle rather than overpowering.

"Nice to meet you," he said to Kate.

"Likewise," Kate replied. "You're from Chicago?"

"Yes."

"It's just, you know, with cybercrime I expected the San Francisco office would handle the case. Silicon Valley and all that."

"Native of Chicago, been with the San Francisco office these past two years."

Was his accent Midwest, Kate wondered? Close your eyes and it could be Obama.

"How come you went west?"

"They needed someone with a law degree in the San Francisco office and I needed a change of scenery."

"Let's give Cody a chance to catch his breath before we start interrogating him," Mac laughed.

"Can I say, how thrilled I am to be in Ireland," O'Neill began. "My father told me our ancestors left County Cork around Famine times."

"Your first visit?" Mac asked.

"Yes."

"Pity," Mac replied. "You missed St. Patrick's Day by two weeks."

"I caught it back home," O'Neill replied. "It's a huge day there, we even dye the Chicago River green."

Kate and Mac smiled.

"Tell us about your investigation," Mac asked.

"I've got a full briefing pack for each of you. It's classified to the highest level of secrecy. It cannot be photocopied or re-distributed."

"Understood," Mac replied.

"Is your CV included?" Kate asked. "I like to know who I'm working with."

"Me too," O'Neill replied, smiling. "Robin Jeffers from Paris speaks highly of you. My CV's part of the brief, I'll be happy to fill in any blanks."

Kate returned his smile. Jeffers had played a key part in breaking her last case.

"Just so we're clear," O'Neill continued, "this investigation should, under no circumstances, be mentioned, or discussed in *any* way with another agency, American or otherwise."

"That's normal protocol," Mac replied.

"I'm under specific orders to convey this instruction," O'Neill said. "Okay," he continued, as he opened the blue cover on the file, "so our operation on KHOURI, Rafiq, started life as a FISA investigation."

By the time they broke up an hour later, Kate had a clear picture of the requested assistance. By then, she knew that the Foreign Intelligence Surveillance Act in the States was enacted to regulate the use of electronic surveillance for collection of foreign intelligence and counter-intelligence.

Kate placed the top secret FBI briefing into her office safe when she returned to base. She would change the code each day until the American operation ended.

"I better talk to the Chief," she said to McNally.

"He's not here," Pete told her. "When he was dropped back, he had a real bug up his arse and took off."

"Is Digger around?"

"In the Cave," McNally replied.

The SIU basement was Digger's domain, dedicated to trade gadgets and trickery. Kate linked up with him there and briefed him on the background to their new case. She ordered immediate reconnaissance of the IT company head office. The plan was to tail the FBI suspect from work, find out where he lived, and start the serious work from there.

"What about Bailey?" Digger asked.

"The Khouri case takes priority over anything else," Kate replied.

"I've identified the Ginger from Cyprus."

"Really?"

"A soldier, stationed at McKee Barracks, just over the wall from Mac's office."

"Shit! What the hell is he doing meeting a scumbag like Bailey."

"Mick Dempsey's his name. Why he met Bailey and the other two is anyone's guess. He travelled back from Cyprus to Beirut with the Arab pair."

"Hussein and Abousamra. Crap! We can't ignore it. Find out as much as you can on him, will you?"

"My source is in a gun club with Dempsey. I'll see what I can do."

"We'll tread carefully with it. I'll show Ron the photo from Cyprus and see if he knows him."

"Will you tell O'Driscoll?"

"Keep it between us for now," Kate replied.

With pressure on for full inter-agency cooperation, an early meeting was inevitable with J2, the renamed Army Intelligence Section. They changed a whole letter from G to J (for Joint) as they operated within the three Defence services, Army, Air Corps and Naval Service. They were the experts when it came to radical Islamic groups and dealt with external threats to the country. The Khouri case thrust Kate into a whole new world. She knew little of ISIS, apart from press articles, but didn't want to come across as ill-informed.

She sought out Detective Tom McManus in the afternoon, not for his translation expertise, rather to pick his brain. He was one of her favourite people. A force interpreter, he was a gifted linguist who spoke three European languages effortlessly. He had accompanied her to France on her last case and his flawless work ensured a seamless operation in a volatile situation. He lectured a European Studies course part-time at Dublin's American University and had an extensive knowledge of Middle-East affairs.

"A lot of Arabs are calling the emergence of ISIS the end of Sykes-Picot," McManus told her.

"Remind me who they were."

"During the First World War, Mark Sykes, a British civil servant and François Georges-Picot, a French one, drew up a secret plan to carve up the Middle East between France and Britain, two of the big colonial powers at that time."

"Of course!" Kate exclaimed. "They drew the borders of the modern nation states in the Middle East."

"People in the West may have forgotten them but the Arabs haven't. Look at history and you'll see that those borders have been contested ever since."

"And ISIS want to smash them."

"Precisely. One of the first videos they put up on the

Internet had a bulldozer cutting through a sand rampart delineating the Syrian-Iraqi border. A handwritten poster that featured in the video declared *End of Sykes-Picot.*"

"It's about more than territory, though," Kate ventured. "There's the Sunni-Shia factor. Why are they such deadly enemies?"

"Well, Sunni and Shia politicians do work together in some countries but a bit like Northern Ireland and the Catholic-Protestant dynamic, relationships can be prickly."

"What's the difference, anyway," Kate asked.

"Between Sunni and Shia?"

"Yes."

"It goes back to a seventh century schism about the succession to the prophet Muhammad. The Shia went with Muhammad's son-in-law Ali; the word, Shia, is derived from *Shiat-Ali,* or followers of Ali. The Sunnis believed the successor to Muhammad should be chosen under Arab tribal tradition and went with his companion, Abu Bakr."

"And they're still fighting over it?"

"That's a simplistic interpretation," McManus replied, "There's lots of theories about where ISIS grew from. Nobody doubts what they're trying to spread and who their main backers are."

"Go on."

"There's a worldwide battle raging for the soul of Islam and Wahhabi oil money is fuelling extremism."

"The Saudis."

"Exactly! People forget that the kingdom only came into existence in the 18th century but was crushed by the Turks. A World War One alliance that the Wahhabis formed with the Brits to defeat the Ottoman Empire, enabled them to regenerate and re-conquer the holy cities of Mecca and Medina, a century after losing them. Then they hit oil."

"And another century on, ISIS is surging through the Middle East imposing the Wahhabi take on Islam— convert or die."

"That battle will wax and wane," McManus said. "It's always been the way."

"I just want to figure out what they're planning in the here and now."

"Good luck with that," McManus replied.

By four o'clock Kate had joined Digger at the mobile command post in a West Dublin business park. Her first day back on the job, constrained by management requirements, felt different. Mac's attention was diverted to many other areas and she sensed an unspoken expectation to keep O'Driscoll in line, whilst getting on with her own job. Being on the frontline, in this case, glancing surreptitiously from the tinted windows of Digger's van, felt more satisfying. They waited for the target to exit the dull, grey brick company headquarters in the leafy business park. She spent the first hour repeatedly looking at the suspect's photograph, committing his features to memory. Until five o'clock the van blended in with other service vehicles in the car park. As it thinned out, their presence became more obvious and Digger alternated to a new position. Angie took up a slot in the car park and thirty minutes later reported their target on the move. He took a bus that dropped him to Blackhorse Avenue, close to McKee Barracks and walked from there to Smithfield, an old markets area, transformed for 21st century living into a mix of apartments and offices. The old red brick buildings on the east side of the square were scrubbed up and a viewing tower had been built on top of a former distillery chimney. The few social housing units that survived now seemed incompatible with the shiny new glass-fronted hotel opposite. The western edge of the square accommodated blocks of contemporary apartments. Kate stayed with the operation until the suspect entered a large apartment block with shops at ground floor level.

"This is goin' to be a nightmare," Digger moaned.

"Why?" Kate asked.

"Every apartment around here is snapped up," he replied. "Gettin' an observation post will be hell."

"Mac said to spare nothing, take him at his word."

"Does O'Driscoll know the score?" Digger asked.

"Report to me. I'll deal with him," Kate replied.

"Gotcha!" Angie came over the radio.

"Location?" Digger asked.

"Sixth floor, at the rear."

"Bollox," Digger swore.

"If it was easy, any idiot could do it," Kate laughed, before she exited the van. "Get Sexton to help out, he grew up just across the river."

"What about the FBI dude?"

"I'll let him know we've housed his boy."

Kate returned to her office and dialled her mother's number.

"Katie," her mother answered with delight. "I hope they've given you an easy first day back on the job."

"No complaints," Kate replied.

9

Earlier the same day, Bailey drove Slasher to his favourite pub, The Leaping Hare. By the time they got there, the coherent, switched-on boss had vanished, replaced by a sour, snarling version. For as long as Bailey had been the gang's enforcer, Slasher was coked off his head most days. His trial for assaulting a Garda was due to start at 11 a.m.

"Have a drink for fuck sake," Slasher said, his left leg keeping up an involuntary jerk that refused to rest.

"You know that's not my game," Bailey told him. "You should lay off it, too."

"What are ya? A fuckin' monk? Have a drink."

"I've a coffee coming."

"You're a real fuckin' buzz kill, d'ya' know that," Slasher moaned, throwing back a shot of Jägermeister.

"What was that?" he suddenly asked.

"What?" Bailey asked.

"I heard a noise, there's someone in there," he said jabbing a finger in the direction of the room next door. "I'm tellin' ya."

"Take it easy, I've someone on the door, they'll check it out."

The Leaping Hare was in their Dublin heartland. They were in the upstairs lounge and Bailey knew for certain that the nearby room was empty. Slasher's drugs gang supplied the south side of Dublin city and most big towns outside the capital. His old man let it be known that while he was away, he wanted his son to take over and Slasher soon cemented control over the gang. Don Bailey became his right hand man, his enforcer. Nobody messed him about and he hoovered up Slasher's dealer debts in record time.

Bailey looked at his boss's dilated pupils as he talked non-stop. Two of his gang, who took care of business outside Dublin, sat impassively at the same table. Without warning, Slasher aimed a kick at it, tipping it over and sending glasses, cups and bottles flying.

"Youse aren't listenin'," he roared.

One of the henchmen patiently set the table upright, while a barman arrived and swept up the mess.

"Take it easy," Bailey said to him. "We don't need any more attention."

"Are ya fuckin' sayin' I'm a problem, are ya?" Slasher said, squaring up to Bailey.

"All I'm saying is you've a trial starting. Sit down, for God's sake."

"Awh righ. D'ya have any news from the Arabs?"

"Later," he told his boss and changed the subject to more immediate matters. "Three dealers are late with their money, is that what you're saying, lads?"

"Who's supposed to be takin' care of those dozy bastards?" Slasher demanded.

"I am," the one closest, replied.

"Get it sorted by tonight, ya dopey fuck."

The thug nodded agreement in Slasher's direction.
The wired gang boss reached out, grabbed his nose and
twisted hard. It broke with a loud crack and blood
cascaded down the wounded henchman's tee shirt.

"Fuck sake," the bloodied thug roared in pain, "there's
no need for that."

"I want to see *more* of that," Slasher roared, wiping
blood from his fingers, "with fuckers who think they can
keep me waitin' for me money."

Bailey remained calm and told the two, "Leave us
alone, would youse."

"When was the last time you slept?" he asked Slasher.

"Sleep is for losers."

"That's shite talk."

"Talk to me about these Arabs. What are they sayin'?
Are we on?"

"They can't say yet."

"Ya fuckin' serious? Do they want it in fuckin' writin'?"

"Nothing like that. It's just that…"

"Just fuckin' wha'? Are they doin' a deal or not?"

"They're not like us. They're bigger, more, you know,
military like."

"So fuckin' wha'?"

"The guys we met in Spain have to take it back and
kind of, have it approved. Check out that everything we're
telling them is right."

"For fuck sake! I want this done before…"

"I'm doing my best. You know I'll mind the house,
anyway."

"Don, I trust ya with me life, bud, but this is massive
and I want to make it happen. My brief told me, even if I
get the jail today, he'll get me out on bail, pendin' an
appeal."

"Drink up, we're late already."

Bailey drove Slasher to the ultra-modern Courts of Criminal Justice on the edge of the Phoenix Park. They met his senior counsel in the circular foyer on the ground floor, where barristers congregated to talk to clients, largely ignoring suites of consulting rooms the new building provided. Around them, clusters of worried-looking people stood soaking up their barrister's final instructions.

Slasher's senior counsel told him that their main defence was going to be offence. They would use the hospital photos of injuries he sustained while in custody to allege police brutality and coercion. "The fruit of the poison tree," his counsel trumpeted. "If I can get your custody ruled unlawful, any evidence that flowed from it will be inadmissible."

When the court clerk read them out, Slasher acknowledged the charges of aggravated assault and obstruction of a peace officer in the course of his duty. He pled not guilty and resumed his seat as the prosecutor began his statement of facts. It had all happened on a day Slasher had grown tired of the overt tail that followed him everywhere he went. He had spent the afternoon with his regular prostitute, snorting copious lines of cocaine throughout a four-hour stay. When he copped his watcher as he exited the apartment block, he flipped. The agitated hoodlum launched himself at the detective and before assistance arrived he had inflicted a couple of cracked ribs. There was also a concussion injury from punches he landed before a tactical baton swept him to the ground.

Medical evidence backed up testimony that the accused was out of control and violent. The toxicology screening revealed the level of cocaine in Slasher's bloodstream spiked towards the higher end of the scale associated with heavy users. The CCTV footage from the cells area of the station, showed a highly agitated defendant

requiring four officers to restrain him. His defence counsel
called just one Garda witness, the victim of the assault, and
accused him of heavy handed tactics. The judge was unimpressed. The outcome seemed destined for a slam dunk
when, during his summing up, she encouraged the jury to
believe the evidence before their eyes in considering
whether excess force was used during the prisoner's
restraint. Past six o'clock when the jury went out, they
needed little convincing and brought in a guilty verdict
after a thirty-minute recess. The judge imposed a five-year
custodial sentence and Slasher was taken down.

Bailey left the court immediately and made a rapid phone
call. He wiped the handset clean and dumped it in a
rubbish bin. As he walked to meet his driver, he crushed
the SIM card he had extracted and threw the pieces in the
gutter.

Gerry Buck drove him to his kick-boxing clubhouse
where he changed into a black tracksuit, and pulled on red
boxing boots. He wrapped a small towel around his neck
and tucked it into his tracksuit top. Then he grabbed a
rope and began skipping; slowly at first, building up an
even rhythm. The swish of the rope altered subtly from
time to time as Bailey criss-crossed his arms in a routine
learned in his early boxing years. With a furious final burst
of speed other boxers eyed enviously, he completed his
warm-up. He restricted his training session to ten minutes
on each of the heavy punch bags. He showered and
changed quickly, endorphin-fuelled after his workout.

The day was turning from a good one, into a great one.
He had promised to pick up his sister, Rachel, at her
beauty salon in Temple Bar and prided himself on never
being late.

Slasher's prison transport arrived at Portlaoise Prison, seventy kilometres out of Dublin, late in the evening. He didn't make it to the newly built modern facility. His new home would be the grey granite jail that the British built in the 1830s. Despite decades of upgrades, the basic structure in the old jail of cell blocks on three landings had remained unaltered. It was classified as the high-security wing and housed IRA prisoners for three decades from the 1970s. Since the turn of the century, it contained a mix of IRA Dissidents and high-risk members of organised criminal groups. For security reasons, the prison authorities segregated them onto separate landings.

As Bailey walked into Rachel's salon, she was spritzing hairspray on her final customer. She was twenty-three, with a teenage-slim figure. Not considered one of the pretty girls during her turbulent schooldays, she used heavy beauty salon make-up every day to present an attractive face to her customers.

"Why don't you have your hair cut?" she suggested. "Ella here is new, she'll do you before quittin' time."

"No bother," Ella said, as she pulled out a fresh black gown and indicated a chair to Bailey.

"Do your head massage, Ella," Rachel advised. "Brother, you're goin' to love this."

The reality of Slasher's situation hit home as he was measured, fingerprinted, photographed, and details of his tattoos recorded. The final leg of the committal process was an interview. In the hope of getting medication to soften withdrawal, he fessed up to his coke addiction. He named Bailey as the only person he would allow visit or seek permission to telephone from the prison.

"You'll share a cell with your old man," the screw told him. "Take your shower before lockdown." Slasher nodded glumly.

Other prisoners stood with their faces pressed against the wire on Landing Two as Slasher was led along. They stared at the upper landing where an IRA prisoner was being chased. The older guards ignored the commotion, recognising the jailhouse ritual of dunking a prisoner due for release.

Gene Fulton embraced his son when he arrived at the cell.

"I need a shower, man," Slasher said.

"We'll go together," his father replied. "Our landing has only five minutes left in the showers."

Cheers erupted from the landing overhead as Slasher mooched along the walkway towards the showers, towel and shower gel in hand.

"Make it snappy," the screw at the shower room entrance told them.

Bailey closed his eyes and relaxed as jets of warm water hit his forehead. He rarely felt so calm. The new stylist massaged his head for ten minutes while shampooing his hair. He listened as draining water gurgled down the plug-hole. Ella brought the chair upright and tousled his hair with a warm, white towel. She then swivelled the chair to face the mirror and for a brief moment her denim blue eyes met his slate greys. Since his deadly deed in Spain they had lost their lustre.

"H-how would you like it?" she stammered.

"Razor it," he replied.

When Bailey confirmed the €200,000 contract to the IRA Dissident group, orders were rapidly relayed to the prison. A junior supervisor on the IRA landing sealed the Fultons' fate when he gave in to pleadings from the celebrating group to hit the showers early. The screw guarding the shower room door turned a blind eye at first when two prisoners blocked the entrance. Seconds later as exuberant shouts distorted to primal screams, it was too late. Smuggled blades melded into plastic toothbrush handles created razor-sharp shivs that sliced through the Fulton's throats before they realised what was afoot.

The screw hit the panic button and tried to push past the two blocking prisoners. As bright red blood spurted from their severed jugulars and streamed across the shower room floor, the killers continued to hack their victims in a frenzied attack. Before an intervention squad of prison guards pushed through and uncovered the crime, the murder weapons were wiped clean and forced down drains.

"Two inmates badly slashed," the squad leader yelled into his radio. "Get medics up here now."

By the time medics arrived fatal damage had been done. Father and son were pronounced DOA at the Midland Regional Hospital, Portlaoise, five minutes ambulance ride from where they died.

10

Kate spent the early evening eating take-away in her stopgap apartment and reading up on the FBI agent. She was back in the thick of the action and the day had gone well. Sexton had secured an interim observation post, an attic room in the National Museum Collins Barracks. It was further from the target than she fancied, so she deployed a mobile two man crew closer to the Smithfield apartment block, in case the suspect decided to go walka-bout. Stung by Mac's rebuke, O'Driscoll absented himself from his office for the day.

The agent's resumé told Kate that Cody O'Neill won the President's Medallion for Law in his graduation year at Loyola University. She noted he had eighteen years' service with the FBI, so had little or no experience of private prac-tice. He had a five-year-old daughter, Caitlin, but his marital status was classified as separated.

A call from Digger disrupted her musings.

"All quiet in Smithfield," he reported. "Any chance myself and Ron could meet this mystery FBI man tomorrow?"

"Shouldn't be a problem. He seems a bit of a suit and tie type so we need a carefully chosen meeting place."

"Fair enough," Digger replied. "Oh, before I go, did you hear the news?"

"What news?"

"Slasher Fulton and his aul' lad were murdered in Portlaoise Prison tonight."

"Jesus Christ!"

"Kate, things like that happen for a reason. We need to find out what that Bailey fucker's up to or pass on what we know to the murder investigation."

"Let's focus on the FBI case, it takes priority."

"Just free me up to do some enquiries."

"With O'Driscoll breathing down my neck?"

"O'Driscoll doesn't have to know."

"We'll reassess tomorrow."

O'Neill was staying at a Ballsbridge hotel, not far from Kate's apartment and she rang him to suggest meeting there. She showered and changed into light linen trousers and a blue and white striped tee shirt with mid-length sleeves. Before leaving, she sprayed Dolce & Gabbana Light Blue, generously, on the nape of her neck and the crook of both arms.

He's gone all casual, she thought, ironically, as O'Neill sprang to his feet in the hotel lobby at nine-thirty. He had ditched the tie in favour of a fresh white shirt, top button popped, and dark trousers with a pencil-sharp crease down the centre of each leg.

"Thank you for meeting me," she said.

"My pleasure," he replied.

The lobby was almost deserted and he had selected a table at the fringes.

"Would you like a drink," he asked.

"A sparkling water would be fine," she said.

He returned from the bar with two.

"Staying off the hard stuff," Kate said.

"I don't imbibe much," he replied. "Mom told me Gramps drank enough for a few generations. He died before I arrived."

Kate smiled in reply.

"So, good first day," O'Neill began. "Your crew did great."

"We did okay," Kate replied. "I don't like it when things get too cosy. Let's see what the next few days bring."

O'Neill laughed softly.

"Two of my guys want to talk to you," Kate said, after they clinked 'Sláinte'.

"We can do that."

"How about you come to the National Museum tomorrow and I meet you there?"

"Sounds good."

"Museum opens at 10 a.m. so, let's say midday. The LUAS tram stop is right outside."

"Okay."

"I'll link up with you and take you to the OP to meet the two Detective Inspectors running the operation on the ground. Dress touristy, okay?"

"Sure."

They chatted for the next hour and O'Neill was disarmingly open with Kate about his family situation. Mum and Dad were both retired, she from teaching and he from the city of Chicago police department. His father was in remission from battling cancer. O'Neill had married his high school sweetheart, Marilyn, but that hadn't worked out. His long work hours drove her into the arms of another lawyer she'd met at a Pilates class. Their divorce papers were awaiting his signature on his return. They had one common acquaintance, Robin Jeffers, the FBI Legal Attaché in Paris. O'Neill was in the running to replace him when he vacated the post.

Next morning, Kate drove to the National Museum with Sexton. O'Driscoll had excused himself from another management meeting and Mac gave Kate a pass to focus on the FBI case.

"IRA Dissidents carried out that double murder in Portlaoise," Sexton told her.

"Settling scores?" Kate suggested.

"Dunno."

They parked behind a store room and made their way to the OP where Digger was already in situ. The action had switched to the suspect's work and his crews were deployed on nearby roads.

"Everything okay?" Kate asked.

"Fine," Digger replied. "Guy walked to the bus stop, caught the bus, and went to work, that's about it."

"Good. We'll discuss it more when Cody gets here."

"Oh, it's 'Cody' now," Digger mocked.

"Grow up," Kate replied. "Where does last night's murders leave Bailey and Slasher's gang?"

"Angie told me the drugs unit she was with for a few months picked up bits and pieces on Bailey," Digger replied.

"What about him?" Kate asked.

"A smart cookie," Digger said. "He runs the streets; keeps the dealers supplied and collects the money."

"His sister, Rachel has a hair salon and beauty place down in Temple Bar," Sexton piped up.

"Angie had a look around it. Nice place, wouldn't have come cheap," Digger said.

Kate smiled at Angie's initiative. "How did she get in?"

"Got her nails done or somethin'," Digger said.

"So Bailey flashes the cash," Kate said.

"No, he's the opposite," Sexton answered. "Not flashy at all, drives an ordinary car, a six-year-old Toyota, doesn't go in for showy clothes either, it's jumper and jeans most of the time."

Although a bit stiff and straight-laced, Sexton had grown on Kate. She liked his unrivalled knowledge of Dublin criminals.

"Doesn't drink or smoke," Digger added.

"What about his connections?" Kate asked. "Who is he running with?"

"Very hard to pin down," Sexton said "he seems to talk to players from all the main gangs at one time or another."

"Any links with the Dissidents?" she asked Digger.

"If he has a connection, I'm not aware of it," Digger replied. "Angie says he's smart; definitely surveillance conscious."

"I spoke to people who knew him as a nipper," Sexton said. "He was part of the Francis Xavier Boxing Club in Crumlin until his late teens."

"He looked fit when I saw him," Kate remarked.

"When he began running with Slasher's gang," Sexton continued, "the club asked him to leave. By that time, he was even training some of the younger lads."

"Anything else on him?"

"An ex-detective I spoke to told me that he had tried to get information out of Bailey, more than once, but no dice. He also told me his family circumstances were bad."

"How bad?"

"Absent father, alcoholic mother," Sexton replied. "She

was on the game until she died."

"Do you know what age Bailey was at the time?"

"Eighteen," Sexton replied.

"And his sister?"

"Fourteen."

"Did he look after her when the mother died?"

"Far as I could find out, he did," Sexton replied. "She was doing a bit of gear for a while, but he got her back on track and into a private school. Then he paid for the beauty school courses, ten grand a pop."

"A scumbag with a heart of gold," Kate said.

Her phone rang.

"I've just paid my entrance fee," O'Neill told her. "Where do you want to meet?"

Kate met him in one of the exhibition halls. His concession to looking touristy was a dark windcheater and floppy hat. Unnoticed, they moved away from the public areas and took the back stairs to the attic OP, where Kate did the introductions.

"What's Rafiq up to this morning?" O'Neill enquired.

"Gone to work after a quiet night in," Digger answered. "Cody, can you… Is it okay I call you Cody?"

"Sure thing!"

"Is there anythin' peculiar about this guy that might give us a heads-up on what to expect? Small details make a big difference."

O'Neill reiterated much of what Digger knew already. Rafiq Khouri was born in 1991 to fourth-generation Lebanese parents in New York. Devout Muslims, they ran a small restaurant in Brooklyn. Rafiq began attending coderdojos when he was eight years old and word had it that the guy was a star programmer in the IT world.

"How did you tag him as a security threat?" Digger asked.

"You know much about cyber security monitoring?"

"Enough to know it's not the easiest job in the world."

"We're finding more and more groups using non-traditional communication that by-passes monitoring targets," O'Neill said.

"So, if you want to intercept 'stealth' communications you need a live lead."

"Most radical groups know we monitor phone and internet traffic," O'Neill resumed. "They're ditching traditional communications for new ways of connecting. Gaming console messaging is one such. It's how we landed Rafiq, or The Dark Prince, the pseudonym he uses when playing Call of Duty."

"Away from the Internet, can we expect him to get up to anythin' unusual?"

"You've seen the guy, he doesn't exercise, sits in front of a screen twelve hours a day. The jury's still out on what he's up to."

"So the whole Cloud Data Centre scare is just speculation," Kate observed.

"The fact he works in one has to be significant."

"Indeed!" Kate replied, unconvinced.

"Some kind of webmaster, plotting a takedown of global systems or facilitating stealth communications between the active cells planning attacks," O'Neill said, "we're fluid in our analysis."

They talked about possible targets ISIS may have eyes for.

"The largest data capacity submarine cable in the world runs from Long Island in New York to County Mayo in the west of Ireland," O'Neill said.

"I read about that," Digger replied. "A low-latency and ultra-high bandwidth fibre optic cable, 5,250 kilometres of it. Amazin'!"

"And what are you suggesting?" Kate asked.

"If it were damaged, global stock markets would be seriously disrupted," O'Neill replied.

"Not an easy target," Digger said. "I'll check it out, but as far as I know that cable makes landfall in Ross village, at a large underground enclosure. From there it connects to the onshore cable network with high-capacity links to the UK and mainland Europe."

"Maybe Rafiq is part of a bigger picture of planned attacks in Europe," O'Neill suggested.

"Have you approached the company?" Kate asked.

"Too early," O'Neill replied. To Digger, he said, "If we can assist on the technical side, just ask."

"This is the first 'stealth comms' interception case we've come up against. We might need your technical people to talk to telecom company techies."

"Just let me know what you need."

Digger nodded his appreciation.

"We're running blind, if we can't see what he's doing in that apartment," Kate said.

"You'll need a distraction to get him out," O'Neill said. "He's super-sensitive about his personal security."

"A fire drill, maybe for his floor," Digger mused.

"The guy's tetchy about anything out of the ordinary," O'Neill said. "You'd need to take his entire block onto the street."

Kate winced.

"Let me look into it," Sexton suggested. "I've a mate in Dublin Fire Brigade."

"Could I ride along when you find an ingress to the apartment?" O'Neill asked.

Digger looked to Kate.

"We'll work out the logistics and get back to you," she replied.

Briefing over, Sexton walked O'Neill back to the public area. He deposited him at the Soldiers and Chiefs exhibition tracing a period of Ireland's military history from 1550 to the modern day. When he returned, Kate was preparing to leave; Pete McNally had texted that O'Driscoll had arrived.

"I better get back," Kate said, "but before I do, talk to me about drug routes."

"Most of the cocaine getting into Europe comes from South America via west coast African countries like Guinea Bissau and northwards to Spain," Sexton replied.

"And then what? Irish crims living on the Costa del Sol ship it here?"

"Mostly, but it's a muddled picture. Many of the Irish criminals that go down there have shown a capacity for making deals with their English counterparts. They're making big money—fast."

"Is Bailey going freelance?"

"If Bailey's running drugs from the Middle East, then it's a new route," he told Kate.

She briefed him on the linkup she and Digger observed between Bailey and three unknown suspects in Cyprus.

"If it's not drugs; why is Bailey talking to two known members of Hezbollah?" she asked.

"Your guess is as good as mine," Sexton replied.

Before she reached base, Kate rang Dan Whatney, the CIA Liaison in the US embassy in Paris.

"How're ya settlin' back in?" he asked.

"Finding my feet. Can we chat about our mutual interest in Lebanon?" Kate asked.

"What d'ya want to know?"

"The guy I saw in Cyprus is a scumbag involved with a dangerous Dublin drugs gang. What about the Beirut pair?"

"Both Hezbollah. What's your guy's current status?"

"His former bosses, a father and son were murdered in prison last night. Their gang controlled the south side of Dublin and most large towns outside the capital. Last night's murders puts Don Bailey top of the pile."

"Jeez Kate, sounds like ya should be talkin' to the DEA."

"Too early to say. We're trying to work out why Bailey met the Beirut suspects. Any ideas?"

"Did ya identify the second Irish guy?"

"We're working on him but we think he…" Kate hesitated. She hadn't touched base with the Army about Dempsey yet.

"What?"

"He might be military."

"Army? What's goin' on there?"

"We don't know for sure, it's early days. Let's keep that between us for now, okay?"

"You got it. Kate, I'll keep my eyes and ears open for anything that I think could be connected, but right now, I got nada."

She reached SIU's underground parking and used her shiny new swipe card to enter. O'Driscoll's black Lexus was already in the number one parking spot. Juggling two complex cases and keeping a weather eye on what he was up to was a big ask. The prospect of sharing the Beirut intelligence with the investigators on the Fulton murders worried her. With arrests came interrogations and one slip might feed the information back to Bailey. She locked her car, refocussed her thoughts onto the FBI case and strode towards the lift.

11

The two gunmen lying in wait for 'Doc' Carroll, northside Dublin's ruthless gang leader, allowed him exit his bullet-proof BMW and walk towards his heavily fortified house. Carroll had dropped off his youngest child to pre-school and copped the ambush a split second too late. He was in open ground, a free fire zone.

The planner had laid out the daytime hit meticulously. He figured by ten o'clock, the housing estate's roads would be quiet and that would limit the chances of collateral damage. Kids would be in school; their parents back indoors. To the executioner, all that mattered was neutralising the target.

Eye witnesses told investigators of hearing a number of rapid shots. A burst from an assassin's sub-machine gun had felled Carroll. Witnesses reported that after the initial burst, they heard no further shots; just the victim screaming, "Don't shoot." Their statements made no sense to investigators, until a home security video revealed a second shooter coolly finishing the job with a double tap to the head from a handgun with a silencer. The pair of assassins then calmly walked through a nearby alley to a waiting car and escaped. The burning Honda Civic was located within ten minutes, three kilometres from the crime scene.

Later the same day, D-I Ron Sexton updated Kate on the killing as they sat in an almost deserted pub in the west of the city, nursing insipid coffee. Digger and Angie joined them as early evening drinkers dropped in on their way from work.

"A week on from the Fulton murders," Kate observed, "now this!"

"Nobody's connecting Bailey to it yet," Sexton said.

"If he's behind it, what the hell is he up to?" she asked. "Is he trying to take over the city?"

Sexton replied, "Doubt it. No single gang is big enough for that."

"Angie found an interestin' titbit," Digger said, as they pulled over two low stools to perch opposite Kate and Sexton. He was taking over from Sexton for the night shift and overlapped an hour.

"First, talk to me about Rafiq," Kate said.

"Still at work, there's a unit watching," Sexton replied.

"Anything coming from the apartment?"

"Nothin' worth talkin' about," Digger answered. "Gamin' and chattin' to his family back in the States on Skype."

Earlier in the week Sexton engineered the evacuation of the Smithfield apartment block. Two micro cameras, one in the living room and the other in his bedroom, were now giving them a live feed from the apartment. Cody O'Neill accompanied Digger during the covert fit out and requested blanket coverage. Digger disagreed;

arguing that putting in additional devices heightened the risk of detection. Kate concurred. Sexton babysat Khouri's case freeing Digger to chase up their lead on Mick Dempsey.

"What's this titbit on Bailey?" Kate asked Angie.

"I asked my old skipper in drugs if I could scan the surveillance logs on him," she explained. "And last year Bailey was lost on three separate occasions not far from Jafar Hajj Nasri's house."

"The Money Man?" Kate queried.

"One and the same," Angie replied.

Nasri had lived in Dublin for over twenty years and was suspected of having strong Al-Qaeda connections. Kate's last case confirmed him as an active player. Over the years, he had met many Jihad fighters who visited Ireland from Iraq, Afghanistan and the conflict in Syria. A successful businessman, his import enterprise sold nuts and spices to wholesalers but he was also a Hawaladar, hence the Money Man tag. The hawala system offered ordinary folk an 'informal' way to transfer money between countries that bypassed banks. It operated throughout the Arab world and Asia.

"Any sightings of them together?" Kate asked.

"Nope," Angie replied.

"What dates was he 'lost' near Nasri's?"

"Over a year ago, I've got the dates back at base."

"We were watching Nasri last year," Kate said. "I find it hard to believe he had other stuff going on."

"He's a resourceful man," Digger reminded her.

"Rather than speculating on it," Sexton cut in, "why don't we see if we can make any of it stand up."

"Let me think about it," Kate replied.

"What's to think about?" Sexton said. "Leave it to me, I'll suss it out."

Kate liked the direct way Sexton operated, he didn't hold back.

"Not this time," Kate replied. "I'll chat to Mac and we'll discuss it later."

"What about the soldier?" she asked Digger.

"Dempsey's being discharged, I'm told," he replied.

"He's quitting the Army?"

"He's hit the retirement age. My mate has got him work with a security company."

"Any Bailey connection in his background?" Kate asked her two D-I's.

"None established," Sexton replied. "I'm talking to a contact at the weekend."

"What do you mean?"

"Years ago, I heard a whisper that Gene Fulton had a shit-hot guy looking after weapons. It nagged the hell out of me that I could never figure out who it was."

"And you think it could be Dempsey?" Kate asked.

"He might be a fit," Sexton replied. "What are the Army telling us about him?"

"I haven't asked yet."

"Why?"

"If I ask, I'll have to explain the whole Hezbollah connection. If I do that, we might lose the case."

Sexton nodded.

"With the FBI keeping us tied down, the Army might pressurise the Commissioner to have Dempsey's connections investigated and push us out of the picture," Kate elaborated.

"Do it themselves, even," Sexton added.

"Fuck that," Digger swore. "Amateurs!"

"I'll sort something out," Kate ended the discussion.

Mac now controlled agent handling, and Kate drove straight to his office. He confirmed SIU still had a live connection close to Nasri and called the agent's handler, Detective Gerry Grealy, to check out the Nasri/Bailey connection Kate had suggested. He verified the pair had met once, twelve months earlier.

———————

The next day, at McKee Barracks, Sergeant Mick Dempsey handed in his application for permission to retire from the Army. *It was the way the Army worked,* Dempsey reflected, *you almost had to seek permission to use the toilet.* His commanding officer ticked the 'granted' box and issued discharge papers. He shook Dempsey's hand, thanked him for his service, and wished him well. Dempsey walked to the Quartermaster stores where he handed back an assortment of old uniforms and two pairs of boots. The store clerk wrote out a receipt and pushed it across the counter. Thirty years of his life signed off in a matter of minutes.

As he crossed the parade ground towards the barracks gate a final time, Dempsey expected the experience might leave him feeling downbeat. However, the recent job proved he had lost none of his planning skills. It raised his spirits and paid €10,000. When Dempsey told Bailey about swinging the security job, employed where he could be most useful, he threw in an extra five hundred euros.

Dempsey saluted the sentry on duty and walked out the pedestrian gate with a pep in his step, heading straight for the bookies.

12

Next morning at Garda HQ, Kate read the invitation to attend her UN contingent's medal ceremony in Cyprus and put it down on Mac's desk.

"It's up to you to decide if you go or stay," he told her. "It's a big day for your old contingent."

"They'll send on the photos," she replied. "I'm staying put."

"That's item one out of the way," Mac smiled.

"What's with the grin? Item two?

"Mr. O'Driscoll is out of our hair and you're taking over the Unit for the moment. What do you make of that?

"Whoa, wait! How come O'Driscoll's out of the picture?

"GSOC is publishing its report on Zoom's death tomorrow and O'Driscoll is heavily criticised in it."

"What's happening with him?

"Well, we know why he's been absent these past few weeks. He's been circling the wagons."

"What do you mean?

"The Commissioner was all set to shift him to a desk

job until a call from the Minister's Private Secretary 'changed his mind'."

"What the hell?"

"O'Driscoll starts in Special Branch tomorrow, back to his old job, as the Minister requested.

"Absolute jerk," Kate replied. "He's as good as gotten away with it."

She returned to SIU and straight to O'Driscoll's old office. She pulled photographs from the wall and crammed them into a cardboard box before dumping the contents of his desk drawers on top. Satisfied that any physical evidence of his tenure was erased, she opened two windows and watched the curtains billow.

The news was out; Pete McNally peered around the door and asked, "You moving in already?"

"I'm going nowhere, just getting rid of the junk" Kate stated, firmly. "Close those windows in an hour, transfer the phones and lock it up."

"What about that?" McNally asked, pointing to storage box on the Chief's desk.

"Dump it in the storeroom," she replied. "Let him ask if he wants his crap."

Mac sprung a surprise in the late afternoon, arriving unannounced at SIU as Kate sat in on the briefing for the evening crew. Since she was going to miss out on a medal ceremony in Cyprus, he had ordered that the souvenir be collected from the HR section.

"You gave ten months of your life to UN service," he pronounced, as he pinned the medal on her lapel. "Unfortunately, you couldn't join your contingent comrades to celebrate it, so we're doing it here."

Whistles and cheers greeted the ceremonial award.

"Settle down," she jested with her audience, "this doesn't mean we all go drinking."

When she got home she changed and went running. The day had been emotionally draining and she wanted to clear her mind. She needed to put O'Driscoll in the past rather than agonise over how he had played the system and won yet again. She was halfway through her stretching routine when the caretaker rang to tell her a delivery had arrived. Intrigued, she took the lift and met him in the foyer.

"An American fella dropped this off for you," he said, handing her a bottle of champagne.

There was a card, 'Hi Kate, to celebrate your contribution to making the world a safer place. Thank you for your service, Cody.'

"When was this delivered?" Kate asked.

"Minutes ago," the caretaker replied. "Very polite man, he got back into the taxi and left."

Kate thanked him, returned to her apartment and checked her freezer for ice. Five forlorn cubes sat in the near empty tray. She grabbed her phone from the kitchen counter and dialled out. Trapping the phone on her shoulder, she placed the champagne bottle into a basin of water and dumped the precious ice around it, securing it with a kitchen cloth.

"I can't think of anything more depressing than drinking champagne alone," she told O'Neill.

"Kate," he exclaimed. "I thought you'd still be celebrating with the gang."

"Nope, but I guess you've been talking to Mac.

"Assistant Commissioner McEnroe updated me on your personnel changes."

"Why not stop by for a glass of bubbly?"

"Okay, great. I guess I'll turn the cab around."

Kate rolled up her exercise mat, showered in record time and changed into a white blouse and blue jeans. She sprayed on her Dolce & Gabbana Light Blue, and checked her look in the bedroom mirror. *I'm giddy as a teenager*, she thought.

"Try to ignore the chaos," she told O'Neill, when he arrived. "This is a stopgap for another few weeks."

"It's good," he replied. "Thank you for the invitation."

"No, thank you for the thought."

"Sincerely meant," he replied, as he sat on the edge of a small sofa. "I hate how my country rides roughshod over the UN, when it suits. Look at all the conflicts the UN has calmed since it was founded."

"It wouldn't be my career choice," Kate replied. "Will you do the honours?" she asked, handing him the champagne.

He popped, poured, and actually proposed a toast to world peace.

"Didn't Bill Murray do that in *Groundhog Day* when he was trying to woo Andy McDowell?" Kate teased.

"What are you saying?"

"There must be better toasts."

"To the end of bullshit!" O'Neill said, raising his glass.

"I'll drink to that," Kate winked at him.

They clinked on it and sat on the uncomfortable couch, chatting about the time-consuming and tedious Khouri case.

"Your Mr. O'Driscoll is mighty interested in progress with Khouri," O'Neill observed.

"When did he speak to you about the case?"

"He called to the embassy last week. I had no choice but to bring him to my office."

"That's the first I'm hearing of it," Kate replied.

"It was just a quick chat really," O'Neill said. "Asked

me for a heads-up if anything major was coming down the track."

"Son of a bitch! He's worried about his bloody shares."

"He's out of the picture now, in any case. Let me refill your glass."

Kate was relaxed in O'Neill's company. He suggested taking her to dinner but she told him it had been a big day and would rather eat in. Her local Thai restaurant came up trumps. Forty minutes after ordering, they delivered an aromatic package to her front door. The pair unpacked the dishes and spread them around the coffee table, then sat on cushions either side. Kate lit candles rather than lights as the evening gloom advanced.

When they finished, she cleared away the dishes and fetched the champagne from the kitchen. She knelt at the coffee table and shared what remained between their glasses. "Thanks for a lovely evening," she said, kissing him lightly on the cheek.

He took her hands in his and drew her close.

"It's been wonderful," he said, kissing her lips.

Unruffled, Kate responded passionately and they rolled onto the rug. After moments of fervent floor wrestling, she led him towards her bedroom. As they reached the door, O'Neill swept her into his arms and stepped gingerly into the unruly room.

In the semi-darkness they eagerly undressed each other, the novelty of shared nakedness feeling exhilarating. As O'Neill tenderly kissed her neck his musk was intoxicating and arousing. They surrendered to the rhythm of their bodies, with short gasps becoming more urgent until their union peaked and they crumpled in exhausted satisfaction. They lay together kissing and caressing until their breathlessness subsided. He broke the spell with a final kiss and slipped out of bed. Kate was already dozing when he leaned over and whispered that he had to leave. Muttering her goodbyes, her senses caught his freshly showered scent.

Bailey felt confident that meeting his northside rivals was a risk worth taking. He wanted to face down his enemies, show them he feared nobody. For his plan to work, Carroll had to go. Low on funds after the Fulton job, he had dangled a carrot in front of the ex-soldier and the rest was history.

Today's meeting was set sixty kilometres north of Dublin, at the edge of the commuter belt towns. He was picked up in a hotel car park and had agreed to come alone. He didn't want one of his own gang getting twitchy and starting a war. One of his rival's gang searched him before letting him anywhere near Doc Carroll's replacement.

"You have some fuckin' balls askin' to meet us, today of all days," the thug told Bailey.

"I appreciate you showing up," Bailey replied, nonchalantly pulling a chair from under the kitchen table.

"Oh we'll always rock up," another replied. "Ya here to tell us why ya topped Doc?"

"Who do I talk to?" Bailey asked, as he turned the chair around and leaned his arms on the back rest. "One big gorilla or every monkey in the room?"

"Answer the question: why was Doc whacked?" the wannabe boss at the top of the table replied.

Bailey came back fast. "Do you really think I'd be here if I had anything to do with that?"

"You had your own boss done in jail," another thug said from the opposite end of the table.

Bailey shrugged, "Everyone's a detective."

"Answer it," the main man said.

"I'd nothing to do with Slasher dying. He was offed because him and his aul fella owed the IRA. When they came looking to have their debt paid, he told them to go fuck themselves."

"That's not what we heard."

"Well you heard wrong. We were like brothers, me and Slasher." Bailey pitched it perfectly, his face a veil of sincerity and sadness, as he spoke of his former boss.

"It's a bit convenient an' all," the main spokesman piped up again, "you showin' up like this, the day after Doc gets whacked."

"Look, all I want to do is assure you I had nothing to do with Doc. Everyone here knows I respect territory."

The ragbag gang around the table shrugged.

"I don't want ye feeling that ye need to lash out to prove a point," he continued. "When my plan kicks in, this tit-for-tat shit has to stop."

"What plan is that?" the wannabe boss asked.

"It's there for you, if you want to be part of it," Bailey told them.

"Part of what exactly?"

"A business that includes export as well as import."

"What da fuck ya on about?"

"We do it right; we can control product going into Liverpool, Manchester, Newcastle and Birmingham as well as Dublin."

"What makes ya think, ya could do that?"

"Contacts I have are interested in a deal. They just want to know we can deliver."

"We're listenin'."

Staying cool was critical and Bailey waited for the bickering to die down before he planted the seed. Just like the ex-soldier's plan for Doc Carroll, holding your nerve was the key. Dempsey told Bailey that he had collected enough bodies with the UN in Lebanon to know that no-one caught in a free-fire zone survived. They had waited for their target to move away from his car before Dempsey felled him and Bailey completed the job.

As he left, Bailey believed the meeting had gone well and the extra bodies he needed would come on board. He laid out just enough information to reel them in but needed funds, much more than these northside monkeys could ever cobble together. Making the grand Arab plan work would craft his future.

———

"Excuse me," Kate said as she yawned and stretched.

The previous twenty-four hours was a blur and Sexton had just concluded his report. He related how the previous night, Bailey had met with the murdered 'Doc' Carroll's gang.

"Bailey would know some of them to talk to, individually," he explained. "But we've never seen him risk meeting an entire gang before."

"You gave the go-ahead to follow Bailey?" Kate said to Digger.

"Guilty as charged!" he replied. "You weren't answerin' your phone."

"Out of power," she replied, defensively. "It was a good call. What about the FBI case?"

"Runnin' like a military operation," Digger replied. "We had housed the suspect in Smithfield when Ron got word on Bailey. Jane was unimpressed, but I came in early, took over on Khouri, and gave him a unit to tail Bailey."

"What's Khouri up to?"

"Last night he was on his PS4, gaming and chatting," Digger replied.

"Do we know with whom?"

"No. We can see he creates a party, a kind of group and communicates with whoever is in it."

"A group chat like with Skype?"

"Kind of. He has two options with the party; restrict it to friends only or open it up to friends of friends, that way anyone can join in. He does the latter but also switches between chatting and playing his game."

"Did you ask the FBI for assistance in trying to intercept the group chats?"

"O'Neill knows about it. It's happened regularly in the past, apparently."

"What did he say?"

"Said that when they tried to run the software PlayStation supplied, on an intercept programme, it didn't work. They think Khouri altered the coding."

"That's the first interesting development since the case began," Kate said. "What about Bailey?"

Sexton opened his journal and scanned his notes. He knew the territory better than most and explained how all the Dublin gangs were on edge since a rumour floated that 'Doc' Carroll had been whacked in revenge for the Fultons.

Kate continued. "If that's the case, why would Bailey meet his rivals now?"

"It's very odd," Sexton replied. "Early intel indicates that he contracted Doc Carroll's killing."

"Tell me about last night's meeting."

Sexton described the gathering at a secluded house north of Dublin, which had been a nightmare to cover. The northside gang, hyper-sensitive to another attack, had most of their number out covering access roads around the meeting place.

"Any idea on who was inside to meet Bailey?"

"We sighted Doc Carroll's main sidekick and three others coming out of the house afterwards."

"I guess this means we're taking on Bailey as a second case," Kate said.

Sexton and Digger agreed.

"We're going to need more bodies," Sexton said.

"I've got a list of nominees for training," Digger advised. "I can set up a week-long crash course. After that they can learn on the job until the dust settles and we get a chance to complete their training."

"Do that," Kate agreed.

13

Mac was livid when Kate told him that she was taking on Bailey. She reminded him of her promised autonomy and argued that SIU were the only unit that could hope to uncover Bailey's scheme. Mac reluctantly authorised two weeks to work the case but insisted that Rafiq Khouri continue to receive priority. If nothing definitive came up on Bailey, he ordered her to share all the intelligence with the team investigating the Fulton murders and let them take the lead.

Running a training course in tandem with two high pressure cases stretched SIU to the limit. Kate sanctioned the overtime spend for the training week but as it progressed she worried about keeping her crews fresh. Towards the middle of the week, Digger popped his head into her office.

"Do you want to rally the troops before we head out?" he asked.

He had rounded up candidates with an expressed interest in surveillance and put them through the wringer.

Kate always talked with training groups to encourage their effort and thank them for trying out for SIU.

"Where are we at with this?" Kate asked, as they strode along the corridor.

"We've finished the theory bit and done some field work," he replied. "We've another day on the street comin' up, a few hours' sleep, then an all-nighter. We'll have them whittled down by Friday afternoon."

"How's it looking?"

"Most are still a bit nervy; the next 24 hours will sort the wheat from the chaff."

By Friday afternoon Digger had reviewed the performance sheets, made up his mind, and forwarded Kate his recommendations. From twenty candidates, two men and two women, were selected, the ones he felt were ready to give surveillance a shot. The newbies would have to prove their worth over a two-year probationary period.

Detective Gerry Grealy stared out the car windscreen as he tried to assess his agent's mood and get a bead on him. He took a bite of his burger and threw what remained back into the bag. It was almost a year since he had been given the task of handling Danesh, his Pakistani agent, who was devouring every scrap of his takeaway as they spoke. Grealy sorted out any immigration hurdles Danesh encountered, ensuring the visa extending his stay in the country was validated. He was a valuable SIU resource who reported on the activities of Jafar 'Hajj' Nasri, aka the Money Man.

"Something is not right with him at this time," he told Grealy.

Grealy was, by now, scoffing his chips, grabbing four at

a time with his large fingers. He licked them clean of salt and vinegar, before replying.

"Just a sec," he said.

The top of his head skimmed the grease stain on the roof lining as he twisted in the driver's seat. In contrast, Danesh barely cleared the passenger headrest. Grealy leaned over and retrieved a voice recorder. He checked the rear window and scanned both sides of the dockside car park. Nobody seemed to be taking an interest in them.

He pressed the record button, before resuming eating his chips. "Now," he asked, "how do you mean something's not right?"

"He lose his temper all the time. Being around him is like walking on hot coals."

"Why?"

"You have to walk carefully; say wrong thing, it set him off."

"Is the business in trouble?"

"I think it is good. He take on another worker."

"So what you're saying is that business is good but he's on edge all the time?"

"This is how he is."

"Is he getting you to do anything outside your usual stuff?"

"Not really," Danesh replied, "except…"

"Don't fuckin' hold back on me. Last time it earned you a bloody nose. Give me all you've got."

"I drive him in the country."

The drive took place two weeks earlier on a Sunday morning. Danesh explained that Nasri had instructed him to take the M7 motorway from Dublin. When prodded, the agent outlined that they had driven for twenty-five minutes and then cut off the main artery.

"Bundle of Sticks!" Danesh laughed. "This was the place."

Grealy knew that time spent with an agent was precious. He didn't like wasting it; he had to read the body language and react to the information the agent offered. He couldn't afford time wasted talking nonsense.

"What are you on about?" he growled.

"This is the name of the place I turn."

"Bundle of Sticks? Did you see a sign?"

"Yes, at roundabout."

"Did you turn left or right at the roundabout?"

"I go all the way around and take the last road."

"So, a right turn. Where did you go from there?"

"Near to a town."

"What town?"

"I do not know. I do what Boss tell me—turn left, drive slow."

"Did you drive into the town?"

"We did not go in town. We turn left at roundabout with flowers and then we drive in countryside."

It wasn't much help, roundabouts on approaches to most towns had flowers planted on them.

"Why did he tell you to drive slowly?"

"He want to take picture, so I stop, actually."

"A picture of what?"

"Horse farm."

"A stud farm, was it?"

"A place where the racing horses are."

"Was your boss sitting in the front seat beside you?"

"No, he in back, he write something on paper after he take picture. Maybe, he buy horse, soon."

"How far out from the town was the horsey place you stopped at?" Grealy asked.

"Five kilometres, I think."

Before letting him off, Grealy got the agent to repeat the story. He didn't interrupt, instead concentrated on making note of anything that might help identify the location. He then drove twenty-five minutes out of Dublin on the M7 motorway which brought him into Kildare County. He was aware that there were lots of stud farms here. He called a mate in the local traffic corps about the oddly named roundabout. He solved the mystery. It was off the south Naas motorway exit and a right turn there, sent you towards Newbridge town. Grealy drove on, trying to recreate the journey the agent had described. As Newbridge approached, he turned left on the outskirts, at the Pfizer factory.

The landscape soon confirmed that he was in stud farm country. In addition to the natural hedges, field boundaries were delineated with post and rail timber fences. Seven kilometres out of town Grealy drew up outside Ballycleary Stud. It had a tree-lined avenue and a large sign on the gates warning that entry to the public was strictly forbidden. Ballycleary House, a grey Palladium pile, stood at the end of the impressive driveway. It was surrounded by scaffolding and seemed to be undergoing a major renovation.

The main yard lay to the right of the dwelling house. Grealy could make out the boxes around the yard where the thoroughbred bloodstock was housed. Behind the house it looked like several fields had been made into gallops; four horses were on a track, kicking up sand as they sped along, kept to a steady pace by their riders. Grealy soon lost sight of them as they disappeared behind high hedges. Alongside, was a full-blown race course, including a series of jumps. It was flat season, so the obstacles were pulled to the side of the course. Six workmen with wheelbarrows sought out any foreign objects on the ground and prodded the luxuriously thick grass surface with forks to improve drainage.

He had no interest in gambling, was clueless when it came to horseracing and unaware that Vincent Cleary, owner of Ballycleary, was a successful trainer. His most important client was a Saudi national. His Highness Sheikh Muhammad Bin Salah Al-Naqeeb had stud farms around the world which included substantial investments in Ireland. Local rumour was that his money was paying for much of the renovation at Ballycleary House and stud. When Grealy copped a figure at the edge of the yards peering in his direction through binoculars, he knew it was time to go. He picked up a road map, scanned it quickly, and drove off slowly.

Mick Dempsey made a mental note of the registration number of the grey car that seemed to tarry a little too long near the entrance to Ballycleary House. It was his first week in his new job and he dutifully recorded the vehicle number in a daily incident log. The stud was pestered by punters hoping to see the horses in training and assess their form. Vincent Cleary didn't tolerate it and instructed his security company to swiftly move on any interlopers. Dempsey didn't care about long-term job security, he just needed to demonstrate diligence for a few more weeks.

By the time Grealy met Kate, he had swapped registration plates on his car. It was a standard security measure for agent meetings. Kate was en route from checking in with Digger when Grealy called and they met up at the Pope's Cross car park in the Phoenix Park.

"Why would Nasri scope out a stud farm?" she asked.

"No idea," he replied. "He also mentioned that his boss is out of sorts, these days."

"What's that supposed to mean?" Kate asked.

"The agent doesn't know. Anything in particular you want me to do?"

"Tell your agent to check in every day. If Nasri goes near the stud farm again, he needs to tell you immediately."

———

Don Bailey expected surveillance of some kind; he was used to it. Usually, after leading his pursuers on a merry dance for an hour or so, he could pick them out. In the weeks since Doc Carroll's murder, he sensed he was being watched but couldn't flush anyone out. For a while, he thought it might be some of the northside gang following him. Two days of checking their whereabouts put them out of the picture. Bailey then figured it had to be cops, different to the usual ones. He dumped all his phones, picked up fresh ones and wasted valuable time each day on anti-surveillance.

Something familiar struck him about the face he caught glancing in his direction on a day he sat in a Temple Bar café staring out the window. He did a double-take when he noted the cyclist again next day and ordered a second coffee. To a casual observer, the guy in cycling gear was just another bike courier on a coffee break, but Bailey was now certain he was being watched. The second coffee gave him a throbbing headache and as he stood up to leave the half-finished cup, it hit him.

He sat down again and removed a folded photo from his wallet. Smoothing the sheet of paper out on the café table, he smiled. The prostitute's debt pay-off was about to reap dividends. Bailey recalled what she had told him. Her client was a cop; now the same guy had turned up close to him, two days in a row.

He made a quick phone call and waited. Ten minutes later the SIU newbie watching the café noted Gerry Buck, Bailey's driver walking in carrying a plastic bag with unidentified contents. Inside, Bailey walked to the toilets and extracted a large envelope from the packet purchased. He popped the A4 sheet and a scribbled note into it. As he sealed the envelope, he gave Buck precise instructions. They walked out of the café together and while Bailey went on a distraction walkabout, Buck carried out his boss's order.

Newly appointed detective, Jonathon Mooney, Jonny, to his mates was in his element. He had permission to grow his hair long and was encouraged to remain unshaven most of the time. He loved his new surveillance assignment and felt he was fast growing into it. The cycling didn't bother him, he was young and fit.

The target was on the move. He called in the direction of travel and soon others took up the chase. When he saw an envelope taped to his bike he figured it was a marketing ploy, someone cashing in on the city's growing cycling population. He slid it off and tore it open. After a quick glance at the contents he closed it again and put it inside his jacket, his hands unsteady as he undid the bicycle lock.

His head buzzed as he cycled towards the rendezvous with van driver, Pete McNally. How best to play it? It had only been one night, while morning sickness spoiled his partner's interest in sex. He had been out on the town with his old unit, but was heading home early when he picked up the pro. She wasn't the usual sort; she was classy looking and he had been too pissed to notice that the fancy accent didn't come naturally. Her true inner city accent had emerged when they got to the hotel.

Fucking bitch, he thought, *must have photographed me while I dozed.*

Then, there was the recent photo of his one night stand. It horrified him. She looked ten years older than he remembered. The note that accompanied the picture was in a childish scrawl. 'Shame if this showed up on the Internet,' the first line read. Underneath, there was mobile phone number to call.

His partner had become his wife and their baby daughter, Orla, was the most important thing in Jonny's life. He knew the right thing to do was to take the threat back to D-I Sexton and confess all. But he was Jonny Mooney, after all; he felt confident that he could keep it under wraps and hit back at the prostitute trying to blackmail him.

Audrey Kelly figured the two guys in the navy car for punters, at first. Past midnight, they had kerb-crawled long enough to make her edgy, as she worked the rough end of Benburb Street.

"You doin' business?" the passenger shouted. In reply, she turned, hesitated, and then nodded. They beckoned her towards the car and as she approached, the snatches of conversation she overheard, worried her.

"Is it her, are you certain?" the driver asked.

"Deffo," the passenger replied. He stepped out of the car and flashed an identification card in her face. "Garda Síochána, get in," he told her, opening a rear door.

"What the fuck's this," Audrey laughed, as she slumped into the back seat. "A crackdown?"

The days of being rousted by vice squad detectives were mostly in the past. These days it was uniforms she spoke to and they knew her by name. They were community patrols, sound, they cared about the girls' welfare rather than focussed on their profession. From time to time, Audrey gave whatever information suited her purposes on who was pushing drugs in the locality.

"So what's the craic, Jack?" Audrey inquired, as they drove off. "Where are youse two goin' to take me?"

The two cops cracked up.

"Dirty-minded fucks," Audrey spat in reply.

"We need you to answer a few questions," the cop in the passenger seat said.

"Fire away, Andrew, I've nothin' to hide."

"All in good time," Detective Andrew Timmons replied, annoyed that the quick-witted prostitute had noted his name from the badge. He turned and looked from the old mugshot photograph in his hand, directly at her. "What's your name?" he demanded.

"Audrey Kelly," she replied.

Minutes later, the car swung off the city street into a red brick building's basement. They didn't bother turning on lights in the dilapidated underground space and her ordeal began with an intimate body search. The two cops forced her face-down on the car bonnet and ripped her bra and thong off. Then they dragged her to a disused cell block. As one cop clanked closed an ancient cell gate behind them, the other spread a photo on a bench in front of her.

When he shone a torch on it, she had tried not to react. The dozy cop, Audrey thought, that's what this is about. She couldn't help the involuntary smirk, but it incensed her jailers. One pushed past her out of the cell and she heard water running. Without warning, the driver grabbed her hair and yanked her out to another pitch black room. As they closed in on the running water sound, she tried to stall, but his grip propelled her forward. He forced her head under the water, while his partner trapped her flailing arms. The water continued flowing into the deep sink, replenishing spills, as they repeated the dose.

Eventually, Audrey reluctantly gave up her story on using the photo to clear her debt with Don Bailey. An hour after lifting her, the two cops dumped her, shivering, on the footpath of her night time beat. Volunteers from a homeless soup run came on her bruised body twenty minutes later and called an ambulance.

The following day Jonny Mooney walked confidently into the Chief Superintendent's office at Special Branch. Office staff were used to seeing him coming and going. O'Driscoll was president of the Garda rugby club and Mooney was one of the team's rising stars. He closed the door and sheepishly drew up a chair in front of the Chief's desk.

"Sir, I can't tell you how much I…" he began.

O'Driscoll held up his hand and stopped him.

"The prostitute is not your problem," he said.

Silence hung in the room as Mooney digested the news.

"Don Bailey is," O'Driscoll concluded.

With her boss transferred, Kate was parachuted into his slot at a conference of European Intelligence Services in Madrid. Formal exchanges of intelligence occurred routinely, but robust intra-services relationships were essential to ensure that less obvious intel flowed freely between security services and police forces. Maintaining continuity was a challenge when new faces appeared and the acquaintance cycle began all over. Kate worried about how she would be received into what sounded to her like an old boys' club.

She was picked up at Barajas airport and ferried to her city centre hotel. First to arrive, her driver, cum bodyguard, suggested a visit to the Prado Museum and lunch. Was it because she was a woman, she wondered? She dismissed the notion and welcomed the distraction before the business end of the trip began. The driver used his police badge to usher them past long queues so that Kate could take in as much as possible during the whirlwind visit. She loved the Rubens, Rembrandt and Bosch works but *Las Meninas* by Diego Velázquez was her favourite.

The Baroque-style snapshot of the *Infanta Margarita*, daughter of a Spanish king, was painted in 1656. It was a sombre, yet sensual work, set in the artist's studio; the young princess and her entourage seemingly just dropped by for a visit. For Kate it played like a photograph; the skin colours were true and the *Infanta Margarita* looked directly at the viewer. Even Velázquez stared out from the canvas.

"It seems he's searching for something that's out of reach," Kate commented, as she studied it.

"One of the most loved paintings in Spain," her driver remarked.

Kate's meeting began at 2 p.m. when a fresh faced Colonel took his place at the head of a large conference table. His name was Antonio Garcia and he moved the meeting along at a smart pace. Each country had received an advance copy of the latest terrorist threat assessment against Europe. The biggest challenge to police and security services was weighing the possible fallout from the conflict in Syria. Videos were showing up on Islamic sites showing radicalised European youths exhorting their national Muslim brothers to join the Jihad. Garcia outlined some additional intelligence from Ceuta, the Spanish colony close to the Maghreb in North Africa. They had succeeded in stopping two young women in recent days at the border as they tried to leave to join the Syrian conflict. Insignificant, he conceded, compared to the hundreds travelling from Europe.

He invited questions and comments, before suggesting acceptance of the report's contents. Kate couldn't mention the ISIS case she was running; O'Neill's total ban on sharing the intel outside the FBI saw to that. A consensus was agreed that the European state of alert remain just below its highest level in most countries. The highest was reserved for when specific intelligence indicated an attack was imminent.

Meeting over, Garcia asked Kate to join him in his office on the second floor.

"I am happy to meet you," he began. "Our French colleagues speak highly of you."

"Thank you," she replied, a little taken aback. "It's my first trip to Madrid since college; I love your beautiful city."

"It's not bad," Garcia replied. "I am from the south, so it will never feel like home to me."

"Are you long in the post?"

"Just over one year. I learn all the time."

"It's a steep curve."

"I ask you to come here because I have a case I think you can help us with," Garcia began.

He explained how the Guardia Civil had been investigating radical Islamic activities around Malaga. It was centred on a Lebanese Sheikh, who, according to sources, was radicalising youths at a local mosque. Their sources told them that the Sheikh had a strong following in Hezbollah-controlled parts of Beirut.

While he lived in a villa near Benalmadena they had gotten an agent close to him for a few months. Back in November, the agent had gone missing. Four weeks after he disappeared the villa was put up for sale. Fishermen's nets retrieved the agent's body in February. There wasn't much left to work with from a forensic perspective, however, dental records confirmed his identity. Examination of the skull showed that he had been executed, a single shot to the back of his head.

"He was the gardener at the villa," Garcia explained. "We're still answering questions from a judge on our handling of him as an agent."

"And you think there's a connection with us?" Kate asked.

"For months we photograph everyone who calls to the villa. The agent put a camera in the garage for us."

"You've viewed footage from that time?"

"Precisely! These are photos I would like you to take back home and show to your field officers. They might recognise the men in them."

He slid an open envelope across the desk and Kate tipped its contents out. They were good quality prints. She fanned them and began to scrutinise.

"We have shared with the UK, France and Germany, as a priority," Garcia explained. "They tell us none of the suspects are known to them."

"Oh," Kate exclaimed.

"What? You recognise?" Garcia left his chair and came around to Kate's side of his desk.

"We know this one," she replied, "we're working on him at the moment, but it doesn't make sense, he's not a radical Muslim, he's a criminal."

Garcia nodded.

"Don Bailey is his name; he's a major drug dealer in Dublin."

Garcia scratched his head. "You're right, the Sheikh is unlikely to risk getting mixed up with drugs. But many criminals get radicalised in prison."

"Bailey's never been in jail. And I seriously doubt he's been radicalised."

What really startled Kate wasn't Bailey's image. It was the guy about to slide into the car with him. The last time she saw him, she scrambled for safety soon afterwards. She couldn't tell Garcia that passenger with Bailey was Aazim Hussein, a senior Hezbollah player in Beirut. She would have to get back to Whatney, the CIA's Paris liaison and see how he wanted to play it. The Spanish would learn the news eventually, but the Americans had taken risks to identify the suspects and it was their call on when and how the intel was shared.

"What can you tell me about the day the photos were taken?" Kate asked. "What were the Sheikh's movements?"

"Do you have anyone on your staff who can read Spanish?"

"Yes," Kate replied.

Garcia made a quick phone call.

"I'm getting you copies of the surveillance logs for the day our agent disappeared. I will also get you some video from the garage. This is a big breakthrough."

Kate worried. For Garcia, this identification offered him a new lead in a murder investigation and shed new light onto his enquiry into the Sheikh's activities in the south of Spain. For her, it opened up a vista into the unknown. Bailey didn't touch alcohol, she recalled. Was that an indicator of radicalisation? A leap too far to be credible; Bailey's mother's addiction was the best guess as to why he abstained. There had to be another angle.

Garcia hosted an official dinner that evening. Kate was irked within minutes of arriving as, one after another, her international colleagues congratulated her on the ID. Already Garcia had informed the Brits, French, and Germans. She was annoyed that they knew about it before she had a chance to fully investigate what the connection meant.

At least I filled Mac in, Kate mused. She had also touched base with Cody O'Neill, updating him on another unremarkable day in the Khouri case. His stay in Dublin was becoming open-ended and the embassy had provided him with a nearby one-bedroomed apartment.

She sat next to Garcia who chatted incessantly throughout dinner.

"You know the forensics we recovered from inside the villa," he told her. "They are very good."

"Really?" she replied. "What kind of evidence did you gather?"

"In the basement where we believe our agent was held and interrogated we retrieved a 9mm slug from the floor boards. DNA from chair also. "

"Down the line, if you get a suspect, that will be invaluable," Kate agreed.

Later, as the old boys' club flocked towards the bar, Kate bid everyone an early good night. Late-night schmoozing wasn't her style.

Next morning, she pulled on her running gear and jogged in the local park for half an hour, enjoying the early morning sunshine. As she stowed her briefcase in the overhead compartment on the return flight, she winced from her earlier exertions. Time for a new sports bra, she decided as she buckled her seat belt and turned her phone off.

She had no idea where the case was headed. Bailey was somehow implicated with the people who were suspected of killing a Spanish police agent months earlier. Nothing from SIU surveillance gave any hint of him having such far-reaching connections. Cabin staff began their pre-flight safety routine as the plane was pushed back from its stand. The engines revved as it started to taxi; Kate grasped the seat's armrests and closed her eyes.

In Dublin, Don Bailey was comforting his sister. She finally stopped wailing and took a sip from the coffee his driver had picked up at a nearby café.

"Rachel, what exactly happened?" he asked.

"I was just openin' up, like, when they came in behind me," she said, slipping a lock of her jet black hair over her right ear.

"Who were they?"

"Said they're Pearse Street, you know, the locals."

"Did they show you a warrant?" Bailey enquired.

"There was one fella givin' orders, he flashed a bit of paper at me. I didn't read it."

"So what happened then?"

"Look around ya, for fuck sake, they pulled the place apart."

The drugs unit from the local nick had been thorough in their search of the premises. Every shelf, drawer and cabinet had been inspected, their contents spilled or tossed. The small office Rachel operated from had been ripped apart. Papers lay strewn on the floor and her laptop had been seized.

"Did they say what they were looking for?"

"Drugs, they said. The fucker givin' the orders said that they'd got a tipoff that I was selling gear."

Bailey stared at his sister, open-mouthed. Her salon was smack in the middle of Temple Bar with its lively nightlife scene and the busy drug trade that went with it.

"I'm not," she shouted. "Fuck sake, I'm not that stupid."

"Rachel, I believe you," he said, putting an arm around her shoulders. "We'll give you a hand to clean up."

"I want something done about this," Rachel said.

"Talk to that complaints office, the Ombudsman, tell them you're being harassed for no good reason."

"What about the tipoff? Ya goin' to find out who did that?"

"Rachel, stay out of my business," he told her.

"Does it look like I can?"

Bailey and Buck spent the next two hours tidying and cleaning with his sister until they had the beauty salon ready for business. Rachel called the two girls who worked for her and told them to return in the afternoon. Only one of them took up the offer, the manicurist quit. Bailey stayed with his sister while she found a temp who could fill in for the lost employee.

When he returned to his car, he scanned the immediate surroundings before checking phones for messages. A mobile Buck had purchased had its first communication; a four word text. Bailey's dull grey eyes narrowed as he read its message — "Don't fuck with ME".

15

Mac shifted in his chair listening impassively to Cody O'Neill. The FBI agent was reiterating his Director's gratitude for the contribution the Garda Síochána was making to the international fight against ISIS. Kate sat in the armchair beside Mac and held O'Neill's eyes as he spoke. She pondered their feisty liaison, and its likely outcome; his return to the States when the case was done.

"I expected more action," Mac said.

"Well, Mr. McEnroe, we're delighted with how well Kate's team is doing."

"But nothing much is happening," Mac replied.

"Honestly," O'Neill answered, "we think things are happening in cyberspace."

"What things?" Kate asked.

"We don't know for sure," O'Neill replied. "What we're picking up back home, convinces us that Rafiq is an important player."

"Can you help us capture what he's doing online?" Kate asked.

"I'm not convinced that would be a wise strategy," O'Neill replied.

"Why not?" Mac interjected.

"Right now, it seems to me that Rafiq is very comfortable in his surroundings. And thanks to your good work," O'Neill said, sweeping an arm in their direction, "we know every move he makes. If we try an online interception, and fail, it might tip our hand."

"That's not accurate, we don't know every move he makes," Kate replied. "We've no clear picture of what he does at work and no idea who he communicates with online."

"Still," O'Neill came back, "what we've got from your good selves is great and very reassuring. The Director would like it to continue."

Kate looked to Mac. If she didn't really like O'Neill, she just might loathe him for this patently simpering performance.

"We started out with what seemed like a quick turn-around, but right now it's not looking that way." Mac said, standing up to indicate the case review's conclusion. "Kate, stay on the suspect; Cody, re-evaluation in one week."

"The raid on the beauty shop doesn't add up," D-I Ron Sexton explained to Kate later in the morning during a catch-up briefing.

"We don't know what prompted it," he added, as she stashed the FBI file away in the safe. "I've asked Angie to make enquiries."

"Okay, keep me informed. What else?"

"After leaving the shop in Temple Bar, Bailey met with two of Doc Carroll's gang for over an hour."

"Do we have any intel on what's behind all this cosiness?"

"Nothing definitive at the moment."

Digger tapped on the door.

"Tom McManus is here."

"Five minutes," Kate replied.

She wrapped up with Sexton; told him to keep the crews he had for the next two days. At that stage, she told him she would reallocate resources to cover Nasri.

McManus skimmed the Spanish surveillance logs immediately Kate handed them to him and outlined the case background. "At cursory glance, it's repetitive stuff," he told her. "I should have something for you by late in the afternoon."

Digger scooped up the garage surveillance DVDs from her desk and an hour later summoned her to the Cave where he cued up footage and pressed play. "So, Bailey's travelling in the back of the car with this Sheikh Nader guy when they arrive at the garage."

"Okay," she agreed, as the sequence began.

"Look at the expression on Bailey's face as he gets out of the car. He doesn't look happy."

"What? Now we're interpreting looks?"

"Hold on," Digger said. "The camera activated on a motion sensor. We see them again when they return. You can see that they've only been away from the car for eight minutes."

"Not much of a meeting," Kate remarked.

"Watch the whole scene when they return," Digger said. "Tell me what you see."

Kate dutifully watched as the images from the Spanish agent's camera played out on the screen. When the car reversed out of the garage, Digger stopped the video.

"Well?" he asked.

"Aazim Hussein gets in the back of the car with Bailey for the return trip."

"Very good," Digger said, "notice anythin' else?"

"There was something different about Bailey."

"Watch it again."

"He's wearing a different shirt when he comes back to the car," Kate said, when Digger stopped the replay. "Same colour but different shirt."

"Excellent, you're earnin' your detective allowance. Any other aspect to it?"

"What happens in eight minutes that made Bailey change his shirt? Why did Hussein sit with him on the return journey?"

Digger played the garage footage a third time while Kate watched attentively.

She nodded as the scene unfolded on the screen before her.

"Hussein seems to be concealing a weapon. He's forcing Bailey into the car and Bailey has three spots, could be blood, on the white belt of his jeans."

"Top of the class," Digger applauded. "If the Spanish agent disappeared the same day, I'm guessin' Bailey did him."

"Why would he do the killing, I wonder?" Kate asked.

"The motivation is as clear as mud but that's pretty strong circumstantial evidence, Digger said, tapping the screen, "that Bailey pulled the trigger."

"What about the rest of the picture?" Kate wondered.

"How do you mean?"

"Why would they hold a gun on Bailey, if he had just done them a favour?"

"That bit, I can't figure out," Digger replied.

Kate summoned Sexton to view the footage. "That's remarkable," he said, agreeing with Digger's analysis.

"Yeah," Kate agreed. "The Spaniards did well."

"No," Sexton replied, "I mean it looks like Bailey actually killed someone."

"Why is that remarkable?"

"The word out there is that he's never done anyone; he's always ducked out of doing the deed."

"Well, it seems that info is wide of the mark."

"Looks that way; I'll mention it at the afternoon briefing so that everyone's aware of the true nature of the beast."

"You can mention new intelligence that Bailey has carried out an execution in the past. Don't say who the victim was."

In the late afternoon McManus came back to Kate with a translation of the surveillance logs.

"Looks like somebody accompanied your main suspect," he told Kate.

When she gave McManus the documentation earlier, she told him the reports concerned an operation on a drug dealer's trip to Malaga. He waited as she read through the description of a second suspect who travelled to Malaga airport with Bailey the day after the episode in Benalmadena.

"Sounds like Slasher Fulton," she said. She called Garcia and asked him to forward any photos from the airport. These confirmed that Fulton was the second suspect on the trip. Garcia agreed to Kate discussing the information with the Americans.

McManus's translation confirmed Bailey's brief visit inside the villa and outlined how he and Fulton spent their final night in Malaga at a lap dancing club. Fulton brought one of the dancer's back to his apartment; Bailey spent the night alone.

They chatted about the possibility of Sunni and Shia connections in the case.

"Are you sure there *is* a connection?" McManus asked.

"We've strong evidence that a Dublin criminal is in contact with a Hezbollah group. We also suspect that he's been in contact, at some stage, with an Al Qaeda suspect in the city."

"The Al Qaeda suspect will be a Sunni; Hezbollah are Shia."

"That's what I figured."

"You'll need more context to figure out what's going on."

As McManus left, Kate thanked him for his input, rang Dan Whatney in Paris and outlined the status of the case.

"Jeez, Kate, that changes everything," he said.

"How do you mean?"

"I'm gonna have to bow out. I don't have jurisdiction anymore."

"I know your London guy looks after Irish cases," Kate said, trying to lighten the mood. "Is there any way you could fix it that you continue with it. It would make sense."

"No can do, Kate. If there's one thing that puts noses out of joint, it's encroachin' on someone else's turf and I ain't gonna do it."

"Okay, will you prepare a case background for him before I get in touch?"

"I can do that; he'll have it this evening. I'll ask him to call you tomorrow."

"Thanks, Dan."

Kate didn't fancy the idea of working the case with Ben Richardson, the London CIA Liaison. He had only made one trip to Ireland since his appointment a year earlier and impressed nobody. His initial meeting with Mac was scheduled to last an hour but he cut it to twenty minutes. An opportunity had come up, he explained at the time, to meet a 'colleague' from the British embassy. Mac was dumbstruck at Richardson's tactless approach and his general lack of knowledge on the terrorist threat in Ireland. It was unsurprising that his assistance was seldom sought. She chatted to Mac about it and decided to invite Richardson for a face-to-face to try and reboot the relationship.

Kate waited until the commuter traffic eased before heading home. She tried to feel positive about Richardson's impending visit. He promised to fit it into his schedule, a week hence. The lack of urgency wasn't a good omen.

Close to her apartment, she paused at traffic lights opposite Saint Vincent's University Hospital and noticed lights still on in the reception of the breast check clinic. She indicated right and turned into the clinic car park. Her new training bra hadn't helped and while she knew her increased workload meant less time to work out, she didn't like the tenderness she felt lately each time she trained. There were no lumps or bumps, but then Aunt Greta had only noticed dimples before her diagnosis. Kate's mother lost her only sister to cancer a year later. The cheery receptionist smiled and explained nobody waltzes in off the street expecting to book a mammogram. A referral from her GP was required before anything could happen. Kate thanked her and tapped another note-to-self into her phone to make an appointment the following day.

Before she started her car, her phone beeped a text message from Betty Fitzpatrick, her old college roommate. Despite hectic lifestyles, they'd kept in touch in the years that followed Kate's college buddy completing her masters in financial risk management. During the years Betty spent in London, they kept each other up-to-date on how their lives were panning out. Since her return to Dublin to work in corporate banking, they'd met up and rekindled their college friendship. After a rowdy first night drinking together and promises to stay in closer touch, the unrelenting nature of Kate's last case forced her to cancel many coffee dates.

Outside Garda colleagues, Betty was the only friend that Kate shared her work phone number with. *Hi Kate,* the text read, *Prince Charming popped the question, need a bridesmaid. Call me, Fitz.* Kate groaned and tapped another reminder into her phone.

16

Newbie detective, Jonny Mooney, took his daughter's tiny hand in his as they set off walking at snail's pace along the path. As they reached the neighbourhood park her loud squealing and twisting in the stroller left him in no doubt that she wanted to move under her own steam. Since Orla started walking, that was how it had been. Not yet two years old and stubborn as a mule. He loved her even more for that. He was due to leave for work in an hour and had adjusted to the couple of hours sleep he managed between shifts and back home with his wilful daughter. Things had gone quiet since he took Chief O'Driscoll's advice and came out swinging against the blackmail attempt. He prayed it would stay that way.

On the other side of town, Gerry Buck smiled as he put the finishing touches to the special project his boss had given him. He closed his laptop, grabbed his car keys, and drove slowly out of the council estate. On the journey across town he was hypervigilant, constantly checking to try and detect any trailing vehicles. He didn't cop any and parked up, frustrated, outside Bailey's house, forty minutes later.

Angie perched on a desk edge chatting to her former drugs unit sergeant, feeling at home in her old squad room. Sexton had tasked her with finding out what prompted the raid on Bailey's sister's beauty salon. Today her old skipper was being reticent and she was treading warily.

"Looks like we were set up," he told her. "Now I have fucking GSOC crawling up my arse."

"Where did the tip come from?" Angie asked.

"A Garda Confidential Line call, precise information about product and where the stash was hidden. The caller sounded like someone in the know, that's why we decided to hit."

"Male or female?"

"Male caller, Dublin accent, call came from a payphone in a Henry Street shop. Who the fuck uses them anymore?"

"What did he say exactly?"

"Said there was at least a key of coke stashed there. Given her brother's form, we had no trouble getting a search warrant."

Angie asked if he still had a recording of the call and he gruffly told her that their copy had been seized by GSOC's investigators. He slapped the desk and said he had a prisoner awaiting interrogation. As he departed, she asked permission to use his office phone and noticed the mobile left behind on the office desk. A quick search of the voice recorder found the file she wanted. After sharing it to her phone, she stuck ear buds in and listened as she strolled

the corridors of her old stomping ground. Although preoccupied, she nodded to acquaintances along the way, as the
recording went through the preliminaries; the date of the
call, name of the call-taker, and name of the Garda who
made the copy. When the caller's voice came on, Angie
stopped dead. She ducked into the women's toilet, found a
cubicle and listened back to the recording several times.
She then called her colleague and told him to pick her up
two streets away from the station.

"Any progress?" Detective Jonny Mooney asked Angie,
as she hopped into the car.

"Nah, GSOC beat me to the punch," she
said. "Drive."

"Fuckin' assholes," he replied, as he pulled into traffic,
"sometimes you wonder whose side they're on?"

"They're calling the shots on this one. Let's get back
to base."

Angie joined Digger in the cave when they got back.
She shut the door, locked it and then scribbled on a pad.
The note said *Sweep*. Digger nodded and systematically did
an electronic sweep of the room over the next twenty
minutes. They chatted nonchalantly while both scrutinised
every nook and cranny of the room for bugs.

"Clear," he finally said. "What's up?"

"We could have a big problem," Angie said. "Listen to
this, not on the speaker."

Digger put on headphones and listened.

"This is the call that brought the raid on Bailey's sister's
place," he said, quietly, when it ended. "Is there somethin'
I should be hearin'?"

"Does the voice remind you of anyone?"

"It's a Dublin accent, the caller's tryin' to disguise
his voice."

"Now, listen to this."

She played him the conversation she had recorded in the car.

"What do you think?" Angie asked.

"The Dublin accent is there but it's a stretch to say more than that."

"Can you run voice biometrics against the two recordings? See if you can get a match?" Voice biometrics worked by digitising a profile of an individual's speech. By capturing tones in word segments, collectively, they identified the speaker's unique voice print.

"I doubt it, there's too much background noise in your recordin' which, incidentally, I'd delete immediately," he said. Voice biometrics had helped identify suspects in the past but Digger was cautious.

"What do you need to make a comparison?" Angie asked.

"The confidential line recordin' is fine; I can model that one. I'll need an equally clear recordin' to do the same thing with Jonny."

Later in the day Angie arranged for Mooney to call Digger seeking five items of equipment. Digger recorded the call and when he printed off the voiceprint model he called Angie.

"Let's talk to the boss," he said.

They played both recordings for Kate and then Digger explained the voiceprint analysis.

"There's some divergence in the model from the confidential line recordin'," he explained, "that's because the caller's distortin' their voice, you can hear it."

"What are you telling me?" Kate asked. "Are they the same voice or not?"

"The deliberate distortion rules out a perfect match," Digger replied "but there's enough in it for us to be worried."

Kate called in Sexton, who had supervised Mooney since his arrival.

"He's been fine; very good actually, nothing to indicate a problem with him," Sexton reported.

"I selected him for the trainin' because Zoom recommended him, over a year ago," Digger said.

"Okay," Kate said, finally, "we start working on Nasri from tomorrow. Switch Mooney to that job. Digger, if he's dirty, get him out, fast."

"What about GSOC's investigation?" Sexton asked.

"For now all we've got are strong suspicions," Kate replied. "I'm calling it that State security could be compromised if I inform that office at this point."

"Leave it with me," Digger said. "I'll do some nosin' around."

Make it quick," she told him. "I'm the one holding the baby."

When Bailey received Mooney's text message following his sister's shop being turned over, he knew that he had two options. Attack or retreat. Retreat wasn't in his DNA. Over the next week he recycled the routine that had previously flushed out the young cop. Nothing showed up and he only got silent treatment from the text threats he sent.

He lost patience, knowing that each day drinking coffee and sitting around waiting for action was another day he was unaware of who was watching him. So, he changed tack. His internet addicted driver was a gaming maestro and Bailey put his skills to good use. He laid out in detail what he required and swore Buck to secrecy. The tech-savvy hoodlum recognised the warning as no idle threat. He created a simple website and called it www.offsideoutrage.com. He designed it to appear like a women's group initiative to *out* philandering partners.

Digger went after the errant detective with a vengeance. The day after identifying him as high risk Digger located the 'burner' mobile phone that he figured Mooney was using, as no suspicious calls had shown up on the other phones he checked. He quickly identified the number and Kate convinced a nervous judge to issue a warrant to intercept all its traffic. The first intercept was a picture message. The screen grab showed a photo of the dozing detective alongside one of Audrey Kelly. The tagline read *Garda abuses a woman he's paid to protect.* When Digger tried to access www.offsideoutrage.com, it flashed up a message 'website under construction'. The text message assured Mooney that the website would soon be live. It gave him a 24-hour ultimatum to arrange a face-to-face meeting.

As he and Kate examined the message, things began to fall into place. You didn't need to be a genius to connect the dots leading back to Bailey and Kate had promised the judge an update on progress. He was in chambers preparing for his morning in court when she rang him.

"We've intercepted a threat from the criminal party this morning," she explained.

"Very good," the judge remarked. "I'm glad my warrant assisted your investigation."

"Thank you for your confidence," Kate replied. "The difficult part for us is working out our next move."

"Difficult in what way? If you can link the threatening party to the phone sending the messages, there's plenty of charges to bring him before a court."

"I'm confident we can do that. The problem is the main suspect is also a major target in a complex international case."

"You don't want to show your hand at this stage."

"Precisely!"

"Superintendent, allow me some time to speak to a colleague and I will come back to you."

"Thank you, Judge."

Kate was at a loss to figure out what he had in mind but ten minutes later he rang back.

"Superintendent, you want to resolve this matter as discretely as possible, am I correct?" the judge asked.

"Absolutely," she replied.

"What about the GSOC investigation into the raid on the beauty salon. They cannot be kept in the dark forever."

"If we can sort this out, prudently," Kate said, "I will ensure Detective Mooney admits his part in the affair."

"Fine," the judge replied. "Here's the view of an esteemed colleague who is quite brilliant when it comes to libel law."

Kate listened while the judge outlined a suggested plan of action. Most good ideas are simple and this one was such. Use the law against the criminal. Not the criminal code, rather the civil one. They went over how the data SIU possessed could link Bailey in a chain of evidence to the offending phone. The judge's lawyer friend offered to prepare the necessary paperwork, post-haste.

When Mooney arrived for work, he was steered into Kate's office and his choices made clear. He broke down sobbing, whimpering that he was only trying to save his marriage and readily agreed to sign the paperwork. It would allege libel against Don Bailey and seek €1 million in damages, should the offending website go live.

SIU had been watching Bailey overnight. Digger drove the lawyer's summons server in an SIU car disguised as a taxi. He dropped him close to Bailey's house and as the target closed his front gate, the process server pounced, served the papers and jumped back into the taxi. Each succeeding step went as predicted. Bailey sought legal counsel. The two sets of lawyers consulted and assurances were sought and exchanged that removal of the publication threat meant the end of the affair.

Incensed by Mooney's approach to O'Driscoll for advice, neither Kate nor Mac were surprised that the guidance he offered was skewed, to say the least. The approach to the GSOC office required delicate handling.

Above all else, it trumpeted independence as its most vital asset. Kate asked Mac to smooth the way with the chairman and with a road map in place to end the affair, she accompanied Mooney to the GSOC office where he admitted making the phone call that triggered the raid. The chairman assured Mac that the thoroughness of their investigation meant Rachel Bailey would be waiting a while to hear the outcome.

When the wayward officer's confession was done, Digger sat silently in the rear seat with him, while Kate drove back to SIU. The place was deserted, apart from Pete McNally. Digger had already seized the detective's service weapon and he supervised Mooney while he cleared out his locker. Without ceremony, Kate handed him a transfer order, reverting him to uniform duties. Whatever disciplinary proceedings followed would await GSOC's deliberations. Digger escorted him to the Honda 500cc bike he used to get to and from work. He stayed with him while he donned his helmet, kick-started the machine and exited the SIU car park for the final time.

Mooney took the long route home, trying to clear his head before he spoke to his wife. He cut the engine as he approached the driveway. Little Orla howled the house down whenever she heard her Dad's motorcycle approach. He pushed the bike the final few feet to the up-and-over garage door and opened it as quietly as possible. The strong-willed tot had a well-established routine of being first to greet her Dad. An engine roar triggered her immediate reaction and the race to the door leading from the kitchen to the garage began in earnest. The mother waited until she saw a chink of light under the doorway which told her the main garage door was open before she released her impatient daughter.

Little Orla waddled back into the kitchen soon after and told her Mum, "Dad-dee sleep."

"Don't be silly, darling," her mother replied. "Daddy's just home early. He's putting his old bike to bed."

"Sleep," she insisted.

"Let's go see," her Mum said, taking her hand and heading into the garage. Horrified when she noticed red liquid dripping from the child's other hand, she bent down and picked her up, saying, "What on earth have…?"

Then she noticed the feet, sprawled close to the garage door, and jolted to a halt. A sheet hanging on the improvised clothesline strung from one corner of the garage to the other partially blocked her view. She pushed it aside and saw her husband's body slumped against his motorcycle, a weapon alongside in a pool of blood.

"Oh Jonny!" she screamed.

17

When Digger passed the news to Kate, they drove immediately to Mooney's house, neither able to utter a word. They
turned off the busy airport road and located the cul de sac
where he lived. Scenes of crime tape strung along the front
hedge delineated the eerie spectacle. An ambulance waited
in the driveway and four patrol cars were parked on foot-
paths, either side of the road.

The ambulance crew was inside, consoling Mooney's
wife. Her parents had arrived and provided a distraction
for the child. Digger and Kate ducked under the tape and
flashed ID to the Garda at the front gate who logged them
into the crime scene record.

"We've closed the garage door, head around the back,"
she advised.

A photographer was setting up a strobe in the garage
when they looked in. Digger crossed himself and invoked
God's mercy on his fallen colleague, muttering, "*Ar dheis Dé
go raibh a h-anam,*" Blood that had pumped from the single
bullet wound to the right temple stained the concrete floor.
The lead investigator, the D-I from the District Detective

Unit, stood on a small patch of grass in the back garden talking on his mobile.

"He chose the thinnest part of the skull," Kate overheard, as the D-I scrutinised them. "There's a large artery runs directly underneath."

Kate indicated she needed a word and he wound up his call. She led him to end of the garden and outlined the day's earlier events.

"Balls! In that case, I'll have to turn it over to GSOC," he said. "At least we know why the poor bastard lost it."

"Will you do some door-to-door enquiries, anyway?" Kate asked.

"Do you think that's necessary?" the D-I asked.

"Never hurts," she replied. "There's something not quite right …"

"Stop!" the D-I interrupted. "This isn't your fault. Don't try to see things that aren't there. The poor bastard topped himself."

They walked into the garage and continued speaking quietly.

"We seized his service weapon this morning," Kate whispered. "Where did that one come from?" she asked, pointing towards the garage floor.

The weapon beside Mooney's body, hadn't been moved.

"It looks like a Sig," the D-I replied. "Maybe he took it from a colleague's locker. We'll wait for Ballistics to arrive before we touch it."

Digger was standing close to the crime scene photographer as he went through his routine. The tech was scrolling through the images, ensuring he had all the angles covered.

"That's odd," he said, talking to himself. "I'll go again."

"What's up?" Digger asked.

"I'm getting shadow from the sunshine coming through the fanlight over the garage door. Without flash fill, you can't see it, but when you compensate…"

"Show me," Digger asked.

They scrolled through the images. On normal setting, nothing seemed out of place. However, when the tech used flash fill and over exposed the images, scuff marks showed up on the garage floor.

"It's probably just Jonny's motorcycle boots," Digger suggested. "He'd strike the ground hard enough steppin' off the bike every day."

"These look like recent marks and the pattern suggests a scuffle. I'm shooting the whole scene again and forensics can scrape samples."

The first twenty-four hours of the investigation provided answers to many questions. The main one being that ex-Detective Mooney didn't die of a self-inflicted wound. Eye witnesses reported seeing a second bike, the one his daughter heard, with a pillion passenger drive up to Mooney's house shortly after he arrived. No shot was heard. When Kate learned as much, she asked Ballistics to compare the round that killed Mooney with the two slugs extracted from Doc Carroll's skull. A silencer had been used in that murder and Sexton's intel linked it squarely back to Bailey's gang. Ballistics confirmed Kate's hunch. Bailey had crossed a line. Everyone had to watch their back.

Over the following days, Kate and Sexton attended the daily case conferences at Mooney's local station. Commissioner Fox ordered that no stone be left unturned in bringing the killer to justice. Chief O'Driscoll flatly denied any knowledge of Mooney's blackmail problems and claimed that rugby had been the sole topic of conversation during the visit to his office.

The first week of the investigation drew to a close with a case review at his local Garda station late on a Saturday night. There was no tangible evidence to connect Bailey and he was laying low. All the intelligence pointed in his direction but investigators had so far failed to convert any of it into evidence. The review dragged; Kate listened restlessly, as the chief investigator nit-picked his way through the job sheets. She messaged Cody O'Neill, cancelled their dinner date, and trudged out of the meeting, an hour and a half later than expected, feeling despondent. If Mooney was going to get justice, she thought, she would have to deliver Bailey.

Digger rang before she reached her car in the station yard. The main suspect had been sighted at a café not far from his house. A red mist of righteous fury enveloped Kate.

"What's the address?" she asked.

"We're on him, leave it to us," he replied.

"Digger, tell me where he is," she insisted.

"His local chipper."

The Kingfisher Café was in the middle of Crumlin on the other side of the city. Kate jumped into her silver BMW and roared along the M50 ring road, until she reached the turn off. She throttled back as she worked out a strategy. Next stop, Crumlin Children's Hospital, she smiled. The guy in charge of the staff car park was ex-Garda Tom Cunniffe. Years earlier, he had walked Kate along her first beat and they had kept in touch. With two kids in university, Cunniffe needed to work a crappy night shift rather than sit back and enjoy his retirement. She explained her needs and he handed her a blue lanyard with a hospital pass dangling on the end of it. He explained the hospital layout and pointed towards a corridor.

Kate walked rapidly through ground floor corridors until she found an exit. She pulled on a tan beanie and hailed a taxi. To complete the transformation, she popped on a pair of black, round-rimmed glasses, gave the driver the destination, and asked him to wait while she ordered.

The Kingfisher had two rows of tables and chairs running down the centre. Booths with red seating, hemmed them in on both sides. Six teenagers, boisterous from whatever cheap brew they had consumed, clustered around a single table in the middle. Kate asked for a fish and chips takeaway and pushed into a booth while it was prepared.

Bailey was in another, furthest from the counter. Kate observed him slurp water from a litre bottle, between bites of his fish supper. Buck, his driver, sat opposite, leaning over and talking incessantly in a low tone. Bailey was clean shaven, dressed in fresh clothes, and appeared unruffled. Wherever he had spent his week out of sight, he hadn't endured any discomfort.

Kate's antagonism increased by the minute as she surveyed Bailey. She noted his wariness; his seat commanded a view of the front of the café. Cars on the street outside attracted his attention, as did every customer who walked through the door.

Her phone vibrated a text message — *don't engage*, Digger warned.

A-hole's daring us to arrest him, she tapped in reply.

Let the bastard stew, came the instant retort.

Kate remained seated until the Italian owner held up her order. He spotted the lanyard as she paid and shovelled an extra scoop of chips into the bag. "For our friends at the hospital," he smiled. Kate smiled a thank you, and noted Bailey's quick sideways glance as she exited. Fifteen minutes later she thanked Cuniffee, handed back the hospital pass, and wished him *bon appétit* as he tucked into the fish and chip supper she left behind. Getting close to Bailey eased some of Kate's frustration. It was past midnight when she made it to O'Neill's apartment. He had a table in the tiny kitchen laid out, a forlorn single red rose at the centre.

"You must be starving," he said.

"Let's skip to dessert," she suggested.

Mooney was buried with State honours two days later, hundreds attended his funeral. Kate's biggest challenge was holding back her crews. The numbness felt following Zoom's death a few months earlier had subsided but Mooney's killing rekindled it. A desire to strike back at Bailey raged through the unit. She needed to harness that energy and focus it. Nobody went to the pub after their colleague was interred; Kate called a full unit briefing.

The jammed briefing room crackled with tension. Most were seated, some stragglers leaned against walls. Kate sat at a top table, in the centre of a group with Mac, Digger and Sexton. She asked for a case update and Sexton began in his usual precise manner. A burnt-out motorcycle, located two kilometres from Mooney's house, was confirmed as the getaway vehicle. There were no fresh leads, although a number of job sheets were still outstanding. The investigators were hopeful that forensics would give them leads they could follow up.

"How did the killer know where Jonny lived?" a voice asked from the crowd.

Uneasiness crept into the room.

"Was he followed?" another added.

Sexton looked towards Kate for guidance. "Tell them," she said.

"Someone from Bailey's brief's office duped a legal clerk working for Jonny's libel barrister into supplying his address. They said the court services required it."

"Bullshit!" a few voices echoed.

Kate stood up as Sexton resumed his seat. Straight away she was hit with questions as to why Bailey hadn't been arrested. She told her squad it was a tactical decision.

"Maybe Bailey thinks he's covered his tracks well. No one doubts he ordered Jonny's murder but it's a diversion; he's got something else going on. That's where we'll get him. We need to be patient, box clever and figure out what that is."

Around the room, restlessness, feet shuffled, heads dropped.

"We *don't* do revenge," she said, and paused a beat, to let it sink in. "But we *never* give up."

She paused and looked to Mac.

"Commissioner, do you wish to add anything?"

"You're doing fine," Mac replied.

Kate paused and looked around the room slowly.

"No one rests until Don Bailey is either locked up or zipped up in a body bag. Any more questions?"

There were none.

Sexton took the cue and announced, "Briefing for the working unit in ten minutes."

Bailey needed to sustain his hard man image and the hasty plan B had been instinctive. The slap-down of his clumsy blackmail attempt forced his hand. One of his gang had a stolen bike stashed and getting the cop's address was ridiculously easy. Once again, Dempsey proved a brilliant tactician. He supplied the weapon, drove the bike and warned Bailey to get it done swiftly, make it look like suicide. It nearly ended in catastrophe when the cop saw him coming at him in the bike's wing mirrors. Bailey was caught off-guard by his victim's strength in the struggle, so he used the second weapon and tossed the Sig on the ground.

Following the job, he had gone offside, avoiding his own house and those of accomplices. While the search was on to locate him, associates were being picked up and questioned for forty-eight hours before release. The north-side gang complained long and loud about the extra attention they were getting. Killing a cop in a shootout was one thing, doing it premeditated, at his own house, was plain dumb. Bailey felt confident that he couldn't be linked to the crime and returned home a week later to await the inevitable. His driver picked him up and he decided to eat locally. Some of the local rats would report his reappearance and he could get the arrest done and dusted. When nothing happened he figured it was business as usual.

Kate returned with Mac to his office when the unit briefing concluded. The government was being lashed in the press for taking its eye off the ball in tackling organised crime and Commissioner Fox wanted updates on SIU's commitments and resources. The stagnant FBI Khouri case was still top priority and O'Neill hadn't offered Kate any hope that it would change any time soon. It left her with mixed feelings.

"Rousing speech," Mac grinned.

"How did your meeting about Dempsey go," she asked.

Mac had agreed to talk to the Lt-Colonel Shaw from J2, Army Intelligence. Shaw told him that Mick Dempsey had been a good soldier and 'cool under pressure,' was a recurring comment on annual evaluations. Shaw never referred to the gambling addiction that blighted Dempsey's military career.

"What did you tell him of our interest?"

"I told him we had seen him meeting a Dublin criminal," Mac replied.

"Did you say where?"

"No. I told him the criminal was of intense interest at present."

"When was his final overseas tour?"

Mac looked through the three-page army report. The first page dealt exclusively with document handling caveats, so he ignored it. He spotted the information at the end of the second page.

"He was in Lebanon from June to December last year. Returned home, served out his last few months next door in McKee Barracks, and retired in April."

"So he was in service when Digger and I saw him in Cyprus back in October."

"Yes. What are you thinking?"

"In Cyprus we sent home a monthly UN situation report. The Army must have somewhat similar reporting."

"And you think there might be something on Dempsey in a report?"

"Not necessarily in a situation report, but if he's mentioned at all, there might be more behind the main one. There will be other records, local ones, those are what we need to dig into."

"Shaw will want to know why," Mac sighed.

"I'll leave that up to you," Kate said.

"If I mention the Hezbollah connection it will set alarm bells ringing."

"If they were doing their job correctly, the officers should know who their personnel are associating with over there. I want to find out what happened with Dempsey on that final tour."

"I'll ask, maybe not quite so bluntly," Mac smiled.

They discussed the impending visit from the London CIA liaison, Ben Richardson. He had agreed to dedicate a whole morning of his overnight visit to Dublin to meeting Kate and Mac.

"Did he say why he was staying overnight?" she asked Mac.

The Dublin to London connection was one of the most lucrative for the airlines that serviced it. There were over twenty flights out of Dublin every day.

"Says he's taking a friend who has moved to the Dublin embassy out to dinner."

"Do you believe him?"

"Why wouldn't I?"

"There's something about that guy I don't like," Kate frowned.

"Let's try and keep it civilised. You know we've worked well with them before and we're going to need them again."

"It's just… he's a smarmy creep."

"We're taking him to lunch," Mac said, "so pick somewhere nice."

Two days later, Kate parked up in a central Dublin side street before walking with Richardson and Mac, the short distance to the Chapter One restaurant. The morning meeting with their visitor had ended early. Even making a special effort, she couldn't warm to the guy. Was it the way his arms flailed constantly as he spoke, or the slicked back style he favoured on the blond hair that capped off his pointed head? She couldn't be sure, but what she really disliked was his lack of interest throughout their meeting. He portrayed himself as an expert on all things Middle Eastern and made much of the fact that one of their guys had been injured in identifying the two Hezbollah suspects in Beirut. He was unaware that 'their guy' had assistance on the day.

"How is your colleague's recovery going?" Kate asked.

"Look, I have no idea. I can't even tell you his name. Can we get back to business?"

"Shoot," Kate replied.

"Everyone's focussed on the Islamic State, people forget Al Qaeda are still a force to be reckoned with," Richardson said.

"We monitor Al Qaeda suspects living here on a continuous basis," Kate told him.

"I've been trying to figure out how, in the name of God, Jafar Hajj Nasri managed to evade justice after last year?" he said. "Makes no sense to me."

It wasn't the first time Richardson had brought it up. He was fixated on the case. "Given what that guy almost pulled off, there's a lot of people back home would like to put him in a room and spend a few hours with him," Richardson jabbered.

Mac cut the discussion dead, telling him that not arresting Nasri was a tactical intelligence decision, not up for discussion.

While their lunch was superb, the atmosphere around the table was stilted. Chapter One was Kate's favourite restaurant and as she exited the women's rest room the maître d' beamed in her direction.

"Kate, we haven't seen you in a while. Have you been eating with the opposition?"

"No, no, John, I've been working out of the country," she replied. "Back home again, now."

"Your guest seems like hard work, if you don't mind me saying."

"You're very perceptive," she laughed.

"It's okay for you," he continued. "We have him back again this evening."

"Really?"

"Yeah, he booked a table while you were inside. The embassy has an account here."

"Good luck," Kate smiled as she headed back to the dining room. She stopped momentarily and then walked back to the maître d'.

"John, would you call me discreetly when he arrives. I'm supposed to make sure nothing happens the guy while he's in town."

"Not a problem," he replied, with a conspiratorial wink, as Kate pressed a ten-euro note into his white-gloved hand.

Kate rang her mother later that evening and explained, in passing, how she had been feeling a bit lightheaded during the week. Almost immediately she regretted mentioning it.

"It's the way you eat," her mother scolded, "you're probably a touch hypoglycaemic."

"Great! What's that?"

"It's a diet thing, no big deal, really. Pay more attention to what you eat and you'll be grand. Don't leave any longer than three hours between your meals."

Kate listened.

"More nuts and Greek yoghurt," her mother told her. "Fish too, it's got as much protein as meat and quarter the fat."

"I'll try it for a while and let you know how I get on."

"Do it for a few weeks. Then you should notice an improvement."

"Okay thanks, Mum, I'll keep you posted. Almost forgot, remember Betty Fitzpatrick?"

"Fitz. Of course."

"She's getting married and she's asked me to be bridesmaid. I'm meeting her tomorrow."

"Katie, that's wonderful. When's the wedding?"

"Don't know yet, not for a while I'd reckon. Knowing Fitz, she'll want everything planned down to the last detail."

She hung up, thought about going for a run, but talked herself out of it. She still hadn't gotten around to booking an appointment with her GP to arrange a mammogram and stuck a post-it note on her fridge as a reminder. Tired of her cramped living conditions, she couldn't wait to get back into her own apartment. She was hungry, despite having eaten well at lunchtime. She went to the fridge and found milk well past its 'use by' date, a small pot of yoghurt and a loaf of sliced bread that had seen better days. She could have gone shopping; there was a supermarket just a kilometre away. Instead, she reached for the phone and ordered her favourite, Chicken Pad Thai with cashews from the nearby restaurant.

She was munching through noodles when the maître d' rang her to confirm that the noisy American had made it for his evening meal. Kate asked if he was alone and learned that he had an English gentleman for company. Kate left what remained of her noodles, called Digger, and gave him the go ahead. Three hours later he called back.

"Whoever that was," he said, "he's not an American."

"I knew that already," Kate replied. "What happened when they left the restaurant?"

"Richardson went back to his hotel."

"The other guy?"

"Caught the last flight to London."

"Did you get photos?"

"We sure did."

"Okay. Good work. See you in the morning."

Kate wondered what Richardson was up to having a clandestine meeting in Dublin. He was based in London and yet whoever he met had caught a return flight back there. She was too tired to figure it out.

18

Digger showed her the photos of the mystery dinner companion first thing next morning. Richardson and he were about the same age, early thirties. Digger captured the images as they left the restaurant. Both wore jeans and jackets, white shirts without ties. An informal evening, or so it appeared.

"Was he carrying anything?" Kate asked.

"Travelled light, nothing but an evening paper," Digger replied.

"What do you think?"

"Spook, I'd say."

"Fits the bill. Why the hell meet him over here?"

"What do we do with the information?" Digger asked.

"There's nowhere to go with enquiries. I'll talk to Mac about it. Could there be an innocent explanation to the whole thing?"

Digger's unconvinced expression told her he thought otherwise. He checked his notes and concluded the brief. "Richardson's companion travelled under the name C. Osbourne," he scowled.

"No enquiries, okay," Kate emphasised. "All quiet with Nasri since we took up on him?"

"Quiet as a pub on Good Friday, we're seein' him goin to work in the mornin' and comin' home in the evenin'. Nothin' else. Two of my crew called in sick this mornin' so we won't have any cover on him until late afternoon."

"Okay," Kate replied. "I'll talk to Grealy at the end of the week and see what his agent has to say."

Digger nodded. "Let us know if anythin' worthwhile comes up."

By eleven o'clock, Kate was sipping coffee with Fitz in a Wicklow Street corner café in Dublin city centre.

"Four weeks!" she exclaimed. "You're getting married in four weeks."

"July the fourth actually," Fitz confirmed, laughing.

"Jeez, Fitz what's going on?" Kate demanded. "What's happened to the minute-detail-planning risk analyst?"

"When we started to plan our wedding my family freaked us out, trying to take over everything," Fitz replied, shaking her head.

"Most parents are like that," Kate replied.

"I think Dad wanted to make it the social event of the year, invite all his bank buddies. So, we hijacked our own wedding; scouted Dublin hotels for cancellations and got one for the fourth of July. We've invited the people we really want to be there and now, all that's bothering my folks is that people are going to think I'm pregnant."

Kate laughed. She liked Fitz from the moment they met in their first politics lecture. They were polar opposites. Fitz hated sport, but loved meeting people. She dragged the reticent Kate into many college societies, including the

College Historical Society, a competitive debating club known as the Hist, where both starred in their graduation year. Tall and angular, Fitz still dressed impeccably and her stunning auburn hair was as long and sleek as it had been in college.

"We're having a civil ceremony in the hotel," Fitz explained, as she pulled up a picture of her husband-to-be on her smart phone and showed Kate. "Colin's his name, he's an artist."

"Wow, talk about being swept off your feet. You kept that quiet."

"We met in London and got together when Colin came home. What about you? Anyone special?"

"Well," Kate began. Before she could stop herself, she blurted out her recent dalliance with an older man. She didn't dish all the details but the afterglow was obvious.

"Tell him how you feel," Fitz suggested.

"It's complicated," Kate said. "I've got an hour to spare, want to browse and get some ideas on what to wear?" she suggested, changing the subject.

"Don't you need an appointment to get near wedding shops?" Fitz said. "And I was hoping to lose a few pounds first."

"You're fine, for God's sake. Let's give it a go, who dares wins."

In the first wedding shop a snooty assistant eventually conceded that she had no incoming appointments and agreed to let Fitz try on. The stifling heat in the place made Kate uncomfortable. However, as Fitz fitted one after another dress, Kate cheerfully admired different aspects of each one. Fitz laughed that her mother would disown her she didn't bring her along for actually choosing *the dress*. Kate would be the only bridesmaid and agreed to fit different colours to give Fitz ideas. They settled on a royal blue number, and as she slipped it off in the changing room, her stomach convulsed and she spewed mocha and stomach acid down its front.

"Oh my God!" the saleswoman shrieked, as the odour permeated into the shop. "You've ruined it!"

"Get a towel, you silly woman," Fitz cried as she raced into the changing area. "I guess we're definitely taking it now," she said to Kate.

Kate had tears streaming down her face. "I don't know whether it's the puke or if I'm actually crying."

"Ah," Fitz laughed. "Memories of our first Trinity Ball."

"The smell is about right," Kate laughed, accepting the towel from the disgusted saleswoman. By the time Kate was cleaned up and changed, Fitz had sorted out a strategy for the dress with the manager.

"I've got to get back," she told Fitz. "I'm paying for that dress. Call me when it's ready and I'll pick it up."

"Yeah, yeah," Fitz replied. "I've to go get in shape in four weeks, you never have to worry."

In contrast to everyone else sprinkled around the 100-acre site, Jafar Nasri's corpulent, suited figure seemed ill at ease close to the horses. The smells offended him. The bloodstock sale he had been instructed to attend was taking place at Goffs, a company that had auctioned horses in Ireland since 1866. Their 21st century sales rings were a half hour drive out of Dublin, close to the M7 motorway. Goffs took care of their top buyers, many received free accommodation, while other sponsors took care of their transport needs. Over the two-day sale, in excess of €11 million would change hands. Nasri had been unaware the place existed until instructed to pay it a visit.

He had no idea what his tormentors meant when they told him he would fit in with the other 'Sunni dogs' attending the sales. When catalogues were continually pushed in his direction by sales staff it became apparent to him that Saudi Arabs were welcomed with open arms. The sale turned out to be a national hunt auction with only steeplechasers offered. Buyers were mainly English, Irish or French and if the Sunni Arabs, his tormentors had in mind were buying today, they were doing so through agents.

The animals were housed in stable boxes located in corrals spread across the site. Stable hands exercised them up and down pathways. The horses trotted along with a graceful *swoosh* of motion as they passed Nasri. He went to the parade ring where the pedigree bloodstock were shown. Then he walked to the indoor amphitheatre sales ring where he mingled awkwardly with the flat caps and padded gilets. He watched as horses were led into the paved sales ring, lot numbers on their rumps, and shown by stable lads as bidding carried on, sometimes building to a frenzy. It was the only part of the entire business that interested him.

While Nasri had no interest in the business being conducted, he diligently noted the layout of the place. He checked entrances and exits, where the car parks were located and noted the helipads where two helicopters sat idle. He then called his driver and told him to come pick him up.

He trudged down to his basement when he got home and unlocked a cupboard where he kept a satellite phone. He had received it weeks earlier from a red-haired man, who had visited his warehouse, unannounced, and didn't introduce himself. He advised Nasri to switch it on at six o'clock and when he did, he found out his younger brother had been kidnapped. Nasri scanned his layout notes as he powered the phone up and walked out into a tiny court-yard at the side of his house to get coverage. When it kicked in, he rang a number in Beirut to report his obser-vations. Towards the end of the conversation he asked:

"What about my brother?"

"He still eats our food," he was told.

"I must speak with him."

"Insh'Allah, another time."

Disconsolate, Nasri powered the phone off when the call ended and locked it away. He could see no way out of this bind; he would count on the grace of Allah to keep his brother safe.

In the evening, the agent who had driven Nasri to Goffs, called his handler seeking an urgent rendezvous. The information he passed on earned him a small bonus. Next day, Detective Gerry Grealy's rotund frame filled a chair in Kate's office as he related what he had learned about Nasri's trip to the bloodstock sales.

"Does the agent have any idea what the trip was about?" Kate asked.

"Not a clue," Grealy replied. "He still thinks his boss is out of sorts, not himself, if you know what I mean."

"Not really."

"The agent says his morale is low."

"What the hell's that supposed to mean?" Kate asked.

"He said that he seems weighed down with worry."

"Is it the business?"

"I checked his Revenue returns for last year, his profits are up."

"So the business doesn't explain it."

"I made some enquiries with Goffs," Grealy continued. "I know the head of security there. He let me run through the CCTV footage for the time Nasri was around the place."

"Any joy?"

"He was strolling around, is all. No interest whatsoever in the horses didn't even have a sales catalogue."

"So what was he doing?"

"In all honesty, if it was anyone else, I'd say he was scoping the place."

"Can you get me the footage?"

Grealy liked to impress and like a magician producing a rabbit from a hat, he pulled a DVD from his pocket. "Any chance of me getting a bonus?"

"I'll tell the boss you've been a really good little agent handler," Kate replied.

"The 'little' part, I like," Grealy laughed, as he ambled out of the office.

Digger dropped by the squad room in the late afternoon. He was making up the numbers with his crew working the night shift on the Nasri stakeout. Kate invited him to study the footage with D-I Sexton.

"He's definitely scopin' the place out," Digger said, "and he's no good at it."

Sexton agreed. Nasri threw furtive glances at almost every camera he passed, making little effort to hide the fact that he was having a good nose around.

"Any ideas?" Kate asked.

"Are we ruling out robbery?" Sexton asked.

"Rule nothing out," Kate replied.

"Planning a hit on somebody attending the sales?" Sexton said.

"Maybe," Kate said.

"Are they thinking of snatching one of the nags?" Digger suggested.

"A repeat of the Shergar case," Kate said.

The Provisional IRA had kidnapped the prized stallion from stables only fifteen kilometres away from Goffs in 1983. The animal was never seen again.

"I can't see that," Sexton said. "The horses being sold here have little performance history. They're bought on the basis of pedigree, in the hope that a good trainer can get the best out of them."

"What about Nasri's recent activities?" Kate asked.

"Nothin' remarkable; goes to work, comes home, mosque on Friday. The wife looks after the kids," Digger said. "Nothin' on the phones to raise suspicions."

"There's one thing that chimes with other reports," Kate said.

"Horses," Digger agreed.

"The report of him taking photos near Ballycleary Stud," Kate said, "when was that?"

"Three weeks ago," Digger replied.

"So, whatever he's at, it's something connected to horses," Sexton said.

"Or *someone* connected to horses," Kate replied.

Kate walked to the whiteboard on the wall opposite her desk and called for status reports on the three targets they were covering. She wrote #1 Priority above Rafiq Khouri's name. "Status?" she asked her two D-Is.

"Stable, I suppose, is the best way of describin' it. Goes to work, eats in at night, pizzas mostly," Digger replied.

"Has he made any contacts?"

"None observed," Digger explained.

"Commissioner Fox wants this case wrapped up. Whatever it takes, are his exact words," Kate added.

"O'Neill's gettin' a tech guy over to see if we can break his communications."

"I'm aware of that," Kate replied.

"How come?" Digger asked. "He only rang me this morning,"

"He told me last night. We do speak from time to time," Kate said, immediately regretting her narky tone.

"I see," Digger said.

Kate wrote #2 Bailey on the whiteboard and called for reports.

"Met two more gangs recently," Sexton replied. "A tout says he's told them to be ready to move at short notice."

"What does that mean?"

"The tout said whatever he's planning he wants to make sure everyone can handle a weapon," Sexton said.

"Are we getting any audio from Bailey's meetings?" Kate asked.

"He's movin' around," Digger answered. "He's not usin' any of Slasher Fulton's old haunts."

"And there's nothing further to connect Bailey and Nasri?"

"Not a dickey bird," Digger replied.

Finally, Kate wrote #3 Nasri in the last column. She inserted a large question mark under his name. "So, STABLE, BUSY and DON'T KNOW is current status on targets," she summarised.

The Khouri case devoured most of their resources and they were stretched to cover Nasri at all. Digger argued that given his history, it was worth persisting with cover on him for a few more days.

Sexton mentioned intelligence that a Birmingham colleague talked about during a New Scotland Yard conference he had attended the previous week. They were picking up ripples of an Irish gang supplying gear into Birmingham. It was small but growing.

"Did you discuss it with the Drugs Unit yet?" Kate asked.

"Rang the D-Super when I got back but he's just pissed he didn't get the trip to the Organised Crime conference. Wouldn't talk to me about it; told me to put the intelligence in writing and send it to him."

"Mee-ow!" Kate laughed. "Presumably we're talking about ecstasy, heroin, and methamphetamines?"

"The lot," Sexton replied.

"Is the Beirut Sheikh funding Bailey?" she pondered. "And if he is, what's Bailey doing for the money?"

Sexton shrugged.

She recalled the first time she saw Bailey in Cyprus, considering him just another vicious criminal. She knew now they had something in common: single bloody mindedness and never backing away from a fight.

19

Next morning Digger was pissed off when he finally opened his eyes. Because of his stripped back team on Nasri, he had put in a fourteen-hour shift making up the numbers. He had been asleep an hour when Jane shook his shoulder.

"*Is mian Padraig leatsa*," she told him.

Irish was the spoken language in the Rooney household. Their children were fluent speakers and attended an exclusively Irish-speaking school.

"Tell him I'll call him back," Digger mumbled.

"He says it can't wait," Jane replied. "And I've to get to work in an hour." She loved the job she started nine months earlier in a café at a local shopping centre.

"Holy Christ!" he exclaimed, grabbing the phone. "*Dia dhuit!*" he gruffly greeted his brother.

"*Dia is Muire dhuit*, Grumpy balls," Padraig returned the traditional greeting with interest. "Have ye somethin' goin' on at the minute?" he continued in Irish.

"We've somethin' goin' on all the time. What are ya on about?"

"No, I mean have you somethin' big?"

"Look, I'm just off nights, I'm wrecked," Digger said. "What are you talkin' about?"

"Are the Yanks over doing somethin'?"

"Listen, Padraig, spit it out whatever it is."

Digger's brother had followed him into the Garda Síochána. He was a uniform sergeant based at Shannon airport on the west coast. Maintaining public order at the airport was his brief and monitoring the clusters of protest groups ensconced there, stole large chunks of his time.

Despite a neutral stance in international conflicts, the Irish government had agreements in place with its American counterpart that allowed stopovers of military flights en route to the Middle East or conflict zones, further afield. Some media dubbed Shannon, 'the little US military base in the west'.

"One of the hairy Marys here was tellin' me about somethin' odd she saw an hour ago," Padraig began.

"What was that?"

"She said one of the 'funny' planes came in, taxied to the freight side of the airport and three black vehicles drove off it."

"So what?" Digger said.

"She swears that someone from the airport fire service opened an emergency exit gate furthest away from the terminal and allowed all the three yokes drive through."

"That's odd, if it's true," Digger said. "Do you believe her?"

"Stuff she's told me in the past has turned out to be true," Padraig replied.

"So no immigration or customs checks?"

"Straight out the gate is what she told me; a 4x4, a kind of minivan yoke and a square looking sedan, all black."

"What does she mean by a 'funny' plane?"

"A grey yoke with barely any markings at all; a rarity these days. The prisoner planes, I remember, looked the same."

Amnesty International reported that the CIA had landed many times at Shannon en route to interrogation centres dotted around Europe while the US operated its rendition policy with militant Islamic prisoners.

"Listen," Digger told him, "I'll make a few calls and see if I can find out anythin'. Either way, I'll buzz you back."

Digger rang Bill Twomey in the Emergency Response Unit. It was the SWAT, trained and used for armed interventions.

"Bill, have ye anythin' special goin' on?"

"I wish; it's too quiet lately. I'm running out of ideas to keep everyone going."

"Anythin' planned with a sister agency?" Digger said.

"Nothing."

Digger relayed the message he had received from his brother. Twomey agreed that if the report was accurate it was very odd. Maybe the Army were doing something, he ventured, and omitted to tell anyone about it. He took the description of the vehicles and promised to relay it to patrols he had out in the city curbing gangland violence.

Digger went back to bed. He lay on his back, trawling his memory to link the report to something concrete. He dozed, drifting back to the plains of slumber from where he had been dragged. Before he got there, a thought hit him that made him sit bolt upright. He rubbed his face and checked his bedside clock. He had only been out for five minutes. He leapt from the bed and took a cold shower. He stepped out, shook his head, spraying the bathroom mirror and stared at his unshaven reflection.

He towelled off quickly and called Twomey back. He

spoke the code word, *misneach,* it meant *courage* in Irish. Then he called Kate and repeated it. They both knew the drill: do not trust or use your phone until an immediate face-to-face rendezvous.

"I've got to go out," he told Jane, as he made coffee in the kitchen. He intended sipping it en route.

"I'm about to leave for work," she replied. "You're supposed to pick up the kids from school in the afternoon."

"I've got to go, it's urgent."

"You spend more time with her than you do with us. You even have a photo of two of you on your phone."

"Jane, not now. That photo—oh, it doesn't matter."

"It's true."

"What about you and this James bloke, ye're together a lot."

"It's Jay."

"Jay, Jim, Jimmy, whatever. Ye've got very chummy."

"He needs me."

"Does he?"

"For his business! Look let's not do this now, you're tired."

"His business?"

"Yes, I'm helping him build up his business. You didn't like me out front, so I do stock control and tax returns now."

"I never said nothin' about you servin' tables."

"Your look said it all, anytime we talked about it. When you've rested, we need to chat about it."

"I've got to go."

Jane sighed and scratched her head. "I'll get Liz to pick up the kids from school and I'll collect them when my shift ends."

"Thank God for good neighbours," Digger replied, grabbing his keys.

"We have to talk," Jane shouted after him, as he exited the front door.

Digger met Twomey and Kate at the designated meeting place, the Cricket Ground car park in the Phoenix Park. All three sat in Twomey's BMW SUV. Six foot three, with a rock hard body from years of strength and conditioning training, Twomey's presence dominated the vehicle. He sat with one hand on the steering wheel, as Digger retold his brother's story.

Kate said nothing until he was done.

"Jesus, Digger, do you really think an intelligence agency would be that stupid?"

"If I'm right, this is a rogue operation. You said so yourself. Richardson is fixated on Nasri and bringing him to book for what he did last year. I don't like the meeting the prick had with that spook, when he was over here. Now, just a week on and we have activity at Shannon that nobody knows about. Something's off."

"Does the Army know anything?" Twomey asked.

"I need to discuss it with Mac first and he's in Brussels at a heads-of-service meeting," Kate replied. "He's not back until late this evening."

"What happens in the meantime?" Digger asked. "What about my crew?"

"I'm not taking drastic action on a hunch," Kate replied.

"Never stopped you in the past."

Twomey stared out his side window, as Kate let the comment go.

"How many patrols have you in the city tonight?" she asked him.

"Why tonight?" Digger intervened.

"If there's a smash and grab operation planned for Nasri, as you seem to believe, it'll happen in darkness," Kate said.

"True," Twomey added. "Trying a daylight extraction would be insane."

"Of course," Digger agreed, rubbing his face. "I'm a bit punch drunk; only an hour's sleep."

"I'll have two SUVs patrolling the city, four in each," Twomey said. "One north side, the other south side."

"That should be adequate," Kate replied. "Digger, you need to get some sleep."

"I'm headin' over to join my crew now; I'll get some kip while I'm there."

"I'll get Sexton to release some extra bodies to you," she told him.

"Tell them we've switched radio channels," Digger said as he headed back to his car. "We're on 6 now."

In the late evening, dark cumulonimbus clouds brought the night down early as Mac touched down at Dublin airport on the last Brussels flight. Kate picked him up and pulled into an airport layby to brief him. Torrential rain began to hammer down onto the soft top. The convertible had seemed like a good idea in Cyprus, now she hoped its roof wouldn't leak.

She was tuned in to Digger's crew reports throughout the evening. All was quiet, Nasri had returned unhindered from work and nothing suspicious had arisen during the day. She gave Mac a situation report.

"Did you talk to anyone?"

"Who would I talk to?" she replied. "I'd be laughed out of town."

"So Digger thought, a friendly agency might be

sending operatives onto our territory to abduct a 'person of interest' to them?"

"I thought it unlikely."

"Ring Ben Richardson," Mac ordered.

"Do you think that's wise?" Kate asked.

"It's very unwise not to," Mac responded.

She called the number. A pre-recorded message told her that Richardson's phone was powered off.

"Did you mention it to Cody O'Neill?" Mac asked.

Kate's expression darkened, "Not answering his phone all day, so I called the embassy eventually. They said he was out of town."

"Had he mentioned anything about going back to the States to you?" Mac asked.

"Not a word."

"Try Whatney," Mac said.

"He's told me he wouldn't encroach on Richardson's turf."

"Ring him anyway," Mac insisted. "We have to bottom it out, one way or the other."

Whatney answered, in jovial form on hearing his friends.

"What's cookin' over there?" he asked in his Texan drawl.

Kate laid out the information they had regarding the plane and its unusual cargo. As she told him about their meeting with Richardson and his fixation on Nasri, his mood changed.

"Jeez Kate, I can't believe you're sayin' all this," he said. "We've shown nothin' but goodwill to you guys."

Mac cut in.

"Dan, you've been upfront with us all the way," he said. "We can't say the same of Mr. Richardson."

"What d'ya mean?" Whatney asked.

Mac told him of the meeting Richardson had a week earlier with the unidentified English man.

"Maybe he was just tryin' to smoke out the Ruskies," Whatney suggested.

"I'm sorry, Dan?" Mac said.

"You know, meetin' someone he needs to meet, outside London, that place is crawlin' with Russian spooks."

"Dan, are you saying the CIA uses our country for espionage?"

Whatney went quiet and then came back.

"Mac, I don't like where this conversation is headed, I thought we were friends."

"We are, and as a friend we're asking you to put in some calls and reassure us."

"I'll see what I can do," he replied and hung up.

Radio crackle began as their call to the puzzled CIA man ended. One of Digger's crew close to Jafar Nasri's house had seen a black Chrysler sedan do a drive-by. Digger ordered another change of radio channels.

"Jesus Christ! What have I done? I should have listened," Kate exclaimed, as she gunned the BMW and shot out into sluggish airport traffic.

She put in a flustered call to Twomey.

"We're in position, close by," he assured her. "Digger's got a nose for these things and I pulled my two patrols to Harold's Cross. I have uniforms on standby to cordon off a combat zone."

"Hold on, I've an incoming call," Kate said.

"Gotta go anyway. We're low on numbers to take three vehicles, but we're deploying now," Twomey advised.

"I'm getting stonewalled," Whatney told them. "Nobody's tellin' me anything."

"Okay, Dan," Kate said, "thank you for trying."

"Word of advice, Kate, if someone's doin' something stupid, they'll be usin' contractors," Whatney cautioned. "Those fuckers are deadly, you guys take care."

20

Nasri lived in Harold's Cross, an inner suburb on the south side of Dublin. The houses were mainly built in the 19th century and Nasri's was a classic brown-bricked, two-storey-over-basement dwelling. SIU's observation post was in a block of modern apartments that overlooked it. Mac re-evaluated the intelligence with Kate as she drove. Both felt the absence of satisfactory American response, coupled with the suspicious activity close to Nasri's house, justified their decision. As Kate dodged around slow moving traffic near Christchurch Cathedral, Mac authorised Twomey, if engaged, to initiate a full-force response. The command was barely cold when all hell broke loose.

Twomey chose the combat zone with an expert's eye for detail. One side of the street was lined with houses, mainly in darkness; most residents retired for the night. He would direct the action to the opposite side, the side boundary of Nasri's back garden. He had eight foot soldiers on hand.

Digger's team alerted him that the 4x4 and minivan were approaching. The black sedan, a Chrysler 300, positioned itself on the main drag, alongside the side street exit. When Twomey gave the order his team swung into action, hemming in the two vehicles. The contract operatives reacted as expected when the road ahead of them was blocked. They revved their engines hard and tried to reverse out of the trap, pushing against the ERU jeep that had closed the door behind them. As instructed, it held the convoy in for fifty metres and then released its chokehold. It swung sharp left into a side alley allowing the spooked convoy reverse down the street where Stinger spikes deflated their tyres. One of Twomey's men popped up from a basement and fired a solid slug shotgun shell into the 4x4's engine block, disabling it. Smoke and steam billowed from the front of the crippled vehicle. The minivan's engine was still running. Twomey exited his command vehicle and roared a 'Surrender weapons' order over a bullhorn. He waited seconds. Nothing happened.

"Last chance!" he warned. "Throw down your weapons and exit the vehicles."

The driver window of the 4x4 rolled down a click and two handguns were pushed out onto the street. In the same instant, smoke canisters were tossed in Twomey's direction from the passenger side of the vehicle. He dropped to ground to catch the action that followed. The doors of the 4x4 flew open and figures in dark combats ran towards the minivan. Twomey glimpsed the running boots and then saw two tumbling objects bounce in his direction.

"Grenades!" he warned his men. It was a classic tactic, trying to break contact from the ambush. His team were in full battle gear and trained to counter it. Their tinted eyepieces would guard against the flash, the respirators against the gas that would be deployed. Their helmets had built-in ear defenders and mics so that Twomey could still communicate. He dived behind his command vehicle, head

down, shielded from the explosion. The blast was deafening, even with ear protection. He steadied himself and
called for a status report. Everyone was still standing. He
peered through billowing smoke to confirm what he
expected and grinned as he saw the final dark figure from
the 4x4 pile into the minivan.

They were fleeing. They would expect their run-flat
tyres to take them out of the immediate danger zone. He
had hoped for as much and planned a countermove. As the
minivan door slid shut, the engine revved loudly and it
reversed fast towards the main drag. The jeep he positioned in a narrow side street had a front bumper of rein-
forced steel. It rammed hard into the rear of the minivan,
sending it spinning like a top. When it finally came to a
halt buckled around a lamp post, the van's engine cut out.
The ERU team descended on it, instantaneously shattering
the windows and windscreen. The black Chrysler took off
from the bottom of the street. Ken James, Twomey's
second-in-command chased, but it had gotten a head start.
He relayed details to the reserve Twomey had called up for
city patrol, then raced back to join the main action.

"Out," Twomey ordered, yanking open the sliding
door.

The failed contractors knew what to expect and didn't
resist. As they exited, Twomey's men kicked them to the
ground and disarmed them. He called up a prisoner transport and after a thorough search, dumped each one into
the rear.

Minutes later, Digger came over the radio to Kate, who
had parked in a side street and walked with Mac to where
the prisoners were being loaded.

"Target has company."

"Specify," she ordered.

"Press."

"Roger!"

The smoke was clearing in the street as Kate and Mac arrived and surveyed the toll.

"Call Whatney and brief him," Mac told Kate. "When the media ask what's going on here, tell him I'm classifying it as a joint counterterrorism training exercise."

The journalists who interviewed Nasri at the front door of his home also spoke to other alarmed residents on the street, awoken by the chaos. Some of the scribes recognised Mac from his time in charge of the capital and fired questions in his direction. He was ready, and batted barbed queries away with reflections that operational demands meant training had to be kept as realistic as possible. Mac patiently explained to the assembled media that he couldn't forewarn the residents of the street; that would be counterproductive. It would also risk images spreading on social media suggesting that a real terrorist attack was taking place in Dublin. All the journalists were from print media. He was grateful for that and planned on departing before any television crews arrived. He addressed each question the journalists fired, but stopped short of identifying what other organisation was involved. He hoped he had sufficiently played down the episode to puncture media interest by the time the questions dried up.

21

On Kate's orders, Digger filmed the battle and photographed the aftermath, a street littered with debris. She arranged for a recovery company to lift the crippled vehicles and take them to a nearby station. When a specialist search team he had called in completed their sweep of the street for evidence, Mac used contacts in Dublin Corporation to switch a city centre clean-up crew. In quick time, the suburban street was scrubbed clean of debris and once more, peace descended on the sleepy neighbourhood.

The rush to manage the kickback from the rogue operation tipped into the early hours of the morning. When everyone was accounted for at the scene, Kate briefed Whatney who asked for an hour's grace before getting the politicians involved. She gave him thirty minutes. An hour after the showdown, Twomey's city patrol located weapons and boilersuits dumped in a field, close to Dublin airport. It triggered a frantic sweep of the airport carparks which located the Chrysler. Unseen CCTV cameras recorded images of the four occupants and two were hauled off a

London flight. The other two remained at large. The best guess was that they had headed towards the border with Northern Ireland. The captured operatives were photographed and fingerprinted. Kate retained the details, there would be no official record of their detention.

The political fallout was controlled and kept behind closed doors. Kate and Mac were in the Commissioner's office at 6:30 a.m. Lost sleep showed on Commissioner Fox's face as Mac recapped the events of the previous night. Fox had spent the hours following the incident, strategising with the politicos. As the magnitude of the situation dawned, the Taoiseach's office took control. This was a political nuke with potential to sour relationships with a long-time ally. The US government wanted at all costs to avoid a public falling out. Morning newspapers ran modest reports on their inside pages with the biggest, the Irish Independent, going with a headline that read *Chaotic Garda Training Exercise Alarms Dublin Residents*. However, there was no avoiding reality; armed US agents had breached the country's sovereignty and the violation had to be addressed. Mac's quick thinking at the scene had bought time, but already journalists were sniffing around reports of a weapons find near the airport and a commotion on the late London flight.

When Whatney got back in touch, he had the CIA's director on a conference line. Mac spoke to him. The director assured Mac that the operation as described to him, had no official sanction. He explained that in the short time available to him, he had been able to get some indications to explain what happened. It appeared that a group of over-zealous Homeland Security agents had managed to rope Ben Richardson, his London liaison officer, into a 'dumbass' scheme to spirit a person of interest to US agencies, out of Ireland. He assured Mac that

Richardson would be on the first flight out of Britain to the US. That he would be leaving CIA with a boot in the rear, was a given.

A political decision meant the DPP would direct no charges against the captured operatives. Kate had ordered a local armed unit to surround and detain their aircraft at Shannon. As dawn broke over the west of Ireland a convoy of three ERU jeeps entered the airport, drove onto the plane in turn, and offloaded their cargo. The airport was slowly coming to life. As he unlocked the front door, the duty-free shop's manager picked up a bundle of Irish Independent newspapers. He was arranging them on their display stand as the non-descript aircraft roared down the main runway and climbed high over the Atlantic.

At Mac's office later in the morning, Kate argued for a full investigation to find out if any local agency had aided the stymied operation. She was feeling miserable. She had ignored her instincts, taken a safe management route and been caught out. The tension of the previous night and loss of sleep didn't help. The advice from her mother on improving her eating habits was in the toilet.

Given the complexities of radical Islamic terrorism and the fact that Irish soldiers served on frontlines in Lebanon and the Golan Heights, she reckoned there was a good chance that J2, the Army's Intelligence wing had been either bullied or cajoled by an American agency into repaying an old favour. The fact that there had been no phone call from them to enquire about the incident deepened her suspicions.

"Any word of Cody O'Neill?" Mac asked.

"He called late last night, all apologies," Kate replied.

"What's his excuse?"

"He said his father had taken a turn for the worse and he had to get home double-quick."

"Was he ill before O'Neill came over?"

"In remission from cancer; he had told me as much. It seems its back with a vengeance."

"And he just up stumps like that; doesn't bother to call anyone?"

"He said the San Francisco office told him to focus on his family. An agent was supposed to get in touch, but forgot to call me."

What Kate omitted was that she had located a text from O'Neill on her private mobile. It had been sent well before the action at Nasri's house, telling her that he had a family emergency and was returning home for a short stay.

"Nice to know other people screw up from time to time," Mac said.

"O'Neill will be back early next week. He's bringing a tech with him so that we can make a serious attempt on Khouri's communications."

Back at SIU, Kate went to the women's room to freshen up and was washing her hands when Angie walked in.

"Hey," she said, "didn't expect you in so early."

"Couldn't sleep," Angie replied. "Fucking freaky night!"

"You can say that again."

"If you don't mind me saying, you look shit."

"Would you expect anything different? After a night like that!"

"It's not a sign of weakness to see a doctor, you know," Angie chided.

"Tell that to some of the men in my rank," Kate laughed.

They had the place to themselves. A large mirror ran the length of the wall behind them. Kate leaned against the white countertop as Angie looked in the mirror, checking out the dark circles under her eyes.

"We look out for each other, right," Angie began. As she spoke, she placed a pregnancy test kit on the sink next to Kate's hand. She pulled away in alarm.

"Are you joking?"

"Deadly serious. These past weeks you've been chewing Rennies and visiting the loo a lot. Maybe I'm wrong, but if there's any chance you might be pregnant, you should find out."

Kate felt her cheeks flush. Had she been careless? Her mind flashed back to the wedding shop with Fitz. How did she miss the obvious? Recurrent queasiness had bothered her for a while, until it eased a week earlier. It resurfaced when Digger shared his suspicions on Richardson.

"How come you carrying this around?" Kate asked, lifting the kit.

"We're trying for a baby," Angie replied. Her partner was an Emergency Department nurse who worried all the time about the job Angie did.

"Eileen's doing all the hard work. This is our second try and we're on tenterhooks waiting to see if we're successful this time around."

"I hope you get good news," Kate replied.

"Hang onto the kit," Angie said, as she patted her hands dry.

Kate steadied herself against the countertop and regained some composure.

"I don't think I'm pregnant, but thanks for your concern."

"No problem," Angie replied and strolled out.

Kate re-entered a cubicle and took the test. The instant

she read the positive result she resolved to follow her instincts. Don't panic, get more information. Before returning to her office, she phoned her doctor and made an appointment for later that afternoon.

She tried to sift through paperwork but her concentration was shot. Her phone rang continually. She was on autopilot, fending off queries without having to think much. She couldn't believe she hadn't thought of the possibility of being pregnant herself. As lunchtime approached, she made up her mind. She called Digger.

"Did you get any rest?"

"Dead to the world for the last ten hours," he replied. "I'll see you shortly."

"I'm feeling a bit crook," she explained. She'd picked up the idiom from Aussies she worked with in Cyprus. It described exactly how she felt.

"Are you going to see the doc?"

"I've a four o'clock appointment. I'm going home to rest."

"Don't worry, I'll mind the house," Digger replied, sounding chirpy.

"About last night…"

"Go home and look after yourself. We can talk later."

"Alright."

Kate rang Mac and told him she would be out of circulation for a few hours in the afternoon. She drove across town and shopped in her local supermarket before returning to the tiny apartment she called home for a few more days. Her own apartment would free up at the end of the week when her tenants returned to Dubai. She couldn't wait to get back to its comfort and familiarity. Her mother had promised to come down for a few days to help get the place set up again.

She changed clothes, pulled on sweats and packed

away her purchases apart from the soup and bread. She turned on the small gas ring on her cooker and began warming up the broth, then cut slices of the traditional brown soda bread. Feeling a chill, Kate wrapped a blanket around her shoulders and sipped spoonfuls of the warm soup while pacing between her kitchen and sitting room. In contrast to her own apartment's view of Dublin Bay, this place offered nothing. The window in the main room stared across a car park at another apartment block. She began to feel queasy and put the soup aside. Still peckish, she paced the square room munching mouthfuls of the crusty bread.

Her unique job meant everything to her, without it, she would feel rudderless. A termination would make the problem go away but she dismissed any consideration of it. Something deep in her soul coloured the prospect of new life as bright and welcome. Dealing with the practicalities would be a whole other ball game.

"You're five weeks gone, if the information on your last period is accurate," Doctor Sarah Sheridan told Kate, later in the afternoon. "How do you feel about that?"

"Like a walking cliché," Kate replied. "A single woman with an unplanned pregnancy."

"Don't do yourself down, Kate, that's not you."

"It's just…" tears flowed. Doc Sheridan offered tissues and Kate wiped her face. "For the first time in my life, I'm unsure what to do next."

For the next thirty minutes, despite a packed waiting room, the meticulous doctor talked over Kate's dilemma. She gave her a sick note; a vague gastro anomaly, the 'official' reason for the enforced three-day absence. On her way home, Kate informed Mac of the sick note but told him twenty-four hours rest should suffice.

She packed an overnight bag, drove to Dundalk, and shared the news with her mother.

"You're not shocked?" Kate asked.

Margaret Bowen hugged her daughter tightly in response. "I'm thrilled," she said. "You'll have to go easy now."

She had met some of Kate's previous boyfriends and liked all, except Charlie, the most recent one she knew about.

"You can tell me about the dad when you feel ready," her mother told her. "In the meantime, here's what you need to do."

An endless stream of advice followed, about, eating well, reducing stress, staying healthy. When Kate rang her sister Norrie, she was eager to know more about the father, but she just told her it was complicated.

"Someone from work? Not married, is he?"

"He's American; can we just leave it at that."

Mary D'Arcy, a psychologist who assisted Margaret Bowen at the local Rape Crisis Centre, dropped by for coffee the next day. They were best friends and she had helped steady Kate when post-traumatic stress from her last case threatened to push her over the edge. Kate didn't buy that her dropping in was coincidental, but welcomed the chance to chat. When Sexton rang in the evening with intel that Bailey was arranging some sort of weapons deal with persons unknown, she packed her bag, hugged her mother, and headed back to her other life.

22

Kate smiled when Digger briefed her on his investigation of the intel Sexton had picked up. He had scrambled crews for an early morning deployment on three suspects' houses. At 06:15 the crew watching Jack Lockhart, an IRA Dissident, reported a pickup. He immediately switched his two other teams to the pursuit. At 07:35 the pair parked up near a roadside chuck-wagon to buy breakfast. They ordered and paid for two jumbo breakfast rolls, took a number and waited with other customers. An Asian chef, worked furiously behind the chuck wagon owner. He fried the bacon, sausages, eggs and other trimmings which the owner then squeezed into an enormous split bread roll. One of Digger's crew cut the line and shouted an order for a coffee. Shouts erupted from angry customers, telling him to get in line. The detective kept the argument going just long to distract Lockhart and his driver while Digger attached a tracking beacon underneath their car. As the morning wore on, the operation spilled out of Dublin, into neighbouring counties.

In another rest room tête-a-tête with Angie earlier in

the morning, Kate confirmed her instincts as correct. Like a playground pal, Angie jumped up and down on hearing the news whisper shouting "Yay!" Kate pressed a finger to her lips to shush the celebration. Calmed down, she agreed to keep quiet until Kate felt ready to share the news with everyone else.

Acting as head of SIU was wearisome for her. She absented herself from the management meeting but called Mac to brief him on the Bailey case.

"Dan Whatney rang me yesterday," Mac began. "Said he couldn't get you on the phone."

"I had it turned off. Have you forgotten that I'm supposed to be on sick leave?"

"Slipped my mind. How are you feeling?"

"A lot better, thanks. What did Whatney want?"

"Expressing the CIA's gratitude — again, for the way we dealt with the *invasion*. The Director wants to come over to thank us in person."

"Anything else?"

"Whatney's going to deal with the Bailey case until it's over. They're referring to it as the Nader case."

Kate briefed him on Bailey's rejuvenated networking with Dublin gangs. Another SIU crew had tracked him as he spent the early hours, busy conducting anti-surveillance. He had linked up with gang cronies and appeared to be following a lead car containing two Dissident IRA suspects that Digger's crew had picked up earlier.

"Keep me posted," Mac requested.

⸻

Nasri was incensed at the paucity of newspaper accounts concerning the events close to his house. He had spoken to different journalists for over an hour after his terrified family had been woken up. He had given them good leads that should have sent them querying American involvement. He supplied photographs he had taken on his smart phone from top floor windows but the hacks were unimpressed with the blurry, smoke-filled images.

Sources back in Saudi alerted him that he was on a secret *most wanted* list in America, one that the public would never see. He was convinced last night's full scale battle at the rear of his house was connected to that. Nobody in Ireland seemed to give a damn. While his wife accompanied their children to school next day, he dug out the Sat phone and called the contact number in Beirut.

"Someone tried to attack my house last night," he said.

"Not us," the voice replied.

"Your actions bring danger to my family," Nasri pressed on.

"Your Sunni dogs kill our Shia brothers every day. What do you want?"

"Understand, I cannot assist you anymore, forces will be watching."

"Nothing has changed."

"The risks are great, too big; I will draw attention to you."

"Do you want to see your brother again in this life?"

Nasri sighed.

"Wait for contact."

"I want to speak to him."

"What you *want* means nothing. Contact one week from today."

Nasri switched off the unit and returned it to its hiding place. He dragged himself upstairs, slumped into an armchair and waited for his driver to return with his wife in the family car.

While the Spanish trip opened Bailey's eyes to the fact that he was a cog in a much larger machine, he felt a new bravura. Since commandeering Slasher's gang, he had taken out his main rival and dealt lethally with a cop who crossed him. He was still standing, untouchable. During a second overseas visit, Bailey had passed Nader's emissaries the message that he had recruited an effective group, capable of carrying out their plan. He warned his Arab paymaster that the deal was dead, if they messed him around on payment.

The secret to keeping his new associates onside was to keep them busy. Before leaving Dublin, he had been driven around aimlessly for two hours. Nothing showed when he lingered at different locations to try to pinpoint anyone following him. It was risky getting into bed with the Dissident IRA. They were a motley collection, but he chose the group that came up trumps in dealing with the Fultons and could access the weapons he needed.

Straying from his usual stomping ground made Bailey twitchy. His driver followed the lead car and ended up in a farmyard. An elderly hayseed emerged from a rundown cottage but didn't speak, instead he pointed towards a shed where other cars were parked behind large round straw bales. Bailey got out and donned a pair of hiking boots from the back seat of his car. Jack Lockhart joined him as he threw his town shoes into the back footwell. Tall and skinny, he didn't strike Bailey as much of a revolutionary. His face was long and angular with a pasty complexion. An attempted comb-over of limp, mousey-grey hair completed the anaemic look.

"We walk from here," Lockhart snapped.

"Right, let's get moving," Bailey replied.

Bailey followed him through an opening in a hedge at the rear of the farmyard.

"Is it far?" someone from Bailey's group shouted.

"A fair stretch of the legs," Lockhart replied. "Keep your voice down; we don't want the world to know we're about."

They encountered no one. The meadows they crossed were waist high with lush green grass as farmers waited for a weather window to commence silage making. As the landscape changed, they squelched for an hour through rough scrubland, full of thick green bulrushes. Coniferous forest plantations came into view as they veered towards higher ground, but the terrain underfoot remained the same. Most of Bailey's associates had come unprepared. They complained long and loud about the murky water that spilled freely into their trainers. Bailey figured that somewhere close by, there had to be a valley or gulley used for weapons training. Instead, their journey ended in what looked like an abandoned farmhouse.

"What's the story?" he asked Lockhart.

"Patience, Mr. Bailey."

"Patience me bollix, when do we fire the weapons?"

"We value our security," Lockhart began. He took Bailey into the decrepit parlour of the old dwelling house. "We won't risk one of your bozos coming back and showing Special Branch where we train. We wait here til darkness and then move."

"How the fuck are we supposed to fire guns in the dark?" Bailey asked angrily, feeling duped.

"Trust me, weapons will be fired. You want these lads to be able to shoot leaving here, that's what you'll get."

Bailey grabbed Lockhart's neck in a chokehold. "If this is a fucking set up, you'll be the first one I do. Then I'll shoot the other muppet."

"Mr. Bailey," Lockhart replied calmly, "I can assure you there's no trap. The training will be done in an old coalmine five miles from here. It's been ours for years, we want to keep it that way."

"What about food, these fuckers are grumbling already," Bailey said, pointing towards the kitchen.

"There'll be grub later. You'll be collected at dusk. The training will take as long as it takes, then we'll guide ye back to your cars."

"You could have told me all this in advance."

"That's not *our* way," Lockhart told him.

By the time thick cut ham sandwiches were delivered in the late afternoon, Bailey almost had a mutiny on his hands.

"Jaysus farmer's food," the city slickers grumbled. "What a fuck-up."

The only thing that kept the disgruntled group from abandoning ship was the reality that they didn't know their way back to their transport.

23

At Dublin airport, Kate watched the Terminal 2 arrivals door open and close for an hour before Cody O'Neill finally came through.

"Well, this is a pleasant surprise," he beamed, kissing Kate on the cheek.

"I thought we should talk," she replied.

"God, yes," he replied. "I was briefed on what happened. What a total mess."

"Of course, but…"

A kid in a grey suit, crumpled from travelling, sidled alongside O'Neill. He looked like he graduated college five minutes before leaving The U.S. and was wearing his first work clothes. He had a brand new black trench coat slung on his arm.

"Kate, this is Special Agent Gary Birchall, he's going to work on the communications side of the case."

"First trip to Europe?" Kate asked, as she shook his hand.

"Yeah, Agent O'Neill told me you get a lot of rain over

here," he replied. "And my mom insisted," he added, holding up the trench.

"Can't argue with that," Kate smiled.

"Let's chat in the car," O'Neill suggested.

"Sure," Kate replied, knowing the opportunity to break her news had just evaporated. As O'Neill put his case in the car, Kate enquired about his father. He just shook his head.

It was approaching noon when Lockhart's car went to ground. Digger stalled action for fifteen minutes, then sent a three-woman team with Angie as lead, to locate it. They cautiously approached the rural cottage where Digger's tracking signal had stopped moving. Hunkered behind a hedge, thick with untamed brambles, Angie searched until she found a gap in the vegetation to scan the farmyard. A rusting plough lay in one corner, a redundant hay turning machine stood in another with blue paint peeling off it in layers in layers. She watched and listened until satisfied that there were no dogs on the loose, then leapfrogged her team between outhouses in the crumbling yard until they made it round the perimeter into the hayshed. They found three vehicles stashed among straw bales. There were two pairs of shoes thrown in the back of Bailey's car hinting that the group had taken to the fields. Angie quickly located trampled grass nearby that confirmed as much.

Digger gave her the go-ahead to follow the trail and report to him when it ran cold. He needed more information on the locality. The pursuit had taken them well out of Dublin, through the neighbouring county, Wicklow, and onward into Carlow. They were close to its border with three

other counties. The isolated location fitted with the type IRA
Dissidents used for training. He rang Murt Butler, the Detective Inspector in charge of the terrorist intel analysis unit.

"We're workin' on Don Bailey, Murt," Digger began.
"He's brought us into south Carlow. We don't have sight of
him at the minute; do you know any suspects in the locale
that he might be visitin'?"

"Bailey's not my side of the fence."

"Jack Lockhart led the way here," Digger came back.

"Oh, I *am* interested to hear of Lockhart and Bailey
meeting up. Never good news when the Dissidents and
crime gangs get tangled up."

"Any ideas on where they might be headed around
here?"

"Lockhart's never far away whenever the Dissidents are
training."

"Trainin'?" Digger replied.

"We know Lockhart controls some Real IRA arms
dumps. Maybe Bailey's buying or renting guns from him."

"That's what we're tryin' to find out. Any safe house
around here?" he asked, giving the GPS coordinates.

"Let me work on it. I'll get back to you."

Angie's group reached the edge of arable land. They
would have to encroach onto open ground to progress
further and Digger told them to hunker down and await
orders. Half an hour later Butler rang back.

"There's an old coal mine not that far from where you
are," he told Digger. "If they're doing anything with
weapons, it will likely be there."

"Thanks Murt, we'll check it out."

Stranded in an exposed position, a summer downpour
soaked Angie's group. They found shelter under the
spreading branches of a chestnut tree on the opposite side
of the field and waited for orders. Eventually, Digger rang

and told Angie to have everyone hike back to where they had ditched their transport. They did it in double-quick time and met the rest of the team in the decaying hayshed of a long abandoned farm. Despite the surrounding trees, Digger was conscious that they were in an exposed rural location and their presence wouldn't go unnoticed for long if they hung around. He briefed the crew on the new scenario: the likelihood that a weapons exchange or training was the probable reason for Bailey's sortie into the country. He spread a map on the bonnet of his car and indicated the location of the disused coalmine.

"It's over there," Digger indicated, pointing west.

His team scanned the location with binoculars through a side of the shed long stripped of its galvanised sheeting. The rusty outbuildings of the disused coalmine were located on a hill with a six foot high chain-link perimeter fence to prevent entry. Marshy ground lay on two sides where tufts of green bulrushes pushed up out of sodden soil. There were trees to the rear on high ground and it fronted onto approach roads that offered no concealment. It was difficult terrain to traverse; impossible to do so, unseen, in daylight and treacherous to cross at night.

"We're goin' to have to set up an OP with sight of the mouth of mine," Digger said.

"Where do you suggest?" Angie asked.

"Not sure yet," Digger replied. "I'm meetin' Pat Fleming shortly. He's local and I'm hopin' he'll guide us."

He ordered Angie and her crew to take their meal break in the shed and dispersed the rest of his crew to roads within a five-kilometre radius of the old mine.

When he picked up his old mate at the rendezvous point, Digger marvelled at the fact that Fleming had barely aged since they first met. During basic training, they shared a room for six months in Templemore

Training College before being assigned to the same Dublin station for on-the-job training. Although their career paths had diverged sharply, they had remained buddies. Fleming's motivation in joining the Garda was to assist ordinary people in sorting out life's troubles. Digger's intention was solely to go after the bad guys. After five years' border duty, Fleming had settled in the village of Clonegal where he established himself as a durable community figure. He was uncompromising in prosecuting drunk drivers and his sub-district's two publicans quickly discovered that he would keep his word to close them down if they persisted in serving customers after closing time. When Fleming caught Northern Irish thieves in the act of loading twenty cattle belonging to a local farmer onto a truck, it cemented his standing with the community. Not much happened in the area that didn't reach his ears.

He was intrigued when Digger called and asked to meet him away from the tiny station and house he occupied next door. As instructed he used his wife's car and parked up in a forest car park. Pete McNally sat at the wheel of the only other vehicle there and signalled Fleming to climb in. As it manoeuvred away from the forest clearing, Digger began the briefing.

"Pat, this is top secret at the minute, but we need to locate these fuckers, fast."

"I see your language hasn't improved."

Fleming had studied three years at Maynooth Seminary for the priesthood before realising that his vocation lay in a different uniform. He looked hardly a day over twenty-one, with flame red hair trimmed to regulation length, and a stocky frame that exuded strength.

Digger smiled and continued. "We followed a Dublin drugs gang down here; we think the Real IRA is rentin' them guns or givin' weapons training. Any ideas on where they might do either?"

"I don't need that nonsense around here," Fleming replied. "There's only one place they could fire weapons without being seen or heard and that's in Morgan's Mine."

"Is that the old coal mine I've heard about?"

"There's only one. Locals named it after Morgan Jones, a Welsh miner, who died there back in the forties."

"We need to set up an OP to see what's goin' on."

"There's a stand of fir trees to the west of the entrance," Fleming explained. "That's where I'd use."

He pointed it out to Digger on the map, who worked out the coordinates and contacted Angie.

"Take the newbies and get over there before dark. Bring night sights, stay alert, and don't expect any action until dark. Text for comms."

"Roger," Angie replied. "I'll message when we're set up."

"You haven't mentioned what are you going to do, if you see them going in," Fleming said to Digger.

"Observe and report."

"What? You're not going to arrest them and seize any weapons?"

"Pat, whatever else happens tonight we won't be takin' them on around here. This is part of somethin' bigger."

"You know you won't hear any sound on the surface, if they are firing off weapons underground," Fleming explained. "If you want to confirm what went on down there, you're going to have to go down and investigate."

"And you're sayin' to do that we're goin' to need proper gear."

"Exactly, and someone to guide ye."

"You puttin' in for overtime?"

"I'm saying, I'm here if you need me."

"I'm jokin'," Digger laughed. "I'll talk to Twomey and get an ERU team down here on stand-by."

"I'll need to talk them through what gear to bring."

"Thanks, Pat. We'll work somethin' out on the overtime."

"Beats chasing cattle rustlers any day of the week," Fleming laughed.

At dusk, Angie and her team skirted the open ground and set up on the edge of the fir trees. Heavy black clouds that brought torrential downpours all afternoon had merged into a threatening sky. To the west a massive bank of rain swollen blackness blotted out any chance of catching the sunset. Before they left the shed, they picked up waste dumped as people snacked during the briefing. Angie dug out a dry sweater from her bag and changed. SIU's newbies, Rebecca Kingston and Joan Murphy, complained that no one had told them to bring a change of clothes.

"Becky, you've learned something today. Surveillance is about expecting the unexpected and being prepared for it," Angie told her.

Angie didn't ask if the girls liked their new nicknames, Becky and Joanie. Both were fitness freaks, Angie liked that about them. Becky ran marathons, and Joanie trained for triathlons. They donned camouflage gear for trekking through the forest and with their roles well-rehearsed, the newbies got the hide set up before the downpour began in earnest. Torrents of water streamed off the rain sheet keeping the worst of the weather off them while Angie focussed on setting up the cameras, video and stills, and the powerful binoculars that gave them a good view of the mine entrance.

"*Ready to rock*," she messaged Digger.

The weather remained foul as darkness fell and the spotter team settled in for the long haul.

"Is surveillance always this miserable?" Joanie whispered to Angie.

"It's all about the end result," Angie replied. "Nothing beats slapping the cuffs on someone you've tracked for weeks."

They listened intently to traffic sounds on nearby roads. The rain hammering off their overhead protective sheet made it doubly difficult.

After two and half hours of nothing, Joanie suddenly whispered, "Movement."

"Location?" Angie asked.

"The mine entrance gate shifted a few seconds ago."

Angie clicked on the digital night vision monocular. Their view to the mine entrance was unobstructed, so she chose the 5x42 unit that performed best when it had clear terrain ahead of it. It was a generation-4 night vision device, which gave a sharp outline of activity in the darkness and the black-and-white display didn't strain the eyes. Their hide was about 400 metres from the mine and Angie knew they needed starlight to get better images. From that distance, in total blackout, there was no chance of reading the registration plates on the van that dropped the group. She counted ten individuals, as they darted from the gate and disappeared into the mine shaft. When the gate closed, she switched off the night sights. It was their 'Rolls Royce' unit, but it devoured battery power and she didn't want to drain it immediately. Becky and Joanie kept watch as Angie messaged Digger. Two tedious hours later she sent another text.

"Group departed."

"Certain all hostiles off scene?"

"Counted ten in — ten out."

"Roger. We'll wait half an hour and then go in with Twomey and crew."

"We've got your back."

"It's a warren down there," Fleming told the search team at a hurried pre-deployment briefing. "We're going to have to take it real slow."

"What's the height of the tunnels?" Twomey asked.

"There's two main ones that are five foot nine. The rest I'd say would struggle to make four foot," Fleming replied.

"Okay," Digger said. "One pair per tunnel, let's go."

As they entered the mine, Twomey noticed a small soiled statue near the entrance.

"What's the story?" he asked Fleming.

"St Barbara, the miner's patron saint. Miner's going on a shift rubbed her foot and said a silent prayer that she would keep them safe."

"Didn't work for Morgan Jones," Twomey said, dryly.

"Maybe he forgot to rub the relic," one of his team sniggered.

Digger zipped up his boilersuit. "Let's get on," he said quietly.

They split into pairs and took three tunnels. The two men Twomey sent down the small tunnel hunched over immediately on entering it. Digger agreed a ninety-minute rendezvous back at the entrance. He set off down one of the bigger tunnels with Fleming.

"How did miners spend a lifetime workin' down here?" he remarked, after twenty minutes of walking at snail's pace.

"There was no choice back then," Fleming replied.

They scanned the floor for any evidence of earlier visitors but found nothing. The minutes trickled by as they inched their way along the dank tunnel.

"How far in are we now, d'ya think?" Digger asked, as they completed three-quarters of an hour.

"Well, the pit is over a hundred feet underground and this tunnel runs for about a mile and half."

"Any risk of the roof collapsing?"

"The old miners told me they felt safe enough. The solid rock made for a sound roof."

"What about the water? It's seeping out of the walls everywhere."

"It's a wet pit. They had pumps on all the time when it was being worked. If we see the rats leaving we'll know it's time to go."

"Rats?"

"Of course, you're underground. In the old days, the miners fed them crumbs so that they would stay near enough to them to give them an early warning of trouble."

A hundred metres further on Digger's foot kicked something metal. Excited, he shone his torch on the object before angrily kicking the rusted oil can further up the tunnel.

"Fuck this," he said. "This place is givin' me the creeps. Let's head back and meet Twomey."

"Language!" Fleming admonished.

When they reached the rendezvous they found Twomey's blackened face beaming at them.

"Have you been diggin' coal or what?" Digger asked.

"Go look in a mirror," Twomey laughed. "We found these down that tunnel," he said, handing over a handful of spent shells and hitching a thumb over his right shoulder.

"What calibre?"

"12.7mm, they've been firing semi-automatics down there; pistols too."

"Lead the way," Digger said.

By the time the search party emerged, the rain clouds had rolled back to reveal a sky filled with stars and a sickle moon hung low on the south-west horizon. Angie's night vision image was sufficiently enhanced for her to fire off quick frames of the grimy group; souvenirs for when the case ended. Becky began dismantling their gear. She scrolled through the images captured earlier, before packing the cameras away. "It doesn't add up," she said. "I know four of these scrots, they're just scumbags from the northside gang."

Digger arranged a pick-up with his transport away from the mine. He dumped the bag of spent rounds in the back of the van. Then he slipped off the grimy boilersuit and used a soggy towel to wipe his coal-slaked face. Later in the day, ballistics experts confirmed that Bailey's shadowy cabal had used a rag-bag of weapons, some misfiring.

24

When Kate contacted Whatney days after the Dublin fiasco, they didn't dwell on their recent shared history. Politicians were dealing with the fallout from Richardson's failed operation. An immediate outcome was that the Paris CIA Liaison added one more country to his European brief. She interrupted him as he drank coffee and scoffed *pain au chocolat* at le Petit Plateau, a small café close to the Seine.

"What a life you have, Dan," she teased.

"Cut a guy a break, will ya," he laughed. "I'm dashing between meetings."

She was still scrambling for clues as to what Bailey was planning. Where did Nasri fit into it, if at all? The visit he made to Goffs bloodstock sales was out-of-character behaviour and totally unexplained.

"Is there any update on the profile of your person of interest since last year?" Whatney continued.

"Just that strange visit he made to the bloodstock sales a few weeks back."

"What about that?" he asked. "Looked like he was casin' the joint, is that right?"

"We don't know for sure but he wasn't buying horses. Coupled with that, we've picked up that he's been taking photos at a nearby stud farm."

"What do you know about the family background?"

"Not much, the Brits gave us some general background," Kate outlined. "The family has fingers in many pies in Saudi but they couldn't find any radical connection."

"They're Hawaladars, right. That puts them into contact with a huge spread of people," Whatney mused. "They must be known, far and wide."

"Do you have any assets in Saudi that could dig a bit deeper into them?"

"Remind me where they're based."

"Jeddah on the Red Sea, as far as I know."

"Yeah that's right," Whatney said. "Makkah province; two million Muslims pilgrimage there annually."

"Can you make something happen there?" Kate asked.

"Well the Director has told us to spare nothing for the Irish, so I'll do my best."

Kate hung up without discussing possible collaboration between Shia and Sunni rebels. Bailey's connection to the Shia Sheikh Nader was confirmed, but the link with Nasri was tentative in her view. Grealy's agent was adamant the pair had met a year earlier, however, weeks of SIU surveillance had yielded no connection.

Kate called Garcia, the Guardia Civil Colonel in Madrid. Sexton's enquiries had confirmed that Don Bailey had made another foreign trip just before he got busy at home. He had used a holiday charter flight from Belfast to travel to Barcelona. She had passed the information to Garcia immediately but had heard nothing in reply.

"You read my mind," Garcia replied. "We are final-ising a translation for you just now."

"A translation of what?"

"A report on your suspect, Bailey."

"What about him?"

"We confirm him at Barcelona airport from the charter you told us about," Garcia explained. "Later the same day we confirm him crossing at Le Perthus in a hire car."

"Where's that?"

"It is a small town on the Spanish/French border."

"Have you passed it to DGSI?"

DGSI was the French Security Service, it dealt with domestic terrorism.

"Just a minute," Garcia said. "I get the report. Okay, yes we tell the DGSI and they use road tolls to track the car's journey to Nice, the same day."

"Did you trace him leaving Barcelona?"

"No, he flew from Nice to London on the last flight that night."

"Great work, Antonio," Kate said.

"Thank you. If Bailey comes in our country again," Garcia told her, "we will arrest him for the murder of our agent at the villa. Nader and his accomplices also."

Kate thanked Garcia for his assistance. He gave her the go-ahead to discuss the case with DGSI. It was a given that she would update him with the outcome. Kate waited to digest the full report and when it came through in the late afternoon, she called Yves Fenaux at DGSI headquarters in Paris.

Bailey struggled to keep things on track. The weapons training had been infuriating. By the time they got everyone down the mine, they were cold, wet, and hungry again. Some of the weapons Lockhart's associates brought along were in bad nick and misfired. It took an hour to get those with no firearms experience instructed in the basics. The light down the tunnels was pitiful due to Lockhart's cheap torches. When it came to firing the AK47s, he told everyone to just aim straight down the tunnel and blast away. At least with the pistols, he set up targets and shone his best lights on them. Bailey collected a tenner from each of his gang and then doubled the pot for the best shot. It cheered the gang up until his driver won the money.

He detested being told to meet and take instruction from the foreigner in Harold's Cross. Still he had little choice but to follow the programme laid out by his puppet masters. They had done their homework on him and he strongly suspected the Arab businessman of taking the photograph of Rachel's shop. The call to meet up had come to an old mobile used by Slasher Fulton. Bailey had been dumping phones on a weekly basis but Buck picked up the voicemail. Apart from being Bailey's driver, his job was to keep his boss connected. He kept the old phones charged and checked them every day. When Bailey returned the call, Nasri's voice was unmistakeable. He told Bailey they needed to meet face-to-face and arranged to meet in a city centre café.

With Digger spending the day working with Special Agent Birchall on the FBI case, trying to break their target's PlayStation communications; Sexton ran the surveillance operation that picked Bailey up as he left the housing estate where he lived. He was at ease working the streets of his home town. The surveillance crews he guided worked seamlessly and seldom dropped targets. It was rarely easy due to the bureaucratic process of regular warrant applications lagging behind Bailey's regular phone switches. The delay meant SIU missed Nasri's call.

However, when Buck dropped him at the top of Dawson Street and drove around the block to a multi-storey car park an SIU crew had him in sight. Sexton cut Buck loose to focus on Bailey, who set off on foot towards Trinity College, cutting across Duke Street, into Wicklow Street and into the Powerscourt Town Centre, where he browsed shop windows trying to smoke out his pursuers. Sexton called up Becky and Joanie to follow the target into whatever café he chose, but he exited the centre, walked twice around the block before using the side streets to head towards George's Street.

Becky was busy, staying ahead of the target, when she spotted Nasri entering a small coffee shop in the George's Street Arcade. Sexton ordered her to go in after him. Not far away, Joanie still had Bailey in sight. Inside the café, Becky joined the queue. She watched as Nasri ordered coffee and asked the assistant if he could borrow the *Financial Times* that sat on the counter. She nodded assent and he tucked it under his arm before walking towards the basement with his coffee.

Becky took a stool at a side counter and surveyed the room. She copped Bailey's driver, sitting alone at a table and sent a text to Sexton to alert him. He ordered the fledgling surveillance officer to sit tight upstairs and watch out for Bailey. Ten minutes later, he duly arrived. Outside, Joanie continued to browse through the arcade's market stalls. As Bailey queued, he checked out the clientele and exchanged a nod with his driver. Then, he ordered a sparkling water and headed for the basement. Angie was in a car, two streets away and called Sexton.

"We should check it out," she suggested.

"We've put them in the same basement at the same

time," Sexton replied "that's surely proof enough. I don't want to let a newbie get exposed."

"I'd like to see it," Angie said.

"Bailey's driver's in the café," Sexton said. "It's too risky."

"Let me give it a go."

Sexton reluctantly agreed and ordered Becky to leave when Angie arrived. Angie donned a red tee shirt with a large slash down one side. She topped off the outfit with a faded blue denim jacket. She removed the tiny stud in her nose and replaced it with an altogether cheaper looking half 'U' model. Finally, she gelled and punked her hair. By the time she got to the entrance of the George's Arcade, she had slowed her walk to a shuffle. Nervous stallholders kept an eye on her as she passed. She pushed open the café door and queued. Bailey's driver had disappeared and Angie figured he had left to pick up the car. She ordered a coffee and slapped fifty cents on the counter.

"You're €1.50 short," the cashier insisted.

"Look, it's all I've goh," Angie answered, accentuating her Dublin accent.

"Then you can't have it," the cashier retorted.

"Jaysus sake, show a bir a compassion," Angie complained.

From the other end of the counter, the manager caught the exchange. He walked slowly up to the cash register. "If I let you have the coffee to-go, will you leave?" he asked.

"Awh righ," Angie answered.

He poured the contents into a paper coffee cup, popped a plastic lid on top and handed it over. "Now, on your way," he ordered.

"I need the jax," Angie said and shuffled away from the till.

Before the manager could stop her, she began edging

down the stairs towards the toilets in the basement. Bailey's driver halted her progress when he suddenly showed up on the midway landing, arms folded.

"No junkies," he shouted. "Fuck off." Behind her, the wimpy manager threw his arms in the air.

"Fuck sake," Angie replied, without making eye contact. She turned and mooched slowly back upstairs towards the irate manager, who escorted her off the premises. She shuffled out of the arcade into a nearby side street. When she felt confident no one was taking any interest in her she called Sexton.

"Bailey and Nasri are deep in conversation downstairs in that café."

"Anything else?"

"Bailey's on edge. He pocketed what looked like a photo when that bastard, Gerry Buck stopped me."

25

Kate recognised Yves Fenaux's number when it flashed up on her office phone. Their paths had crossed over a year earlier. In a pressure cooker situation, Fenaux was icy cool and trusted Kate's instincts. He was suave, easy on the eyes and most important, spoke good English.

"*Bonjour, Kate, tu vas bien* ?"

"I'm good, and you?"

"*Ca va, ça va*! So, Kate, we are working for you again."

"Working together again, perhaps," Kate laughed.

"Your Mr. Bailey, he gives us much to think about."

"Really?"

Fenaux explained that they had run facial recognition software against CCTV footage from Nice airport and gotten hits. They picked Bailey up handing back the hire car keys and later as he waited for the London flight.

"Something interesting happened while he waited," Fenaux explained.

Bailey received a phone call and immediately walked towards a toilet block. The DGSI double-checked passenger lists for flights that arrived while Bailey was at the airport. Their software scored two further hits, picking out Hussein and Abousamra travelling on false passports. They had flown in from Jordan fifteen minutes before Bailey received his phone call. An hour later CCTV picked up the Hezbollah suspects speaking to a receptionist at a private jet charter company.

"No sightings of Bailey talking to them?"

"None."

"Have you interviewed the receptionist?"

"Of course. She explained that the pair wanted to find out about a short-term jet hire at Nice. You know how long in advance to book, cost, that kind of thing."

"Was she suspicious?"

"On the contrary, she's asked the same questions several times every day."

"Hardly a coincidence; Bailey being there the same day."

"Unlikely, we think it was carefully planned. We examined the scans of the Jordanian passports the suspects presented and they are exceptionally good quality."

"Finding a good travel document forger in the Middle East isn't exactly difficult."

"I agree. We'll send on a full report."

"Do you have any thoughts on what they might be planning?" Kate asked.

"We know that ISIS eats into the Hezbollah finances and that they try to find new ways to raise funds. For this case, we have no specific intelligence."

"Bailey's background is almost exclusively drugs. Our intel is that Bailey is trying to expand his distribution network into several UK cities."

"So perhaps, he intends to take his supply from the Bekaa Valley."

"Maybe."

"DGSI will hold the case, if we believe the money from any drug importation is being used to fund terrorism."

"You've told Garcia about Nice?"

"Not yet but I will, it is normal protocol," Fenaux assured her.

———

Mac was less and less concerned with operational matters as Commissioner Fox leaned on him for day-to-day managerial support. Kate still considered him her main mentor, her go-to guy if she needed guidance. In a late afternoon briefing at his office, he told her J2, Army Intelligence had supplied the reports she requested. She filled him in on Bailey's meet up with Nasri and the suspected meeting in Nice.

"Now I'm really worried," he said. "Have you any idea what's on the cards?"

"Too early to say."

"Bailey's Islamic contacts make no sense."

"At least Fenaux's holding onto the case. We can use a similar justification, if it turns into a drugs' importation job. You know, funding international terrorism, etc."

"Why did you need these reports?" Mac asked, sliding four manila folders across the table.

Kate opened the first one. "We have very little on this ex-Army Sergeant Dempsey. His personnel record told us he was a good soldier, but we know nothing of his overseas service. These situation reports, from his last tour in Lebanon, might yield something."

"Want me to enquire with Shaw if they know what Dempsey did when he left the Army?" Mac asked.

"Digger tells me he found work as a security man. Let's not show our hand for now.

Kate brought the J2 reports home. Over the previous weekend she had moved back into her old apartment. The departing doctors had been perfect tenants and before they left had the place professionally cleaned. She convinced her mother that she didn't need to come to Dublin to help her move in. Instead, she paid the caretaker to shift the heavier boxes and by Saturday night Kate was settled again.

She threw the J2 reports on the kitchen counter when she got in and showered before changing into sweats. She had vowed to devise a healthy eating plan soon, but for that evening she resorted to ordering in her usual Chicken Pad Thai. When her order was delivered twenty minutes later, she brought everything into her lounge and sat on the floor so that she could spread out the reports on the floor as she read them. Hormones had switched her preference from cashews to peanuts in the dish and, as usual in recent weeks, she ate every scrap of the huge portion of noodles. She ran a hand over her stomach at the end, uncertain if what she was feeling was the beginning of a bump or just bloating from her carbo bash. She considered inviting O'Neill over to see the place and get a chance to talk properly with him. Since his return, Special Agent Birchall shared his apartment. Kate also picked up a certain reticence from O'Neill, all their contact had been perfunctory. She dismissed the notion and focussed on the reports.

Most were monotonous, repetitive from month to month. They described the number of patrols carried out in the IRISHBATT sector of operations. Checkpoints mounted were described in terms of size, location, and activity. Incidents occurring were described in bland, terse terms. It had been a quiet six months for the contingent. No casualties and just low-level incidents. Kate skimmed the *civil affairs* sections of each monthly report. It described the Army's interaction with the local civilian population. She knew from her own UN experience that it would be run-of-the-mill stuff. In the final monthly report, Kate came across an innocuous entry featuring Sgt. Dempsey. She was annoyed that Lieutenant-Colonel Shaw hadn't bothered to read the reports and highlight it for her. It would have spared her the tedium. It seemed the Commandant writing the report threw the paragraph in as an afterthought:

Sgt. Dempsey reported an interface with two locals whom he had met during a previous tour. The contact consisted of an invitation to share a meal with the men, together with a local family. The Sergeant was commended for his initiative in deepening the trust between IRISHBATT and the indigenous population.

The next morning Kate rang Mac and told him that she wanted to follow up the report. He told her it was time to mend fences and speak to Shaw herself. She bowed to the inevitable and called the J2 number.

"Lt. Col. Shaw, this is Kate Bowen," she said when his phone answered.

"Detective Superintendent Bowen, it's been a while."

"Indeed! You were kind enough to pass some reports to Mac; I'd like to discuss an aspect of one of the reports."

"Ah, they were for you. Assistant Commissioner McEnroe didn't say."

"Is that a problem?" Kate asked.

She wondered if he was this frosty with everyone. She'd never found him any other way.

"Indeed not. How can I help?"

"Do you have a copy of the report?"

"I have the original," Shaw replied.

Kate asked him if the identities of the men Dempsey met were known. Shaw told her there was nothing further on the file other than what she had read. However, he told her he knew the author of the report and agreed to contact him to see if he had any contemporaneous notes that might fill in the blanks. By afternoon, he was back in touch.

"There's nothing to that report, Detective Superintendent," he told Kate. "Turns out that on an earlier mission, Sergeant Dempsey had coached football with the two chaps involved when they were in a local orphanage."

"I see," Kate said. "Did your Commandant friend note their names by any chance?"

"Yes. Do you have a pen?"

"Shoot!"

"Hussein was one guy, first name Aazim, and the other chap was called Musharraf Abousamra."

"Thank you very much, Colonel," Kate signed off and hung up.

"Yes!" she shouted.

Dempsey was the pivotal link to Bailey's Middle East connections. She called Mac and filled him in.

"You're going to have to brief the Army on the Hezbollah background here," he said.

"Not yet," she replied.

"If anything breaks before we tell them, we'll suffer."

"We'll let them know soon, but I need to work the intel to try and figure out what's being planned. In any case, Whatney's going have to give the go-ahead to share it."

"Agreed, but we brief the Army before we tell any other agency, okay?"

"I'm not a dummy," Kate replied. "I know the rules; you don't have to spell it out."

He laughed and hung up. Kate pushed back into Mac's old chair, hands clasped behind her head. She had commandeered it for its built-in back support since her pregnancy was confirmed.

Her instincts had been spot on; the trail led back to somewhere in the Middle East. Bailey was immersed in something more deadly than a straightforward drugs deal. Kate was more determined than ever to stop him.

PART II

26

Vincent Cleary threw open his bedroom curtains as his yard came to life. Horses whinnied and poked their heads out as stable hands opened the top half of the boxes. Ballycleary Stud had been in the Cleary family for over sixty years. Vincent's grandfather, Jimmy 'Schooner' Cleary bought the house and one hundred acres in 1950 from an Anglo-Irish family whose fortune had dwindled and they could no longer afford its upkeep. 'Schooner' Cleary had just retired having been Irish Flat jockey champion ten years in a row. He acquired the 'Schooner' handle when a wealthy owner gifted him a yacht for winning a third King George VI Chase at Kempton for him in his final year as a professional rider. The elder Cleary flogged the vessel and used the proceeds to put a deposit on the house and yard that would become headquarters to a modest training operation.

He struggled financially throughout the fifties as Ireland remained a largely agricultural country. In the sixties, industry expanded, the economy prospered and businessmen invested spare cash in bloodstock. When one of Cleary's charges won the Aintree Grand National, the family name entered racing folklore. A year before he died, Schooner turned the business over to his son, John.

In his first decade, all told, John trained over a thousand winners and transitioned the business through the turn of the century. As his training operations slowed, the number of winners dwindled. When the economic crisis began to bite in 2008 he passed the baton to his son, Vincent. Although an avid horseman, Vincent had never ridden professionally. His large frame, a gift from his mother's side, meant he had no hope of ever making the crazy weights required of jockeys. He enjoyed riding out from the yard in the early mornings. Late spring, early summer, were his favourite times of the year. Being part of a string of horses riding out among the bright yellow clumps of gorse on the Curragh plains was a glorious feeling. Apart from occasional squeals or bucks from some of the animals, it was the most tranquil part of his hectic day.

By the time he took over, Vincent knew the business was struggling financially. The infusion of new owners, prompted by the early century economic boom, quickly dried up. Vincent Cleary decided that the only way forward was to focus on quality. His knowledge of equine lineages, what made them great, how it could be tweaked in breeding, caught the attention of wealthy owners. His sister, Stephanie, qualified as a veterinary surgeon, and completed a graduate programme in Equine Sports Medicine at University College Dublin before joining the business. She analysed poor performance, determined causes and recommended remedies or sale for the horses concerned. She passed on to her brother the knowledge gained on genetics and exercise physiology. Her daily focus was the treatment of diseases and injuries that impacted on the performance of their equine stock. The result of their collaboration was sensational. During Steph's first season with the business, from forty-two horses, Vincent Cleary produced an incredible seventy-five wins. It didn't go unnoticed.

Certainly not with Highness Sheikh Muhammad Bin Salah Al-Naqeeb. Despite being thoroughly modern, portraying the exotic Arabian prince came easy to him. In reality he was one of three thousand princes in the Saudi royal family. Al-Naqeeb was educated at a private grammar school in the UK, then Cambridge University and finally the Royal Military Academy at Sandhurst. He maintained a personal website which documented his educational achievements and charity work. His royal status even afforded him the platform to see his poetry published in Arabic. The deferential attitude shown him during his early years in the UK amused. However, as Al-Naqeeb matured through his twenties and into his thirties, he recognised the conceit. The object of the deference was to divest him of some of the vast sums of money at his disposal.

Oil was his family business and through decades of change, Saudi Arabia retained its status as one of the world's largest petroleum producers. In accordance with the Sharia law, which governed land ownership in the Kingdom, all land was ultimately owned by the state as entrusted to it by God. Al-Naqeeb's uncle, the king, administered God's patrimony in trust. When his overseas education was completed, the young prince became an important part of the family business.

He was tasked with exploiting his renowned charisma and charm to ensure that the Saudi Kingdom remained a dominant voice in OPEC, the group of oil-producing countries that set global prices. Although its influence had waned since the global oil crises it provoked in the seventies, world governments still paid close attention to OPEC pronouncements.

The jet-set lifestyle left him unfulfilled. Despite a team of PR handlers, British media tagged Al-Naqeeb as just another pampered royal. It was an unfair generalisation and his strongest desire was to change that perception and to create a more positive narrative outside the Islamic monarchy. His love of horses, developed before he was shipped off to Britain for education, gave him an outlet. A chance meeting with Vincent Cleary during the 2010 Irish Derby at the Curragh turned the page on a glorious new chapter in his life.

They had spoken at the winners' enclosure and Cleary invited him to visit his yard before he returned to the UK. When Al-Naqeeb rang him late on Derby evening to accept, Cleary suggested that he come for breakfast next morning and ride out with some of his charges. Al-Naqeeb agreed, and early next day he mounted one of Cleary's best steeplechasers.

"Walk for ten minutes and then we trot," Cleary had told the group before heading out.

It was the height of summer and the sun was burning off the early morning mist on the green Curragh plains where they were headed from the yard. Two security guards travelled close behind in a hired Range Rover, content that the ten foot hedges on either side of the gallops offered privacy. Al-Naqeeb was absorbed by Cleary's tales of animals that he had advised owners to purchase based on his belief that he could transform them into champions.

"Steph is so good with the horses," Cleary told him.

"She spots little problems before they become big ones. To a trainer, that's invaluable."

"But, you, you must advise the owner to purchase or not to purchase before you know the animal at all," Al-Naqeeb smiled.

"Well, round here, they say it's in the blood. My family has been doing it for generations."

The rest of the morning went swimmingly from Cleary's viewpoint. The Sheikh wanted a gallop before the ride ended and the group obliged. They brought him to the practice track and settled on a one mile chase over flat ground. Despite riding a steeplechaser, the Sheikh's horse somehow won the day. Over breakfast, he asked Cleary if he would come to Saudi to meet his extended family. Two weeks later in Riyadh, Al-Naqeeb made him an offer which Cleary couldn't and didn't refuse. In return for purchasing and training future champions for his family, the prince would pump substantial funds into Ballycleary Stud. The injection of cash turbo-boosted Cleary's operations and five years later he had enough money to renovate the old house.

At eight o'clock on an overcast Monday morning, Vincent Cleary stepped out a side door of his house into a small courtyard where an obstacle course of cement mixers, wheelbarrows, and other builder's tools greeted him.

"Where's the foreman?" he asked one of the workers.

"Out the front, last time I saw him," came the reply.

Cleary walked around the side of the house, his feet crunching on the gravel underfoot.

The foreman was near the front door poring over a plan with two of his crew and gesturing towards the roof.

"I thought you promised me this would be gone by

now," Cleary said, indicating the scaffolding. "The prince is due in a few days."

"We discovered that the lead in the valley between the main roof and the one to the side needs replacing," the foreman replied. "It's what's causing the leak in the rumpus room. We'll need to keep the scaffolding there until we've fixed it."

Cleary's American wife had set aside a large room in a wing of the old house that had lain unused for years, as a playroom for their two young children. He was forty when he married his bride, ten years his junior. She understood that most of the money they earned would be ploughed into the business but insisted that it wasn't spared when it came to the children.

The prince would be staying two nights at Ballycleary, a first, and Vincent Cleary wanted the place fit for royalty.

"I want it done and dusted by Thursday at the latest," Cleary said.

"We might have to do a few late evenings, Mr. Cleary," the foreman replied, "but we won't let you down."

"The Lodge?"

"It'll be finished today."

"Let's take a look."

His Saudi benefactors requested that Cleary renovate one of two lodges on the property, exclusively for their use. The old hunting lodge was within walking distance of the main house and looked pristine as Cleary strolled around inspecting the fresh paint. The prince had hired an interior decorator to furnish it to his taste. He was due tomorrow to ensure everything was as the prince intended.

The influx of funds to Ballycleary Stud had been good for the neighbourhood's economy. Cleary retained a local landscaping company on a semi-permanent basis. They planted extensive copper beech hedging on its approaches.

The rows of semi-mature trees that went in along either side of the main avenue were carefully nurtured and had grown to give the place an imposing, almost stately, appearance. Vincent Cleary did not ride out that morning, his attention consumed by other matters. He watched as a white Toyota 4x4 parked in the visitor area alongside the yard. He walked over and greeted his guest.

"Wally, how are things with you this morning?"

"Couldn't be better, Vincent," his jovial guest replied as he removed his shoes and slipped on a pair of green wellingtons. "Now let's get this done and I'll get out of your hair."

Vincent Cleary had known Walter Dolly for many years, mainly from meeting him at local golf club functions. The retired Commandant had been a logistics officer with a transport corps at the Irish Army's HQ in the Curragh Camp. His fondness for taking a gin and tonic at the nearby club house at any hour of the day was widely known and curtailed his promotion prospects. Five years earlier, Dolly resigned his commission and set up a private company, Equus Security, specialising in the needs of the horse racing industry. To most trainers, he was a likeable character, who employed well trained ex-soldiers to do the job of securing their yards. Apart from an occasional round of golf, physical exertion didn't feature much in Dolly's weekly schedule. His portly figure was ample evidence that the programme had not been adjusted in a while.

"So, you're having his Highness the Sheikh, stay over next weekend, is that right?" Dolly began.

"That's it Wally. We need everything ship-shape during the visit. No slip ups."

"Of course! That's why you employ us."

"You're going to have to link in with Sheikh Al-

Naqeeb's security team. Whatever they want, give it to them."

"Vincent, that's all taken care of; I've been in touch with them these past two weeks. We're professionals."

"Great! Now tell me what you want to view."

They walked through a shallow pool of disinfectant before entering the first concrete paved yard where two young stable hands groomed a pedigree stallion. The animal was outside one of the twelve boxes dotted around the square enclosure, prancing around as if on coiled springs. The stable lad moved with the animal holding the reins tightly and speaking softly to it while his female companion made a start on brushing the sleek chestnut coat. Vincent Cleary walked over and took the animal in charge.

"This is Mon Chef," he said, as he stroked the splash of white that ran down the front of the animal's head, calming it down.

"God, a lot of people made good money off him," Dolly replied.

"Retired to stud last year."

Cleary handed the reins back to the stable lad and the pair continued their survey. Dolly knew the layout well but wanted to assess where best to place the two security men he would station there each night of the Sheikh's visit.

"Have you any empty boxes?" he asked Cleary, as they entered the final yard.

"Yards one and two are full. There's two empty boxes side by side here."

"Could I suggest that you do a switch and leave the box closest to the perimeter empty?"

"Why?"

"I like to guard the flanks and it would give me an

onsite base. I'll stick the monitors in there for the extra cameras I'm mounting before His Highness arrives."

"We can do that," Cleary said. "How many will you have working here during the visit?"

"Mick Dempsey will be here in the yards with one other for the overnights. He knows the place by now."

"Is he the one always looking for tips?" Cleary asked with a grin.

"He's sound," Dolly assured him. "He served under my command in Lebanon and was a good soldier. I think that's everything. I'll put a mobile patrol out each night but they won't disturb you."

"What about the Lodge?"

"The Sheikh's personal bodyguards are responsible. My command centre will be on 24-hour alert for the duration of the visit. Don't worry, we'll be ready for any eventuality."

27

Kate was talking to Whatney on her office line when her personal mobile buzzed in her bag. They were brain-storming roles Dempsey might be playing in whatever grand plan Bailey was putting together. Whatney was keen to find an excuse to get over to Dublin on a visit. Kate fished the phone out of her bag as they spoke and unlocked the screen. She agreed coming over would be a good idea, they needed to get Whatney in a sit-down with J2 to discuss the backgrounds of the Hezbollah militants. He gave her the go-ahead to tell Army Intelligence that the CIA had identified Dempsey's associates as part of Hezbollah in Beirut and south Lebanon.

Kate juggled her personal mobile and read its message. It was a slap-on-the wrist text from Holles Street maternity hospital telling her that she had missed her scan appointment and would have to reschedule.

"Crap!" Kate groaned.

"Somethin' up?" Whatney asked.

"I've just been reminded that I was supposed to be

somewhere else an hour ago. I better call and make my peace."

"Okay," Whatney said. "Let me know when you set up the meetin' with your Army guys so that I can book a flight to get over there."

"Will do."

Kate rang the hospital immediately and spoke to the scanning unit scheduler she had mucked about. She got lucky. The administrator was having a bad day. Another patient had just called and cancelled. Kate snapped up the slot, grabbed her car keys, and told Sexton that she would be missing for at least an hour. He agreed to field any phone calls while she was away.

Unfamiliar smells and sounds struck her when she got to the maternity hospital, her first time as anything other than a visitor. She diligently obeyed the wall-to-wall signs banning use of mobile phones and switched both off, before seeking out the scanning unit. An hour later, having wiped her stomach clear of the gel the nurse applied before carrying out the ultrasound, she was walking out staring at a square photograph.

Damn, I better tell Cody soon, she thought, as she viewed the life growing inside her. She reached the car and turned her mobile back on, immediately noticing three missed calls from Mac. She listened to his message and negotiated her way out of the city centre before making the urgent call back requested.

"Everything okay?" she asked.

"No," Mac replied. "Everything most definitely is not okay."

"What's eating you?" she asked, annoyed by his tone.

"What was the one thing I asked you to do with the Army? Remember?"

"What? I'm planning on calling Shaw about Dempsey's pals when I get back to base. Whatney gave me the go-ahead about an hour and half ago; he would like to set up a meeting with them."

"In the name of God, why have you not done that by now?"

"I'll be doing it shortly. What's the matter?"

"Shaw knows already and he's fuming. Whatney obviously reported up the line about the ex-soldier, Dempsey, being a link between Dublin criminals and Hezbollah. It's gotten back to Shaw through their CIA military contacts."

Kate listened intently, put off momentarily by darting traffic around her in Ballyfermot, a working-class western suburb. Surrounding industrial estates disgorged trucks and vans onto the main route at irregular intervals, making it clogged and slow-moving. She pulled into a supermarket car park to focus on Mac's anger.

"I got distracted after speaking to Whatney," she told Mac.

"By what?"

"Something personal."

"You had to run a personal errand and now the Army are seriously pissed with us."

"I'm sorry, I'll sort it…"

"Do nothing. I've apologised for *our* mistake. I'll call him again to reassure him that there was no ill intent behind it, just an oversight."

"Sorry."

"I'm hearing that too much lately," Mac replied and hung up.

Kate leaned her head on the steering wheel to regain her composure. What was happening? She'd never lost focus like this. Suddenly, she felt tears streaming down her face and pulled out a tissue from her open bag to wipe them away. The printout from the scan spilled from it into the footwell on the passenger seat. Kate picked it up, ripped it in four, and dumped it on the passenger seat. She leaned back in her seat and wiped away the tears. She took deep breaths to calm down and think straight. She uncovered the mirror in the sun visor and touched up the minimal makeup she wore.

As she prepared to start her car again, Kate noticed a woman nearby, staring at her. She was closing the boot lid of a battered-looking car having filled it with grocery shopping bags. Before Kate could get her car started, she approached and asked, "Is everything okay, love?"

The car window was closed. Kate opened it slightly.

"Excuse me, I couldn't hear."

"Are you okay?" the woman repeated.

"I'm fine, thank you. I got bad news, that's all."

The concerned shopper stared across at the torn image on the passenger seat and pieced the puzzle together.

"Love, you're not the first and you won't be the last," she said.

"What?" Kate asked.

"The scan, I can see the pieces. You're not overexcited about the news," she persisted.

"No, no, it's not that at all; something else entirely."

"Look love, talk to someone. Don't try and do it all on your own."

"Thank you, you're very kind. I have to run," Kate said, as she closed the window, and took off.

Before she arrived back to her office, Detective Gerry Grealy called.

"Can I call in to see you on my way home?" he asked.

"Sure, Gerry, it would be great to see a friendly face."

"Bad day?"

"The pits! See you in a while."

Before Grealy arrived, Kate had spoken to Whatney and told him that she had messed up communicating the Dempsey intel to the army. She told him that they might need a cooling-off period before setting up a meeting.

"Shit happens, Kate. Don't sweat it," he comforted her.

When Grealy arrived at five, Kate called Digger and Sexton to sit in on the meeting.

"My man tells me Nasri took another trip around that stud farm near Newbridge," Grealy opened.

"When was this?" Kate asked.

"Two days ago," Grealy replied. "The agent said there's a lot of work going on around the place."

"I'm not surprised," Sexton chipped in. "Vincent Cleary has two runners going in the Derby on Saturday."

"Did Nasri do or say anything while he was there?" Kate asked.

"No. The agent said Nasri told him to drive slowly past the place, then loop back onto the M7 and return to Dublin."

"There has to be a purpose to the visits," Sexton said.

"Other than observin' the lie of the land," Digger said, "he can't be pickin' up a whole lot of information on just a drive-by."

"So do you think he's kind of, verifying information?" Sexton speculated.

"Maybe," Digger replied.

"That implies there's another source," Kate said.

"Yup!" Digger said.

"Why? What information?" Kate asked. "What's in Ballycleary Stud that Nasri could be interested in?"

"My gun club mate does security down around there," Digger said. "I could ask him, if you like."

"Do that," Kate replied.

"Do you need anything else from me?" Grealy asked.

"Has your agent said anything lately about Nasri's mood?" Kate asked.

"I ask him every time we meet and it's the same answer every time. He's feels his boss is very down in the dumps, like there's something weighing on his mind."

"All the noise around his house lately won't have helped," Sexton added.

"Yeah, what the fuck was that all about?" Grealy asked.

"Training," Kate, Digger, and Sexton replied in unison.

Grealy grinned and said nothing.

"Thanks for everything, Gerry," Kate said. "Call me if anything changes, okay."

"Can I tempt anyone to a drink," Grealy asked as he stood up. "I'm heading to The Back Door for one before heading home."

"Sorry, Gerry, we're not done here yet," Kate told him.

When Grealy departed, Kate looked towards her two D-I's.

"Any ideas?"

"Looking at the intel we have," Sexton began, "can we conclude that Nasri has some part to play in whatever Don Bailey has been planning?"

"I can't make sense of that connection," Digger replied. "There has to be somethin' we're not seein'."

"I'll shake the trees tonight," Sexton said. He moved freely through his old neighbourhood and maintained sources.

"I'll call Whatney back and see if they can rush through their enquiry on Nasri's family," Kate said. She looked at the office clock; it was 7:15 p.m. "What's happening with the FBI case on comms interception?" she asked.

"A dead duck," Digger replied. "None of the software the young lad tried worked."

O'Neill's IT technician had hit a brick wall as he tried to break Rafiq Khouri's comms set-up. After a week of working with one telecommunications provider after another, he was ready to give up and return to the States to rethink his strategy. Since O'Neill returned, he had been to Mac's office twice, for case reviews. It had been all business; should the interception fail, they would re-evaluate, he explained. Kate had called him once and invited him to meet for a late evening drink. His "Best not" reply confused her.

"Let's take four away from Khouri and put them on the Bailey case," she suggested.

"Don't strip it yet," Digger said.

"Why not?" Kate asked.

"There's been an anomaly with his routine in the past week. I want to check the footage from the hall camera."

"The pizza delivery?" Sexton asked.

"I was told he orders pizza all the time," Kate said.

"He does," Digger replied. "But for the second time in just over a week, he's turned away a delivery, saying he didn't order it."

"Okay," Kate said. "Look into it and let me know."

She checked her office safe, turned off the lights and drove home. After eating, she fished the torn pieces of her scan image from her bag. She placed them on the table and carefully stuck them back together. The tear marks showed but when the image was restored, Kate kissed it. "Our first fight," she whispered, "friends again."

Then she googled 'hen parties' and spent an hour and half scrolling through possibilities. The clock was ticking and to her relief, Fitz insisted that she didn't want a solely boozy girls' night out before her big day. Kate would have to innovate.

28

The following day Bailey met Nasri at the Leaping Hare, his old haunt when Slasher was around. He was unaware that weeks earlier, Digger had spent three hours early one morning, building bugs into light fittings dotted around the walls and into the ceiling. Cameras were too risky he decided and was content to plant audio-only devices. When SIU tailed the pair to the pub Digger was elated; his long term investment was going to pay off. As the conversation began the barman commenced his clean-up from the previous night's drinking. He clink-clanked pint glasses together as he picked them up before plonking them on the counter. The hum of the dishwasher kicked in minutes later. Then the barman began vacuuming the carpet.

"Curse a Jaysus on ya," Digger exclaimed, as he threw off the headphones in the back of his command post van. He gingerly retrieved them, and focussed on picking up any of the covert conversation.

Inside the pub, Don Bailey smiled when Nasri broke the news. It was an involuntary reflex, Bailey couldn't control it; he had waited months to hear it.

"The transfer is made," Nasri said. "This is their message."

"What else?"

"They want assurance everything is ready."

"Tell them, yes."

"They want to know if anything has to change."

"No changes. I will give you a rendezvous time to pass to them on Friday."

"This is all?"

"What about down there? Did you see anything sus?"

"A lot of men were working at the main house."

"Were any of them suspicious? Do you think any of them were Law?"

"I don't know. All the men I saw were doing manual labour."

Digger caught snatches of the conversation. When time permitted he would use software back at base to filter out as much of the background noise as possible. It might enable him to write up some kind of intelligible transcript. For the moment, all he knew was that Nasri had brought news of a transfer, which he took to mean money. From the sound of Bailey's voice, he seemed pleased. The rest of their discussion was buried by the clinking sounds of the bar clean-up.

When Nasri left them alone, Bailey's driver powered up a laptop and connected to the Net. Bailey watched Buck, as his fingers danced over the keyboard punching in account numbers and codes. A triumphant thump later, Buck swivelled the laptop and showed him the screen. It confirmed the message the Arab had passed to him. The €500,000 instalment had been delivered to his Isle of Man bank account. It more than recouped Bailey's outlay in clearing the pitch of Slasher Fulton and his old man and the pittance he paid Dempsey for his mercenary services for the other jobs.

His sister, Rachel, was the only human being that meant anything to him; she was family. No matter what happened, he wanted to ensure she would be safe. She had calmed down since the raid on her Temple Bar beauty salon. With action imminent, he mulled over whether he should leave a note explaining what to do when he disappeared to set up base in Marbella. He hoped she would eventually join him there. In the end, he decided against it. His clear instructions to his solicitor were to deliver a letter to her by hand and then arrange to pay her a regular monthly amount.

Digger put video of the rejected pizza deliveries to Khouri's apartment up on separate screens in the cave and played the interaction from beginning to end. Kate sat on a high stool, with Angie alongside, reviewing the footage.

"Play it again," Angie asked.

"Hunch?" Kate asked.

"Not sure."

All three watched both scenes play out before Digger paused it. "Definitely, the same guy, both times," he said.

"It's Andrew fucking Timmons from Special Branch," Angie said, suddenly. "The baseball cap covers most of his face but I'm almost certain that's who we've got."

"O'Driscoll!" Digger exclaimed.

"What?" Kate asked.

"I bet a pound to a penny, he's behind it."

"Why?"

"Timmons and Thompson are his bully boys; a proper

pair of pricks," Digger continued. "The fucker's tryin' to sabotage the case."

"Jesus Christ!" Kate swore.

"Better tell Mac that the idiot is pokin' his big fuckin' snout in where it's not welcome," Digger said.

"If it's put to Timmons, he'll deny it, flat out," Kate replied. "And the footage isn't conclusive."

"So what? You'll say nothing' to Mac?"

"What was the name of the company O'Driscoll bought shares in?" Kate asked. She tapped a finger against her lips a few seconds, then blurted the name Blue Sky Keys.

As Angie googled it, Kate added, "I read that shares in some of the big cloud companies fell, weeks ago. Usually when the big guys sneeze, everyone catches a cold."

"Blue Sky's shares tumbled a fortnight ago," Angie showed them the screen.

"The bastard's trying to protect his investment, checking up that Khouri's still around," Kate said.

"I prefer the sabotage theory," Digger grumbled.

"Alert the crews on Khouri," Kate ordered. "If either of Timmons or Thompson show up again, detain them."

At four o'clock she held a pre-deployment briefing with her two D-Is before Digger's late crew took up duty. Sexton worried about a pattern of unauthorised takings in the city. High-powered cars, two Audi A4s, a 5-series BMW, a Volkswagen Passat, and two Toyotas, one of them a 4x4, had all disappeared around Dublin in the past week and were still outstanding.

"It's hardly a remarkable pattern," Kate replied.

"Not per se, but I've heard that certain cars are being stolen on Don Bailey's order."

"Anything further on the Mooney murder investigation?"

"There's promising CCTV showing some of the route the bike used in the murder took. Forensics have matched the rubber residue scraped off the garage floor to the soles of four possible footwear types."

"Not exactly a breakthrough," Kate said.

Sexton shook his head.

"Did you manage to clean up that recording from the pub?" she asked Digger.

"The barman ruined my chances, the gobshite, clatterin' around the place," he replied. "All I've managed to get was Bailey tellin' Nasri somethin' about no deviation since the last discussion. He said somethin' about Friday that I couldn't catch."

"When was Bailey in Nice?" Kate asked.

"End of April," Digger replied.

"So whatever it is, it's weeks, maybe months, in the planning," Sexton said.

"If there's no change since Nice, they must have something fixed to aim at; what could that be?" Kate asked.

"The Irish Derby next weekend is an annual event that's fixed in the racing calendar," Sexton said. "There will be a lot of betting at that; a serious amount of cash floating around."

"That don't fit," Digger replied. "I mean who are they goin' to knock off? One bookie, two, three? Nah, it's somethin' else."

"Bailey's connected to Nasri," Kate began. "From the pub audio we can deduce that Nasri is conveying messages from someone else to Bailey. If Bailey's talked about a previous discussion, then there's a good chance it's the people he met in Nice. But why use Nasri? Why not communicate direct?"

"I've no idea, Digger replied. "We're getting nothin' of any value from his phones."

"A Nasri connection with the Beirut Sheikh doesn't add up anyway," Kate continued. "They're the opposite sides of the Islamic divide."

"The target's in the horsey world," Sexton said. "That much is obvious. What we need to do is figure out what target is juicy enough for Bailey to put this much effort into. My money's on a kidnapping."

"Then who is he going after?" Kate asked.

"If Nasri's been looking at Ballycleary Stud, isn't there a good chance it could be Vincent Cleary?" Sexton suggested.

"Is he all that wealthy?" Digger asked.

"I don't know," Sexton replied. "But he runs a big operation down there. An awful lot of wealthy owners have horses with him."

"What? Are you saying they might stump up a ransom?" Kate asked.

"It's worth considering," Sexton replied.

Kate gave the go-ahead to strip four from the FBI case. Sexton and Digger left the office to re-deploy their resources as Kate's phone rang.

"You might want to rethink delayin' that tête-à-tête with your Army guys?" Dan Whatney opened without ceremony.

"Give me a reason," Kate replied.

"Somethin's goin' down, we don't know what. We've picked up a ripple that one of the Nasri brothers is missin' from Jeddah these past few weeks."

"Missing? What does that mean exactly?" Kate asked.

"Disappeared, nobody has seen or heard from him for weeks. The Nasri family is big; Jafar's father had several wives. The best guess-timate is that there are eighteen children, fourteen sons."

"Are you picking up anything on the one who's gone missing?"

"We think it's Youssef, the youngest and a favourite. Nobody seems to know anything outside the family circle. And try as we might, we can't penetrate that."

"We've been getting a read on Jafar Nasri, here in Dublin; that he has been out of sorts for the past few weeks. Nobody knows why."

"Anyone interestin' contact him recently?"

"His phones have been dead, just family at home and business calls at work. We covered him meeting Don Bailey, our main target, on two occasions recently."

"No calls from home about Youssef being missin'?"

"Not a single mention."

"He must know, then. Otherwise, his family would be on the phone talkin' about it. Kate, I think you should get that meetin' set up with the Army, pronto. We need to unearth what that ex-soldier brings to the party. He seems to be a key player in all this."

"Leave it with me," she replied.

Kate sensed an opportunity and called Shaw. She was nonplussed when the Lt-Colonel cut her short as she apologised for her recent oversight. Rather than SIU arrange it, she asked Shaw to host an urgent meeting to discuss Dempsey with the CIA's European liaison people.

Next day, Whatney arrived into Dublin airport on the first Paris flight with the US military liaison, Darrell Jackson, in tow. A green Army Lexus picked them up and dropped them to McKee Barracks at the city end of the Phoenix Park. Kate was next door at Mac's Garda HQ office by 8 a.m. She brought him up to speed on overnight developments.

Dempsey had returned to his small flat in Hanratty Gardens after leaving the pub. Bailey's driver had arrived thirty minutes earlier than usual this morning to pick his boss up and both were travelling towards Dublin's north side. Nasri was on his way to work and usually got to the warehouse by eight thirty. Before Kate concluded the brief, Digger's crew confirmed that Nasri had arrived at his business. Another routine day was underway.

Mac and Kate left Garda HQ at nine o'clock and strolled the short distance to McKee Barracks. The sentry at the rear gates pointed them in the direction of the Officers' Mess, where the meeting was set to commence at 9:30 a.m. in the main conference room. They glanced towards a small jumping enclosure just inside the barracks wall. A rider from the Army's Equitation school was putting a show jumper through early morning routines; the animal's grunts and snorts reflecting the effort of clearing the obstacles placed in its path.

"Master stroke this," Mac told Kate, as they walked along the edge of the square. A drill sergeant, about to commence marching practice, called a company to attention. "When we go in, I'll speak first, okay?"

"Whatever you want."

"After I've done the thank-yous, you continue with the rest of the briefing," he continued.

"Fine."

As they stepped into the Officers' Mess foyer, Shaw greeted them.

"Assistant Commissioner; Superintendent, you're both very welcome."

"Thank you," Mac replied.

"Nice digs," Kate remarked.

"Your first time?" Shaw asked.

"Yes."

Kate read the Lt-Colonel's body language. He was chuffed at the opportunity to host high profile visitors. Mac did his gratitude routine and Kate provided a synopsis of what SIU knew about Don Bailey's activities. Dan Whatney gave a potted history of what the CIA had on the two Hezbollah suspects, Aazim Hussein and Musharraf Abousamra. It was sketchy other than confirming that both were closely linked to a Sheikh Nader, a radical Islamic preacher, who was garnering an increasing following in Lebanon. Shaw then outlined what J2 knew about them.

"When made aware of Dempsey's connections," he began, "we pulled all the reports on his tours in Lebanon, right back to his first tour in '89. We can confirm that former Sergeant Dempsey knows these two suspects since they were youngsters. He came across them at Tibnin, at the orphanage there."

"Great work," Whatney interjected.

"Thank you. We're aware now that he knew them quite well," Shaw continued. "Three separate monthly reports from his tour in 1996 mention his coaching football at the orphanage. Here's a photograph taken at the time."

Shaw distributed copies of the photograph to Whatney and Kate.

"Man, this is really impressive," Whatney said, pointing at the print. "There's Hussein and Abousamra as kids."

Kate studied the eager faces of the two youngsters. It was hard to square the innocent grins with their transformation in adult life. Dempsey was down on one knee at the centre of the shot, his hand leaning on a football, surrounded by beaming young faces.

"That picture was taken before the Camp 56 massacre from Israeli shelling," Shaw added. "Along with others who witnessed the events that day, Dempsey suffered stress as a result."

Before he copped the signal from Jackson, his military colleague, not to pursue it, Whatney asked, "What happened there?"

One of Shaw's deputies, Fitzgibbon, replied.

"We were there as part of UNIFIL, the United Nations Force in Lebanon," he began.

Whatney was intrigued; there was no stopping him now. "*You* were there?"

"I led a Battalion Mobile Reserve patrol that day." The meeting listened without interruption as Commandant Fitzgibbon outlined the horrific events of the day.

"Jesus H Christ!" Whatney said. "Do you recall this?" he asked his colleague.

"One of the Twin Towers bombers referenced it as motivation for revenge," Jackson replied.

"Dempsey served only two more overseas tours, including last year," Shaw replied, taking back control of the meeting. "After retirement he got a job with Equus Security; one of our former Commandants, one Walter Dolly owns it."

"Where's that firm based?" Kate asked.

"Somewhere in Kildare, I believe," Shaw replied.

"Have you spoken to him about Dempsey?" Kate asked.

He fixed Kate with a resolute look as he began. "No, Superintendent, I decided that, discretion being the better part of valour, I would consult the stakeholders before making such a move."

She held his stare, "Good, do please steer clear for the moment."

"As you wish."

The remainder of the meeting was taken up with filling

in the blanks on Dempsey's background. He had been a good soldier; did his job and mostly kept his nose clean. His gambling addiction blocked his progress to higher rank. Despite the barrack room brawls it provoked during his Army life, his overall service rating on discharge was 'exemplary'. Neither Whatney nor Jackson added anything further to what the CIA had provided in earlier reports which amounted to confirmation that Hussein and Abousamra were Hezbollah, closely linked to the radical Sheikh Nader.

The meeting concluded at eleven and Shaw invited everyone to coffee in the Officers' Club bar. Kate accepted a china cup with mint tea from an orderly and chatted to one of Shaw's sidekicks near a window that looked out onto the barrack square. The drill sergeant was inspecting two lines of soldiers lined up in guard-of-honour formation.

"Are they preparing for something special?" she asked.

"The Defence Minister is visiting the Equitation school this afternoon with a Saudi prince, who's over for the Derby," he replied.

They watched as the drill sergeant put his soldiers through their paces, before allowing the squad relax in the 'at ease' position. An officer appeared from the other side of the square at the head of a string of six immaculately turned-out horses. He led them across the parade ground and began practicing lining the animals up alongside the guard of honour.

"Those horses are better groomed than a lot of police I know," Kate laughed.

"The minister is schmoozing this guy, wants him to invest some of his oil dollars in the National Stud in Kildare," the officer explained. "Everything has to be top notch when he gets here."

"Rather you than me."

She returned to the meeting room, retrieved her attaché case and touched Whatney's arm.

"Are you free in the afternoon?"

"Sure, Kate," he replied. "Jackson's going down to the Curragh by helicopter to view an Army Ranger Wing exercise. I have to see the RSO; then I'm all yours."

The Regional Security Officer was the principal security officer at all US embassies. The one in Dublin had Irish roots and cemented them by marrying a local girl.

"Tell McCarthy I said hello."

Whatney rang after six, apologised for the delay and enquired if she still had time for a quick face-to-face before he headed to the airport.

"Sure," she replied. "Will you be accompanied?"

"The RSO is gettin' me to the airport," Whatney told her. "I'm linkin' up with Jackson there."

"Good. See you soon."

An hour later, Pete McNally escorted Whatney from his car directly to Kate's office. The Texan pulled up a chair, sat down and looked around.

"Place ain't changed much since Mac's time," he drawled.

"My budget doesn't stretch to a refurb," Kate laughed. "Where's McCarthy?"

"Outside, talkin' to Pete, givin' us a chance to parley," Whatney said. "The Arabs have a sayin' — *not being able to know something is no proof that it don't exist.*"

"Jeez Dan, that sounds profound, coming from you. No offence!"

"None taken. We need to find out what that son-of-a-bitch Nasri is doin' and we think he might be usin' a SAT phone. If he is, can you intercept it?"

"Let's ask Digger. Hold on, I'll see if he's still down in the cave."

She rang the extension and Digger picked up on the first ring. He was about to leave and spend the night at the Nasri OP. He joined Whatney in Kate's office and scoffed at the idea that SIU budgets might cover satellite interception gear.

"Ya'll familiar with the technology?" Whatney asked.

"I got a demonstration at a trade show in Paris once," Digger said. "I can manage it. Why do you ask?"

"Our Director ordered me to pull out the stops," Whatney said. "I gonna make ya an offer—take or leave it." He leaned back in his chair and shouted towards the door, "Yo, McCarthy, get in here."

"You're looking fresh as a daisy," Patrick McCarthy greeted Kate, as he entered.

"Jeez, Pat, flattery—how Irish have you become! Come on in."

He grinned and walked over to a side table, where he set down the heavy device he'd lugged in. It was a dull grey colour and looked like a sound amp with a carrying handle on top. It wouldn't have looked out of place alongside a Grafton Street busker. He unclipped one side and pulled down a keyboard. The attached screen was secured to the main unit: simple, but clever.

"This is a satellite interception system…" he began.

"It's a first, Kate," Whatney interjected. "We've never shared this type of equipment with a partner agency before."

Kate sat back and listened while Digger and McCarthy discussed interleaving and unique audio coding. They moved on to complicated modulation, and from Doppler shifts to frequent inter-beam and inter-satellite handoffs. When they concluded, she breathed out.

"Well, can you operate it?" she asked Digger.

"Of course! The question is do we need it? Sat phones need line of sight to the sky. As far as I'm aware Nasri makes his calls indoors, but I'll recheck that."

"This gear is down to me," McCarthy said to Digger. "Guard it with your life."

"Trust us, Pat. And we won't even ask what you use it for, the rest of the year."

"Better get you to the airport or you'll miss that flight," McCarthy said to Whatney, quickly changing the subject.

Kate smiled and thanked the two Americans for the special consideration. Pete McNally arrived and escorted them to the SIU car park.

"What do you think?" Kate asked Digger.

"I'd love to get a chance to use it. I'll pull down all the photos of Nasri and check them before I switch the feckin' thing on. For now, I'll stash it in the cave."

29

In the late evening Digger sat poring over photographs in the tiny kitchen of the vacant apartment SIU was using as an OP to observe Nasri's house. Usually rented to college students, the universities were closed for summer and he had persuaded the letting company to delay the badly needed redecoration work. He doubted the students got their deposit back. Angie manned the camera pointed directly into Nasri's backyard. A separate mobile unit was based near the front of the house.

Digger spread out the Nasri photos Pete McNally had printed on the kitchen worktop. His instructions were to print only shots of the suspect making phone calls. As he began poring over them, he immediately excluded any indoor calls. He had brought a large circular magnifying glass and began examining the photos for any tantalising clues. There were shots of Nasri at his house and around his business with his mobile glued to his ear. Digger scrutinised each one minutely.

He took a break and cracked open his thermos of

coffee. He whispered to Angie, asking if she fancied a brew but she declined. He stood up, stretched, and glanced at the ceiling. It had once been painted a magnolia colour, just like every other room in the place. Now it was pock-marked with brown stains. Digger figured that wet teabag fights were the least robust activity the previous tenants got up to during their stay. Stud partition walls had also been punctured.

He massaged his lower back before resuming his scrutiny and moving on to six shots of Nasri in the small court-yard at the rear of his house. In the first one Nasri was staring intently at the mobile in his hand and dialling a number. The next shot in the sequence showed Nasri raising the phone to his ear and Digger had his moment of revelation.

"Watson, get in here."

Angie appeared at the kitchen door.

"What?" she asked.

Digger held up the circular magnifier.

"A little bit Sherlock, don't you think?"

"Come on, what do you want?"

"Look at these two photographs," he told her. "Do you see anythin' different?"

Angie picked up the prints and studied both.

"Use the magnifier, if you like."

"I don't need it. One mobile has a red front and the one he's using at the rear of his house is copper-coloured. You can switch around those covers, you know that."

"Would Nasri strike you as someone who'd bother?"

"No, but his wife or kids might," Angie replied.

"Kids are too young," Digger said. "Any thoughts on the size or shape of the two phones?"

"They look the same to me."

"I think they're different phones. There's something I need to check."

When Digger re-examined the Nasri prints, there was one consistent feature. In all the courtyard phone calls, Nasri always used the phone with the cooper-coloured front. Worth noting was that soon after two of these court-yard calls, Nasri met Don Bailey. Digger was convinced it had to be a Sat phone. When he returned to base at the end of the night shift, he extracted the satellite interception system from the cave and gave Pete McNally a crash course on how to operate it. He talked to Kate about the legal side of intercepting satellite calls. She said she wasn't sure but didn't want to get mired down with Justice Department officials discussing the semantics of what could essentially turn into a trawling exercise.

"Nobody outside the unit knows we have this equip-ment," she told him. "Let's keep it that way and get the stuff back to the RSO before anyone asks."

Before the shift ended Nasri had, as usual, been housed in the office at the rear of his warehouse. Digger briefed Kate on his night's work before heading home to catch up with his children before they left for school.

Sexton coordinated the daytime coverage on Bailey and juggled crews to cover all bases. In his Thursday evening briefing, he emphasised the uptick in Bailey's activity. He had met the new leader of the northside gang on four occasions in three days. The SIU phone intercepts were patchy and grabbed routine intel only. The detectives monitoring the channels detected a mood change in some gang members, a tantalising indicator of imminent action.

Sexton's mother rang him in the afternoon. She had been the strong one in his family. While his father believed most people had a spark of decency, his mother's world-view was more nuanced. She steered her children clear of troublemakers but, never turned away anyone who needed help. Most other mothers in Oliver Bond flats liked her.

"Hi Ma, what's up?" he greeted her.

"Nothin' son, I'm passin' on a message, that's all."

"What message? From who?"

"Doesn't matter who. A car you might be interested in is in a lock-up in Walkinstown."

"Ma, who told you this? I need to know."

Despite Sexton attempts, his mother steadfastly refused to say where the information had come from. She gave him the address and told him she would see him and the family for Sunday dinner as usual. He knew her source was someone in the flats but even working back through the approaches he had made, there was no way of verifying the origin. He had to check it out. Sexton didn't know the Walkinstown area very well but was aware that most of the lock-up garages at the rear of houses were only accessible through cul-de-sac laneways. Checking them unnoticed, would be tricky. He brought his dilemma to his boss.

"Watch the place for the rest of the day," Kate told him. "Digger can take a closer look in the early hours and figure out if it's safe to enter."

At 3:30 next morning, Angie and Digger entered the laneway by scaling the wall from the adjoining convent grounds. They were dressed entirely in black, including balaclavas. Earlier crews had noted the activity in the surrounding houses throughout the afternoon. It was a residential area and by midnight most houses were in darkness. Digger insisted on waiting until after 3:00 a.m. when the chances were that most people would be sleeping deeply. He knew that anyone roused at that hour would take time to adjust. Should they be caught out by an alarm, that vital period of grogginess and disorientation for anyone seeing them increased their chances of a clean exit.

The day crews had passed details of the lock on the shed and told him there were no signs of alarm wiring. Digger and Angie skirted along the walls, stopping at intervals, waiting and listening. When Digger reached the shed he quickly unclipped a set of lock picks and got to work on the security padlock. It was a 70 mm brass block lock with a pin tumbler locking mechanism. Digger picked it in ten seconds flat and carefully slid it off the handle. Angie rubbed oil on the door hinges to kill squeaks and placed a micro camera on the wall to cover the blind end of the laneway before giving Digger a thumbs-up. He tentatively pulled the door open and held his breath; the peaceful night remained undisturbed.

He returned Angie's all-clear signal. She gingerly stepped out of the alley and kept watch through a crack in the door while Digger worked on the blue Audi A4. After ten torturous minutes, he slid out from underneath the car, stood up and whispered into his radio.

"Test transmission in 5, 4, 3, 2, 1."

"Contact confirmed," he was informed. "Signal strength excellent."

"Let's make like a shepherd," he grinned at Angie.

"Getting the flock outta here can't happen quickly enough."

While Angie retrieved her camera, Digger carefully

replaced the lock on the garage door. They retreated silently back over the convent wall and as they reached the playing field, removed their balaclavas. The night-time action prompted an adrenaline surge and the pair jogged lightly to the pickup point.

On Friday morning at Kate's office, Sexton paced the floor impatiently. When she returned from the management meeting, she smiled at him. The early morning news had been all positive; locating the stolen car and fitting the tracking beacon were welcome breakthroughs.

"More good news, I hope."

"I'm afraid not," he replied.

"Let's grab a coffee, actually make mine an OJ," she said, dumping files on her desk and returning towards the squad room.

Sexton delivered the news briskly as they walked down the corridor.

"Something's on today. This morning at eight o'clock, Bailey's driver called to pick him as usual. Or so we thought. He came out of the house wearing a hoodie, as he has been doing all this week, and jumped in the car. Kept the hood up, even in the car."

"That wouldn't be so unusual, would it?"

"No, par for the course. At 9:40 they parked up and went into a house on the north side and stayed there for half an hour. As they exited, one of my lads copped that the way Bailey walked appeared different."

"So, what happened?"

"They got the Traffic Corps to do a stop and confirmed that it wasn't Bailey."

"What else?" Kate asked as she opened the bottle of orange juice and poured it into a glass.

"Are you on a health kick?"

"Who are you, my mother? What else is going on?"

"Looks like the gang has dumped all their phones."

"All of them?"

"Every single one; we're intercepting six and they've been dead since eleven o'clock last night. Not pinging off any mast, anywhere."

"Okay! First, stay on those phones, they might reactivate. Second, I need precise reports — what we know about whom. The whole gang can't have just upped and vanished."

"Okay boss, I'm on it."

By midday, the picture was clearer. The only member of Bailey's gang still in circulation was Gerry Buck, his driver. Kate was annoyed that even Dempsey could not be accounted for. He had returned early from the pub the previous night to his flat in Hanratty Gardens. The SIU duty sergeant was forced to pull his crew out of the area when a street brawl erupted between rival gangs. It sucked in patrol cars from both sides of Dublin to quell it. The mood in the flats was still tense this morning making it difficult to approach without attracting attention.

Kate returned to her office and rang Digger's home number. Jane answered.

"Hi," Kate said. "How are you?"

"Fine, fine," she replied. "How about yourself?"

"I'm good, Jane. Busy, as I'm sure you're aware. Is he awake yet?"

"I heard him stirring a while ago. He had another call, hold on, I'll get him."

Kate quickly updated Digger on the overnight developments. "Everyone's gone AWOL, even Dempsey," Kate told him.

"I know where he might be," Digger replied.

"Where?"

"My gun club mate tells me he's workin' with Dempsey at Ballycleary Stud, tonight and tomorrow night."

"What do you think?"

"Vincent Cleary's not a big enough kidnap target," Digger replied. "At least, I don't think he is."

"Then, what the hell's going on?"

"If Bailey's openin' a new drugs pipeline from Lebanon, maybe it's connected to that. Usin' horses to smuggle drugs into the country, maybe?"

"Doesn't explain the enquiries Hussein and Abousamra made about executive jet hire in Nice. Can you get in here soon?"

"On my way."

Early the same morning, Captain Dick Saunders dropped his teenage son and daughter to their international school and headed back to the little village where the family had settled. They loved Gorbio, their adopted village, perched high in the hills behind Nice. The American had worked for Côte d'Azur Charters for three years. Trained as a combat pilot with the US Navy, he had served in every war the US had involved itself in since the nineties. When he retired at forty-four, he wanted two things; to continue flying and live outside the States for a while. When the offer of a job, based in Nice came up, he felt he'd hit the jackpot. He loved the south of France and the work was straightforward, once you were flexible.

There were forty-two nationalities at his kids' school

but the teacher-student ratio was one to twelve. The location at the edge of a pine forest made it as close to ideal as high school can get. Pleased that his kids settled in quickly, Saunders was stretched to get enough work to cough up the hefty quarterly fees.

After dropping them off, he returned home and treated his wife to breakfast at their local café. They were enjoying coffee refills and chatting with the husband and wife owners when the airline's admin office pitched him a quickie flight to Dublin. His wife groaned.

"We're taking the kids to Gerona tomorrow and that's over five hours' driving. Will you be up to it after flying?"

"Piece a cake, hon," Saunders assured his wife. "Dublin's just a short hop."

"Well, if you really think so."

"We've got school fees coming up next month and I'll be home before you notice I'm gone."

"I'm going to stay and chat to Arlette. She's helping me with my French."

"Okay, hon, I'll grab my bag. See you in the A.M.," he said, planting a kiss on her forehead.

———

As Saunders zipped closed his travel bag, Bailey was settling into a chair at a café over the river from his sister's beauty salon. He had cycled to the hook-up on a blue Dublin rent-a-bike and dumped it at a nearby stand. He sipped coffee and listened while Rachel talked non-stop. Bailey actually liked that about her. Most of it was inane chatter about the customers she had in the shop during the week, but it lightened his mood. Although confident that the diversion he set up had worked, he would keep checking as he headed to his next destination on a Dublin bus.

As the score drew closer, he grew less anxious. The chances of a tout letting something slip diminished as each day went by. He half-listened as Rachel talked about a fat American customer who left a miserable tip, despite receiving extra care and attention. His thoughts drifted towards how his life was about to change. The end was in sight; in the next few hours, the action he would carefully choreograph would transform his future.

When Saunders arrived at Côte d'Azur airport in Nice he was informed that the client had been delayed and that the flight would not be leaving until late evening. He was livid. Now midday, with holiday traffic his home was an hour and a half drive away. He fished a coin out from his right trouser pocket; an Eisenhower silver dollar. He never flew without it since his Dad gave it to him the day he received his wings. The bemused French admin staff watched as he tossed it high in the air. He caught it and flipped it onto the back of his hand. The outcome would decide whether he stuck with his decision to take the charter. Ike's profile headshot stared back.

"Nuts!" he exclaimed. "I go."

"Do you want to log the flight plan?" the manager asked.

"Later, call the maintenance supervisor first. I want to find out what I'm flying."

The supervisor drove him to the largest hangar the company operated and stopped in front of a white Gulf-stream. Saunders did a walk-about inspection. He had flown this bird before; she was reliable. The supervisor told him that during its recent annual service, they had sorted out a hydraulics problem which might have slowed the landing gear's deployment. Nothing else out of the ordinary had shown up. Saunders agreed with the maintenance supervisor to go with 70 percent fuel fill. The Gulfstream had a range of 2,900 nautical miles and the Dublin flight would be a round-trip just shy of 1,600.

Saunders returned to the admin office and logged the flight plan. Given its ad-hoc rather than recurrent nature, it might have proved sticky, but the new flight time simplified matters. He logged the aircraft type, registration number, call sign, number of passengers and cruising altitude into the system, along with the remainder of the obligatory information. He asked the manager for a departure time and scowled when he was told close to midnight. Saunders continued filing the flight details, aware that he would likely get direct clearance to climb to 37,000 feet shortly after take-off. Usually, air traffic controllers authorise such flights to climb incrementally. Tonight, he should attain cruising altitude within fifteen minutes. He expected the flight would have direct clearance all the way which would save time and fuel. After reaching cruising altitude the plan would be to cross the Massif Centrale that dissected central France and keep west of Paris before hitting the coast. Then a short hop would take them across the English Channel and by the time the Welsh coastline came into view, he would already have commenced his descent into Dublin.

"Who am I carrying?" Saunders asked.

The manager looked at his screen and told him that he would have three Jordanian businessmen going out and that he would pick up an extra passenger in Dublin for the return leg.

"I'm going to eat now," Saunders said. "You need to get me a hotel room, I've got to rest a few hours."

"This room, it comes from your payment," the manager told him.

"D'ya' think so, buddy? You knew hours ago that the flight was going to be delayed but you chose not to call me, in case I bailed."

"This is not true."

"It is and you know it. Now get me that room."

30

By late Friday afternoon Don Bailey knew there was nothing to do other than wait for darkness. He glanced around the empty warehouse and contemplated the breadth of what he was about to achieve. The Ford Transit they would use to transport their quarry was set up as he had instructed. A long chain hooked under one of the van's bench seats was connected to a set of open handcuffs. The cars needed to block off roads from any law they might encounter were ready to be deployed.

For long stretches since their first meeting, he had felt hemmed in by the Arabs. They had laid the groundwork well to ensure they got what they wanted. Fair play, he thought, but now he was totally in control. He turned the phone Nasri had supplied over in his hand. The instructions that came with it were not to operate it for longer than ten minutes and to avoid using it from the same position more than once.

Bailey would play navigator for the van driver. He had rehearsed the route and knew every turn and twist to take on the road. The heat of the past few weeks had made doing it a nightmare, but he had been patient. Over the weeks of constant surveillance, he had managed to slip out of the house between three and four o'clock on five separate mornings, without being seen or followed. He had driven the route and tested alternatives. He was 100 percent confident of his end. Timing was critical; until darkness, nobody moved, this was his order. He felt confident that the northside gang would follow it. He prayed Lockhart would do the same.

When Kate received a call from agent handler, Gerry Grealy, at six o'clock she wasn't especially surprised. It was his favourite time to ring and make a late appointment to drop in before heading to the pub on his way home. She had ordered a full unit recall and a frantic, covert search was underway to locate Bailey's gang.

"Can I call in to see you," Grealy asked.

"We're flat out here, Gerry, to be honest," Kate replied.

"I don't like talking on the phone."

"We're going to have to trust it."

"Okay then. You know our mutual friend?" Grealy began, in thinly disguised code. "Well, he told me that he dropped off a phone from his boss to someone you know quite well."

"I understand," Kate replied. "It would be great to have that number."

Grealy read it out.

"That sounds very long. Is it the IMEI?"

"No, our mutual friend said, IMSI."

Grealy explained how the phone had been switched off when the agent received it but the PIN was written on a scrap of paper and stuck to the rear. Before delivering it, the agent had powered it up and noted information he figured could be useful. His initiative earned him another bonus. The address where he dropped it off was the home of one of Bailey's myriad associates. Kate checked the surveillance log and confirmed that Bailey's driver had called to the same address late the previous evening. She thanked Grealy, told him they had an ongoing operation, and asked him to stay alert for anything that could be connected to it.

Pete McNally was immediately animated when she told him about Grealy's intel.

"That's it!" he exclaimed.

"What?"

"IMSI means International Mobile Subscriber Identity. This is the Sat phone Nasri's been using. We need more information about it."

"I'll talk to Whatney."

Kate needed to fill the yawning gaps in their intel. Being confined indoors was driving her crazy and she needed out. Hours earlier, she deployed Digger with a crew of three to Ballycleary Stud. They decided to hold off on a direct approach to Vincent Cleary until they had more information. She analysed her resources and stripped back the FBI case to minimum coverage for a number of hours until they located and neutralised Bailey's gang. At five she rang Shaw in J2 and heard glasses clink in the background. He explained they were having a send-off for an officer heading to the Golan Heights on a UN observer mission. She apologised for the interruption and told him she needed a contact number for Equus Security. Shaw offered to ring his former colleague. She thanked him but said it was best to leave it her.

"Remind me of his name again," Kate asked.

"Walter Dolly," Shaw replied. "Everyone calls him Wally."

Wally Dolly must have had fun growing up, she thought.

With Pete McNally designated to man comms at SIU, Kate jumped in her car and headed for the M7. She rang Digger en route.

"What's happening down there?"

"The place is a hive of activity," he replied. "It looks like they're expectin' a crowd tonight."

"How have you deployed?"

"We're staying mobile for the moment. Has Sexton raised any of Bailey's gang?"

"Nothing yet, it's a game of hide and seek. I'm impressed that Bailey has managed to do this in Dublin."

"He can't stay hidden forever," Digger said, then added, "I'd like to take a closer look around Ballycleary House."

"Shaw's given me the number of the security guy. I'm dropping down to meet him. Maybe he could arrange it?"

"Is that a good idea? There's a lot happening in Dublin."

"I'm climbing the walls, can't think straight."

Digger laughed. "Before I go, what's the story with Khouri? Are you keepin' cover on him?"

"Of course," Kate replied.

"Mmm!"

"What aren't you telling me?" Kate asked.

"Look, don't jump down my neck."

"Go on."

"I got a name for the security manager where Khouri works. He's ex-Special Branch and he did a discreet enquiry for me. He says that Rafiq Khouri's job is to test the companies' systems for robustness against cyber-attack. The company gives him latitude to use their servers to access ISIS sites so that he can look at the software behind them."

Kate was flabbergasted. "Jesus, Digger, making that approach wasn't your call."

"Don't you see? We've wasted weeks tailin' someone who's just doin' their job. We need everyone tonight. O'Neill's messin' us around; the FBI case is shite."

"We don't know that for certain," she replied.

A palpable silence filled the car as Kate hurtled her BMW down the M7's fast lane.

"Call me when you get close," Digger finally relented, and gave her coordinates to punch into her Sat Nav for where to meet up.

Kate was exasperated. The pressure of the last few weeks was rupturing the cohesion she expected from her teams. When she called the number Shaw had supplied, Dolly sounded flustered.

"Yes!" he shouted into the phone.

"Is that Mr. Dolly?" Kate asked.

"Who's asking?"

Kate hesitated, not wanting to spook someone, whose reaction was uncertain. She decided on a ruse.

"Detective Superintendent Kate Bowen here, sir, from the Garda Protection Unit. We're guarding President Higgins tomorrow at the Derby and doing a sweep of the area this evening. Ballycleary Stud is where your company is working over the weekend, is that correct?"

"Yes. What do you mean by a sweep?"

"Just a threat analysis exercise, sir. It won't take too long."

"Look I am up to my tits here. We're expecting a VIP in the next hour; can't this wait?"

"I can be with you in half an hour, sir. Then I can cross you off my list."

Kate picked up Angie en route and thirty minutes later, they drove slowly down the stately avenue of Ballycleary House. The place looked magnificent. The freshly mown grass glistened emerald green in early evening sunshine. Flower beds in full summer bloom provided a riot of colour as the avenue opened onto the gravelled driveway at the front of the house. Before reaching it they were diverted to the visitor parking area where a short tubby man with a flushed red face stood waiting beside a white Toyota SUV.

"Are you the protection detectives?" he asked.

"Kate Bowen," Kate said, showing her ID. "This is Angie."

"Walter Dolly," he replied, shaking hands with them both. "What do you need to know?"

Kate and Angie decided to stick to basic enquiries. Kate requested a layout plan of the house and grounds, which Dolly supplied immediately. Angie enquired about the number of guests coming to the evening reception. There were over a hundred people expected. While Dolly glanced around continuously, she ran through a list of questions that she and Kate had concocted. By the time they were ready to leave, Kate was aware that the security men's main job was to guard the yards where the bloodstock was housed. A monitoring base was set up in one of the boxes close to a yard exit and there would be a mobile patrol in the fields, twice or three times during the night. When concluded, she thanked him for his cooperation.

"By the way," she asked, "who's your VIP?"

"His Highness Sheikh Muhammad Bin Salah Al-Naqeeb of Saudi Arabia," Dolly replied.

"And who's he, when he's at home?" Angie jested.

"A prince from the Saudi Royal Family and a big wheel

in OPEC, I'm told," Dolly replied. "Mr. Cleary trains all his horses here at Ballycleary."

Kate remembered the expected guest at the Army barracks the previous day and wondered if they might be the same person. She deferred putting the question to Dolly in case it piqued his curiosity.

"You've a nice evening for it, at least," Kate said, as she headed for her car.

"There's heavy rain due overnight. The going for the Derby is expected soft to yielding."

Back in the command post, Kate swallowed two iron supplement pills Doctor Sheridan had prescribed, and washed them down with a bottle of water from her shoulder bag. She also downed the folic acid tablets the GP insisted she take for the first twelve weeks of her pregnancy. Digger had badged a security patrol in an industrial estate, close to Newbridge town and found parking for Kate's car in a small garage. As she screwed tight the lid on her water bottle, she took in the command post's cramped confines and unventilated odour. She smiled and savoured the feeling of being back where she belonged.

"Want a coffee?" Digger asked, as he examined the layout map.

"Naw, I'm good with water," she replied. She parked her annoyance at Digger's unauthorised Khouri case enquiry and focused on what lay immediately ahead.

Her mobile rang as Digger's phone vibrated a text alert simultaneously.

"The car with the tracker is moving," Sexton told her.

"Tell the crew to stay well back and keep me posted," Kate told him, a beep alerting her to another incoming call.

"Action," Digger smiled.

"Hi Gerry," Kate chirped. "Didn't expect to hear from you so soon."

The agent handler's message kicked off a frenzy of activity. Grealy told her that his agent had been ordered to drive to Nasri's warehouse, open it up and switch off the alarm. His orders were to roll down the shutter at the front, but leave it unlocked. Nasri told him to find somewhere nearby where he could stay out of the sight and await orders.

"He was told to turn off the CCTV," Grealy said. "But I told him to just turn the monitor in Nasri's office off and leave the system recording. You never know, we might get away with it."

On Kate's order, Sexton immediately deployed units into the streets around Nasri's warehouse. An hour after Grealy's call, a dark blue Ford Mondeo arrived, most of its registration plate covered in mud, obscuring all the letters and some numbers. Jack Lockhart, the dissident IRA suspect was in the passenger seat. From the partial registration details, Sexton identified that the vehicle belonged to an IRA sympathiser from Kilkenny.

"Has to be weapons," Kate said. "Bailey's gang is tooling up."

She rang Twomey and told him she needed an ERU team on standby.

"We're stretched, Kate," he told her. "We've the British Prime Minister coming in tomorrow morning for the Derby and we're preparing for that. We're also providing protection to a Saudi guy at the moment."

Justice Department officials frequently requested the ERU for close protection work on high-profile visitors. It was the kind of suit-and-tie duty that Twomey's men didn't much relish.

"Can you get a unit into Harold's Cross for the next

few hours?" Kate asked. She told him they would likely be confronting a mixed IRA, criminal gang with an unknown quantity of weapons.

"I could pull my night crew in early," he replied.

"Great!" Kate replied. "Let me know when you're in place."

She briefed Mac.

"Has anything shown up at the stud farm?" he asked.

"Nothing so far; I'm in the neighbourhood with Digger plus three. Dempsey's working security at Ballycleary over the weekend. It doesn't mean necessarily that the action will be there, but it's worrying."

"Since you're close by, why not approach the owner and talk to him?"

"I don't want to raise undue concern. I've talked to his security and have a picture of their deployment."

"Adequate?"

"Not to repel any kind of determined attack."

"Keep me posted."

Kate re-evaluated her resources. She stripped a crew of four from the Khouri job and allocated them to Sexton at Nasri's warehouse. The FBI case was down to bare bones. She was taking a chance, but felt she had little choice, given the circumstances. O'Neill's reticence of late irked her—her trust evidently erroneous.

"Dempsey's the joker in the pack," she said to Digger. "We need to figure out if he has anything going on? Have you sighted him?"

"Not yet. We've done a few drive-bys and when dusk sets in, myself and Angie will get close to the house. We'll watch and see if we can find out if he's up to anything."

"When you're in place, I'll allocate the newbies, front and rear. Until then, they stay mobile — ten minute sitreps."

Digger nodded. As Angie drove slowly, heading on another drive-by, a quick glance out the rear window told Kate rain wasn't far off, the evening sky was darkening rapidly.

She called Twomey. He was distracted with the British PM's advance protection team carrying out on-site checks and reviewing security arrangements for the visit. It was due to start early on Saturday morning and included a trip to the Curragh to see Ireland's richest horse race.

"Is the Saudi guy you're looking after called Sheikh Muhammad Bin Salah Al-Naqeeb?"

"That's him. He's been to Goffs and the National Stud with the Defence Minister today. Oh, I just got word, my guys are in place at Harold's Cross. Sexton's the on-scene commander."

"Perfect; chat later."

While frantic covert police activity played out around them the citizens of Dublin went about their usual Friday evening business. John Kilkenny had started coaching junior soccer before his own playing days ended. His current under-10 team was showing well in competition. The soccer coach glanced over his shoulder as he replaced the padlock on the forty foot container that served as their dressing room. All the youngsters had been collected and he figured the approaching car had taken a wrong turn. As the passenger window wound down, he saw a hooded figure staring at him. Before he could react, the thug leapt out and opened the back door of the car.

"Don't make a fuss, John, get in," he said, menacingly.

"How do you know…?" Kilkenny protested.

"Just get in the fuckin' car," he ordered, eyes darting left and right.

As he slumped into the back seat, another hooded man stuck a revolver into Kilkenny's side. His captor leaned over from the front and spoke to him in a calm, calculating voice. "We know you've a young lad at home, his mother's with him and he's asleep. Do as we say and no one will get hurt. Do anything stupid and ye'll all suffer. Are we clear?"

Kilkenny nodded.

"Number four will stay with Gertie, til we're done."

"I'm not a bank manager," Kilkenny said. "I'm a flying instructor. I think you've made a mistake."

"No mistake," the thug replied.

In a nearby housing estate, number four settled into a brown leather armchair as Gertie Kilkenny sat motionless in the chair opposite.

"Stick on the telly," he said in a thick Dublin accent. "It's goin' to be a long night."

31

Bailey startled when the phone sitting on the dashboard squawked into life, like an activated alarm. He grabbed it, silenced its strident ringtone, and answered. The charged up, pay-as-you-go unit had been purchased the previous day by his driver. He recognised the incoming number; his sister's shop. He had given her the number when they met for coffee earlier. He didn't welcome the distraction, not this evening.

"Jaysus, you're hard to get hold of," she said.

"Rachel, what's up?" Bailey replied. "I told you this number was for emergencies only."

"No one's answerin' any of the other bleedin' ones."

"Okay, look sorry for barking at you. Do you need something?"

"No, I'm just passin' on a message is all. Your friend, Jack, rang the shop just before we closed and asked me to tell ya that he's waitin' to see ya."

Bailey's stomach churned but he remained calm. "Was he a country sounding fella?"

"Yeah, definitely a culchie, like," Rachel laughed. "I'll text ya his number."

"Fair play, Rachel, thanks."

"I'm all closed up now," she told him. "D'ya fancy goin' for a drink or somethin' later?"

"Maybe another night, Sis, okay?"

"Is everythin' alright? Ya sound different."

"Everything's coolio. Better go ring this muck savage."

Rachel laughed and told her brother she would call him on Sunday afternoon. Bailey rang Lockhart immediately.

"What da fuck you at ringing my sister?"

"Nobody else is answering," Lockhart replied. "I know where she has the place, it was my only option."

"What's your story?"

"We're in position for the last hour."

"The last hour? You were told nothing moves til dark."

"You have your timetable and we've ours," Lockhart replied.

"It will be dark in another hour. Stay put 'til then."

"Remember who calls the shots, Mr. Bailey. We don't take orders, we give them. Maybe the people coming in to meet you later tonight would prefer to do business with us."

Bailey's head buzzed, he struggled not to shout. Apart from Lockhart using his name on an open line, he clearly knew something of his plans. Someone had talked. Had he been double-crossed? Had the northside gang struck a side deal? It was too late to change anything now; he had no choice but to stay put.

"If you want to live to see tomorrow, do as we agreed," he warned Lockhart.

"We're leaving here at midnight."

"If you leave before meeting my lads; I'll put a bullet in your head. That's a promise, not a threat."

Lockhart didn't reply, but hung up. Bailey threw the phone into the glove box, jumped out, and violently kicked the front wheel of the van.

"Dopey bastard!" he swore under his breath. "He's fucking dead!"

The industrial estate where he was holed up was patrolled by private security and he needed to stay out of sight. There was nothing to do but wait. He had ordered no contact until the first weapons were picked up. Using clean mobiles, each crew would then report to him that they were underway. The northside gang had two cars already tooled up from their own weapons stash: two sawn-offs, a Glock 19 machine pistol, and a .357 Magnum revolver. They were waiting on Bailey's instructions.

Kate couldn't understand why nothing was moving at Nasri's warehouse; undoubtedly the location for a weapons handover. Sexton had entry and exit points to the small industrial estate under observation for hours. By late Friday evening nothing suspicious had come or gone. The beaconed car had crossed the city; the SIU tracking vehicle stalking it all the way. It identified a stop made at a north-side gang member's house. The tracking crew followed orders and stayed well back, so they had no idea what transpired at the address. Its current location was on the north side of the city and it looked likely it was headed towards the M50 ring road.

At Ballycleary Digger and Angie had set up OPs either side of the main house by the time the VIP arrived. Kate manned the command post on her own leaving the newbies as a mobile backup, on standby close to the stud. Digger uploaded photos he snapped of the prince stepping out of a black Mercedes onto the broad sweep of gravel at the front of Ballycleary House. Kate noted the prince's jet black, immaculately groomed hair. He wore a light grey two-piece suit, a sky blue shirt, and a grey silk tie. No doubt the work of a private tailor, the suit sat perfectly on the prince's narrow frame. Kate had checked out online photos of him in Arab robes which made him appear taller. The bodyguard who opened the rear passenger door was a head taller than him and Kate estimated he was over six foot.

A second bodyguard appeared and raised an umbrella as Vincent Cleary descended the porticoed entrance steps before greeting the prince with a firm handshake. Digger's final photo showed a beaming Cleary directing the prince towards the house. He confirmed that the ERU detectives on protection duty had parked on the yard side of the main house. Kate was wary of Dempsey spotting any contact between Digger and the crew, so she decided to keep their operations running separately. The detectives were aware SIU colleagues were somewhere in the neighbourhood, but from experience they knew not to seek details.

Angie had reported sightings of Dempsey as he patrolled the yards. Everything appeared in order as rain began to cascade down. The two experienced surveillance officers were prepared for the bad weather and wore waterproof jackets and leggings in summer camouflage colours of dark green and brown. While Angie watched the yards, Digger's position gave him a view of the dining rooms and lounges. The main house was a hub of light and noise. Digger observed waiters moving between rooms with trays of canapés and drinks. He dug an energy bar out of a rucksack and tucked in.

The armed Garda presence at the house alarmed Bailey when Dempsey informed him of it. In a quandary as to how best to deal with it he asked for advice.

"They're just sitting in their car at the side of the house," Dempsey replied. "It's pissin' down rain here, I don't think they're goin' to budge. Do it right and ye'll disarm them, no bother."

"We'll just shoot the cunts," Bailey replied.

"No, that'll alert the house. Gettin' to the main man after that would be near impossible. Without him, no payday."

"Either way," Bailey came back, "I'm not calling anything off."

He was relieved when the first crew Lockhart armed, checked in at eleven. The thunderous rain on the galvanised roof of the warehouse had been driving him mental. The northside crews were mobile; one had grabbed the body they would need for later. Two calls to go, then he could quit this place. Bailey walked to a loading bay at the rear, activated the SAT phone and dialled the number supplied.

Kate was relieved when Sexton told her that a car had arrived at the front of Nasri's warehouse and driven in when the rolling door was lifted. She had barely hung up when Pete McNally rang, his voice urgent.

"Listen to this," he said. "Hot off the presses."

Pete hunched over the satellite interception system keyboard and pressed play on the recorded conversation of Bailey and another voice speaking in halting English. Kate figured the accent for Middle Eastern. The call had already been converted to text and Pete e-mailed a copy. She scanned the transcript on the command post laptop as she listened to Bailey begin the conversation.

Caller 1: We will be ready in under two hours. Will you accept delivery?

Caller 2: Yes, transport is on the way.

Caller 1: Good. Payment is on delivery.

Caller 2: We know this.

Caller 1: Fine. Will I see you or the other one?

Caller 2: Insh'Allah, both of us, my friend.

Caller 1: Next call will be five minutes before hand over. Be ready.

Caller 2: We will.

Call ends.

"Mac's here," McNally told Kate.

"Put him on."

"Where are we at?" he asked.

She briefed him on what they knew. The first car with two of Bailey's mob on board departed Nasri's warehouse within minutes of arriving. At 11:30 p.m. Sexton reported another car driving in and departing five minutes later. Both were followed at 12:12 a.m. by Lockhart and his IRA buddy who headed for the M7 motorway.

"Do you think they're headed in your direction?" Mac asked.

"Can't be sure. It's awfully quiet around here since the reception ended. Can you talk to Grealy and see if any CCTV recorded at Nasri's.?"

"Will do," Mac replied. "I'll let you know."

Mac called back inside five minutes.

"The agent is too scared to go near Nasri's place."

Kate mulled over the dilemma. It was pointless pushing Grealy into a corner and risk exposing his agent.

"Get a warrant and do a covert search of the place before you get Nasri involved," she advised.

A hasty phone call to the on-call judge's court secured it. Although taken aback by an Assistant Commissioner showing up in his court to swear an information for a routine search warrant, he didn't delve into the case background. Pete McNally raced towards the warehouse and when Mac called him to confirm they were legal, he headed straight to Nasri's office, and gingerly turned on the monitor. He pressed play and video of Lockhart checking weapons before handing them over to Bailey's gang flickered onto the screen. The images would be a slam dunk against the stars of the show. Meantime, the gang would have to be confronted and disarmed. Pete removed the DVD, turned everything off and informed Mac and Kate as he drove back to base.

Mac arranged for a uniform patrol call to bring Nasri to his unsecured warehouse. On finding the CCTV system turned off, he cursed his incompetent staff for forgetting to activate it and for leaving his business exposed. The uniforms noted Nasri's statements word for word and thanked him for his cooperation.

Kate informed Digger.

"Lockhart's armed them, two AK47s, a pistol, and a submachine gun."

"Anything further on what they're goin' after?"

"Bailey's spoken to a foreigner on the Sat phone and they expect to link up later."

"The Arabs?"

"Sounds like. We've no sighting of Bailey. As far as we know, he's still in Dublin."

"The Arabs are on the way?"

"Seemed like that."

"Maybe it's a drugs drop. A first run."

"Sexton says the gang is heading south, this direction. I'm calling it as a kidnapping and the prince is the target. I'll get a contact number from Twomey for the ERU protection detail. We're going to need them."

As Kate signed off, Dan Whatney's number flashed up and she answered instantly.

"Hi Dan, make it fast."

Whatney laid out what he had heard from their Beirut station. The station chief had flashed a message to CIA stations worldwide. Intelligence from a credible source indicated that Hezbollah had advanced plans to kidnap a prince from the Saudi Royal family.

"Nasri's younger brother was a bargaining chip," Kate said quickly.

"Exactly," Whatney replied. "Oh, before I go; have you heard anything about the French operation tonight down in Nice?"

An urgent radio message from Digger interrupted.

"Dan, the shit's hitting the fan here. Got to go. Call Mac and tell him about that French op."

"Did you order the ERU escort to leave?" Digger demanded.

"Negative."

"A few minutes ago one of the prince's bodyguards came out and gave them a thumbs-up. They've just started up and sailed out the front gates."

"Oh shit, Whatney got me before I could call Twomey. The prince is definitely the target. I'm deploying Joanie and Becky to front and rear of the house and I'm getting closer myself."

Kate delivered the orders rapid fire and told the

newbies to report when they were in position. She climbed awkwardly from the rear of the command post van into the front seat and started the engine.

Sexton informed Kate that Jack Lockhart's car had veered off the M7 at junction 11 onto the M9. Kate ordered him to stay on Bailey's cars. He told her the beaconed car had stopped moving, within striking distance of Ballycleary Stud. Kate found a field entrance and parked up. She was less than a kilometre from the stud.

"Bailey's going after a VIP at Ballycleary and we're thin on the ground. Meet me here, ASAP," she said giving him the Sat Nav coordinates.

Twomey was in the unit's quiet room when Kate got him. He was trying to catch a few hours' sleep before rising early to greet the incoming British PM's security detail.

"Why would your crew leave Ballycleary Stud?" she asked.

"We agreed with the prince's bodyguards to provide an escort while they travelled from A to B and to stick around until he retired for the night."

"We believe there's going to be an attempt to snatch him tonight."

"Christ on a bike! How come we're only hearing this now?" Twomey replied, fully awake now.

"The pieces only came together in the last few minutes. Don Bailey's behind it."

"I'll get my guys to go back there, pronto," Twomey said.

"Tell them to link up with your unit from Harold's Cross, they're with Sexton who's almost here."

"Who have you got on the ground?"

"Digger and Angie have been in position for the last few hours at either side of the house. There's lights on in a separate lodge to the back and I've deployed Joanie and

Becky to cover the front and rear of the house. I'm waitin' to hear from them."

"Will you see anything coming soon enough to call the cavalry?" Twomey asked.

"It's a poxy night; the rain makes it impossible to see very far. It works for us and against us. There's a complication."

"What?"

"One of the security men working at the stud is almost certainly part of Bailey's gang."

"Shit! I'll talk to Kenny and call up the stand-by crew."

Kate ordered Digger to observe and report *only*, given that they would be outnumbered and outgunned by Bailey's gang.

At SIU, Mac signed off his call to Yves Fenaux. They were old buddies from a leadership course in the FBI's Training Academy at Quantico, Virginia. Mac's ability to speak his language cemented their friendship.

"What did Fenaux say?" Pete McNally asked.

"They raided an apartment in Vieux Nice this evening. A local with Lebanese parents is in custody. Fenaux thinks there's a connection between the suspect and the two that Bailey met at Nice airport a few weeks ago."

"How does he figure that?"

"They found a contract for a charter of a private jet during the search of his place. It left Nice an hour ago, heading for Dublin. The guy they arrested is a pilot with a local air club."

"Get Kate on the line," he ordered Pete.

He briefed her on the worrying development.

"I've tried Vincent Cleary's landline and it's dead," Kate told him. "His mobile phone came back with a 'powered off' message."

"You're going to have to get to the house and warn him," Mac advised.

Kate conferenced in a call from Twomey. She briefed him on the communications blackout at Ballycleary. All three agreed that if an attempt was made to get a hostage out of the country it would probably be from an airport close to Dublin.

"We're going to need air support to deploy," Twomey replied.

"I'll talk to Shaw and get back to you," Mac told them, as urgent bursts of radio traffic cut in from Kate's command post.

When he rang Twomey back he told him, "The Ranger Wing has a squad on stand-by at Baldonnell for the British PM's visit tomorrow with two Westland AW 139s and crews with them through the night. As far as Shaw's concerned, whatever we need is ours."

As they spoke, Mac heard the familiar clunk as mags were loaded and rounds breeched, as ERU weapons were readied. "We're loading up. With lights and sirens we'll be at Baldonnell in ten," Twomey said.

"Get everything you can in the air," Mac ordered him. "We're going to need it."

32

Detective Rebecca Kingston had been ecstatic when selected as one of the chosen few to join SIU. Tonight, the rookie surveillance officer contemplated whether any of the crap they endured was worthwhile. When the boss ordered herself and Joanie to take up positions on either side of the main house, they groaned at the thoughts of leaving their comfortable car. Keeping the front and rear approaches to the house under constant observation was their task. By the time she found a place to hunker down, Becky was already cold and wet. She chose a field drain for cover. The weather blotted out the sound of any wildlife, but something was sure to be scavenging around. Being alone was tension-filled and brutal.

When she made out four armed men running fast on the opposite side of the field, she hadn't completed her set-up. She froze. It was too late to do anything other than pray they couldn't see her. The rain that been pouring down since nightfall, drove hard into her face as she lay flat on a ground sheet. She had just wiped the lenses on the night vision binoculars and observed that the furtive group were clad in boilersuits and balaclavas. All wore combat boots. Two were carrying assault rifles, one had a sawn-off shotgun, and the final one carried some type of handgun.

Her view was far from ideal but any movement to adjust might be picked up. Becky waited until they disappeared from view and then sent a group wide warning text. Seconds later, ambient light from the yards and main house was sucked out of the night. Becky flashed another text—*Lights at main house gone out.* Digger replied: *Roger, standby-switch to radio, observe and report.* To Joanie, Becky flashed a *U OK?* Digger came back immediately—*NO personal msgs.* Becky acknowledged via radio.

"Report, please," Kate radioed Digger. She had no view of the stud from her temporary parking.

"Stand-by," he replied.

He could see what had occurred and scanned the main house trying to make sense of it.

"No genny kickin' in," Digger reported. "Assume it's part of the plan."

Kate called Sexton.

"How far away are you?"

"One kilometre back according to sat nav. Do you want us to blue light it?"

"No, stay dark. We need to get a handle on what we're facing. I'm just ahead of you; link up and follow me in."

"The protection car has linked up the ERU squad with us. They know the layout, let them take the lead."

"The power has just been cut at the main house. There's no sign of a backup generator kicking in. That means the front gate probably won't open," Kate cautioned.

"Digger says there's a track alongside the main entrance, we'll use that and come in through the yards."

"We have to take down Dempsey before he warns Bailey."

"Estimate ten or more with him," Sexton replied. "We see you now, follow us."

Kate pulled the lumbering van out the gateway and struggled to catch up with the convoy as it sped towards its destiny.

Bailey buzzed on adrenaline. The approach to the house had gone exactly as he and Dempsey had planned it. The ex-soldier cut the power and sent his security buddy to check out why the backup generator had not kicked in. He had disabled it earlier and as his buddy knelt and found the severed diesel fuel lines, Dempsey knocked him senseless with the metal folding stock of an AK47. The gang cuffed the unconscious guard and pulled a strip of duct tape across his mouth. Bailey had intercepted Equus Security's mobile patrol. He caught the middle-aged ex-soldiers dozing in their Land Rover and drove it through the fields back to the yards. When they reached the one nearest the house, he passed the captives to a couple of northside thugs, who trussed and secured them with their unconscious colleague in the rear of a horse transport truck.

Bailey eased the Land Rover out of the yard as Dempsey walked alongside. The thug with him sported one of yellow High Vis jackets taken from the security guards, Bailey wore the other. The 4x4's headlights dazzled the prince's bodyguard who showed up close to the rear of the house. He shouted to Dempsey, enquiring what was wrong. He appeared unarmed and Bailey slipped off his High Vis and slid unnoticed from the cab. Dempsey called to the bodyguard that they were working on the emergency generator. As the guard strained to catch the explanation, Bailey edged along the wall of the house, keeping to the shadows, listening intently to the exchanges.

"Repeat please," the guard asked Dempsey, shielding his eyes from the headlights as he walked towards him.

"Hands where I can see them," Bailey ordered as he pounced, ramming the Glock hard under the guard's chin. He liked the silencer; it gave the weapon a lethal appearance and had proven invaluable. "Search him," he ordered Dempsey, his eyes never leaving the prisoner.

"Clear."

"Inside," he ordered, opening a side door to the main house.

Once in the hallway, Bailey struck the bodyguard hard on the side of the head with the Glock and dragged him to a nearby utility room. Dempsey jumped into the jeep and pulled it alongside the porch door.

Digger opened the side entrance gate and Sexton's crew ditched their cars behind the hedge that ran up to the stud farm yards. They pulled on bulletproof vests and raid jackets, and hunkered behind the cars. Kate lumbered through the gate in the command post and instantly worried it might get bogged down as she pulled off the gravel track onto the grass verge.

"Boss, we need you here at the command post," Digger said as he huddled with Kate, poring over the stud layout plan in the rear of the van. The ERU team leader, Ken James, looked over Digger's shoulder and listened as Kate rapidly drew up a plan of action.

They double-checked each step and seconds later, the pair jumped out and ran crouched along the gallop track where Digger lay flat, striving to get some kind of view through the thinner base of the hedge. James was a national judo champion, a block of solid muscle, although he didn't appear much taller than Digger. An unruly mop of curly blond hair sprouted from underneath his squad baseball cap. He turned it back to front as he lay down beside Digger and peered through a night sight.

"Fuck it, Kenny," Digger swore, "I can't see a thing."

"I need to breach that outer yard, if we're to launch an assault on the house," James told him.

"Base, can you check the flanks," Digger asked Kate.

Tango Bravo 1 — Angie, reported no sightings. Tango Bravo 2 — Becky also reported no further activity since the four bodies transited her area minutes earlier.

"Base to Tango Bravo 3 — sit rep?"

No reply came. Joanie was south of the house but Kate didn't have an exact location. Five minutes earlier, she had reported all-clear. Kate tried again. No reply.

Please answer, Joan—a text message from Becky. Still nothing came in reply.

"We've got to get to her," Becky came on the radio.

"Hold your position," Digger growled. "Do not move. I repeat do *not* move, until further orders."

Kate cut in. "I'm redeploying Tango Bravo 1 to locate Tango Bravo 3. First Aid responder accompanies, go now."

"Roger that," Digger acknowledged.

"Tango Bravo 2 hold your position," Kate repeated. Some of Bailey's gang came from that direction. Chances were they would try to exit the same way.

Digger told James that the only confirmed sightings they had was a group of four. The Land Rover with the Equus mobile security team had the engine running and headlights on close to the main house but the rain obscured any chance of verifying its occupants.

James re-joined his squad, laid out the plan, and slapped the roof of the ERU transport to get it moving. They moved stealthily towards the yard, sloping alongside their armour-plated transport as it crawled towards its objective. As they turned towards the yard entrance a burst of sub-machine gunfire sprayed them. Five dimples of shattered glass instantaneously punctuated the bulletproof windscreen. The driver, unscathed, threw the car into reverse as all three colleagues alongside the vehicle opened up, returning fire with drilled precision.

They reached the shelter of a solid block barn wall as Digger crawled rapidly in the direction of the action. They hadn't taken any hits, apart from the Volvo, and even with the obscured windscreen it was still functional. James ordered that it be left in place to block any attempted exit from the yard.

"Fire is coming from one of the stables," he told Digger.

"Can you see which one?"

"The left corner, as you face down the yard entrance."

"Okay, standby."

Kate told Digger there was a feed store further along the block. If they could penetrate that, they could outflank the gunman guarding the yard.

"I need coverin' fire while I move with James' team. What weapons have you got?" Digger asked Sexton.

"Everyone has a personal issue Sig Sauer pistol and we've two Uzis. I'll empty a mag from my Sig in the stable direction."

"Use Uzis — short bursts — start when I'll tell you."

Digger moved fast with the ERU team after the first Uzi burst. Sexton's crew were taking return fire. Rounds pierced the skin on the Volvo's front passenger door, but were deflected by the armoured plating. Whoever was in the stable, was measured and calm, no signs of panic. In the stable boxes, horses agitated by the commotion whinnied and kicked out; another eerie distraction. Crouched behind the stables, Digger advanced the group; operating on night sights they cracked the feed store door open and scattered cautiously inside. It was clear. James eyeballed the yard and assessed the terrain. The noise from the horses helped. Any box with an animal was unlikely to harbour a potential ambusher. The assault started with an Uzi burst from Sexton, then James' team spilled out into the yard, a pair either side. They provided cover while James sprinted towards the target box and lobbed a flashbang. The deafening noise from the grenade heightened the spooked horses' agitation to fever pitch. James dove into the stable box and kicked the sub-machine gun from the screaming thug, writhing on the ground.

"Shut to fuck up," James said, as he knocked him cold.

Inside the house, Bailey and his accomplice made rapid progress to the first landing where they paused. They heard voices upstairs and went in their direction.

"Where's the feckin' torch?" a male voice said.

"I'll get candles set up," a woman's voice replied.

She was calm until a burst of gunfire from the yard shattered the eerie calm that the pitch darkness cast over the house.

"The children!" she screamed.

"Jesus Christ Almighty!" Vincent Cleary said. "Hit the panic alarm. I'll go see what's going on."

"It's not working," Gloria warned her husband, as she repeatedly pressed the bedside button. "Hit Emergency on your mobile."

"Don't bother," Bailey said as he entered the room. He reached out and grabbed her hair. She screamed again.

"Leave her alone," Cleary shouted from the other side of the pitch black room.

Bailey and accomplice wore night vision goggles. While Bailey dragged Gloria towards the door, his accomplice clubbed her husband with a rifle butt and knocked him senseless. He hit the floor with a sickening thump. His attacker retrieved the mobile phone and turned it off.

"Don't hurt him, don't hurt him," his wife cried out in the darkness.

"Do what we say, when we say it and no one needs to get hurt," Bailey told her, as she twisted in his grip.

"Nice ass!" Bailey's accomplice remarked.

"Get out," Bailey ordered him. "See what's going on in the yard."

He turned his attention to his hostage. "What's your name?"

"Gloria."

"We don't want to hurt you, Gloria," Bailey told her, his mouth close to her ear as he spoke. "We want your guest. Tell us where he is."

"Don't hurt my children," she pleaded.

"I don't have time for this," he said, tugging hard on the hank of hair he held tightly. "Tell us what room your guest is in."

"The lodge."

"The what?"

"The lodge behind the house."

Bailey cuffed her hard in the mouth. "Are you fuckin' with me, bitch?" he snarled.

"No, no, honestly," she whimpered, as blood trickled between her lips.

"Is he alone?"

"As far as I know."

"The guest is in the lodge behind the house and you think he's alone. Is that right, Gloria?"

Bailey's accomplice, poked his head back in the room. "Are ya ridin' her or what?" he leered. "We need to move."

"Get two more from the yard to guard the jeep, *now*. He's not in the house." Bailey snapped.

"Now, Gloria, if I have to hit you again, it will hurt," he said yanking his hostage's hair to show he meant business." What do you mean, as far as you know he's alone?"

"He has a secretary. I don't know if he's with him."

"He's a bum boy prince, is he?" Bailey snorted. "Put clothes on," he ordered, easing his grip.

Through night vision goggles in the pitch black room, Bailey watched her as she opened a wardrobe and scrambled until she found a pair of jeans. She pulled the nightie she wore over her head and used it to wipe blood from her mouth before flinging it into the wardrobe. Momentarily naked, her pendulous breasts distracted him as she zipped up the jeans and then pulled on a sweatshirt.

When he exited the bedroom, he passed Gloria Cleary to his partners in crime. "Put her in the jeep," he commanded. To his northside collaborator, he shouted, "You come with me."

They ran towards the lodge and cautiously approached a side door. It was locked, but flew open when Bailey kicked it hard and the jamb splintered. The pair edged warily towards the bedroom at end of the corridor. When they ducked inside, they found it empty. Bailey indicated that he would take the right hand side of the room while his accomplice checked the other. Bailey's side had a door leading to an en suite bathroom, there were wardrobes opposite. Glock held in both hands, he checked under the bed but found only a void. His accomplice foraged in the first wardrobe but came up empty-handed. Tentatively, Bailey entered the en suite bathroom. Inside, he pulled a shower door open and pointed his weapon into the cubicle. It was empty, but as he closed the door his eye caught a movement in the bath behind.

He reached in and pulled a body out. The terrified captive wore silk pyjamas. He held his hands in front of his face to fend off blows as Bailey slapped him hard either side of his head. The captive then placed his hands behind his head, fingers interlaced, in a gesture of surrender.

"He's here…" Bailey began.

A muffled grunt from the bedroom stopped him dead.

"Kneel," he ordered the terrified prince. "Move and you're dead."

He pressed his back against the bathroom wall and advanced towards the noise. Furtively, he peered into the bedroom. The bodyguard kneeling on the prince's bed, was holding down Bailey's accomplice, one hand clasped vice-like over his mouth. With the other, he used a scimitar dagger to slice across his neck. Bailey pointed and fired a burst at him. When he saw the aggressor drop to the floor he dived over the bed and fired again. The bodyguard didn't stir.

Breathing heavily, Bailey ripped the goggles from his accomplice's face and leaned over him. His eyes stared wildly at the ceiling and blood arced from the slash wound across his throat, splattering Bailey's balaclava. The sickening gurgling sounds he was emitting confirmed he was a lost cause. Bailey lurched back into to the bathroom and emerged pushing the prince ahead of him, gun pressed to the back of his head. He held him at the doorway, checked outside and then yanked him out to the corridor.

"Leaving, leaving, action stations, action stations," he called into his radio.

"Where's our mate?" Bailey heard someone shout at him, as he reached the jeep.

"Dead," he replied. "Forget him, we're rolling."

"Take or leave?" Dempsey asked, pointing to Gloria Cleary.

"Take," he replied. "Insurance!"

33

Captain Dick Saunders silently cursed himself for not acting on intuition and passing up the flight. He was unsettled by the Jordanian passengers his station manager had introduced as he checked their travel documents. In the hours before the flight, the third passenger had dropped out; urgent business in Nice the explanation. It didn't much matter to Saunders that apart from 'please' and 'thank you' the pair spoke only Arabic. He didn't need to form lasting relationships with his passengers. It unnerved him that the business suits the pair wore looked incongruous and neither seemed comfortable.

Another detail nagged him as Nice ground control authorised start up and push back before passing him to the tower for taxi clearance. Apart from one client dropping out and his passengers' dodgy suits, something else was off; what the hell was it? Their regulated departure time had altered and at thirty minutes past midnight, Nice tower told Saunders he was clear for take-off. With wheels up he was immediately passed to Lyon air traffic control who gave him direct clearance to Dublin.

Twenty minutes later he had attained cruising speed at five hundred miles per hour and levelled off at 37,000 feet when it hit him. The passports! He had watched the station manager giving the travel documents a cursory glance before returning them to his high-paying clients. The cover of each one appeared brand new. If these were much travelled businessmen as suggested, it was stretching credibility to believe that both had changed their passports at precisely the same time. Another nagging discrepancy.

The French-Algerian manager had tried conversation, but their dialects differed too much for them to communicate effectively. During the pre-flight briefing, Saunders advised his co-pilot and cabin steward to be alert for changes of demeanour and to warn him if he had any suspicions.

When the steward's warning came, it was too late. They were 110 miles out of Dublin and had started the descent. The steward told him via intercom that he needed a face-to-face. Saunders clicked open the cockpit door and glanced over his shoulder. He was horrified when he saw his passengers unmasked as hijackers with a weapon pressed against his colleague's throat. A harmless letter opener from the airport scan now revealed itself as a lethal weapon with a razor edge forged on one side.

"Don't hurt him," he pleaded.

Saunders couldn't have anticipated the next move. The hijacker pushed the steward aside and swiped the weapon across the co-pilot's neck. The stricken airman screamed in agony, clamping his hand over a gaping wound. Blood spewed freely onto the instrument panel. As the hijacker made to strike a second time Saunders grabbed his wrist and stopped him.

"I lose him, I lose the plane," he shouted. "I'm not

fucking kidding. Strike him once more and I'll dive bomb this bird into the sea."

Saunders was eye-to-eye with Hussein, close enough to smell the garlic on his breath and read the manic intent in his eyes. Saunders tightened his grip.

"Do as I say, I let him live," Hussein snarled. "Any tricks, I cut him again and you will listen as he dies."

Saunders ordered the cabin steward to help him remove their wounded colleague and they lifted him from the cockpit into the first aisle seat. Blood spattered copiously onto the white leather seats as he screamed in agony.

"You're going to be okay, Jack," Saunders assured him as he tore open a large ambulance dressing from the first aid kit.

"You, in cockpit, now," Hussein ordered.

"Finish the bandaging first," Saunders ordered the cabin steward, "then lean the chair back and elevate his feet. Stay strong," he urged them both.

He returned to the cockpit, strapped himself into his seat, and disengaged auto-pilot.

Hussein read from a piece of paper.

"Show primary destination," he demanded.

Saunders pointed him towards the GPS readout.

"Now," the hijacker said, "enter secondary destination."

As he called out the GPS coordinates, Saunders punched in the numbers. He was confused; the numbers told him that he was still flying to Dublin.

As Ken James' team breeched the final yard without resistance, Digger raced from the second one to join them.

Muffled sounds coming from a horse transporter parked in a corner distracted them momentarily.

"What do you think?" James asked Digger.

"Probably Dolly's security men. If they're makin' noise, they're alive, we'll free them later. Let's focus on gettin' to the house."

Crouched behind a low wall, Digger and James peered gingerly over it to assess what lay ahead of them. The black Land Rover was pulled up near an open side door, its engine running and a distressed looking woman sat motionless in the rear seat.

"Oh fuck, no," Digger groaned.

James adjusted his night vision binoculars and saw a hooded gunman stall at the rear of the house. Accomplices were scattered around the tiny yard, one in guard position behind the 4x4. The gunman scanned the yard methodically, received thumbs-up from his henchmen signalling the coast was clear.

The hooded suspect emerged from the darkness dragging a pyjama clad man towards the jeep and bundled him into the back seat. "Leg it," he roared at the rear guard who had jumped into the driver seat.

"That's Bailey and Dempsey," Digger said to James, "we're too late." Dempsey revved the 4x4's engine and it shot towards the open gate of one of the fields.

The hooded figures guarding Bailey's vehicle while it loaded, now ran towards the courtyard exit. There were four in all, armed with a liquorice allsorts of weaponry. The miniature camera on James' helmet sent grainy images to Kate in the command post.

"Take them now," she ordered.

"Light them up," James commanded his team.

The tactical torches the ERU team carried had LED conversion heads that increased the light output to six times that of regular two D-battery flashlights. As the concentration of brilliant light hit the group, James aimed a rapid burst from his H&K MP7 sub-machine gun over their heads.

"Armed Gardaí!" he shouted. "Drop your weapons."

The gang froze and tore off their night vision goggles.

"Weapons down, *now*," James repeated.

Three complied, one ran. A red dot followed him an instant before a single shot dropped him.

"Secure the prisoners," James ordered.

Kate had pulled Sexton's crew back to their cars and they shot past her to block the escaping jeep.

"Tango Bravo 2 to Base."

"Go ahead," Kate told Becky.

"I'm following the rear lights of that Land Rover. It's headed towards Tango Bravo 3's area."

Kate acknowledged. "Search party is out there. Hold your position."

Becky punched the sodden ground in frustration. She had heard the earlier exchanges of gunfire and knew they were in a highly volatile situation. Then she heard Ken James shouting at someone to surrender and shuddered when a shot rang out shortly afterwards. She felt she was losing it and couldn't tell if the wet streaks across her face were tears or just the miserable fucking rain. She needed to get to her friend.

"Tango Bravo 3 located," Angie's voice came over the radio, minutes later.

"Status?" Kate asked, urgently.

"Bad head gash and shook up, but still with us," Angie replied.

Over the next few seconds Becky wiped her eyes

continually as she scanned the landscape for hostiles and struggled to stay professional.

"Tango Bravo 1, vehicle approaching position, stand by."

"That's Bailey, Dempsey and the hostages," Kate warned Angie. "Don't engage — observe, and report."

Angie pulled a camouflage ground sheet over Joanie, and pressed herself flat to the mucky ground as the first aider scuttled down a field drain out of sight. The Land Rover sped through the centre of the field before exiting through a gate on the opposite side.

"Tango Bravo 1 to Base. They're switching vehicles. New vehicle is a white Ford Transit van. The blue Audi's with it."

Angie called out the reg. plate details she could see in the fleeting glance. She confirmed that the Land Rover now appeared to be empty. The first aider resumed patching up Joanie. He placed a pad over the severe gash to her head and secured it with a bandage. Kate sent a backup team in Becky's direction and told her to swap places with Angie in taking charge of her friend. Becky took off running the instant she received the order.

Kate focused on coordinating the chase cars. They ran into a road block five hundred metres from the stud. The first car was sprayed with shotgun blasts that took out a front tyre. Minutes later on the opposite side of the stud farm, a second mobile was fired on, this time by a burst from an assault rifle. Unlike the ERU's Volvo, none of SIU's transport was bulletproof. When the driver took a shoulder wound and crashed, Kate ordered the rest of the chasing pack to back off.

The Transit with Bailey and hostages headed towards the M7 motorway, the blue Audi A4 followed close behind. When Sexton heard Angie's report, he jumped into the tracking car and gave chase. Kate reversed the command post out to follow him. Digger and Angie raced to join her and Ken James pushed into the rear of the crowded van as it lumbered out the stud farm's side gate.

Bailey sat in the single seat closest to the van's sliding side door. His silk pyjama-clad hostage sat opposite casting furtive glances towards the blacked-out window. He was manacled to the bench seat with handcuffs and shivered as he stared at the figure sitting opposite in the bloodstained balaclava. In the seat behind Gloria Cleary sat with her hands resting on her knees. They bound together with two black cable ties. A slash of duct tape pulled across her mouth, rendered her mute. Dempsey followed Bailey's orders to drive within the speed limits and do nothing to draw attention.

Motorway light leaked in from the front of the van and cast the prince's face into light and shade as they drove. His eyes never left Bailey.

"I'm an infidel to you, I suppose," Bailey said to him.

The prince shook his head.

"Don't worry you'll be back among your own, soon enough."

The prince's expression, raw fear and confusion, amused Bailey.

"Name your price," the prince muttered.

Bailey shook his head.

A raindrop pattern streaked the front of Gloria Cleary's sweatshirt as tears rolled down her face. Her neck muscles tightened and her breathing grew rapid. Bailey leaned over and ripped the tape from one side of her mouth.

"What?"

"I have asthma," she sobbed. "I'm having an attack, I can't breathe."

"Not my problem."

"Leave the tape off, please," she begged, between gasps. "That way my breathing will get back to normal. I won't scream, I promise."

Bailey acceded, but left the tape hanging from her cheek as a warning that the concession was temporary.

"I can't feel my hands," she told him. "These straps are pulled far too tight. They're cutting off my circulation."

"This isn't a fucking holiday."

"I want to be able to hold my kids again. I'll do whatever you order."

Bailey shifted out of his seat. He unholstered his weapon and stuck the muzzle to the prince's left ear as he moved into the seat beside her.

"Do anything stupid and he dies first, then you," he warned her as he used a knife from his belt to cut the ties.

"Thank you," she replied and began rubbing feeling back into her hands.

"Hold onto the bar at the back of that seat," Bailey growled. He pulled two fresh cable ties from his belt and secured her hands. "Now shut the fuck up!"

"ETA, ten minutes," Dempsey shouted from the front seat.

Dublin city loomed on the horizon and as the Citywest Bridge came into view he startled when he noticed the Air Corps base awash with lights at two o'clock in the morning.

"Must be night exercises," he said over his shoulder. "Never fancied them."

"Night exercises?" Bailey pondered, as he stared out the window.

Kate made a tactical decision and switched Sexton. He would return to Ballycleary House to interrogate the prisoners and manage the crime scenes. After a hurried rendezvous on the M7 hard shoulder Angie jumped into the tracking car driver seat with Kate beside her, Digger and Ken James crammed into the rear. Kate prayed the beaconed car wouldn't turn out to be a decoy as she called Twomey.

"What's your status?" Kate asked.

"We're airborne, two Air Corps choppers, one with an Army Ranger squad. The Garda chopper's on city patrol, if we need it."

Briefed by Mac, Lt-Colonel Shaw had arrived at the Air Corps base to direct the military side of the operation.

"Where do you think a plane might attempt a pick-up?" Kate asked Twomey.

"That Nice flight Mac mentioned is due to land at Dublin pretty soon. We've Air Traffic Control on alert to keep us posted."

"Beaconed car is veering left at Citywest," Digger butted in.

"Direction of travel?" Kate asked.

"Going onto the R136. That will bring him towards Lucan and eventually onto the M4; he can still make Dublin airport from there. He's avoiding the M50."

"Get closer," Kate ordered.

Angie floored it. In the rear seat, Ken James gripped a grab handle and clung on. Digger was too preoccupied with his technology to notice; they couldn't lose their only lead. They swept past convoys of trucks and reached the turnoff four minutes after their prey deviated onto his new course. It was a link road with traffic lights and roundabouts at regular intervals. It worked in their favour; once through the first two, Kate shouted, "Slow down, they're up ahead at the next lights."

The blue Audi A4, that Digger and Angie tagged a few nights earlier, was tucked in tight behind the white Transit. As the lights changed, both vehicles pulled off slowly and continued on a track that would bring them towards the M4. Not much further up the road a right turn would take them towards Dublin airport. Digger relayed the news to Kate.

"We have contact," Kate told Twomey.

"I'll get the Garda chopper crew to establish visual contact overhead but stay well back. If they abandon the vehicles we'll need its thermal imaging cameras."

"Good thinking," Kate agreed.

Twomey's squad was circling within five minutes of Dublin airport.

"What if it's not Dublin airport?" he asked when she updated him.

"Where else could it be?"

"I don't see how Bailey could hope to get out of a major airport without confrontation," Twomey mused.

"He's proven that confrontation doesn't put him off. Where else is there?"

"Dublin Weston Airport is only up the road from where you've turned off," he told her.

Kate was annoyed she hadn't thought of it; she had taken a flight out of it years earlier with a Garda Flying Club buddy. It grew from a grass strip aerodrome in the 1930s when it opened, to take on a new life in the 21st century as the country's only executive airport, going after corporate business.

"It's closed at this time of night, surely," she ventured.

"I'll ask the pilot to check it."

"Vehicles turnin' left, left, left onto M4," came Digger's urgent voice.

The pilot in Twomey's chopper switched radio frequency.

"Weston Tower, Weston Tower, this is Alpha Charlie One Niner." No reply.

"Weston Tower, Weston Tower, this is Alpha Charlie One Niner, do you read?" The tower was coming into view but nothing came back on the radio. None of the runway lights were on.

Twomey raised binoculars and peered through the front of chopper.

"The lights in the tower are on but we're too far away to confirm if anyone's there."

"I'll come round and take a look-see," the pilot replied.

He flew over the vast expanse of Intel's Ireland campus, located a few miles from the airport, and came in low towards the tower. As he approached it, everyone on board caught the series of red flashes from the lights on top of the tower.

"Someone's in trouble," the pilot said.

"What do you mean?" Twomey asked. "I can't see anyone in there."

"The red light flashes mean the aerodrome is unsafe and aircraft are advised not to land there," the pilot replied.

"Christ on a bike, something is already in play here."

He passed the news to Kate.

"Target leavin' motorway at junction five, left at junction five," Digger's voice confirmed their fears.

"It ends at Weston," Twomey said.

34

In the control tower, John Kilkenny was focussed on doing everything demanded of him. He fretted that back home his son would wake and see the unwelcome guest holding his mother hostage. The thugs who forced him to open up the air traffic control tower spoke little throughout the night. They used designated numbers to communicate amongst themselves. One and two were guarding him, number three was outside in a car. Kilkenny ran a small flying school at Weston and reckoned his big mouth had landed him in it. During many hours spent in the cockpit together, most learners listened to tales of near misses and scary moments from his previous life as an air traffic controller at Dublin airport.

The circling helicopters of the last few minutes spooked the gang. As his captors dived for cover he had managed to activate the warning lights. When number three reported them, Kilkenny convinced his captors that they activated automatically if an aircraft flew too near the terminal building. A phone rang and jolted him from where he was sitting on the floor since the choppers arrived.

"Talk to me," number one answered.

"Get the gate unlocked," Bailey ordered. "We're approaching."

"Thanks be to Jaysus!" he replied. "I can't wait to get out of here."

The security man who had opened up for Kilkenny was bound and gagged in the staff locker room. Number one rang his accomplice waiting in the car and told him to get the entrance gate unlocked.

———

Saunders' Navy training kicked in on return to the cockpit. Primary objective — evaluate your enemy. He played for time; made much of wiping his colleague's blood off the instrument panel. He figured the guy reading the scrap of paper had limited aviation knowledge. As Saunders' right hand flicked switches and pushed buttons on the panel, Hussein queried everything.

"What you do?" he asked.

"Changing radio channels for approaching Dublin."

"No tricks."

"No tricks," Saunders sighed.

He didn't do it straight away. He let the hijacker see him use a selection of instruments before he sent the hijack transponder code. The reaction was immediate.

"Côte D'Azur Charters three Whiskey Zulu this is Dublin, please confirm you are squawking 7500."

"Good morning Dublin, that is affirmative."

"Côte D'Azur three Whiskey Zulu descend to five thousand feet and await instructions."

"Côte D'Azur three Whiskey Zulu, descending to five thousand feet."

"Wind is 270 degrees, six knots."

"Roger."

In the control tower at Air Corps HQ across the city, Lt-Colonel Shaw looked across at the air traffic controller who had suddenly become animated. They were on a live feed from Dublin airport's radar.

"An inbound flight has just squawked the hijack code," the controller shouted as he looked up from the screen.

"Details?" Shaw requested.

"He's about four miles out. ATC Dublin is clearing the decks for his arrival. The pilot's a Yank."

Shaw called Mac and relayed the information. Mac knew the procedure; he had done enough hijack rehearsals when the ERU was just taking baby steps. The airport police and fire crews would shepherd the flight to a remote part of the airport until its status could be verified.

"The hostages are at Weston," he told Shaw. "I'm en route there."

"I'll inform ATC Dublin," Shaw replied.

A Westland AW139 hovered over the north end of Weston as Army Rangers abseiled from the aircraft. The pilot held it steady and they spilled out in seconds, he jettisoned the ropes and banked steeply away from the airfield. The Rangers fanned out to secure the perimeter.

Angie pulled their car in tight to a hedge just outside the airfield's open gate. They had seen the lights of the van and Audi disappearing towards the small terminal building. Apart from a light in the control tower, it was in darkness. A second chopper hovered low at the far end of the airfield and then flew off. It was Twomey's unit, which had also rappelled and regrouped. Twomey told Kate to hold off encroaching onto the airfield until they had assessed their opposition. Mac and Pete arrived in a backup command post van and pulled in tight behind the tracking car.

Kate briefed Mac and waited anxiously for Twomey to come back.

"Perimeter is secured. We're on deck, approaching the terminal," he reported, minutes later. "Three vehicles on one side of the terminal. The chopper overhead is telling me that all hostiles are now indoors, with the two captives."

"A hostage negotiator is en route. Nobody leaves the terminal building, meantime. Understood?" Kate told him.

"Roger."

"Everyone wears raid jackets, okay," Twomey warned Kate. "I don't want friendly fire downing anyone."

Already wearing hers, she located two bulletproof vests in the boot and threw them to Mac and Pete, then found two spare jackets. They were emblazoned, front and back, with GARDA in large gold letters. She zipped hers up and pulled it over her tiny bump. For an instant, she pondered the dual risk but dismissed it.

"Shaw told me the Nice flight squawked the hijack code a few minutes ago." Mac informed Kate.

Kate passed the news to Twomey.

The full emergency plan activated at Dublin airport. Fire tenders and airport police trucks parked at their designated deployment stations on the apron awaiting instructions from the tower. Nearby Beaumont Hospital was put on notice to prepare for incoming casualties. The senior air traffic controller ran the show.

"Côte D'Azur three Whiskey Zulu this is Dublin, descend to three thousand feet."

"Descending to three thousand feet."

"Wind is 275 degrees, gusting ten knots."

"Roger."

Earlier foul weather had cleared the east coast. Saunders had a clear view of the city as he approached over the Wicklow Hills. Strings of lights, north at Howth Head and south at Dunlaoghaire Pier reached into the Irish Sea and cupped the bay.

"Destination is now secondary location," the hijacker told Saunders.

"I can't just fly blind; I might collide with another plane."

"Do it," the hijacker ordered.

In the Dublin tower everyone strained for the first view of the inbound flight until, finally, the landing lights came into view.

"Côte D'Azur three Whiskey Zulu, you are clear to land, western runway."

"Western runway, copy."

The waiting emergency services started their engines as the plane came into view. They watched it gradually descending, wheels down and prepared to move. At the last minute it aborted the landing and started to climb back into the night sky.

"Côte D'Azur three Whiskey Zulu, this is Dublin, what's your status?"

"Dublin, I got a landing gear warning light. I'm going around, climbing straight ahead to fifteen hundred feet."

"Clear to climb to fifteen hundred feet. We had a visual on your landing gear. Everything seemed okay."

"Copy that. Coming round."

The air traffic controller immediately realised something wasn't right. The plane continued flying straight ahead. In Baldonnell, Shaw saw it also; the plane was headed in their direction. He activated a full-scale response to repel an attack on the airfield. A three-man squad raced to deploy their anti-aircraft missile system. It was the RBS 70 and the crew mounted the surface-to-air missile weapon on its tripod with drilled assurance. If Shaw gave the order, its laser guidance system would guarantee the missile found its target.

Following his GPS directions, Saunders flew downwind and executed a 180 degree turn. In Weston tower Bailey saw them fly past. It was the signal he had waited for and he pulled Kilkenny up off the ground and put the Glock to his head.

"Switch on everything you need to guide him in," he ordered.

Kilkenny turned on the landing lights and activated the radio.

"What's the flight's call sign?" he asked Bailey.

"Fucked if I know," Bailey replied.

"Flight approaching Weston airport, this is Weston Tower, what is your call sign, please."

"Weston Tower, this is Côte D'Azur three Whiskey Zulu I need to land urgently. I have a seriously injured crewman."

Kilkenny's calm voice advised Saunders that he needed to approach the airfield from the east for landing. He watched as the pilot executed another fly past before descending towards the airfield. Around the perimeter, the Army Rangers pushed deeper into hedges out of sight of the approaching landing lights. The jet screamed over-head as it descended rapidly. Small clouds of smoke pillowed and quickly dissipated as its wheels hit the tarmac.

As it slowed and taxied to the end of the runway, Saunders' voice came over the radio.

"Weston Tower, I need to disembark my injured

crewman immediately. Permission to taxi to the apron," he requested.

His request was met with silence.

"Take us close to tower," Aazim Hussein ordered Saunders.

"Weston Tower, I repeat I need to taxi to apron and disembark injured crewman."

Hussein's phone rang.

"Is what the pilot's saying right?" Bailey asked him.

"One crew is bleeding, yes," he replied.

"Okay, we'll bring you in, get the prince on board. I don't give a fuck about injured crew. Get ready to move fast when the door opens."

"What happens when door opens?"

"I get on board, check the money. If everything's alright, Dempsey will bring the prince up the steps."

"This is acceptable."

"I leave Dempsey's split with you. He wants to travel back with you."

"What?"

Bailey hung up before Hussein could respond. In the command post, Pete McNally informed Kate instantly. She listened to the call and read through the text transcript on the screen.

"Ring the tower now," she told the hostage negotiator, who had arrived on scene.

The tower was crowded, hostages and captors bunched together, all eyes focussed on the jet that was making its way slowly towards the terminal. Nerves were shredded and when the ATC phone rang, the room jumped.

"Answer the fucking thing," Bailey shouted.

"Weston Tower," Kilkenny answered.

"Detective Garda Michael Lynch speaking, put Don Bailey on the line, please."

Kilkenny held out the handset.

"The caller wants to speak to a Mr. Don Bailey."

Initially nobody moved. Bailey had the prince held in a tight grip, his face close to the window of the tower watching the plane turn at the end of the runway.

"Who is he and what does he want?" Bailey shouted at the terrified air traffic controller.

"He's Detective Lynch from the Garda Síochána," Kilkenny informed him. "He wants to speak with Mr. Don Bailey."

"Not interested," Bailey replied.

Kilkenny passed on the message. He listened carefully to the response then addressed Bailey again.

"Mr. Lynch says to tell you that your position is hopeless. The airport is surrounded by soldiers and the Garda are here in force. Your only option is to surrender."

Bailey grabbed the handset from Kilkenny. "Get fucked," he roared.

The five gang members left with Bailey panicked. They snarled orders at each other as they rushed to cover off doorways to the tower.

"Calm to fuck down. Nothing happens while we have these," Bailey said, pointing to the two hostages.

"What happens when the prize prince is gone?" number one asked Bailey.

"We'll still have Gloria here."

"I'm gettin' on that fuckin' plane," Dempsey said.

"Shut the fuck up," Bailey said. "I need to think. Call that fucker back," Bailey said to Kilkenny.

Kilkenny brought up the incoming call list on the phone screen and called the last number. When it rang, he handed the phone to Bailey.

"Here's the deal, I let you take the injured crewman off the plane and you let it leave."

"Michael Lynch is my name, you are Don Bailey, right?"

"No, I'm Mick the Divil. Who do you think I am?"

"That's fine. I need to be sure."

Kate, listening on a second line, gave Lynch a thumbs-up confirmation.

"Now Don, here's the situation. The airport is in total lockdown. Nothing gets in or out until we're done here, do you understand that?"

"Do you understand that I've got two hostages here? There's a few more on that plane with two twitchy fuckers guarding them."

"I understand. I need you to know that we can resolve this situation without anyone else getting hurt."

"That's down to you giving us what we want."

"Let's start with the injured crewman. Let's get him out of the equation. I'd like to bring up an ambulance and get him looked after."

"We can do that. Now, if I see anything suss, people are going to die, do you get that?"

"Don, no one needs to get hurt. Let's get this organised in a way that everyone knows what's happening."

"Just keep your dogs on a leash."

Twomey's team moved furtively to one end of a nearby hangar. With the airport ablaze with light, moving around covertly was impossible. They needed to get closer to the terminal and going through the hangar was his only option. He picked the lock and held his breath as he nudged the door open. Inside, it remained pitch black and his four-man team clicked their night sights on and spread out as they worked towards the opposite side that would bring them within a sprint of the terminal building. Twomey rang Kate for an update.

"I've got to penetrate the terminal as quickly as possible," he told her. "Where are we at?"

"Lynch's trying to get an injured crewman off the plane. We've got ambulances at the gate."

"Could we use that distraction to try snatch the hostages from Bailey?" Twomey asked.

"Too risky," Kate replied. "We have to consider the pilot and crew."

"Make sure the ambulance drives slowly and flashes its blue light coming in. I need all the time I can get to bridge the gap from the hangar to the terminal."

"Could do that. Stay on the line; I'll put my phone on speaker and you can hear Lynch talking to Bailey."

Twomey peered out the hangar door. A fly past by the Garda helicopter confirmed that all suspects were crammed into the tower.

"That thing flies past here once more," Bailey said to Lynch, "we'll fucking fire on it."

"Don't do that, Don," Lynch replied calmly. "I'll see if I can get it to back off."

"No second warning," Bailey replied.

"Don, we're going to start the ambulance rolling soon," Lynch began. "We need you to tell whoever is on the plane to open the door and allow ambulance personnel remove the injured person."

"Don't go anywhere 'til you're told to move," Bailey replied.

"Don, time is not our friend here; we need to remove that injured person from our situation as quick as. It will make things easier."

Bailey hung up. Lynch waited patiently. Pete McNally sat at the rear of the command post hunched over the sat phone interception system.

"It's a trap," he exclaimed.

"Slow down," Kate urged. "What's a trap?"

"Read this," he said. "Bailey's just told one of the kidnappers that when the ambulance arrives, they'll rush the prince on board and then the plane goes. They're going to use the ambulance staff as fresh hostages."

"Stay tuned and keep us briefed," Kate said. To hostage negotiator Lynch, "Stall for time."

She passed the news to a huddle of Mac, Digger, Angie, and Ken James. Twomey was listening on an open phone line.

"We have to switch places with the paramedics," James suggested.

"Very high risk," Mac said.

"Good idea, Kenny," Twomey chipped in. "If we're to free the hostages, that's our only way of getting close enough. Get four of our lads to change gear straight away."

"That won't fly," Digger said. "ERU men would be too obvious."

"I'm a trained first responder," Kate said. "I'll take the doctor's place; I'm sure I could pull off a cursory patient examination."

For a moment, Digger stared at Kate, recalling the stunt she pulled weeks earlier with Bailey in his local chipper. He decided to leave it in the past.

"I'll do nurse," James replied.

"Let me take the doctor role," Angie suggested to Kate. "You know it's the best idea. You hang back and call the shots."

"Angie," Kate replied, "both you and Digger have been covered in muck most of the night. You'd never pull it off at close quarters."

"What about Kenny?" Digger asked. "Bit bulky for a nurse, don't you think?"

"We'll make do. The blond curls will sell it," she smiled.

"I'll drive the ambulance, then," Digger said.

"I'll ride shotgun," Angie added.

"This is all very high risk," Mac said. "What about the hostages on the plane? If their captors see an intervention outside, they're as good as dead."

"Digger, do you think we could use the ambulance to scatter Bailey's gang?" Twomey asked.

"We'll give it a go," Digger replied.

"If you disorientate them, I'll lead the Rangers in behind and hit the plane at the same time. Kenny, the prince is yours, get to him and secure him. Give me a few minutes to set this up."

Kate listened as Lynch rang Bailey back and spoke to him slowly and patiently, explaining that the ambulance crew were making final preparations and needed a little extra time. The plane made it off the runway and taxied towards the apron.

35

Kate checked with Twomey, who told her they were moving into position and needed maximum distraction. She recapped roles with everyone one last time before Digger eased the ambulance into motion. The clothes they had exchanged with the paramedics were not a perfect fit, but she hoped the kidnappers would have too much on their mind to notice. Digger activated the ambulance warning lights and intermittent blue flashes slaked the terminal's creamy wall as they slowly approached it.

"Where's that fuckin' ambulance?" Bailey shouted.

"Now Don," Lynch chided, "you can see the blue lights. I need you to treat the medics right, their only concern is for people who require assistance. We need to examine Mrs. Cleary also, Don. Her family tell us that she suffers asthma attacks. Will you allow the doctor see her, please?"

"She's alright," Bailey replied. "The doctor can look at her if he wants."

Bailey wanted the pilot to bring the plane close to the terminal, but Kilkenny warned him that maintaining a safe wing tip clearance was critical. Bailey grabbed the prince and frogmarched him downstairs towards the apron. On the other side of the aircraft, none of them observed the rippling movement in the grass as Twomey and the Rangers crawled ever closer to where the aircraft was turning.

"Bring her as well," Bailey shouted to his paranoid collaborators.

Dempsey walked alongside the captured royal, directing him down the stairway. They stopped on each landing and scoped the terrain ahead. The noise from the approaching jet was deafening.

Twomey's unit used the noise as cover to move between the hangar and the side of the terminal building. They hunkered down parallel to where Bailey's gang had parked up and disabled their vehicles as they lay in wait to make their next move. The team leader clipped a tactical mirror onto an expandable ASP baton, moved to the edge of the terminal and used it to peer around the corner.

The gang gathered in front of the terminal with the two hostages. Digger stopped the ambulance ten metres back. Kate and Ken James stepped out of the rear and walked confidently towards the nervy group.

"Who's in charge?" Kate asked, sharply.

"What do you want?" Bailey replied.

"Get that plane open now, so I can go on board and examine the injured crewman."

"I'm calling the shots," Bailey replied. "You'll do what you're told. Wait here."

Twomey's unit observed the steward extend the steps of the plane and retreat back inside. Twomey and the Rangers remained out of sight at the rear. Saunders cut the engines and shouting erupted immediately.

"Start engines," Hussein screamed.

"I need fuel," Saunders told him. "Without it, we can't fly."

"This is trick."

"No trick. No fuel, no fly."

Kate and Ken James began walking briskly towards the plane's steps. It got them closer to Dempsey and the prince.

"I need to get on board immediately," she said.

"Get to fuck back and wait," Bailey shouted as he cocked his weapon and pointed it at her.

Kate stopped and looked coldly at Bailey.

"My job is to save that poor man's life," she said. "Every second we delay my chances diminish."

"I don't give a fuck," Bailey replied. "Wait here." To Dempsey he said, "Hold him until my signal." Dempsey tightened his grip on the prince's arm.

"Let me go and examine Mrs. Cleary then," Kate called to Bailey.

"Fuck me, you don't give up."

"I need to take her inside," Kate said.

"Take her to the terminal," Bailey roared at one of the gang. "Don't let her out of your sight."

"Wait here," Kate said to Ken James.

Bailey strode towards the plane. He grabbed a bag from a gang member before bounding up the steps. Hussein greeted him with a nervous nod. Abousamra shifted about dementedly inside the aircraft, continually checking through the windows on either side.

"You can see your prize," Bailey told him. "Money."

"Weapons?" Hussein asked.

Bailey threw the camo bag on a seat. Hussein unzipped it and tossed a Glock to Abousamra. He pulled back the slide on his own to check it was loaded and pushed it into the front of his trouser belt. He then pulled two stuffed black bags from underneath the table between the first two seats.

"It is all there," Hussein told him.

"Hurry!" Abousamra shouted.

Bailey opened the first bag and flicked through the wads of cash on top of the pile. He then dug, elbow deep into the bag and checked the bundles he retrieved near the bottom. To the annoyance of his paymasters, he repeated the process on the second bag. The wads were made up of €500 notes. There were ten thousand of them in each bag, a €10 million payoff for delivering the prince. He dumped a handful of wads onto a seat.

"Dempsey's cut," he said.

He picked up the heavy bags and made for the exit. Hussein stopped him.

"First the prince," he said.

"Dempsey will bring him," Bailey replied. "As I walk down, he'll walk up."

"Hurry!" Abousamra shouted from the rear.

Bailey reached the door and nodded to Dempsey to come forward. Inside the terminal building, Kate examined Gloria Cleary, watched over by one of Bailey's gang. She glanced up and froze in horror as Bailey stalled at the door of the plane. His expression changed to a snarl when he copped the mirror Twomey's unit were using at the side of the terminal.

"It's a fucking trap," he shouted. He raised his weapon and sprayed their position.

"Do the fucker," he shouted to Dempsey. Sheik Nader's orders were explicit. If cornered, they could keep their money so long as the prince died.

Dempsey pulled a knife and jabbed it hard towards the prince's neck. The prince raised his arm in defence and blood spurted from the slash onto his silk pyjamas.

The prince doubled up in pain and Dempsey redirected his lunge towards the prince's back. The lunge never found its target. Ken James leapt forward and dealt Dempsey a neck chop with as much force as he could muster. It laid him out cold. The disguised paramedic then dived on the prince and kept him covered as rounds ricocheted on the ground around them. Bailey's group struggled to react as Digger drove the ambulance hard at them. Angie flashed up two ballistic shields at the windscreen. Digger was driving blind. The windscreen shattered and rounds pinged off the shields. They felt a dull thud as the charging ambulance collided with one of the gang. Digger screeched to a halt at the end of the terminal. Angie jumped from the cab, racked a pump action shotgun, and opened up on the gang. It kept them pinned them down as Twomey's team swept from cover. Ken James ran towards the ambulance, pulling the prince with one hand and firing at Bailey's rag-bag allies with the other.

When Abousamra pressed his face against a window of the plane a Ranger sniper took him out. Simultaneously, Twomey led the charge with a Ranger team that breeched the aircraft's rear door. He tripped and lurched forward into the cabin. The Ranger squad leader behind him caught the full burst Hussein loosed off in response to seeing his friend killed. A round pierced the Ranger's googles and propelled him backwards.

Hussein had fired from the aircraft's door where he stared, murderously, out onto the tarmac chaos. The last thing Mick Dempsey's blurred vision saw as he got shakily to his feet, was his childhood football prodigy pointing a weapon at him screaming something he couldn't hear. The round that killed him blew away a large chunk of his forehead. Twomey heard the *Allahu Akbar* scream, an instant before he tossed a stun grenade into the cabin and the Rangers behind him opened fire cutting Hussein down.

Bailey vaulted the side of the aircraft steps, crawled underneath, and ran out the other side. Digger caught the move and shouted to James to get the prince into the ambulance.

"Get him bandaged," he shouted as he took off in pursuit.

Despite the noise around him Digger roared a warning at Bailey calling on him to surrender. He loosed off two rounds that ricocheted off the tarmac in front of the fleeing felon to catch his attention. Bailey stopped abruptly. He dumped the bags, turned and aimed the Glock. Digger dropped him with a single shot.

Inside the terminal, Kate's guardian kept his pistol trained on her until he saw his comrades in arms scatter and fall. Instantly, he pointed the weapon towards one of Twomey's men and got off three rapid shots through the window before Kate kicked out and swept him off his feet. He hit the tiled floor hard and lay motionless. Kate grabbed Gloria Cleary and raced, crouching down, towards a side door. She hit the emergency push bar exit hard and tried to push outwards. One of the gangs' cars was tight up against it and there was no way either of them could squeeze through the space. She looked across towards the guy she thought she had disabled. He was moving. She pulled Gloria Cleary with her and stayed crouched down as she searched desperately for another exit out of the immediate danger area. She could hear Twomey shouting orders. The plane was filling with smoke, more shots rang out. Kate spotted a second emergency exit and made for it. She hit the bar hard and the door swung open. She pushed her freed hostage ahead and rolled out after her. An instant before the door swung shut, a shot rang out and Kate felt a sharp stinging sensation in her stomach. She grabbed Gloria's sweatshirt and pulled her towards the parked cars.

"Get down, stay here," she told her. "Between the engine block and the building is the best cover."

"You're bleeding," Gloria said.

"Just a scratch."

Kate's heart was pounding, a combination of exertion and fear. She looked towards the shot-up ambulance and hoped Digger and Angie were safe.

"Hostage two secured," she radioed. "Sit rep, anybody?"

"Stay there," Digger told her. "Twomey's taking the plane."

"Get me a first responder if you can."

"You hit?"

"Flesh wound. There's one hostile still mobile in the terminal."

"Stay in cover," Digger told Kate. "He's goin' nowhere fast."

Gloria Cleary squeezed Kate's hand as they sat side by side listening to the mayhem on the other side of the terminal. Intermittent shots rang out from inside the plane, followed by eerie silence.

Twomey, appeared near the plane's exit, stooped over Aazim Hussein's body. Army Rangers frantically tended to their wounded colleague.

"Kate's down, she needs help," Digger shouted to him. "There's one still on the loose inside the building. He might try to grab the controller."

"Leave him to us," Twomey shouted. "Get to Kate."

Relieved as Digger scrambled alongside, she smiled weakly.

"How are ya doin'?" he asked.

"My head feels woozy."

"That's just a drop in blood pressure, you'll be grand."

"Everyone okay?"

"One Ranger down and one of Twomey's wounded from the fucker inside the terminal."

"What about Bailey's gang?"

"All but secured. The dead are not yet accounted for."

"The prince?"

"He got slashed, but he'll live. Angie's tending him."

"Thank God!" Gloria Cleary chipped in. "Is Vincent okay?"

"I'm sure he's fine. We'll check as soon as…"

Kate groaned and twisted to ease her pain.

"Keep this pressed tight against the bleeding," Digger said, taking her hand and pressing a surgical dressing tight against her lower abdomen.

Relief about the hostages coming through unscathed was Kate's overwhelming emotion, as more blue lights flooded the scene. A helicopter landed and whisked the wounded Ranger and Twomey's injured squad member, together with the prince to hospital. Mac appeared beside her, bent on one knee, and held her hand.

"I should never have let you near this," he said.

"Don't worry," Kate mumbled. "Just a flesh wound."

An ambulance drove up and parked alongside. A doctor and paramedics emerged and rushed to examine Kate.

"Let's get these ladies to hospital immediately," the doctor said brusquely.

Kate was conscious throughout and smiled as the paramedic sliced off the blood-soaked borrowed uniform.

"Someone's going to be pissed," she joked.

The doctor's expression was deadly serious.

"Come on, let's get the transfer done smoothly," he urged.

Two paramedics placed Kate on a stretcher and moved her into the back of the ambulance with Gloria Cleary.

"I need to accompany," Angie said urgently.

"Sorry, no room," the doctor replied, closing the door inwards.

The ambulance moved off slowly and the doctor spoke to Kate.

"How are you feeling?"

"My stomach hurts, I'm sore and a bit light-headed," she replied. "Otherwise, not too bad. Just so, you know, I'm pregnant — early days."

A paramedic cut both legs of the uniform trousers she wore and Kate moved as instructed to enable the paramedic to slip them off.

"Fine. We'll go to the National Maternity hospital then."

"Why?"

"You have some bleeding I want investigated."

"Oh no!" Kate exclaimed, as the doctor pulled up the blanket.

Gloria Cleary reached over and squeezed Kate's arm.

"You're in good hands now."

As the paramedic changed Digger's bandage on her wound, tears rolled down Kate's cheeks. She lost consciousness as they wheeled her into the hospital's emergency department.

36

Kate awoke in a private room with lime green walls and a television sat precariously on a hinged bracket opposite her bed, but switched off. She felt tender and sore. Her stomach wound had been cleaned, sutured, and covered with a large bandage. She was bleary eyed, felt dopey and was drifting back to sleep when she noticed her mother sitting in the red leatherette visitor's chair. The previous night Angie had driven to Dundalk and brought Margaret Bowen to the Dublin hospital. She reached out and held her daughter while she wept for her lost baby. The doctors hadn't yet explained the precise reasons for the miscarriage but Kate blamed herself.

"Oh Mum, I should have been more careful," she wept, as her mother wiped away her tears.

Margaret Bowen had raised her two children single-handed; an experience that toughened her. She looked into her daughter's eyes and said, "What's done is done, girl, concentrate on getting well."

The previous night Pete McNally had struggled to keep up with all that was unfolding around him as the action reached fever pitch. Still at base with an Assistant Commissioner for company when the crew watching Rafiq Khouri reported the suspect had left his apartment in a taxi, Pete brought his dilemma to his superior officer. Mac was shocked to learn no backup was available and that Kate had stripped the top priority FBI operation to its bare bones. At that moment she was tailing Bailey and his hostages, events were building towards their crescendo and Mac was about to go mobile in the spare command post van. Confronting her on disobeying his orders was pointless, that could come later; instead he ordered the single crew tailing Khouri to stick with him like glue.

The two-man team duly observed the suspect being dropped at a house in Blanchardstown, a mixed west Dublin suburb that had seen its fair share of gangland shootouts, and had a sizeable immigrant population. The crew parked their transport up the street and watched the house for an hour. Late night dog walkers came and went along the road. The team remained focussed on their task, despite receiving texts about the mayhem unfolding across the city from colleagues. Joe Forde, an SIU newbie, envied his friends, right in the middle of the action while he was stuck out on a limb.

"Dodge round the back and check are there lights on" his veteran colleague, who rarely left the van's comfort, instructed him.

The front of the house was in darkness as Forde reached to the end of the street. He cut right and through a laneway that brought him to the rear of the dwelling. He counted the houses until he reached his target, then gingerly checked the top of the wall for broken glass before hoisting himself up and dropping down the other side. A shed provided cover while he scoped the ground ahead. There were no obstacles to negotiate, so he approached the house slowly, moving in a zig-zag pattern. There was light in the kitchen. As his eyes adjusted he could make out Khouri and three others sitting in front of a laptop. Khouri intermittently tapped the keyboard and he overheard a conversation with another party. Forde figured some kind of Internet call was taking place. It was in a foreign language and the other party seemed to be doing most of the talking. He heard an American voice say, "We're ready." He decided not to push his luck and minutes later, exited noiselessly over the rear wall.

Shortly after Forde got back to the van, the front door of the house opened and a single male exited. It wasn't Khouri, so the SIU pair decided to let him go. Forde watched him all the way and as the suspect reached the top of the road he made a phone call.

"He's ringing someone," he told the elder lemon. "Has he rumbled us?"

"Doubt it, probably calling a taxi. Stay alert."

When an agent handler's late night phone call interrupted Chief Superintendent Raphael O'Driscoll's sleep, he was furious. Short of someone shooting the President, his orders were that he was not to be disturbed after nine o'clock at night. Earlier in the evening, he had dined with his old man's business pals, and the wine flowed freely. His wife was sleeping in the next room, but he didn't much care whether he woke her or not. He tried to focus as the handler told him about the Blanchardstown meeting. The agent had been recruited only weeks earlier when one of his henchmen picked up word in a city centre station that an Iraqi had been arrested with an underage prostitute.

O'Driscoll swooped and recruited him as an agent in return for stalling the statutory rape charge.

He was repaying his debt. O'Driscoll kept the agent off the books and his intel, a closely guarded secret. He wanted to reap the glory rather than passing it up the line and handing another case on a plate to the bitch in SIU. His head reeled when the agent's report spoke of an American at the meeting. He gave orders to hit the house immediately and arrest the remaining suspects there.

When Joe Forde saw a marked car close off the end of the street, he tapped his senior colleague to take a look. Another car was getting into position at the other end. Minutes later, they watched in frustration as Khouri was led in handcuffs from the house. Detective Andrew Timmons, O'Driscoll's bully boy, flicked a middle finger from the Special Branch unmarked car as it passed the SIU van.

Along with Angie, Mac and Digger dropped in to visit Kate before she was discharged. Neither commented on her loss. They all looked worn down from the previous night's chaos. She vowed to get back to work soon and Mac promised to keep her posted. Left unspoken was the dismay that Kate sensed from her two closest colleagues that they were unaware of her pregnancy until it was too late.

She was allowed to leave hospital in the late evening. Her mother ordered a taxi that brought them the short hop to her apartment and cooked, while she lay out on her couch catching up with media coverage of the previous night. It seemed to matter little now. Her phone rang and she saw it was Cody O'Neill.

"Mum, I'll take this in the bedroom," she said.

"No work calls," her mother scolded. "Remember, we agreed."

"It's just a friend," she replied, closing the bedroom door.

"Hi Kate, are you okay?" O'Neill asked. "I called to the hospital but they told me you'd been discharged. I'm so sorry."

The sound of his voice tipped Kate into tears. "Give me a moment," she said.

"If it's a bad time…" O'Neill began.

"No, I just need a moment," Kate said, wiping her tears.

O'Neill waited without saying a word.

"I'm fine," she told him eventually.

"Are you, really?"

"Sore, but I'll survive. I'm sorry about everything. I tried to tell you but the time never seemed right."

"Tell me what?"

"About our baby."

O'Neill greeted the news in silence at first. "Oh my God, Kate, I, I, I don't know what to say. I had no idea."

"Cody, what happened between us, was a moment, a beautiful one," Kate sobbed. "Getting pregnant was an unintended consequence. I had no expectations. I guess it wasn't to be."

"Kate, we had something…" O'Neill began.

Before Kate could reply, he continued. "Then, I went back home and saw how kind Marilyn was, helping Mom care for Pop and we decided to try again."

"I see."

"I'll have to tell Marilyn," O'Neill said.

"Things are, as they are."

O'Neill was silent. Kate excused herself, put the call on hold, and blew her nose.

"Is there any chance we could meet?" O'Neill asked.

"I'll call you as soon as I get the all clear."

"Looks like I'll be headed back to the States soon now that Khouri's out in the open."

"What?"

"With Khouri's arrest."

"Let me talk to Mac and get back to you."

"Kate, I'm so sorry."

Margaret Bowen popped her head into the room. "That didn't sound much like a social chat, to me. Fitz is here to see you. Do you want to chat in here?"

"Give me a few minutes to freshen up."

"Hand over your phone," her mother demanded.

"Mum, I'm not a child."

"You need to rest."

"I know and I will," she said, closing the en suite door. Inside, she dialled Mac and learned how Khouri's arrest had triggered howls of protests from the FBI Director. It had also led to Chief Superintendent O'Driscoll's indefinite suspension from duty.

Aside from Bailey and Dempsey, the rest of his gang survived the airport shootout with varying degrees of injury. Some had already appeared before courts on kidnapping charges. The media printed heroic accounts of how the Ranger lost his life in the raid. The tabloids glorified the fact that Twomey's ERU, along with the Army Rangers, had joined an elite club of Special Forces successful in freeing hostages from a plane hijacking.

The co-pilot succumbed to his injuries before Twomey's assault began. Captain Saunders yanked his cabin steward into the cockpit, as Hussein blazed at Dempsey. It saved his life. Seconds later, Hussein died in a hail of Army Ranger bullets.

Mac coordinated early morning raids at the safe house where the IRA dissident, Lockhart, stayed overnight. He feared his own associates more than the Garda. His rent-a-gun scheme with Bailey was a solo venture, which he knew would not sit well with the people in charge of the embryonic terrorist group. He begged to be placed in isolation while in detention, a request that Mac said would be considered in return for whatever information he could provide.

Sexton had managed the crime scenes at Ballycleary with clinical efficiency. While the lodge remained sealed until the murder scenes were cleared, he drove the outdoors forensic teams hard to complete their work as fast as possible. Neighbouring trainers pitched in to help Vincent Cleary begin the job of getting his stud back up and running. A small army of stable hands from nearby stud farms arrived at Ballycleary to help exercise the horses. Miraculously, none had been injured in the chaos of the previous night. By noon Saturday, Vincent Cleary's builder already had a team on site carrying out repairs. Cleary was driven to Saint Vincent's Hospital in Dublin early in the morning where he was reunited with both his wife and Sheikh Al-Naqeeb. An ERU team now guarded the prince with a full-time protection detail.

In the late afternoon at The Curragh racecourse, a huge roar went up as the Irish Derby winner was paraded in the winners' enclosure. The cheers that rippled around were directed more at the horse's owner who led the animal into the enclosure. The prince insisted on leaving hospital to see the race and a helicopter ride ensured he didn't miss out. Sheik Al Naqeeb had one arm in a sling and Vincent Cleary, sporting a large lump on the back of his head, walked alongside helping him control the horse. Swarms of world press descended on the event and they jostled with sporting journalists for quotes from the winning combination. The investment-seeking Defence Minister made sure to be in every photographer's frame. Gloria Cleary stood quietly in the background smiling, and holding her children with each hand. Their house was out of bounds and the prince insisted on putting them up in a nearby hotel at his expense for as long as they needed.

Digger sealed off Nasri's business premises while another unit searched his house and arrested him. He lawyered up fast and sought bail on the grounds of having to attend a family funeral. Late in the evening of the attempted kidnapping, the body of his brother, Youssef, was found in a Beirut street with a bullet in the back of his head. The video evidence from the warehouse notwithstanding, Nasri's lawyer continued to argue for a humanitarian consideration. He brought a *habeas corpus* application before the High Court, citing coercion as the explanation for all Nasri's actions. It granted him conditional bail, one being that he surrender his passport and sign at his local Garda station every day. The conditions functioned effectively for a week; then overnight Nasri and his family disappeared.

A week on from Kate's discharge from hospital, her mother's constant presence triggered cabin fever. Fitz called in most days on her way home from work and Kate insisted everything with the wedding go ahead as planned.

Kate met the investigation team that Commissioner Fox had appointed to pull the different strands of her case together for court. Four hours after sitting down with them, she wound up her statement to investigating detectives. The concentration of trying to sequence the night's events into order left her feeling strained and she went to the rest room to freshen up. She was drying her hands when Angie walked in.

"Hey there, how are you feeling?" she asked.

"Worn out after that interrogation," Kate replied.

"How's your wound?"

"It was just a graze, not too deep. It's healing fine." Kate said. "Thanks for asking."

Angie pulled at wisps of her hair as she looked in the mirror.

"You're very chirpy!" Kate laughed.

"Just happy things are settling down."

Kate looked at her sceptically. "There's something else."

"Doesn't matter," Angie replied.

"Tell me."

"Seriously, it can wait."

"Angie!"

"It's silly, but I've felt giddy ever since we found out we're pregnant," Angie replied. "We got word yesterday."

"I'm thrilled for you," Kate said, hugging her, "you'll make great parents."

"I don't know, it doesn't bother Eileen at all. Me, I'm scared witless."

"You'll do fine."

"Will you get back to work soon?" Angie asked.

"Next week, if I feel up to it; I've a friend's wedding to get out of the way, first."

Rafiq Khouri spoke little under interrogation other than to ask for consular assistance from the American Embassy. A consular officer arrived at the Bridewell station in central Dublin, explained Khouri's rights to him, offered a list of local solicitors, and left.

"Is that it?" Khouri shouted as the cell door closed.

In the cell corridor, Digger waited thirty minutes, then allowed Cody O'Neill enter. It was unofficial. If he got any intel from him, it couldn't be used in evidence. O'Neill interrogated him the entire afternoon, to no avail. Khouri played the victim of a wrongful arrest, under suspicion for doing his job. He refused to budge from his story that some guys from the mosque had asked him for assistance in contacting their families. Because of insufficient evidence, he was released after three days' detention. The laptop seized during O'Driscoll's haphazard raid was wiped before the raiding party got to it. On release from custody, he picked up an overnight bag at his apartment, travelled directly to Dublin airport and took a flight to London Heathrow. From there he flew to Brussels and dropped out of sight.

Two days later O'Neill packed two suitcases and ordered a taxi to the airport. As he answered his apartment door he picked up one of the cases hoping to hand it straight to the cab driver. Instead, Kate stood on the landing. He dropped the case and rushed to embrace her. Neither spoke, they just held each other until the taxi driver arrived and broke the spell. Kate kissed O'Neill on the cheek and said good-bye.

37

The final weekend in June, just ten days after SIU foiled Bailey's plot, Digger invited Kate around for a barbeque. His kids' holidays had kicked in and weather forecasters spoke of summer beginning, with a fortnight of sunshine promised. The garden smelt of freshly cut grass and smouldering charcoal when Kate arrived. She knew most people there, Mac and all the SIU crew had showed up. Jane did the introductions with everyone else, most of them Digger's school run neighbours. The guy Jane presented as her boss, Jay, seemed pleasant. Digger warned Sean and Maggie that they couldn't jump on Auntie Kate until she was better. Instead Jay took over, enthusiastically joining his girlfriend, at least fifteen years his junior, as they chased kids around the garden. Digger burned burgers and singed chicken drumsticks, shaking his head, as he watched Jay climb awkwardly onto the kids' trampoline.

From his pocket, he fished the letter he'd received the previous day telling him he was under investigation for his role in the Weston airport shootout and threw it among the hot coals. GSOC was crusading again, aiming to prove, with the benefit of hindsight, that things could have been handled differently, better outcomes achieved. He didn't dispute other possibilities, although it pissed him off that people who never faced down the danger got to make the most noise.

Digger looked towards Jane, setting out cutlery as Angie and her partner held hands under the table. All three were chatting to Kate, women's business, he guessed. She would have a similar GSOC letter when she got back to work. He would tell her later that Ballistics had just matched Bailey's weapon to the Carroll and Mooney murders.

"Dan!" Jane shouted. "Smoke!"

"Ah feck!" Digger exclaimed, as he removed two flaming burgers from the grill. Grinning, he shouted, "Grub's up."

Kate's notorious bridesmaid's dress was a snug fit when it was delivered, a week before the wedding. Fitz suggested, if she hadn't anyone else in mind, that Kate bring her Mum as her plus one. They had bonded again during her regular visits to Kate's apartment.

On a warm, sunny afternoon, Betty Fitzpatrick married her artist beau, in a civil ceremony at the rose garden of a city centre hotel. Margaret Bowen beamed with pride as her radiant daughter stood smiling alongside her friend for the wedding photographer. Kate's poses were acts of sheer willpower. She was still in turmoil. While her bullet wound was healing fast, she only caught snatches of sleep most nights before flashbacks invaded her dreams. As the evening progressed through speeches, toasts and the couple's first dance, Kate struggled to maintain the façade.

Her mother, meanwhile, was having a ball. She conspired with the DJ to lead a line-dancing set when the evening threatened to quieten down. Kate felt mixed emotions, pride and embarrassment. What would Fitz's starchy relatives make of it all? Experience, and Doc Darcy's good advice on dealing with post-traumatic stress, taught her not to allow feelings of discomfort develop into a stupor. Ultimately, she shook off her misgivings and raced to where Fitz was seated, grabbed her, and dragged her onto the dancefloor beside her mother.

Kate's mother never let anything keep her down. What's done is done was her mantra. Kate would go all-out to carry on likewise. She would concentrate on getting well and polishing her skills at the job she loved. Meantime, there was the dance; Kate didn't care for it, but never said as much.

"Okay everyone," her mum shouted, as the DJ cued up "Cotton Eye Joe", the country and western classic. "It's stomp, kick, and triple step."

"Hook up," Fitz shouted, encouraging everyone to put their arms around a partner's shoulders.

The lines were ready; the DJ pumped the volume up and Kate's mum shouted, "Here we go."

At Kilis, near the Turkish border with Syria, Rafiq Khouri waited patiently with his minder who had picked him up in Istanbul. It had taken a hot, sweaty day of non-stop travel by car to get this far but now, Aleppo, the centre of the jihad, was just sixty-eight kilometres down the road.

They had switched transport, and waited for the

Turkish Police manning the checkpoint to go inside the station; the signal the local recognised as turning a blind eye. He kicked the motor-cycle into life and headed down the track towards the border with his invaluable recruit clinging tightly behind.

ABOUT THE AUTHOR

T. R Croke is the creator of the Detective Kate Bowen mystery thriller series. During 2017 both prequel novella, THE TRINITY ENIGMA and series starter, THE DEVIL'S LUCK featured in Amazon's Top 100 terrorism thrillers.

He is married to Eva and lives in County Laois in the Irish midlands. Read more at www.trcroke.com.

www.trcroke.com
info@trcroke.com

AUTHOR'S NOTE

There was a massacre of Lebanese civilians on the 18th of April 1996 at the village of Qana in southern Lebanon. It followed a mortar attack against the Israeli soldiers, carried out by Hezbollah militants. The attackers reportedly retreated to a UN compound and mingled with people sheltering there from the village and surrounds. The unfortunate village folk had been ordered by the Israeli Defense Forces to leave their homes due to the fighting.

The IDF responded to the mortar attack by firing the one hundred and sixteen artillery rounds from two nearby batteries. Shells exploded either over the camp, or on impact within it, and one hundred innocent civilians died. Mohamed Atta, who crashed American Airlines Flight 11 from Boston into the North Tower of the World Trade Centre in New York City on 11 September 2001 claimed revenge for the Qana killings as his motivation for involvement in the al-Qaeda attack.

ACKNOWLEDGMENTS

Top billing goes to my editor, Lizzie Harwood. Throughout the development of *The Prize Prince* from draft to final manuscript, Lizzie's positivity and enthusiasm for the Kate Bowen series were inspirational. Her forensic attention to detail was as always, phenomenal.

My eternal gratitude goes to Eva, always my first reader and ardent supporter. Likewise to my proofreaders, Michelle, Susie and my daughter, Emma, thank you for your patience, persistence, and sharp eyes. Tom Croke, former Air Corps and commercial pilot, (and my cousin) generously advised on the flying scenes. Former Garda colleagues read chapters and recommended changes, especially Fergus, who guided me on UN matters and directed me towards new avenues of research. Finally, a big thanks to Andrew, who keeps my http://trcroke.com website updated.

References that proved especially helpful during the research stage included:

"Blood, Sweat and Tears" Clonan, Tom (Liberties Press, 2012) A unique insight into the experiences of the

Irish Army over four decades of UN peacekeeping in South Lebanon. I highly recommend it.

"The Things I've Seen" Marlowe, Lara (Liberties Press, 2010) contemporary history brought to life through the reports Lara filed from Lebanon as a stringer for CNN and foreign correspondent for the Irish Times. Lara's book is a collection of her insightful articles and an invaluable bookshelf addition.

"In The Blood" Holland, Anne (The O'Brien Press Limited, 2009) offered a delightful peek into the Irish horse racing world.

ALSO BY T. R. CROKE

The Trinity Enigma

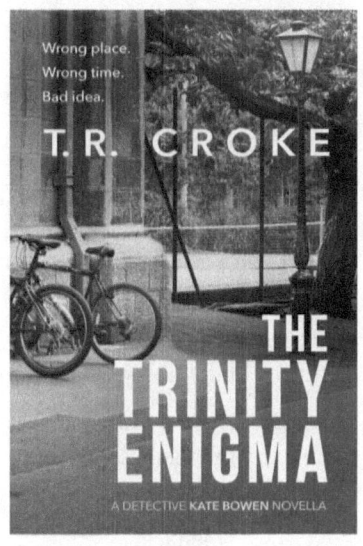

Kate returns to her alma mater, Dublin's Trinity College, to investigate a string of unconnected deaths.

Is a serial killer loose in Dublin's classiest district?

Kate's not convinced… until she sees her old college professor's bizarre witness statement.

Free download Amazon US Amazon UK Apple, Kobo, & others

The Devil's Luck

What happens when two of the world's worst terror groups form an alliance… to hit an unknown target?

When an all-night border stakeout unearths a rogue IRA faction, Kate and her team dig deeper.

Kate knows she needs more than the luck of the Irish to stop this menace.

$3.99 Amazon US £2.99 Amazon UK

Request from the Author

I hope you enjoyed reading *The Prize Prince*. I would really appreciate you taking a little time to leave a review on the website of your choice.

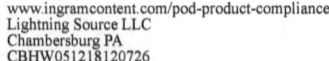